ALSO BY
DARCY COATES

The Haunting of Ashburn House

The Haunting of Blackwood House

The House Next Door

Craven Manor

The Haunting of Rookward House

The Carrow Haunt

Hunted

The Folcroft Ghosts

The Haunting of Gillespie House

Dead Lake

House of Shadows

House of Shadows

House of Secrets

Black Winter

Voices in the Snow

Secrets in the Dark

HUNTED

DARCY COATES

Cover design by Ervin Serrano
Cover images © Martin Benner/plainpicture, Robsonphoto/
Shutterstock, iko/Shutterstock, Ake13bk/Shutterstock

Published by Poisoned Pen Press, an imprint of Sourcebooks
P.O. Box 4410, Naperville, Illinois 60567-4410
(630) 961-3900
sourcebooks.com

Originally self-published in 2018 by Black Owl Books.

Library of Congress Cataloging-in-Publication Data

Names: Coates, Darcy, author.
Title: Hunted / Darcy Coates.
Description: Naperville, IL : Poisoned Pen Press, [2020] | "Originally self-published in 2018 by Black Owl Books"--Title page verso.
Identifiers: LCCN 2019056946 | (trade paperback)
Subjects: GSAFD: Horror fiction. | Mystery fiction.
Classification: LCC PR9619.4.C628 H86 2020 | DDC 823/.92--dc23
LC record available at https://lccn.loc.gov/2019056946

Printed and bound in the United States of America.
VP 10 9 8 7 6 5 4 3 2 1

Sunday, 6:40 p.m.
Ashlough Forest, Cobb Mountain Range

EILEEN COULDN'T HEAR THE bird chatter anymore. She heard only her own ragged breathing, rough like a saw through wood, and her galloping heart.

She stumbled again, catching her foot on a raised root. Her muscles were too drained to keep her upright. She hit the ground hard, branches poking at her side and a rock digging into her collarbone. Eileen grunted, pushed away from the rock, and clutched at the nearest trunk as she waited for the dizziness to fade.

The cool moss felt good under her cheek. A medley of scents—organic decay, fungus, and the strange musk that came from insects—filled her nose. She used it to ground herself as she focused on the rough bark beneath her fingers, the moss against her skin, and the creaking noise of flexing branches in the canopy above.

A twig snapped. It was no more than twenty feet away. Eileen flinched and pressed her lips together to quiet her rasping breaths. She didn't know what had broken the twig. But whatever it was, it had been following her for more than an hour.

She tried to look for it, but the vegetation was too thick. Massive trunks, some hundreds of years old, clustered together, linked by trailing vines and weedy, light-starved shrubs. The sun was close to setting. It desaturated her environment, dousing every color in the same shade of gray.

Leaves crunched as the other being took a step closer. Eileen bit down on a moan. She didn't want to run any longer. She didn't want to be in the forest as the light faded. More than anything, she wished she hadn't decided to go hiking that day. She should have been enjoying her last night in the hotel room, packing her belongings and looking forward to seeing her parents the following afternoon.

Now, she would have given anything to find the path out. She'd been lost in Ashlough Forest for more than five hours. Her water bottle was empty. Her lungs ached. Everything was starting to look the same. She felt like she'd passed the same formations a thousand times, but that was impossible. She didn't know if she was walking toward civilization or away from it. The second possibility filled her with icy terror. Ashlough Forest stretched for hundreds of kilometers, a blanket of impenetrable green and twisting rivers. If she'd strayed too far from the path, she could spend years wandering through the forest and never find her way out.

A bird fluttered away in a frenzy as its nest was disturbed. Eileen looked in its direction, searching for motion, but it was impossible to see through the gloom. She licked dry, cracked lips. "Leave me alone!"

Even to her, the cry sounded pathetic. She stayed huddled at the roots of the tree, pressed against the bark as though it might offer her some protection. Every minute robbed her of more light. She tried not to imagine what would happen when the final traces of sun faded from the sky. She'd only planned for a half-day hike and hadn't brought anything to light her surroundings. She would be trapped in the darkness, surrounded by spiky branches and sharp rocks she couldn't see…and alone with *it*.

Something shifted between two trees. Eileen tried to fix on it, but it was gone before she could catch more than a glimpse. It wasn't small, though. Not a wolf or a wildcat.

There was so little time left. She forced herself to her feet, gasping as sore, bruised muscles took her weight, then staggered forward. In the twisting chaos of the forest, it was easy to imagine paths where there were none. The narrow, clear patches led on for a few feet, sometimes as many as twenty or thirty, then vanished. She knew trying to follow those phantom paths was insane. She still couldn't stop herself.

Dead branches scraped at her exposed forearms and face. She squinted to protect her eyes and stumbled onward. She couldn't hear the other entity following her, but she knew it would be there, waiting for her to stop again. She couldn't stop, though. No matter how dark it grew, she would have to keep moving, keep searching for a way out. If she gave up, she was as good as dead.

Some small animal skittered past her, disturbing dead leaves as it ran. She stumbled away from it as her heart lurched. Behind her, a slow, scraping noise echoed between the trees. It sounded like metal on wood. Eileen's eyes stung, and she blinked them furiously as she began moving forward again.

The scraping noise continued. The volume rose and fell in waves, sometimes so soft that she thought it might have ceased, but then swelling into a horrific scratching and grating cacophony. She didn't think it was a coincidence that the sound had started just as the last scraps of light faded from the sky. She didn't want to cry, but something wet streaked down her cheek.

"Please, please, please." She whispered the mantra with every breath. All she needed was a sliver of hope. A light in the distance, the sound of a car traveling down a gravel road, anything. She would go home. She would tell her parents how much she loved them. She would never take such a risk ever again.

The transition was so gradual that it was hard to say how close night was, up until the moment it swallowed her. She was blind. Arms outstretched, fingers bumping into bark and leaves, she shuffled her feet, trying not to fall. The scraping still followed her. Sometimes directly behind, sometimes to her left, sometimes to her right, but every time it swelled, it seemed a little louder than before.

"Please, please, please." Every muscle shook. Every fiber of her body ached with fear and stress. She began moving faster, not minding as obstacles scraped her hands raw. Her eyes were wide, desperately roving across the tableau of darkness surrounding her. They couldn't see anything, but that didn't stop her from trying.

Her foot hit something hard. A rock, she thought. She'd gained too much momentum and lurched over it, arms outstretched to break her fall. There was no ground on the other side. Just a sharp, steep fall.

A yelp tore free as she tumbled down the incline. Rocks bit into her. She felt tossed like a rag doll, no longer sure of which direction was up or if the motion would ever end. Hands scrambled uselessly for a purchase. She couldn't breathe, couldn't think, couldn't do anything but silently beg for it to stop.

It did. She came to a halt on a rough, rocky surface. Her head swam. Pain radiated from everywhere on her bruised body, but it was worst in her leg. She reached toward the blinding ache and touched something warm and wet.

A sob shook her, followed by another. A noise came from her right. It wasn't the scraping sound, though; it was organic. Running water. She'd fallen down the side of a river. It hadn't been a short fall, though—not the kind she could climb out of. A cliff, maybe.

Eileen clenched her teeth to silence the tears as she felt around herself. She still had her backpack. But it wasn't much help. All it contained were her bathing suit and towel, an empty water bottle, a sketchbook, her cell phone, and her camera.

She pulled the backpack off over aching arms. Every time she moved, the fire in her leg raged hotter. She felt across the fabric until she found the pain tablets she'd stashed in a pocket in case of a migraine. She popped out four and dry swallowed them.

The backpack had been jostled enough that the phone had fallen to the very bottom. Eileen had to feel through her clothes and towel to find it. She pulled it out and pressed the power button. The phone turned on, and her eyes immediately went to the connection signal in the corner. The phone had lost its connection halfway along the drive to the mountain. Every hour, Eileen had taken it back out and tried it again.

It was empty, just like it had been the last eight times she'd tried it. She couldn't help herself, though. She tried dialing her parents' number. It didn't go through. She tried calling the emergency number, with the same result. She scrunched up her face and pressed her palm into her forehead.

She turned the phone around to point its light at her surroundings. Red liquid glistened on her leg. She knew she should do something about it—she just didn't know what. And even if she had the training, she doubted she could do much without any sanitized cloths or boiled water.

The light picked up a rocky, weedy shore. Ahead, as she'd suspected, a narrow river wove between the trees. She looked up and behind herself. A steep slope rose at least ten meters above her head.

The phone turned off, and darkness rushed back around her. Eileen swore and pressed the power button, but the phone didn't respond. She'd known the battery was low, but she hadn't expected it to drain that fast. She tapped the phone against her forehead as fresh tears escaped.

A scraping sound came from somewhere to her left. Eileen lifted her head. Her heart rate kicked up a notch. The sound fell silent then repeated. She could feel herself breathing too quickly, slipping into hyperventilation. She threw the phone into the backpack and dug through its contents to find the camera.

It had been a gift from her grandfather for her eighteenth birthday, shortly before he'd passed away. It was heavy and bulky, and she still didn't understand what all the settings did, but it had a powerful bulb. She found its strap first then used it to drag the camera out from under the towel. It had multiple dials, and she strained to remember which one activated the flash.

The scraping was drawing closer. Underneath the noise, she thought she could hear the crackle of dry leaves and twigs being crushed. She found what she thought was the right switch, turned it, and pressed the button to take a photograph.

It didn't work. The camera clicked, but there was no light. Eileen swore and tried turning the switch in the opposite direction. Another click, still no light. Despite the chilled air, she was sweating. She tried a different switch. This time, when she pressed the button, harsh, polarizing light exploded across the scene.

"Yes. Yes!" She lifted the camera and pressed the button again. For half of a second, her surroundings were brought into sharp relief. She could see the trees, the rocks, and the cliff she'd fallen down. Another flash. She caught glints of light in the canopy as night animals watched her. A third flash. This time, she saw something standing between the trees.

Eileen's breath froze in her lungs. She tried to scramble back, but the pain in her leg exploded, making her gasp. Instead of moving, she lifted the camera again and took another picture.

Something watched her. It was tall and covered in thick black fur, its head tilted to regard her. Eileen's mind froze, refusing to accept what her eyes were showing her. The face looked like it might have once been human, but it wasn't anymore. It was like something out of her worst nightmares.

The scraping repeated. It was moving closer. Eileen pressed the camera's button again, and as light flooded the scene, she screamed.

CHAPTER 2

TODD REFRESHED HIS BROWSER. Eileen Hershberger's Facebook page flashed white for a second then reappeared exactly how it had been before. Her latest status read: *Going on a hike!! Ashlough Forest, one of the most beautiful places on earth! Look out for some photos when I get back to the hotel, lovelies!*

It was eleven at night, and there was only an hour's time difference between his state and where Eileen was holidaying. She'd probably forgotten to post the photos and gone to bed. Irritated, he clicked on another tab to see if anyone had replied to his forum comment. No one had.

He didn't even want to see the photos. Sometimes, if she went swimming, Eileen posted pictures of herself in a bikini. Lots of guys replied to those photos, but Todd didn't. He wasn't there to gawk at her like some mouth-breathing weirdo. He was just worried, like any good friend would be. It was Eileen's last day on holiday, and he wanted to make sure she'd gotten back to the hotel safely.

Spending most of his life on the internet, he found it hard to avoid missing-person stories when they popped up. Sometimes, girls went missing on holiday. Eileen was pretty, she was young, and she was traveling alone. Todd honestly didn't understand why her parents had agreed to the plan. He'd tried to tell her to be safe on the last day he'd seen her, the day before she'd gotten on the plane, but she hadn't heard him. She'd been sitting at the other end of the picnic bench, between Chris and Hailey, and no matter how much Todd had stared at her, she hadn't looked back at him.

He exhaled through his nose and returned to the Facebook page. It was a Sunday night, which meant no one worth talking to was online. He was bored and frustrated, and a gnawing anxiety had started in the pit of his stomach. He clicked Refresh. The page vanished then reappeared. Eileen smiled at him out of the last photo she'd posted, a selfie of herself at breakfast that morning. She'd eaten pancakes. Todd didn't think that was a smart choice. Sometimes, she felt unwell if she ate too much gluten.

Todd scrolled down through her other photos. He'd seen them probably close to a hundred times and knew them all well. Photos of Eileen at her hotel. Eileen on a ferry, holding a floppy hat onto her head. Eileen pointing up at a bridge. She smiled in every picture. That was his favorite part of her—she never seemed to stop smiling, and she never tried to moderate it. Smiling made Todd feel uncomfortable. But not Eileen. She showed off her teeth and her gums and let her eyes scrunch up with delight in every picture.

He found his least favorite photo of her. She was at a club, holding either a mocktail or a cocktail—he hoped it wasn't real alcohol—and leaning her shoulder against a strange guy's chest. The status had been cryptic. "Enjoying my night out, making new friends!"

The guy was tall with broad shoulders and an ingenuine smile. He looked like an ass. Todd didn't know why Eileen had decided to hang out with him. If she was smart—and he knew she was—she would have ditched him quickly. Still, he didn't like how close they were standing together. It made the situation look more intimate than it really was.

He slouched farther back in his chair and chewed on his thumbnail as he kept scrolling. It took a few minutes to get to the photos of her at the airport on the day she'd left. She'd only been gone for two weeks, but she uploaded multiple photos and statuses each day. He didn't want to be paranoid, but it seemed weird for her not to post anything on her last evening.

His phone sat on the edge of his desk. He flicked it on, but the chat window was still empty. Todd always replied to his messages promptly. He didn't understand why other people got so lazy about it. *"Oh, I'm having issues with my phone."* He'd heard that excuse so often, he was sick of it.

He scrolled through his contacts until he found Chris Hershberger then tapped on the icon to write a message. Chris was Eileen's older brother and Todd's best friend. He must have noticed the lack of status updates, too—and unlike Todd, he knew Eileen's phone number.

Todd stared at the empty message box for a moment, his thumbs poised over the keys. He didn't want to come off as weird. On the other hand, he didn't want to beat around the bush, either. He drafted a message.

> Hey man! Sorry to bother you, but I noticed Eileen hasn't uploaded any pics recently. She doing okay? Not sick, I hope?

He reread it, cringed, and deleted it. Chris could get weirdly protective of Eileen and had actually snapped at Todd one time when he'd tried to visit her at her work. Asking about her outright would get him some backlash. Instead, he tried a different tack.

> Yo yo, Chris Columbus! What's up, my man? Anything exciting going down this evening?

He bit his lip. He couldn't tell if it was too much. He was trying to be funny, but funny didn't always come across in text messages. He deleted it again then stood and started pacing. After a moment, he hit on a solution, sat back down, and started typing.

> Chris! Do you have any plans tonight?

He sent the message. It was good, casual and friendly, but asking a pointed question that demanded an answer. He set his phone on the desk, balanced on its end, and leaned back in the chair as he waited for a reply. Seconds ticked by. He began to feel itchy and reached around the phone to refresh Eileen's Facebook page again. No update.

"C'mon, Chris, don't do this to me." He picked up the phone, turning it in his hands, and jumped as it pinged. A new message waited for him: Not much, hbu?

They were having a conversation. That was good. Todd typed frantically.

> Oh, lazy night indoors. I was chatting with some other friends on Facebook and decided to see if Eileen had uploaded any more photos, but...

He bit the inside of his mouth. He was coming on too strong again. Rushing, knowing Chris was probably waiting for a reply, he deleted the message and tried to take a circuitous route.

> I was just wondering if we could hang out some time. Maybe tomorrow?

He sent that message, waited a second, then typed a follow-up.

> Oh wait, you're picking Eileen up from the airport, aren't you? Never mind. We can hang some other day.

Seconds passed without a response. Todd's palms were itching. He hoped Chris hadn't thought it was the end of the conversation. He added another message: How's she doing, anyway? Having fun, I hope?

Chris couldn't get antsy about that. It was perfectly normal to ask about your friends. He set the phone back down and pulled his legs up under his chin. The seconds on his clock ticked by. Todd tapped his fingers on his knees as a frustrated impatience built flames in his stomach. He'd asked a simple question. Was it really too much to ask that his *best friend* reply to him?

The phone pinged, and Todd lunged for it. The message was short, but another followed almost instantly.

We haven't heard from her tonight.

But I'm sure she's fine.

"Oh, you're sure, are you? That's just great." Anger let typos slip into the reply, and Todd didn't try to correct them. Eileen wasn't the sort of girl who would forget to phone her parents. If she hadn't contacted them, chances were she was in serious trouble.

Have you tried calling her?

She said on facebook she was going to upload photos tonight but hasn't.

That's not like her.

When was the last time you heard from her?

The phone stayed silent. Todd glared at the screen, willing Chris to reply, but minutes ticked by with no response. He scrolled back up to read the messages and groaned. They were too much. He should have kept his cool. Now he'd chased Chris away and would probably need to apologize to make things right.

Todd threw the phone aside then leaned back over his computer. He refreshed Facebook a final time. There was no change.

Eileen's parents were nice people, but they were stupid. Knowing them, Todd thought they would sit on their asses and wait for Eileen to call them, when maybe she wouldn't…ever. At least Chris was a bit more intelligent, but he wasn't active enough. He liked to let other people lead. Todd didn't have that luxury. He'd read stories about what happened to girls who were kidnapped. They couldn't afford to wait a few days when every minute was precious. Waiting meant nothing except maybe a body in a shallow grave.

He opened a search engine. A few keystrokes brought up the police station for the last town Eileen had stopped at. Normally, he avoided talking to people over the phone. But for Eileen, he would. He dialed the station's number with shaking fingers and lifted the phone to his ear.

Monday, 9:30 a.m.
Helmer, population 866, at the base of the Cobb Mountain Range

CARLA DELAGO PUT HER head down as she entered the police station. The remnants of a hangover throbbed at the back of her skull. She'd woken up so late that she'd had to skip a shower, which left her feeling sticky and gross. With luck, she could make it all the way to her office without having to speak to another human being.

"Carla! Good morning!" Viv waved from the reception desk. Viv like to wear fake flowers in her hair, and she picked a new arrangement each day. She was perhaps the one person in the entire building Carla liked. If her headache hadn't been so bad—and if she hadn't arrived so late—she would have stopped for a chat. Instead, she managed a thin smile and a wave as she passed the desk. "Morning."

"Decker was looking for you." Viv leaned across the counter and dropped her voice. "It sounded like you were going to get in trouble if he knew you were late, so I said you were out getting coffee."

"Lifesaver." Carla made a mental note to buy Viv lunch as she ducked into the station's back rooms before Superintendent Decker could find her.

Helmer Police Station, serving the town and farms clustered around the base of the Cobb Mountain Range, wasn't a large outpost. The building had once been a courthouse, and relics from the previous era filled the narrow brick halls: wooden doors with aged metal bolts, chips and cracks in the bricks from small earthquakes and innumerable scuffles, and the tangy smell of many generations of people crammed into an over-manned building.

Supposedly, the council was considering moving them to a larger, more modern station. The council was supposedly going to do a lot of things, like deal with the poverty in the area, clean up the river, put some extra regulations in place to stop the tourists from being such idiots, and generally make everyone a little less miserable.

She was being uncharitable, she knew. She lived in one of the most beautiful places in the country. If her office had a window—and if there hadn't been so many other buildings obscuring the view—she could have looked up and seen the majestic Cobb Mountains scoring the skyline. Lush and green, occasionally snow-tipped and surrounded by one of the largest primeval forests in the country, it certainly pulled in enough tourists.

And that was most of her problem. The number of people

in their tiny town occasionally doubled as tourists flocked in to visit the mountain. The nature enthusiasts weren't so bad. They were generally polite and friendly, and they didn't litter. The thrill seekers made her chronic migraines flare up, though. They wanted to hike the mountain. They wanted to ski on the mountain when there was snow. They wanted to treat the town like their own personal hotel resort, get drunk, get into fights, and inevitably destroy property.

A lot of people in Helmer wanted stricter laws about the tourists, but the fact was that would never happen as long as the tourists kept opening their wallets. Snow season was cash season for the town, and a lot of people's livelihoods relied on the college kids who pilgrimaged there.

Carla pushed into the office she shared with two other detectives and slid into her seat. Neither of her colleagues acknowledged her. They had a mutual, unspoken agreement: don't bother me, and I won't bother you. Carla was grateful for their reciprocal dislike of small talk.

Her desk was cluttered with work, which was normal. She discreetly popped two aspirin out of her pocket, swallowed them, then put her head down with the intention of getting through some of the backlog, or at least trying to.

"Delago." Decker slammed the door as he entered, and Carla flinched. She really would have preferred having enough time for the tablets to do their work before talking to Decker. Still, she fixed an alert, energetic expression on her face as she swiveled to face him.

"Morning, sir."

"Where the hell have you been?" He was a tall, blocky man who seemed to live for chewing people out over their mistakes. Salt-and-pepper gray stubble coated his chin, and he wore his hat, even indoors, to hide his thinning hair. That knowledge didn't stop him from seeming intimidating as he loomed over her. Being six foot four gave someone an air of importance, no matter how much hair they had lost.

"Getting coffee." *Thank you, Viv.*

"I don't care if you were getting a lifesaving blood transfusion. Get your ass into this office on time, or I'll make your life hell."

She almost said, "Mission accomplished," but she swallowed the remark. Decker would lynch her for it. Instead, she said, "Sure thing, sir."

"Got a new one for you." He brandished a manila folder. "A kid's gone missing."

"How old?"

He flipped open the file, glanced at the details, and grunted. "Twenty-two."

"Twenty-two isn't—" She bit her tongue and held out her hand. "I'll look into it, sir."

Decker didn't pass over the folder and left her hanging. "Some guy phoned the station last night, demanding we start searching for her, but he wasn't family and couldn't give us any leads. I thought he was delusional. Was going to put it in the shredder, but then her actual family called this morning. Hell knows what that kid was on, though."

"I'll take a look." Her hand still outstretched, Carla wiggled her fingers. She was dangerously close to letting some of her irritation leak into her voice, which would only goad Decker on further. He liked to play mind games, like giving her a week's worth of tasks in one day then reaming her out for not getting through her workload.

He glanced over the other two officers—both kept their eyes fixed firmly on their papers—then grunted, handing Carla the file. "Take care of it quickly. You're on patrol this afternoon. We're still waiting on the Dobson report too."

"I'll take care of it." The words escaped through gritted teeth.

Decker narrowed his eyes, seeming to weigh whether her sass had been enough to reprimand, then mercifully, he grunted and left.

Carla breathed deeply once the door closed, then she flipped the case open and glanced across the details. It was pretty typical, as far as missing person cases went. A college student, Eileen Hershberger, had been uncontactable since the previous evening. According to her family, she'd been traveling across the country, and Helmer and its famous mountain were the last stop on her trip.

They were the only details Carla needed to predict how the case would roll out. Eileen would have been dreading the return to her boring home life and her studies. She would have gone out to enjoy her last night of freedom and gotten drunk. Very drunk. At that moment, Eileen was probably waking up on someone's lawn with a hangover to rival Carla's and a missed flight, to boot.

She would get in touch with her parents, full of apologies and excuses, and the case would be closed.

Carla had created a theorem during her eight years as an officer at Helmer. She called it Carla's Law. If she ignored a problem for long enough, it almost inevitably fixed itself. For better or worse.

She threw Eileen's file to the back of her desk and started on the Dobson report.

CHAPTER 4

Monday, 2:50 p.m.

TODD SAT AT THE back of the Hershbergers' living room. He felt painfully, agonizingly uncomfortable. No one had spoken to him since Chris had yelled at him. If not for Eileen's sake, he would have left already.

He was surrounded by people he had once considered friends. Chris paced near the doorway to the kitchen, where his parents were on the phone to the police…again. Hailey sat in the old paisley recliner, twirling her hair between her fingers so aggressively that Todd thought it might permanently curl. Anna sat at the table, arms folded ahead of herself as she frowned at the wood.

Flint looked bored out of his brain. He roved around the space in erratic patterns, driving Todd wild. Sometimes, he stopped to lean on the corner of Hailey's chair. Sometimes, he passed Chris and gave him a firm nod. He didn't pay any attention to Todd.

Todd had considered them his friends, but they weren't really, he was slowly realizing. He hung out with them often, sometimes once or twice a week, but his only connection to them was through Chris. Eileen, Anna, and Hailey were close, like women often were. Hailey was dating Flint, the idiot jock. They suited each other. Together, they might have enough brain cells for some basic motor functions. Flint and Chris had been roommates in college. The whole lot of them were interconnected, except for Todd. Chris was his lifeline to the social group. If Chris wasn't in the picture, he didn't get an invitation when they hung out.

And now, Chris was mad at him—had actually yelled at him, in front of everyone. It was galling. He had expected Chris to be relieved he had a friend who cared enough about Eileen to offer help, but when Todd had arrived, he'd barely gotten two sentences out before Chris blew up and called him a creep.

He wasn't. He was just worried. It wasn't creepy to be concerned. Maybe things would have gone better if he hadn't brought printouts of all of Eileen's holiday photos, but he'd wanted to show Chris the guy she'd been leaning against in the club. There was a chance the stranger was involved. Why else would he be pushing up against Eileen like they were close, when they clearly weren't?

And now everyone was treating him like a social pariah. They hadn't asked him to leave, but he definitely didn't feel welcome in their little gathering. He was staying, though. For Eileen's sake.

Chris stopped pacing and turned to face the kitchen. Everyone seemed to sense the change in his mood. Hailey stopped twirling her hair, Flint stopped roving, and Anna lifted her head an inch.

Mr. and Mrs. Hershberger emerged. Mrs. Hershberger managed a smile, but it couldn't hide how much she'd been crying. Her eyes were puffy, and her cheeks were pale, even with makeup. "Well, they're still working on it."

"We got the runaround," Mr. Hershberger grunted.

Todd didn't have much respect for either of them, but he liked Mr. Hershberger more. He said things like they were.

Mrs. Hershberger bobbed her head in quick nods and knit her fingers together. "They said there's an active investigation, and… and…"

Chris pulled his mother into a hug. He towered over her, patting her head. They looked ridiculous. "Call again in another hour. And keep trying her cell phone."

"That's it?" Todd spoke in spite of himself. "You've got to do something more. The police are morons. Call the FBI."

"Todd, I swear—" Chris held out his hand, fingers shaking, as he scowled at Todd. "Stop talking, okay, man? You're not helping."

Todd rolled his shoulders and slouched back. If they wanted to let their daughter be murdered in another state, so be it.

Chris turned back and said something to his mother. Her shoulders were shaking. She reminded Todd of a frightened farm animal.

"She's been gone for less than twenty-four hours." Anna laced her fingers together on the tabletop. She sounded like she was speaking carefully. "She might still be on her way home. Someone should be at the airport, just in case. But it might also be wise to explore some other avenues."

Chris looked at Anna over his mother's head. "Got any ideas?"

"If she's not at the airport this afternoon, someone should fly to Helmer to put some additional pressure on the police. In the meantime, we can post a call on social media, asking for information. Use some of her photos. If you have a few hundred dollars to spend, you can target Facebook ads to the people in the town where she went missing."

Chris's face lit up. He pointed at Anna and snapped his fingers. "That's brilliant. We'll do that."

Todd tried not to let his frustration show. He could have told them about social media. Why did Anna get praise for helping, when he'd been trying just as hard?

He knew why. Anna was the golden child. The smarty-pants in a fancy college, studying psychology, as useless as it was. He'd tried to like her for a long while, but the truth was, she liked to pretend she was better than everyone else.

"See if you can find the guy in the photo at the club," he said, but no one listened to him. They were all talking—actually excited, as if that were even remotely appropriate—and gathered around the table as they mocked up a message to post. He approached but didn't try to break into their circle. Instead, he cleared his throat. "Do you want me to wait at the airport for her?"

"Nah, man, I can do that." Chris didn't look up from the

notepad. He was scribbling frantically. "I vote we keep it simple. 'Missing' in huge words then 'please help' below it. We'll need photos of her too. Do we know what she was wearing yesterday?"

"Denim jacket," Todd said. "Blue shirt underneath, cargo pants, and white sneakers. And the necklace she bought from the thrift shop last year."

They all stared at him. He met their gazes, unashamed. "I figured it would be important, so I analyzed the photo she posted at breakfast. Assuming she didn't change—"

Hailey pulled a face. "Maybe we should search for her in Todd's basement."

"Hey," Chris barked, pointing a finger at Hailey. "Don't joke about this."

She lifted both hands, eyebrows raised. "Sorry."

Chris turned on Todd. "Maybe you should be heading home, buddy. I'll text you when we know something. Okay?"

So, they'd finally had enough of him. He smiled, not caring if they saw how much he was seething under the expression. "Sure. Whatever. Have fun making your flyers. She's probably dead by now, anyway."

Angry words followed him as he stormed out of the house. Beneath it all, he could hear Mrs. Hershberger sobbing. He didn't care. They were idiots. Their stupid Facebook meme wouldn't do a thing to help find Eileen. The police were obviously blowing them off. If she was going to be found, someone would need to take action…and no one seemed to care enough about her to do that.

Except for him.

Sitting in his car, Todd looked up prices for plane tickets to Redmond, the closest airport to Helmer. They were only a few hundred dollars. He'd been saving up for an Xbox, so he had enough money squirreled away to cover the flight and a few supplies.

Todd put his key into the ignition, turned it, and accelerated onto the road, tires screeching.

CHAPTER 5

Tuesday, 12:45 p.m.

CARLA'S DAY WAS NOT going well. Gould, the man who normally sat to her right, was sick, so she'd inherited his workload. Decker, the bastard, had dropped by just to laboriously remind her of all of the work she still needed to complete. As if she didn't know. She had a stack as high as her arm.

On top of it all, the missing girl from the previous day hadn't shown up. Carla's Law had failed her; the problem hadn't resolved itself, and the parents had actually flown into town to harass her at work.

Carla felt for them. The father, a stocky man with deep-set eyes, hadn't yelled or even spoken much, but she could feel an intense terror in his voice. His daughter was missing, and he was powerless to do anything about it. His fear was staggering in its intensity. The mother was worse. She'd been crying too much to string more than a few words together.

Carla was terrified of public emotion. As a female officer, she was often sent on tasks where a degree of tact and empathy was required. She'd been responsible for telling people a family member had died, consoling Mrs. Glenn when a punk killed her dog, and responding to a call when a child was found drowned in a pool. Those kinds of jobs inevitably fell to Carla, and she was possibly the world's least qualified person for it. She hated tears. They made her uncomfortable and tongue-tied, and her every effort at comfort fell flat. Apparently, most people considered stilted pats on the back inadequate.

So meeting with the Hershberger parents had been a living nightmare. The father's quiet, desperate stare and the mother's inconsolable sobbing had been too much. Carla had nearly begged them to leave her office. They had achieved their goal, though, even if unintentionally. Carla had bumped up the case's priority.

She sat hunched over her desk, phone pressed to one ear as she waited for the hotel clerk to return. Eileen Hershberger had been staying at a popular tourist hotel in the town center. It wasn't a small place, and spats and belligerent drunks weren't uncommon there. The station got calls for assistance a couple of times a month during the quiet season and a couple of times a week during peak season. Carla had been able to ascertain that Eileen hadn't checked out of the hotel when she was supposed to, and her luggage had been found inside her room.

The big question—the one Carla was trying to get an answer to—was whether Eileen had gone missing in the town or in the woods. She'd had plans to visit a popular trail into the Ashlough Forest that day, and her last Facebook post, uploaded at 9:20 a.m., had encouraged that theory.

But there was a wide window during which she could have gone missing. One of the hotel staff remembered her at breakfast that morning. Her family hadn't known she was missing until she failed to call them after dinner. That left nine hours for something to happen to her, either during the hike or on either side.

To answer the questions of *when* and *where*, Carla needed to figure out how the girl had intended to get to the trail. It was too far to walk to from the hotel room, and there was no evidence Eileen had rented a car. She might have taken a taxi, a shuttle bus, or worse, Uber. Spending her work hours looking into the seedy part of humanity might have darkened Carla's view of her fellow mankind, but she hated the concept of Uber. In her eyes, it was barely a step above hitchhiking. At least taxi drivers had to go through rigorous background checks.

Helmer wasn't exactly a suburban utopia, but it wasn't a hellhole, either. Rapes were more common than Carla liked. Theft reports were frequent. But manslaughter was rare, and when it happened, it was usually accidental, such as drunk driving and bar fights that went too far. Deliberate, premeditated murders almost never landed on Carla's desk.

Still, Eileen was a prime candidate—a young, pretty blond girl with an inviting smile, traveling alone in a strange city. The photos made her look trusting. She was slim, but without any of the muscle that would come from self-defense classes.

"Carla?"

The word was a whisper, and Carla didn't hear it until it was repeated. She turned to face the door, phone still pressed to her ear, to find Viv standing there. The receptionist wore cloth roses in her hair this time. She bounced on her heels and gave a nervous wave.

"I'm free," Carla said, not moving the phone. "What's up?"

"Sorry to bother you, but we've had another call from that guy. Todd Marson. He's becoming, uh, agitated. He says you're not returning his calls."

Carla let her head drop back and her eyes roll up into her skull. "Tell him to sod off and let me do my bloody job."

"Should I—"

"No, no, don't actually tell him that." Carla pressed her palm into her temple. "I've already spoken to him twice. Unless he has something meaningful to contribute…and meaningful by *our* measure, not his…give him an excuse. Tell him I'm investigating leads or something."

"Sure." Viv began backing out of the door. "He, um, he was very insistent that you investigate a gentleman in one of Hershberger's photos…?"

"Yes, yes, he's mentioned that. Once or twice."

The man to Carla's left, Lau, snorted a laugh. He would have heard some of Carla's phone calls with Todd Marson.

Carla shrugged. "Fact is, that photo was taken on Thursday,

and Hershberger went missing on Sunday. Considering how many people Hershberger would have interacted with on any one day, the significance is minimal."

"Right. Excuses, it is."

Carla gave Viv a thumbs-up then let her smile fall into a scowl as she turned back to her desk. She shouldn't have agreed to sit on the phone with the hotel clerk. She'd been waiting for at least twenty minutes by that point and could have been using the time to make progress elsewhere.

Social media had been a blessing for police officers. In days gone past, a lot of Carla's work would have been based on interviews, he-said-she-said scenarios, and eyewitness accounts. Now, people uploaded their lives to the cloud. There was nothing more satisfying than being able to pull up videos of idiot teens breaking public property—videos the teens had taken and uploaded themselves—in court. Those cases were easy and quick to close.

It had helped her narrow down Hershberger's activity on Sunday, as well. The woman had taken a photo at breakfast, tangible proof that she was safe and well. The status update an hour later could have conceivably been uploaded by a third party who wanted to disguise the hour of Eileen's disappearance, but it didn't seem likely. The tone was consistent with earlier posts.

The conspicuous absence of photos following the hike, while not definite, did point toward trouble either before, during, or immediately after the trip to the forest.

She still hoped Carla's Law would play out and Eileen would be found without the police's help. But they'd passed forty-eight hours since Hershberger's last sighting, and with each passing minute, it became increasingly unlikely that Eileen would be found safe and well.

The phone clicked, and the clerk, breathless, returned. "I'm so sorry for keeping you waiting. But I have something that might help. I called all of the staff members who were on duty Sunday, and one of them remembers Ms. Hershberger. She asked them to phone a shuttle bus that could take her to the Ashlough Forest trails. It was due to pick her up at eleven."

"Good." Carla clicked her pen and held it over her notepad. "I'm going to need that staff member's name and contact details, as well as the name of the shuttle bus company."

CHAPTER 6

Tuesday, 8:10 p.m.

TODD SAT AT THE bar, clutching his drink in both hands. He didn't remember what he'd ordered, but it was a brown liquor in the bottom of a glass and tasted like liquid garbage.

He'd arrived at Helmer the previous afternoon. It had taken some time, but he'd eventually located the hotel Eileen had been staying in, using a photo of her in the dining section as a reference. He'd checked into a room there. The reception and housekeeping staff had both been incredibly rude when he'd asked which room Eileen had been staying in, so he hadn't been able to look for clues in or around it.

Using the photo of Eileen holding the mocktail, he'd hopped through Helmer's eight bars. It had taken him longer than he would have liked. He hadn't wanted to waste money on a taxi, so he'd been forced to walk from location to location. The town wasn't big, thankfully, but it had taken him two nights to find the right watering hole.

His funds were short. He'd paid for the earliest flight he could get, which had cost a premium, and checked in to Eileen's hotel at the last moment, which had cost another premium. He was also paying for drinks at the bar to justify his presence there. He didn't have enough left for a plane ticket home. He would need to lean on someone for that; maybe Eileen's family would look after him when he found their daughter.

In the meantime, his priority was finding the guy in the picture. He had a photocopy set on the bar in front of himself, and every time the door opened, he examined the new arrival.

The more Todd looked at the photo, the more he became convinced there was something wrong with the guy. He was nearly a head taller than Eileen and seemed to lean over her possessively. He looked sleazy, too, wearing sunglasses on top of his head even though he was indoors and a cheap jacket over a plain T-shirt. The photo cut off at his waist, but it looked like he was wearing loose jeans.

Most people said not to judge a book by its cover, but Todd believed a cover could tell a lot about the story inside. He always dressed well, combed his hair, and kept himself clean. He had acne and a large nose, but they weren't his fault. He took care of his appearance.

Guys like the man in the photo didn't take care of their appearance, which meant they probably didn't take care of the stuff on the inside, either. Todd liked to read. He liked to know about current events, even though he very rarely met anyone who was intellectual enough to discuss them. The man in the photo probably cared about nothing except drinking, partying, and hitting on pretty girls. Todd found the attitude repulsive.

It was just a shame that girls always went for the jerks. Because Todd was quiet and not a blowhard, it took longer for girls to notice him and longer still for them to get to know him. But if they took the time to, they would find he had so much more to offer.

Eileen wasn't like the other girls, though. She knew better than to run after the jerks. Gradually, she and Todd had been growing closer. She was still getting to know him, but he thought she was starting to like him just as much as he liked her. He'd just needed a little more time to fully win her over.

The pub was half-empty on a Tuesday night. Todd had been there for nearly three hours, sipping liquor and staring at the crowd. He felt like he was starting to become unwelcome, but it was his only lead. All he needed was for the jerk to walk through the door, then he could get the truth out of him…either with force or without. The other man would have to make that choice.

"Can I get you anything else?" The bartender leaned on the counter. His smile was polite but not friendly.

Todd looked down at his glass. It still had a tablespoon of liquid in it. "I'm fine for a while more. Thanks."

As the barkeep stepped away, Todd let his eyes rove from his glass to the photo. He was prepared to come back to the club every evening if that was what it took, but maybe it wouldn't be necessary. He cleared his throat. "Wait, uh, wait!"

The barkeep turned back to him. "Changed your mind?"

"Uh—" Todd pushed the photo across the bar. "Just a question. I'm looking for this guy. I think he might be a regular here."

The man picked up the photo, gave it a quick scan, and passed it back. "Sorry. I know all of my regulars, and he's not one of them."

"But..." Frustration built. The stranger in the photo *had* to come back. He was the missing piece of the puzzle. Without him, Todd had nothing.

"I don't know the girl, either," the barkeep said. "We get a lot of tourists in here. He would have been in town for a few nights, but you're not going to find him now."

"You don't know that. He...he was here last week..."

"Yeah. I know." The barkeep pointed a finger at the guy in the photo. "See that design on his jacket? He's from a New Zealand college. We had a bunch of them in last week, but they left on Friday. Unless he decided to stay behind, he'd be long gone."

Feeling as though he'd been slapped, Todd opened his mouth then closed it again. If the jerk left on Friday, he couldn't be involved with Eileen's disappearance. Which left Todd feeling as though he was trying to grasp at smoke. He had no leads, no clues, no way to find her, and no way to get home.

"So..." The barkeep drummed his fingers on the bar. "Can I get you another drink or what?"

CHAPTER 7

Wednesday, 7:50 a.m.
Lower Andrea River, base of Cobb Mountains

PETE'S BOOTS MADE SUCKING noises as he pulled them out of the mud. It had rained the previous night, not heavily and not for long, but it had been enough to swell the river. The shrimp were more active after rain. He carried a half dozen small shrimp baskets over one shoulder and a bucket in his spare hand. With just a tiny bit of good luck, he and his wife would be feasting on a platter heaped with crustaceans later that night.

He'd lived in the valley below the mountains for most of his seventy years, but Pete still felt a sense of awe wash over him every time he looked up at the green-and-brown behemoth. He'd seen the valley change. Forest had become farming land, houses had become hotels, and now the unknown, uncrowded fishing places were growing few and far between. But the mountain never changed. It had lived there for an eternity and would probably survive an eternity more as long as the politicians found a way to stop themselves from instigating nuclear war.

The rushing, bubbling river seemed to call Pete forward as he waded through the marshy field. This part of the river was his secret haven. The tourists hadn't discovered it, thank heaven, and no one was using the field that bordered it. But the water was teeming with shrimp. A few hours spent putting down the baskets and scooping up their catch would give him and his wife a meal that would have cost them more than a hundred dollars in a hotel.

Pete took care as he crept down the incline to the riverbank. He was feeling his age. Each year made the slippery mud a little riskier and the threat of a broken hip a little more immediate. He sent up a silent prayer of thanks as his boots touched the rocks bordering the river.

The water was faster and clearer than normal thanks to the rain. He followed the bank until he found the little sheltered, slow-moving corners the shrimp seemed to favor. He dropped a couple of baskets in each. He didn't need to use bait. Shrimp were naturally curious and would explore the new addition to their homes without needing any temptation. Once they passed the narrow opening, they would find the wicker weave made it difficult to leave. Pete could scoop the baskets out, pop their top off, and tip the shrimp into his bucket.

He dropped another basket then straightened to stretch his

back. Something glassy caught the sunlight. The shape was trapped in the reeds and mud of the riverbank, and at first glance, it looked like a small, dark rock. As Pete got closer, he recognized the lens of a camera. He'd once owned one a lot like it.

Pete straddled the riverbank and a submerged stone as he bent to pull the camera out of the mud. It was heavy and looked like an expensive brand. He was used to seeing tourists carrying them, though their popularity had waned in the previous years as handheld phones capable of taking both video and photos won the consumerist war.

He turned it over. A small tag had been attached to the underside. Water damage had bled away nearly all of the ink, but enough remained that even Pete's fallible eyes could figure out the name: Eileen Hershberger. Below that was a phone number.

Pete shook water and mud off the camera and climbed out of the riverbed. An unfortunate tourist had probably lost the camera on one of the bridges upriver. If it was digital, it was almost certainly ruined. If it used real film, it might still be salvaged with a bit of TLC. Pete followed the river to another shrimp haven, dropped the last of his baskets, then took his phone out of his pocket. It was an old model, back from the days when they were competing to make their screens as small as possible instead of growing bigger each year. It didn't show movies or browse the internet, but it would work well enough to call the emergency helpline if he slipped and fell, which was the only reason he carried it.

He dialed the number from the base of the camera and listened to his phone ring. There was no answer, and the phone wouldn't even take a message. Pete tried a second time but wasn't surprised when he got the same result. He was tempted to leave the camera on the riverbank.

It must have spent some time in the river, because it was still dripping. Pete shook off the excess water and tried pressing the camera's button. To his surprise, the bulb went off, saturating the reeds with its harsh flash. That answered one question, at least. The camera wasn't digital, and it still worked. That meant there was some point in trying to find its owner. If Eileen Hershberger didn't answer her phone, he could drop it in at the police station and let them handle it.

Pete slung the strap around his neck and tried to ignore the way the water soaked into his shirt. He began hiking back upstream to see if his first traps had caught anything yet.

CHAPTER 8

Thursday, 11:30 a.m.

CARLA'S WEEK HAD STARTED badly and was getting worse with every passing day. Gould was still out sick, and his caseload remained Carla's responsibility. She'd been yelled at twice by civilians and four times by Decker for being slow. She was actually, genuinely putting in effort, but the universe was conspiring to make her job as difficult as possible.

She'd spent most of the previous day trying to track down leads relating to the Hershberger case. As much as Ms. Krensky believed her neighbor's habit of mowing at six in the morning should be Carla's top priority, Carla was trying to direct her efforts toward the cases that really, genuinely mattered—such as a person who had been missing for four days.

The more Carla dug into the case, the more she developed a pit of uneasiness in her stomach. It was growing messy. Initially, she'd hoped it would be as simple as Eileen growing tired of her parents' overly possessive behavior and running away for a few days. It was no longer possible to believe that. Eileen had been at college for a year before taking the vacation—studying to become a middle school teacher—and everyone Carla spoke to agreed that she had been looking forward to starting the next year. She phoned her parents every evening not because they demanded it, but because she wanted to. She had a healthy social life, no evidence of drugs or debts, and no sketchy boyfriends in the picture.

That left two options: she had met foul play or become lost in the forest. And Carla couldn't even get a feel for which eventuality was more likely.

The hotel concierge said a shuttle had collected Eileen to take her to the forest. Carla had shown the shuttle driver Eileen's photographs, and he claimed to remember her, but she got the sense he was saying what he thought she wanted to hear. He'd made a stop at Eileen's hotel, that was certain; a family had boarded at the same time. Carla was still trying to track them down.

If Eileen had gotten onto the shuttle bus, it would have taken her to the forest. The driver said all passengers—at least twenty—disembarked then, and he had picked up a group later that afternoon to return them home. The driver didn't remember if Eileen was part of that returning group, but he thought she must have been. However, he hadn't stopped back at Eileen's hotel.

It was possible Eileen had gone somewhere for dinner. The shuttle bus made several trips to the forest each day, but if she was planning to hike a trail instead of just sitting and looking at the scenery, Eileen would have had to return late in the afternoon—around five thirty. She might have gotten off the shuttle near an eatery and walked back to the hotel.

That was as far as Carla's tracking skills had gotten her. She'd put out a public request for people to contact the station if they'd seen Eileen on Sunday, but a lot of the people on the shuttle bus were tourists who had already moved on to a new destination.

Carla had requested a search party to start scouring Ashlough Forest, but it was hard to do much with so little information. A dozen trails led through the forest, some twenty-minute round trips, some full-day hikes. Without knowing which trail Eileen had taken, they would need to canvass more than a hundred square kilometers, which was impossible. Helmer Station had a limited police force, and helicopter search missions were expensive enough to hurt their budget. It was hard to argue that resources should be directed toward a search when Carla wasn't completely sure Eileen had gone missing in the mountains.

Decker had agreed to send three men to search the trails. That was the best he would do without more compelling evidence, or at the very least, an idea of which trail Eileen had hiked.

Carla had planned to spend time that day tracking down the tourists on the shuttle bus. If even just one of them remembered Eileen, Carla could narrow down the search. That had been the plan, anyway. She'd walked into the office that morning to see Viv, wearing fake tulips in her hair, waving to get her attention.

"A parcel was dropped off yesterday afternoon. A man found a camera in a river. It has a name on it. Eileen Hershberger. That's a case you're working on, isn't it?"

Carla could have melted a hole through the floor with the sheer strength of her anger. The camera had to be a significant lead, and it had been sitting in the station for most of a day without her knowing. Apparently, no one had recognized the name, and it was considered a standard lost-and-found situation. An officer had tried calling Eileen to tell her to pick up her camera, and it was only after he'd spent most of the day trying to get through to her that someone recognized the name was connected to Carla's case.

The camera could have saved Carla half a precious day. It confirmed that Eileen had gone missing in the mountains. The camera had been found in the lower Andrea River, and the higher parts of the stream ran across several of the hiking trails. Carla was working on the theory that Eileen had dropped the camera in the river. It had rained on Tuesday night, and the flow would have washed it down to the mountain's base.

Carla hadn't expected the girl to own a film camera. Everyone seemed to have graduated to digital, unless they were trying to be hipsters. She hadn't even known that film development shops were still open. A quick search on the internet confirmed that none had survived in Helmer, but one still existed in the next town over, where a camera store still offered film-development services.

The film clerk handed Carla an envelope full of photos. She peeked in at them. By her calculation, there were several dozen.

She was attracting stares by sitting in the camera store, so she took the photos back to the station, where she could look at them at her leisure.

She plopped the stack down on her desk and began examining them. The first pictures had been taken in Helmer. Carla recognized their town hall, their wildlife park, and their theater. Eileen appeared in some of the photos, apparently having asked a stranger to take the pictures for her. She was beaming in every single one. Her face had become uncomfortably familiar to Carla over the previous days.

After that, there was a series of pictures taken from inside the forest. One showed Eileen swimming in one of the natural pools. She had propped the camera in the hollow of a tree and set a delay timer to capture herself splashing in the water. She'd also photographed a waterfall and large trees, as well as a signpost.

Then, abruptly, the tone changed. Eileen had taken photos at night. The harsh flash highlighted branches and leaves, their colors distorted and polarized. The light couldn't cut through the darkness between the nearest trunks. It left great swaths of black filling the pictures.

Carla kept flipping. The remainder of the pictures were almost identical. Sometimes the angle changed slightly. A couple looked in a different direction. But predominantly, the camera was capturing the same scene. They showed the same branches and the same trees.

"Why?" Carla reached the end of the stack and flipped back

to count them. Eileen had used a complete thirty-six-pack of film. The first eight photos were normal—the kind of pictures a young adult social butterfly might take. Then five snapshots of the forest in daylight. The final twenty-three were all taken at night.

Carla might have thought she was using the flash to see her way in the dark, except the position never changed. The angle suggested Eileen might have been sitting when she took them.

It was possible Eileen had been trying to signal someone. Repeated flashes of light directed toward the nearest habitation might have attracted attention…if Eileen hadn't been in the middle of the forest. Carla occasionally spent her weekends hiking in Ashlough, where the trees created a natural filter for both noise and light. Walking even a short distance from the group made a person invisible. If Eileen had heard someone walking nearby—another hiker, maybe—then they would have heard her if she'd yelled. There was no purpose in using light instead.

The final option was the grimmest. Eileen might have been using the flash to frighten off a wild animal. That would explain why the pictures were all facing the one direction. Carla picked one out of the stack and squinted, but she couldn't see anything between the trees. Still, the forest had its share of small predators. They generally weren't aggressive enough to bother tourists, but sometimes an animal got desperate. And if Eileen had been hurt, the smell of blood wouldn't help matters.

Carla looked at her clock. It was closing in on midday. That made it exactly four days since Eileen had last been seen. Four days of freezing nights, no food, and no water. Carla's Law had come back into effect. And she was due for a very unpleasant discussion with Eileen Hershberger's parents.

CHAPTER 9

Thursday, 12:30 p.m.

Entrance to the Ashlough Forest, Cobb Mountain Range

TODD COULDN'T STOP SHIVERING. He gripped the straps to his backpack hard enough that his fingers ached as he pretended to examine the sign beside the entrance to the trails. He supposed it was a pretty painting: brown roads snaked through green trees, with bright blue used to mark the rivers. He was too wrapped up in his own mind to see it clearly, though.

Eileen had to be in the forest. It was the only possible answer. He'd staked out the hotel to see if anyone suspicious tried to come by. He'd shown her photo to dozens of people around town. No one had seen anything. Whether Eileen's disappearance was an accident or part of some malevolent plot, everything pointed to it happening in the forest.

He hitched his backpack a little higher. He'd come prepared. But that didn't stop nerves from twisting his stomach into knots. More than anything, he wished he had his friends with him. The others would probably cause more trouble than they helped, but at least Chris was a solid buddy. Their fight left a feeling of sickness in the pit of his stomach every time he thought about it, so he didn't.

The shuttle bus's doors closed with a whoosh, and its engine grumbled as it rolled back down the road. Most of the people Todd had shared the shuttle with had already disappeared down the trails. He needed to take a moment, though. Ground himself. Figure out a plan.

He'd expected one trail looping through the woods, but according to the map, there were twelve. Some went far into the mountain and were marked "advanced." Shorter loops were "easy." He didn't think Eileen would go for either of those. She kept active but wasn't the type who would spend all day in a forest. That left the middle bracket, intermediary. Four trails bore the tag. He would just have to start with one and work his way through them until he found her.

A lot of the advanced and intermediate trails had big red exclamation points over them, with annotations. He read a couple. *Unstable ground, slippery ground, rockslides, be prepared. Symptoms of a lawsuit-happy country,* he figured. People couldn't sue if there was a caution sign.

Another, larger sign stood before the map, painted in bright reds and yellows to draw attention. It bore a simple, if unfriendly, message.

BE PREPARED

THIS FOREST HAS CLAIMED MULTIPLE LIVES.
WE RECOMMEND THE FOLLOWING
PRECAUTIONS TO KEEP YOU SAFE:

- Bring a companion, if possible.
- Carry extra water.
- Obey all signs and instructions.
- Be aware of your surroundings and possible risks.
- Advanced trails are recommended for experienced hikers only.

STAY SAFE, AND ENJOY YOUR VISIT
TO ASHLOUGH FOREST!

Of course Todd was prepared. He'd read enough about nature survival to know how to handle himself. He returned to the map and chose the highest trail. It crossed a pool, and he knew Eileen liked to swim. That would make a good place to start, at least. He turned toward the forest and stepped through the arch that marked the nature reserve's boundary.

The trees were immense. He knew a bit about plants and thought he could name some of them, but they were older than anything he'd seen before. Three people could have stood in a circle around one of the larger trunks and not been able to hold hands.

He tried not to shiver as the permanent shadows dropped his temperature. He'd brought jackets and blankets in case he needed to spend the night in the forest. He was prepared to stay as long as it took to find Eileen. She just needed to hang on long enough for him to reach her.

She was a strong girl. She wouldn't give up easily. As long as foul play hadn't been involved—he still hadn't discounted the theory that the New Zealand student had stayed behind and lured Eileen into the forest—he thought she would have found a way to survive. He'd watched a documentary about a woman who had managed to live for three years in the jungle. The most important thing was to not do anything stupid. And Eileen wasn't stupid, not like a lot of other girls.

The paths began to fork. Todd took the trail farthest to the right. He was glad to see none of the tourists had taken the same trail. He didn't want company. Finding Eileen would be easier if he was left alone with his intellect and his instincts.

He'd heard it claimed that it was possible for people to know when bad things happened to someone they were close to, like twins sensing when their mirror was in trouble or elderly people knowing when their spouses had passed away. Todd had always thought it was baloney. But as the trail cut him farther off from humanity, he started to think there was a kernel of truth to the concept of some kind of interdimensional link that tied soul mates.

Todd tried to clear his mind enough for it to guide him. He closed his eyes and breathed deeply through his nose. He let the forest's noise surround him: insects, birds, and creaking trees. He tried to imagine an invisible thread leading out from his chest, disappearing somewhere into the forest. It would go on for miles, weaving between the trees, leading him straight to...

Raucous laughter disturbed the stillness. Todd gritted his teeth as he looked over his shoulder. Someone was coming up the path behind him.

"Screw this." He gripped the straps to his backpack and started marching. He had half a mind to confront the hikers and tell them to give him some space. They were out for a nice afternoon stroll. He was on a life-or-death mission. Logically, his needs should take precedence. The only thing that kept him mute was the knowledge that they would probably bicker about it and waste precious time.

The laughter came in intermittent bursts. They were a little way behind him but gaining. Todd scowled at his marching feet. The noise made it impossible to focus. And the more upset he became, the harder it was to pay attention to his surroundings.

Well, there was one place he could go to regain his composure. The hikers would be sticking to the trail like the lemmings they were. He'd always known his search would inevitably carry him off the well-beaten path. It was just happening a little sooner than he'd planned.

Todd threw one final look over his shoulder then stepped off the path and into the heart of the forest.

Thursday, 12:45 p.m.

EVERYTHING WAS HORRIBLE.

Mrs. Hershberger wailed. Carla had never imagined the short, rounded woman could sound so much like an alarm siren, but head clasped in hands, shoulders shaking, and mouth wide open to release those howling, screaming cries, she did.

Carla was horrifically unequipped to help. Occasionally, she picked up the tissue box and moved it an inch closer on the table. She'd tried patting Mrs. Hershberger's back. Nothing was helping.

Her husband wasn't letting any emotion escape, but Carla could see it brewing under the surface, threatening to explode out if the pressure became too great. Once in a while, he would blink and repeat the same series of questions. "Is there anything you can do?" or "Can you send more men?" or "She might still be alive, mightn't she?"

Carla sat on the edge of her desk in a miserable, failed attempt to look more relatable. She clasped her hands ahead of herself and repeated the answers she'd been giving him for the last ten minutes. "Her chances of surviving are negligible. Almost nonexistent."

The words weren't sinking in. Mr. Hershberger stared at the opposite wall, where white paint had been chipped over decades to reveal the gray plaster beneath. They were in the conference room. It wasn't a large space, but at least it was private. Carla didn't want the couple dealing with their grief where strangers could gawk at them.

"But…" His hands, thick and weathered, flexed in his lap. He looked like he was trying to grasp onto something solid. His face was blank and unpleasantly slack. "There must be some way…"

"The mountains are a dangerous place to hike, especially if she strayed off the path. We lose perhaps one or two tourists there every year." Carla fought to keep her face open and placid, even though Mrs. Hershberger's wailing nearly drowned out her words. "Often, we can retrieve them, but not always."

"She wouldn't." He swallowed, and his whole face seemed to quiver. "She…she wouldn't go off the path. She's a smart girl. There's been a mistake. Search again."

"It's been four days. A single night spent outdoors carries a high risk of…" Carla had intended to say *death*, but she didn't think either of the Hershbergers were prepared to have it spoken about in such blunt terms. "Of the hiker passing away. Each additional night increases that risk substantially. We know for a fact that Eileen didn't make it out of the forest before sundown, which means there isn't much that can be done for her. We still have men out searching. They will bring her body home, if possible. But you have to reconcile yourself to the fact that…"

"My *baby* is *dead*." It was the first time Mrs. Hershberger had spoken since the meeting began. She'd lifted her head. Her face was wet with sweat and tears, and her hair had fallen out of its bun to float about her in thin wisps. Her lips quivered, and an immense, furious energy seemed to rise out of her. "My *baby* is *dead*, and you want me to…to…*reconcile myself*?"

"Sorry." Carla rubbed her hands over her arms. "Bad phrasing. What I meant was…"

"Screw you!" Mrs. Hershberger picked up the glass of water Viv had brought for her then threw it in Carla's face. Not just the water, but the glass, as well. Carla flinched as it hit her temple then flinched again as it fell and smashed on the tile floor.

"Screw…" The woman stood, her whole body shaking, her face blotchy and red. "You." She turned and moved toward the door. Her legs were unsteady, and she staggered, bumping into the filing cabinet as she clutched for the handle. Fresh wails began to emerge, hiccupping and miserable.

Mr. Hershberger rose and followed his wife. Not even her outburst had been enough to crack his shell, but he put his arm around her as they left.

"Damn it." Carla wiped wet hair out of her face. "I need a drink."

The Hershbergers' pain would hang with her for days. If there were anything she could have done to help, she would have. But Carla was almost certain Eileen had died on that first night. And if she'd been lucky enough to survive, the second day would have ended her. Eileen wouldn't have brought any kind of shelter or insulation for a day hike. It had rained twice in that week. Being wet when the sun set was as good as a death sentence.

Carla kicked at the shards of broken glass. She was tempted to leave them for the cleaning crew, but Decker would have her ass. She pulled a couple of sheets of paper out of the printer and began scooping glass fragments into it.

"Excuse me."

Carla startled. Mr. Hershberger had reappeared in the doorway, hands clenched at his sides. He seemed to have won the battle against his emotions, and they were now buried so deeply that Carla couldn't see them anywhere other than his eyes. "Yes?"

"I wanted to ask if we could have her photos."

Carla glanced toward the stack of pictures on the meeting room desk. She understood. The thirty-six pictures contained the last few days of his daughter's life. The shots taken in the darkness might even encompass the final minutes. She picked up the stack. "I can release the originals to you once our investigation concludes. Until then, I can scan them and give you a digital copy. Would that be all right?"

He nodded, the movement jerky and stiff.

Carla bit her lip. "May I ask…the camera was an old model. Film, not digital. Do you know why she brought it on her trip?"

He nodded, and even though he looked at her, his eyes stared at a point beyond her head. "It was her grandfather's. He passed away last year. She was making a collage to remember him."

"I see." Carla glanced back down at the pictures. All of the daytime photos seemed to have been taken with great care. "Why don't you head out to the waiting room. Viv will make you a cup of tea. I'll have these out to you in a few minutes."

Carla waited until he'd disappeared down the hallway, then she took a deep breath and turned on the printer.

For the next few minutes, the room was silent except for the whirr of the scanner, the harsh chopping lights that squeezed out from under the lid, and the sound of two of her co-workers arguing down the hall. Carla's migraine was resurfacing. She felt in her pocket for painkillers, but her pack was empty.

A soft tapping noise came from the door, announcing Viv's arrival. She wore daisies that day, along with a sad smile. "Need any help, boss?"

Carla shrugged. "Nah. Just getting these ready for Mr. Hershberger."

"He's out in reception. He's asking if there's anything *I* can do to find his daughter."

"Oh." Carla let her head drop. The machine chugged under her hand, more reliable and helpful than she was. "No, Viv. He's in grief. But there's nothing we can do."

Viv glanced behind herself then stepped into the conference room and nudged the door closed. "Tell me if this is none of my business, but even if she's not alive, can't you try to find her body? That would give them closure, if nothing else."

"Yeah. That's the ideal. And we still have three men out there looking. But realistically, it's a gesture more than a solution."

Viv frowned. Carla picked the scanned pictures out of the tray and began blocking them. "I keep forgetting you only transferred here last year. You haven't hiked the mountain yet, have you?"

"No."

"Yeah, it's not like a nature reserve between suburbs. If you get lost in those woods, chances are you're not coming out." Carla waved a hand above her head in demonstration. "The canopy is so thick that it can be hard to figure out which direction the sun is in. You can't see the sky, and any planes or helicopters can't see you. The ground is uneven and unstable, so you can only really walk in the daylight, or you risk twisting an ankle in a hole or, worse, falling and breaking your head."

"But if we could figure out which path she started on and which direction she was traveling in..."

"It wouldn't help much, because it's impossible to walk in a straight line in there. If she was smart, she would have sat down as soon as she realized she was lost. But our searchers would have found her by now if that were the case. Instead, as far as we can tell, she kept walking. Which means she could be almost anywhere. Don't forget, the ground isn't flat up there. She could have fallen off cliffs. Fallen into a river and been carried downstream. Fallen into pits that aren't visible unless you're right on top of them. And once she's dead, her body isn't going to stay intact for long. Wildcats and foxes will rip her apart, carry limbs in different directions, chew her until there aren't even whole bones left.

When you factor that in, it's worse than searching for a needle in a haystack. It's like looking for a fish in the ocean, when the fish might have already been eaten. It sounds barbaric, but the reality is that most people who are lost in forests are never recovered."

Viv's face had scrunched up. Even after working in the station for a year, she was still an idealist. Carla sighed.

"We have three people in the forest, just in case we find her by some miracle. We also have volunteers searching through the river where her camera was recovered. Right now, my theory is she might have either fallen into a river or been washed into one during the rains. We found her camera, so there's a good chance we'll recover some other relics from her too. Bones or maybe some jewelry."

The scanner shut itself off. Carla retrieved the last photos out of the tray then checked on the attached laptop that all of the images had come through correctly. The whites of the night pictures looked harsher, and the colors of the day pictures were more vivid. She was happy with that and saved them onto the USB drive.

"Want me to take that out to him?" Viv's voice was a whisper. Somehow, she'd become attached to the missing girl. Now she, too, was upset with Carla. *Terrific.*

Carla gave her a grim smile and held out the USB stick. "Thank you. I'll take the chance to catch up on some of my backlog."

CHAPTER 11

Thursday, 3:30 p.m.

CHRIS COULDN'T STOP WALKING. He wasn't supposed to leave the house, so he looped through the rooms like a caged animal. Living room, kitchen, hallway, office, living room. Repeat.

Flint and Anna were in the kitchen, pretending to study. They'd spent most of the previous days there under various excuses, sometimes with Hailey, as well. He couldn't tell them to go, not when they were trying to help, but he hated being pitied. It solved nothing. Pity wouldn't bring his sister back, help his parents handle their grief, or make his brain turn off.

As he passed the study, the computer pinged. Normally, it had headphones attached to keep it silent, but he'd unplugged them since Eileen had gone missing. He'd set up a special email address for people to contact if they had any leads about her whereabouts.

Anna's suggestion of a Facebook campaign had been a little too successful. It had gone viral, not just in Helmer, but across half the country. They had been flooded with emails and messages. A couple were from people who had actually seen Eileen—none on the day she went missing, but from cafes and tourist attractions over the days or weeks before. But those were the minority. Most messages were variations on the same two themes: "I'm sorry to hear about this. I'm keeping you in my thoughts and prayers." Or "Has she been found yet?"

At first, Chris had tried to reply to every message. It was an overwhelming task, and when the Facebook image surpassed a hundred thousand views, he'd given up. Maybe he would come back to it eventually and thank them for their concern when everything had calmed down. But for now, unless they had any actual, applicable information, they would have to wait.

He moused over the latest email and skimmed the message. "This is such a tragedy. I've shared with my friends. XOXO Barb."

The well wishes were nice, and he knew he should appreciate them more than he did, but they were starting to gall him. Each new ping gave him a spark of hope, no matter how tiny, and the platitudes were nothing but a disappointment.

He followed his path back around to the living room. Anna kept her head down, seemingly focused on her textbook, but he felt her eyes follow him every time he passed. Flint was doing a worse job of faking interest in his studies. It was uncommon for the bulky man to spend more than a day indoors, and he couldn't stop shuffling in his seat. Chris hadn't seen Todd since Monday. He didn't know whether to be relieved or hurt by that.

The phone rang, and they all turned toward it. Flint rose out of his seat and followed Chris to the kitchen as he picked up the landline. "Hello?"

"Bad news, champ." It was his father, who sounded like he might actually be crying. Chris felt like he'd been slapped in the face; he'd never heard his father cry before, not even when they had to put down the family dog.

He clutched the phone with both hands and leaned against the wall. "What is it?"

"They found her camera. She was in the forest, like we thought. They say she's gone."

Anna appeared at his side. She carried one of the dining room chairs and gently placed it behind him.

He refused to sit. "Did they find her body?"

"No. They're still looking. But..." His words were interrupted by a choking gasp. The line was silent for a moment, and when he returned, he sounded more like himself. "I don't think they're looking very hard. They say we should start making arrangements for her funeral."

"Dad..."

"I'm sorry, champ. Your mother's not well. I think we'll stay here for a few more days, just in case, but then we'll come home. Are you all right there by yourself?"

"Yeah."

"I'll talk to you later. Take care."

Chris hung up. He stood by the phone for a moment, staring at it as though it might ring again, as though he might pick it up and find out the whole thing had been a weird, elaborate joke, but it didn't.

"Hey." Flint had folded his arms around his chest and was rocking on his feet. "You okay?"

Chris turned away. He wished he'd asked them to leave. He didn't want company; he just wanted to be alone. The house felt too small, too crowded and hot, so stifling that he couldn't breathe.

Anna reached toward his arm. Her voice was hoarse. "Chris, I'm so sorry."

He picked up the nearest object, the kettle, and threw it at the window. The tempered glass didn't break, but it did make a horrible cracking noise as the kettle's plastic base fractured. Neither Anna nor Flint said anything as Chris bent over the counter, teeth clenched to keep a scream inside.

It wasn't grief. For grief, he would need to be mourning. He wasn't yet.

He kicked the counter then stalked away. His friends didn't follow. Chris wasn't grieving, but he *was* angry. The police had sabotaged the rescue efforts. If they'd started searching the forest as soon as Eileen went missing, they might have found her in time. Instead, they'd stalled, made excuses, and pretended it wasn't even a problem. He would never forgive them for it.

The front door creaked as it opened. Chris lifted his head. As irrational as it was, his heart missed a beat as he thought it might be Eileen home at last. But as he stepped into the hallway, he saw it was only Hailey, wearing gym clothes and with her blond hair tied back in a ponytail. She looked like she'd run from the gym two streets over.

"Sorry," Anna whispered from behind Chris. "I texted her when the phone rang. Is that okay?"

He shrugged. It was fine. Hailey was Eileen's friend, too, and she deserved to know as soon as there was news. It wasn't like he had a monopoly on his sister.

The girls hugged and spoke in quiet voices as they retreated to the living room. Hailey had worn mascara to the gym, and it was starting to bleed as she cried. Chris wished he could join in. It might help to release some of the pent-up emotion, but he wasn't the crying type, especially not with Flint staring at him as though he might have contracted a deadly disease.

"I need to sit down," he mumbled and staggered into the living room. The girls were at the table, so he sat in the recliner.

Flint followed and leaned against the wall. The computer pinged again, but the noise was drowned out by Hailey's sobbing.

This is going to be my life for the next few days, Chris realized. He would sit at home, compulsively checking the emails and waiting for phone calls from his parents, while his friends hovered around and grieved.

He thought it might kill him.

An explosion of urgent, intense energy rushed through him like a shock wave. He clenched his fists on his knees. "I'm going to Helmer."

They all stared at him. Even Hailey stopped crying.

"I'm going there to yell at the police." He let the words out without moderation. He knew what he was saying didn't sound reasonable, but now that he'd decided on it, he knew without a shadow of a doubt that he was going to follow through. It felt more rational than anything he'd done in the last few days. "And I'm going to search the forest until I find Eileen."

"Hell yeah!" Flint slapped his knee. "That's my bro!"

"No!" Anna held out a hand toward both of them. "What? No! Chris, you can't do that. If the police can't find her, there's no way—"

"The police aren't even trying. That's the problem! They're *assuming* she's dead. They've given up. But what if she's not? What if she's out there, hurt and waiting for rescue? I've *got* to try."

Anna looked close to tears. "I know you're in pain. But I promise you, this isn't going to help. You won't find her."

"But at least he'll be doing something," Hailey said. She looked to her boyfriend for support. "Right?"

Flint nodded. "Yeah. Go look for her. Then, after, you can say you did everything you could, you know?"

Anna looked between the three of them. She ran a hand over her face. Her tone dropped and lost its force. "I guess I can understand that. You'd be going there as a way to get closure."

"To find Eileen," Chris insisted.

Anna shook her head but didn't fight him on it. "Please, sit for a moment and consider what this actually entails. That forest isn't exactly domesticated. It's dangerous, especially if you go off-path, and especially if you stay overnight. We don't want to lose you too."

"I'll go with him," Flint said. His face had brightened with excitement. He looked like an overgrown puppy. "I'll keep him safe. I can bring down any linebacker any day. I bet I could wrestle a bear if it came to it."

"I..." Anna looked like she wanted to argue but didn't even know where to start. "There are no bears in Ashlough..."

Hailey gasped. "Road trip!"

"What? Hail, that's so inappropriate—"

"No, no, it's not." Hailey fluttered her hands in Anna's direction to silence her. "You don't have enough money for a plane ticket, do you, Chris?"

He blinked. "Uh..."

"You took ages to repair your car when it broke last month, and no offense, but your job sucks, so I figure you're low on cash." Hailey looked delighted with herself. "But I can help. Daddy will give me money if I tell him I'm going on a cultural trip. We can take the van. If we all go, we can take turns driving."

"Okay...that might work." Chris ran his hands through his hair. He *had* used up all of his savings on his car. And his parents weren't likely to spot him the money if they knew what he planned to do.

"It's a stupid idea," Anna said, frowning at the table. "But not quite as stupid as it sounds. Helmer is ten hours away by road. If we leave this evening, we can be there early tomorrow morning. Which is the earliest we could start searching, anyway; even if we caught a flight and got there tonight, it would be too dark to go into the forest."

Flint slapped his knee again. "We'll all go. Four heads and four pairs of eyes will do more than just one."

Chris clenched and unclenched his hands. He felt like electricity was flowing through his veins. "Are you guys sure you want to come?"

"Yes," Flint and Hailey said. They turned toward Anna.

She chewed on her lip for a moment then sighed. "All right. Let's start packing."

CHAPTER 12

TODD FINALLY HAD AN excuse to rest. He'd been walking for what felt like an entire day, though his watch said it was only four in the afternoon.

At least he'd gotten away from the trail and the other tourists. Now that he had some space to think, he knew he'd made the right choice. Eileen wouldn't be anywhere near the trail, or she would have been rescued already. That meant he could reject the man-made paths from his list of places to explore.

He'd found a river. Its bank sloped gently to the water, which stretched on for a way but looked shallow. To his left, just before the stream turned out of sight, a low rushing noise and thin mist told him the river dropped into rapids. He walked along its bank until he found a fallen tree that didn't have too much moss or many insects on it, took off his backpack, and sat down.

When he'd embarked on the hike, he hadn't expected it to

be so tiring. He wasn't a crazed gym rat like Flint, but he wasn't unfit, either. Sure, he had a little bit of pudge since he wasn't a prude about what he ate, but underneath were muscles that could handle any sort of physical obstacle. Still, the hike had worn him out.

He pulled a bottle of water out of his bag. He'd brought several and already drank one. That was no problem, though. Four hours into the hike, he'd located fresh, running water. Just like he'd expected, a smart person could easily find what they needed for survival in the wilderness.

As he quenched his thirst, he looked around himself. The trees were starting to lose their appeal. Everything began to blend together after a few hours of walking. He couldn't understand why people fawned over the mountains when he could see nicer trees in his local park for a fraction of the effort.

He'd been keeping himself pointed west as best as he could tell; the canopy blocked out the sun, so he was guessing most of the time. But he had a pretty good sense of direction and knew he could find his way back to the parking lot without any trouble. He wasn't headed back yet, though. There were still a few hours of daylight left for him to look for Eileen.

He lowered the bottle, wiped a hand over his mouth, and called, "Eileen!"

The word bounced around him, echoing through the trees, but faded within seconds. He tried signaling her every five or ten minutes, but so far, there had been no reply. That was all right. He still had time to find her.

Todd took out one of his energy bars and chewed through it. A bit of fuel was all he needed to get the energy back into his muscles. He would cross the river and keep walking in a straight line. Or as straight of a line as he could make with all the bloody trees in the way.

The wrapper was light, but Todd was trying to minimize his burden, so he threw it into the river. Every gram counted when walking all day. Then he shuffled close to the water's edge and filled both empty bottles. Once they were tucked into his backpack, he flexed his shoulders and tried to gauge the best way to cross the river.

It didn't look deep, and the water wasn't exactly rushing. He would have to get his shoes wet. That was annoying but unavoidable. He rolled up his jeans to keep them dry then waded into the stream.

The water was colder than he'd expected, and he gasped as it washed around his ankles and soaked into his sneakers. He set his teeth and waded deeper. The river rocks were mostly smooth and had looked stable from the shore, but as he stepped on them, they shifted under his shoes. Worse, they were slippery. Todd was forced to pinwheel his arms to keep his balance.

At least the river wasn't too wide. He eyeballed the distance and figured there were no more than fifteen or twenty feet to go. He took three quick steps, hoping to cross in a single burst of motion, then yelped as his foot slipped.

He tumbled into the river and screamed a series of curses as the icy water drenched his right side. Todd thrashed and fought to right himself, only to drop back down as the treacherous rocks unbalanced him.

"Damn it—" Moving more carefully, he stood up. Rushing had obviously been a mistake. If he hadn't been in such a hurry to find Eileen, he would have done the sensible thing and crossed slowly. Todd flicked wet hair out of his face and resumed the trip, making sure each foot was planted firmly before taking another step.

The cold was turning his feet numb. The riverbed dropped unexpectedly, and water wrapped around his knees. Todd spat into it. He hadn't expected the current to be so strong, grabbing his legs and trying to drag him downriver. He looked to his left. The drop-off was about thirty feet away; it didn't look steep, but he preferred to avoid it, regardless.

He tried to speed up, nearly lost his balance, but managed to right himself again. He was glad no other tourists were about. They would probably laugh at the way he picked each foot up above the water like a prancing pony. Well, they could laugh if they wanted. His mission spoke for itself.

The water was growing deeper. It was partway up his thighs. He had to lean into the flow to keep his balance. But he was almost halfway across the river. Just a little farther, and it would get easier again…

His foot landed on another unsteady stone, and when he tried to catch his balance, the water yanked his feet out from under him. He fell into the river again, but this time, he only grazed the base. When he got his head above water, he'd already been dragged ten feet downstream.

Todd cried out. He thrashed, trying to swim toward shore, but couldn't tell if he was making any progress. He tried to stand. The water wouldn't let him. Every time he tried to get his feet toward the ground, the immense pressure dragged them away again.

He swallowed a mouthful of the freezing water. The dull, droning roar was growing louder. He threw a look over his shoulder and saw spits of water shooting into the air where the river became a slope. Beyond them, boulders rose above the water, unmovable despite the beating the river delivered on them. They looked painfully jagged.

Adrenaline gave his legs energy to spare. He kicked and touched the riverbed. It slowed his slide by a fraction but not nearly enough to stop his momentum. The edge was so close that it was suddenly all he could hear.

Todd tried to yell, but water got into his mouth. He panicked, waving his arms and legs in every direction, trying to grab onto something to right himself, but the river had grown deeper.

Then he hit one of the boulders jutting above the water. The impact crushed him, but he latched on to the rough stone. When he pulled, he could get his head above water and gulp in oxygen.

The shore seemed an eternity away. Todd tried to reach for it, but the water threatened to tear him off his perch, down the slope, and into the jagged stones. Instead, he tightened his grip on the stone and crawled up the boulder. His muscles screamed in protest as he pulled himself free from the river's insurmountable pressure.

Breathing was easier once he was free. Todd huddled on top of the boulder, clinging to one of its protrusions to stop himself from sliding back into the stream. He was shaking from shock and cold, and his head hurt from where it had hit the stone. His ledge wasn't flat enough to rest on, but at least it was dry and safe.

Todd blinked water out of his eyes. The bank to the right—the one he'd come from—was at least twenty feet away. The bank to the left was closer but not by much. He'd underestimated the river's breadth and its strength. And as he looked down at the water that frothed white around his stone, he didn't know if he could reach either shore.

A miserable, frightened whine escaped between gritted teeth. The adventure was no longer exciting. Already, his wet clothes were starting to chill him to the core. The sun wouldn't take long to set. What would happen to him then? Would he freeze on the rock or grow so numb that he just slipped into the stream?

No one would pass that way. He'd gone too far off trail. He eyeballed the closest shore, the one to his left. The river would get shallower as it neared the bank. If he could leap far enough, maybe he would escape the snatching, dragging influence of the water.

It was worth a shot. Todd carefully rose until he stood on the rock, balanced precariously on the uneven surface. He looked from his feet to the shore and back, building up his courage, then crouched, leaned forward, and jumped.

CHAPTER 13

Thursday, 7:00 p.m.
Douglass Highway, heading toward the Cobb Mountain Range

HAILEY DROVE THE VAN. She wasn't a steady driver, and they'd already had two near misses, but Chris didn't want to complain. Her father had lent her his van under the belief that she would be the only one using it. Flint sat shotgun, his feet up on the dashboard. Chris and Anna shared the back seat. Anna had made a brief comment about how, if they crashed, the deploying airbag would force Flint's leg bones into his torso, but he hadn't put his feet back on the floor, and Anna hadn't pressed the issue. She just occasionally scowled at him.

None of their families knew what they were doing. Chris had told his parents he was going to stay at Flint's house for a few days and that he needed some time, uninterrupted, to grieve.

Anna shared a dorm at her university. She'd emailed her professors to tell them she needed a few more days before returning for classes. Flint's parents thought he was going on a camping trip and hadn't asked any further questions. And Hailey had told her father she wanted to explore Stratford, the culture capital of the state. Happy his only daughter had showed some initiative, he'd given her both the van and a line of credit, which she'd promptly withdrawn to purchase supplies. Chris had to admit there were some definite perks to having rich parents.

He felt good. About as good as he could with his family in tatters, at least. Being on the road, moving toward a purpose—it was so much easier than sitting at home and doing nothing. There would be no one to monitor the emails, but he seriously doubted they would get anything useful out of it, anyway. At best, someone might have seen Eileen on one of the trails…and in that case, they would go to the police before replying to a Facebook post.

Anna seemed to think the trip was just a way for Chris to placate his conscience and get some closure. Hailey and Flint both acted like it was an adventure. Chris was more optimistic than Anna but not as lackadaisical as his other friends. He knew the chances of finding Eileen were slim, and he knew the search would be hard. But he also knew there was still hope.

He had her photos. After a brief phone call to confirm his parents planned to stay in Helmer for at least a few more days, Chris's father had uploaded the scans of the pictures Eileen had taken on the day she went missing. Anna had printed them out.

Now she and Chris examined the pictures in the back of the van, making notes.

They'd put aside the pictures of Eileen enjoying her holiday. It was a little too painful to look at her bright smile, knowing what was going to happen to her just a few days later. The twenty-three photos taken during the night were both confusing and distressing but not much help, either. They showed ten or so trees, some branches, and scraps of brown. The scenery was too dark and too vague for them to have any chance of pinpointing her location based on it.

But then there were five photos taken along the hiking trail. One at the entrance. Two of trees she'd passed along the way. One of a signpost marking a fork in the trail. And one of her swimming in a pool.

Anna had printed a map of the trails leading through the forest, and they were trying to piece together the trail Eileen had taken. Based on the photo of Eileen swimming, they had ruled out nine of the trails simply because they didn't go near any pools. That left three possible paths: two intermediate and one advanced.

"We can probably cross out the advanced trail," Anna said. She'd brought out her reading glasses and had propped them on the edge of her nose. With her straight brown hair, she reminded Chris of a librarian who had terrified him when he was a child. "The intermediate trails are both short enough to be completed in three or four hours. She arrived at the park around midday, and I'm guessing she would have planned to go home on the last shuttle, at six. So, to allow enough time to enjoy the walk and go for a swim, she would have picked intermediate."

"You're probably right," Chris said, only for Hailey to speak over him.

"Unless, you know, she wanted an adventure."

Anna frowned at their driver. "Sorry?"

"She's been talking a lot lately about stretching herself. Striving to reach the next level." Hailey shrugged.

In the two hours between agreeing to go on the trip and getting into the van, she'd showered, straightened her hair, changed, and applied makeup. Chris knew better than to complain to a woman about her spending time on her appearance, but it was hard not to feel bothered when he and his other friends had been kept busy buying and packing supplies.

"Like a midlife crisis?" Flint asked.

"More like a reinvention of herself." Hailey grinned at them in the rear-view mirror. "Haven't you been reading her Facebook posts recently? They're all about taking the road less traveled. Daring to open doors that other people leave closed."

Anna looked like she'd had a revelation. "She's right. Eileen changed the poster above her dorm bed a couple of weeks ago. It used to be her favorite band, but now it's a picture of a woman climbing a mountain."

"And that's why she went on this trip in the first place," Hailey continued. "To try something new. To take risks."

"Still..." Chris motioned to the map. "Hiking up a giant mountain range is enough of a new experience on its own, isn't it? She's not crazy. She'd take the path she could complete in a reasonable amount of time."

Anna was looking at the photos with fresh vigor. "I'm starting to think maybe not. I don't think she would have planned it in advance. But once she arrived at the park, she would have been confronted by a map of the different paths. It would be like giving her a choice—do you want to take the easy road? Or push yourself? Which one would she choose, Chris?"

He hated Anna's logic. Begrudgingly, he looked toward the camper van's ceiling. "She would push herself."

"Yes. She'd choose an advanced path. But she wouldn't spend so long out there that she'd miss the shuttle back. The advanced paths are intended to be all-day hikes, so instead of trying to go all the way to its end, she would have planned to explore and enjoy as much of the path as she could before turning around."

Hailey snapped her fingers. "That's how she got lost. She wasn't there to hike a road—she was there to explore. I bet she would step off the path if she saw anything she wanted to know more about—like a tree or a bunch of pretty rocks. Maybe one time she went too far and couldn't find her way back."

"She's not stupid," Chris said, hating how defensive he sounded.

"No, she's not." Anna passed him the photo of the pool then pointed to a spot of blue on the map. "Here, I bet it's this body of water. I'm guessing that would be about an hour into the trail. She's not stupid, but she doesn't hike much, either. Getting turned around in the forest is easier than you'd expect. She was probably taking all sorts of precautions, but all you need is one small, insignificant mistake. Like sitting down in a clearing for a few minutes and forgetting which direction you came from. Guess wrongly, and suddenly you're in trouble. I bet something like that happened to her."

Chris held the photo of Eileen splashing in the pool. The water was crystalline, the plants looked green and healthy, and Eileen was laughing. He tried to swallow, but his throat was too tight. If she really was dead, he hoped the process hadn't been too drawn out.

"So…" Flint broke the silence. "We go down the super-hard path?"

"I think, weighing everything up, that's the most likely option." Anna wouldn't meet Chris's eyes. "But remember, it's still a tiny, tiny chance that we'll find her. Even if we can follow her up to where she became lost, it's been four days. She could be anywhere by now."

Chris didn't like the insinuation. He turned back to the map, focused on the long, snaking trail that looped through the forest. If she was anywhere near it, they would find her.

Thursday, 8:40 p.m.

TODD, WEARING BOTH SPARE jackets he'd bought, couldn't stop shivering. He'd stripped off his wet clothes and hung them over a tree branch to dry. He hadn't thought the forest could get so cold at night.

The sun had set an hour before, and he'd stumbled through the darkness, trying to find a place to sleep. It was an insane task. Before stepping into Ashlough Forest, he'd imagined what spending the night there might entail. He would find a clearing, gather some dead wood, and start a campfire. He could cook any food he caught or gathered and keep warm overnight.

Nothing had gone according to plan. There were no patches of clear ground. Everywhere he looked was nothing but a mess of heaving roots poking out of the ground, weedy, grassy plants, and endless vines. He'd gathered some dead sticks. They had felt faintly damp to the touch, which wasn't a good sign. He'd brought a box of matches, but they had been in his back pocket when he fell into the river.

He knew he was supposed to rub two sticks together to start a fire. He'd tried that for twenty minutes until his hands were aching and pricked full of splinters. Zero sparks. The wood was too wet. If he had been in a proper forest, he was sure he could have found dry branches that would work.

The longer he stayed in Ashlough Forest, the more he became convinced that the environment wasn't *right.* Everything was too crowded. When plants died, they didn't stay dead like in the nature reserves around his house. There, dead plants made perfect firewood. In Ashlough, dead plants *grew* things. Everywhere he looked were funguses and mosses, and teeming insects spilling out of the wood.

That was another thing he hated. Insects were everywhere. When he rested his head on the ground, he could have sworn he could hear the marching ants. There was nowhere to sit or lie down that didn't put him on top of a spider or a centipede.

He was huddled in the small hollow of a tree's roots, with his knees pulled up under his chin to conserve warmth. He'd brought a flashlight, at least, and kept it on to light his surroundings. Its beam was small and felt painfully weak against the oppressive night. He kept it roving across the trees and vines.

Strange animals called to each other from the boughs above. He thought some might be bats, but it was hard to be certain.

They got close, sometimes, chattering right over his head. They fell silent when he pointed his flashlight at them.

He kept reminding himself Eileen was suffering through the same night alongside him. Once he found her and carried her back to town, they would be able to talk about the experience. It would be a chance for them to bond, finally, and perhaps grow closer than friends. After all, he'd walked into a living nightmare to save her. She would be grateful. Maybe even enamored. Wouldn't that be hilarious? For once, *she* might be chasing *him*.

Something scraped against a tree to Todd's left. He twisted, looking around the trunk he'd leaned against, but his light couldn't pick anything out of the gloom. He settled back down. There was too much *life* in the forest. He was a fan of nature, sure, but only when he could see it. Being surrounded by countless busy animals while he was blind left him feeling vulnerable.

At least now no one would call him a coward. He might not have Flint's stupid muscles, but if anyone tried to compare them again, he could always say, "Did Flint spend two days in the wilderness with nothing to survive on except his wits? No? Then shut the hell up."

The thought made him laugh. He could only imagine the look on their faces.

The scraping noise sounded closer. Again, Todd leaned around the tree. He panned his flashlight across the area. It picked out the same shapes he'd been seeing all day: tree, tree, shrub, tree, vine, tree. Still, he felt uneasy. The scraping sound didn't seem natural. "Hello?" He waited then cleared his throat. "Eileen?" he called out more loudly.

Seconds ticked by. Frustrated, he huddled back against the tree and pulled his phone out of his pocket. The screen flashed to life at the click of a button. His battery was down to thirty percent. Hidden in the folds of his backpack, it had been protected from water damage, and he had been trying to call for backup since he'd escaped the river's grip. His cell phone wasn't getting any reception, though, which was ridiculous. *In this modern day and age, how is there any place on earth that doesn't get reception?* He'd toyed with the idea of climbing a tree to see if that helped, but he'd been too cold and sore. And in the dark, he would have no idea what he was putting his hands on.

The scraping noise sounded like it was almost on top of him. Todd stood, flashlight held ahead of himself with shaking hands. "Hey, is anyone else out there? If you're an animal, you can screw right off."

The scraping sound came from behind a tree with an immense trunk easily large enough for three men to hide behind. Todd wet his lips and circled it, keeping as much distance between himself and the trunk as possible. If someone was on the other side, they were mimicking his motions, circling the tree to remain hidden.

"Hey, you ass! Answer me!"

His throat was growing raw. Maybe he'd gotten sick when he fell into the water. They said all sorts of germs could live in there. If he couldn't find Eileen the following morning, he might have to make his way back to town just to get checked out by a doctor.

Todd had circled the tree completely. He could neither see nor hear anything unnatural. Disgusted, he spat on the ground and moved toward the nook he'd planned to sleep in. As he stepped around the tree, he was confronted by something that seemed to have crawled out of his nightmares.

It was immense. Seven feet at least. Clumped fur hung from broad shoulders to graze the ground. Luminous eyes glittered out from a twisted, shadowed, inhuman face. A long, clawlike appendage extended from its arm and shone in the light of the flashlight. The creature reached out and scraped the claws against the tree's trunk.

Todd ran. A scream tore its way out of his raw throat as he dashed through the forest. He could hear the creature coming after him, crashing through dead leaves and snapping branches. His light flashed up and down in erratic arcs as he pumped his arms, and each step was a gamble. He hit a tree, bounced off, felt blood flowing down his face, and kept running. The ground dropped away, and he stumbled as he fell. He caught himself on a fallen tree and clung to it as he gasped in terrified breaths.

Everything hurt. His head throbbed. Still clutching the flashlight in his shaking fist, he directed its light over his shoulder, toward the slope he'd just stumbled down.

The figure loomed out of the darkness—coming straight for him.

CHAPTER 15

Friday, 3:30 a.m.
Kogarah Road, heading toward Cobb Mountain Range

"CHRIS. CHRIS. WAKE UP."

He groaned, grunted, and lifted his head off the van's door. The vehicle might have been an upper-market model, but its shock absorbers couldn't stop the whole thing from rattling as it bounced over the rural road. Even with his jacket balled up as a pillow, it had made for an unpleasant, uncomfortable sleep.

Anna had turned on her light, and Chris blinked against the glow. She sat pin straight, still wearing her glasses, with the photos and maps scattered on the seat between them. She was looking at him strangely.

"What?" he mumbled. "Did I snore?"

"No. I need you to look at this. I need to be sure I'm not going crazy."

He sat, stretched, and felt his back pop. Hailey was asleep in the passenger seat, her perfectly straightened hair getting mussed every time she shifted. Flint was driving, but he was starting to look tired. They would need to switch duties soon.

"Did you sleep at all?" he asked Anna.

"I tried, but I can't."

"You'll be tired tomorrow."

"I know. Now look at this. I honestly can't tell if I'm onto something or if I'm becoming delusional." She held out a page to him. It was one of the pictures Eileen had taken at night. As far as Chris could tell, there was nothing different about it compared to the other twenty.

"What am I looking at?"

"This shape, right here." She jabbed at a bunch of leaves that had caught the camera's flash. They were buried between two trunks and not as well illuminated as other parts of the scene.

Chris looked at the blur carefully then nodded. "A branch. Okay."

"That's what I thought at first too. But look at this." She placed another image over the first. The blur was no longer visible.

"Okay, I'll need you to walk me through this." Chris rubbed his face. "The branch…is gone?"

"That's just it. I don't think this is a branch." She shuffled around in her seat to face him and held out another photo. "At first I thought the flash didn't reach far enough to show it. But look here."

Chris took the page. The splotch had returned…but in a different place.

He held the two pictures side by side. They both showed the shape between two tree trunks, but in the first, it was close to the right-hand tree, and in the second, it was close to the left.

"And then there's this." She passed him a fourth picture, where the shape appeared in the upper-left corner. It was unmistakable, yet it had somehow moved five feet to the left. "Those are the only three pictures I can find it in."

He clutched the pages until the paper crinkled. "What is it?"

"I'm not certain, but look closely. Doesn't it look a bit like a face? Those parts would be the eyes…"

"Yeah, I think I see it. But it's not like any face I've seen before."

"Hey," Flint said from the driver's seat. "Let me see."

Chris held out the pages, but Anna pushed them back into his chest.

"Not while you're driving."

Flint groaned. "But Ahh-naa…"

"No. We'll show you and Hailey when we park." She turned back to Chris. "If I'm not drastically misreading this, it means there was something in the forest with Eileen."

"Something?"

"Or someone." She leaned closer to look at the pictures again. "Though you're right, it really doesn't look human."

"Animal? It looks a bit like a wolf in this one…"

"No wolves in Ashlough Forest. And besides, it's too high.

Look, the pine needles here give a bit of context. A wolf wouldn't be more than three feet off the ground. This is…"

"At least six feet," Chris breathed.

"Try seven. It's massive."

"Bear?"

"No bears, either."

"What the hell is it, then?" Chris was reminded of who was behind the camera, and he felt like he might throw up. "What did it do to Eileen?"

Anna looked just as helpless as he felt.

"Seriously, guys." A whine had entered Flint's voice. "You're killing me here."

"When we park," Anna snapped. "I'm not letting your ADD-ass crash and kill us all."

Chris had never heard her snap at her friends like that before. The pictures must have unnerved her more than he'd thought.

Anna let him sit in silence for several minutes. He slowly leafed through each picture, hunting for the strange blotch of white, but it only appeared in those three pages. He blew out his breath, put the papers aside, and ran his hands through his hair. "Okay. We don't tell my parents about this. They're upset enough right now. But when we get to town, we take this to the police."

"Ooh, look at Mr. *The police are incompetent, we can't trust them*," Flint cooed.

Chris kicked the back of his seat. "Cut it. I don't like the police, but if we can get them to see what we see, they can mobilize a force ten times larger than us. It would be wrong not to try."

"He's right." Anna nodded, looking excited. "They might not care about just one tourist going missing, but if there's something in the forest that could be a threat to other hikers, they're much more likely to take action."

"We're certain it's a *thing*?" Chris asked. At Anna's look, he shrugged. "It doesn't look human. But it's not like any animal we know of, either."

"Maybe the police will know. Maybe there will be reports of—I don't know—people playing pranks in the forest. Maybe that's all it is? Some big joke."

Chris pushed his balled-up jacket up under his head and rested against the door. He pretended to go back to sleep, but his mind was buzzing. He wished he could believe it was a prank, but that was impossible. Eileen had taken the photos alone, at night, off trail. Whatever was between the trees had lingered there for a while. The time stamps between the first and third pictures of it were nearly twelve minutes apart. He suspected it had been stalking Eileen in the other photos, too…hidden behind trees, out of sight, being warded off by camera flashes.

A horrible, sinking feeling flooded his stomach. Chances were, by that point, they weren't on a rescue mission. They were on a revenge mission.

CHAPTER 16

Friday, 4:45 a.m.

TODD STAGGERED, STUMBLED, AND fell to the ground. He was bringing air into his lungs in hurried, desperate gasps, but the oxygen wasn't moving through his body quickly enough. His head ached. His throat was raw. He was half-blind, and his flashlight batteries were nearly drained. It offered less light than a glow stick.

He felt like he might drop dead of exhaustion. He didn't know how long he'd been running. He only knew that every time he tried to stop, the creature would find him. He didn't know how. He was blind in the dark, but the monster, whatever it was, never failed to track him down.

He had lost his backpack. Several times, he'd tried to circle around to find it. But the forest was like a maze. He had lost both his sense of time and his sense of direction. Without his backpack, he had no water or supplies.

He'd spent the first few hours panicking. Now, he was just trying to survive. If he could find the path and find his way out, he would gladly leave and never return. Not even for Eileen. It wasn't like he was abandoning her; he'd as good as confirmed she was no longer alive. She was a smart girl, capable enough to live in the forest for days or even weeks if it came to that, but she wouldn't have been able to outsmart this monster.

That was what was following him; he was certain. A monster. He'd seen its poison-green eyes. He'd stared into its twisted, demented face—the face of something that had risen out of hell. It moved nearly silently. And it found him, time and time again, no matter how far he ran.

Todd staggered a few more steps. His muscles were spent. There was a small hollow between two trees. The way the vines grew over it created a small hidey-hole. He dropped to his knees and crawled into the gap, eyes closed and lips squeezed together to protect against the ichor and grime that showered him. The space wasn't big, but he could curl into a ball and be completely surrounded by plant matter. He turned off the flashlight.

Vine leaves scratched at his exposed skin. He dragged in gasping, painful breaths and waited for the burning to leave his legs. Now that he wasn't moving, he was starting to feel the cold. Something moved across his cheek, and Todd swatted at it. Spider or insect, he couldn't tell, but it left a smear of goo on him.

The heavy scraping noise echoed between the trees. Todd

opened his mouth and tried to breathe as slowly and silently as he could. His body was begging for oxygen, but he knew he could survive that. He didn't know if he could survive being found.

The sound was drawing closer, as it always did. That was how it started—just quiet, distant scrapes that gradually drew closer and homed in on his position like a missile. The creature always let Todd run. It was so immense that he felt sure it could chase him down and catch him if it wanted to, but it didn't. It only approached in steady, unerring steps.

He hadn't dared to find out what would happen if he let it catch him.

Now, the scrape came from less than twenty feet away. From his position, Todd could see a patch of ground ahead of his hidey-hole. There was very little light anywhere, but without his flashlight, his eyes were starting to adjust.

The creature stepped into view. There was very little of it to see. Its head was covered with long matted fur. Its body was tall and wide, but it held a human-like posture, head lifted toward the sky. Its body was covered in the same fur; it flowed down to its feet like a thick cloak and masked the monster's true shape. The claws caught the thin light. They protruded from where the creature's arms should have been and extended nearly to the ground. The monster lifted one of its appendages and ran the claws across the bark of a tree. They created the sharp scraping noise that had plagued Todd all night.

He pressed his hand over his mouth and nose to muffle his breathing. Terror made him shake uncontrollably. If the creature came toward him, he didn't think he could get to his feet in time to escape it. His legs had locked into place and refused to move, no matter how ferociously his heart pumped.

The creature continued walking. Its movements were so smooth that it almost seemed to float. It was moving parallel to his hiding place, though, and in a minute, it would pass him.

Todd's heart was so loud that he was sure everyone within ten miles would hear it. Another insect dropped onto his neck and began crawling down to his collarbone, but he made no moves to squash it. He couldn't tear his eyes away from the inhuman being stalking through the clearing. A little farther—just a little more—and it would have passed him. He could hide in the cubbyhole, safe, until morning.

It stopped. Its head rotated slowly, smoothly, to look straight at him. The glint of green eyes, almost luminous, flashed out of the bedraggled locks hiding its face.

Todd tried to scream. No sound left him. They met each other's stares, unblinking and unmoving. Then the creature threw back its head, as though in feint of laughter, and slunk between the trees. Todd tried to follow its movements, but it had vanished within seconds.

He didn't understand. His light had been turned off. He'd kept silent. The plant cover was thick enough to almost fully conceal him. He couldn't imagine the monster could smell him among the thick odors of organic decay.

But it had found him nonetheless. And…left?

He didn't dare move in case it broke whatever spell seemed to have fallen over the forest. The area seemed almost unnaturally quiet. Except for the insect crawling across his neck, he couldn't sense any movement.

He couldn't believe the monster had just left him. It had been following him for hours. It should have finished him off then and there.

The answer came easily enough. It hadn't really *left*; it was just waiting, hidden between the trees, perhaps. Or maybe it had already circled around to lurk at his back. It was toying with him. Enjoying his terror. Waiting for him to make the first move before it pounced and brought him down with a swipe of those terrifying claws.

Todd closed his eyes and pressed his hands over his head. A sob struggled out of his throat. He was as good as a sitting duck. And he would have to move eventually.

CHAPTER 17

Friday, 9:00 a.m.

CHRIS PULLED HIS BEST jacket out of his duffel bag and shook it out. It had become creased during the drive, but there was nothing he could do for it now. He put it on.

They had pulled into a parking lot for the grocery store opposite Helmer's police station. The station hadn't been easy to spot, despite the sign above its doorway. It was a strange, narrow brick building with two floors. Bars lined the windows, and the only door that could possibly be the front entrance looked like it was for a closet.

The building might not have wowed them, but Anna had emphasized the importance that they, at least, make a good first impression. They were young adults between the ages of twenty and twenty-three, a demographic not especially known for commanding respect. Looking like they'd slept in a car and spilled fast food sauce down their shirts—which Chris had—would only get them dismissed much more easily.

"How do I look?" He fluffed his jacket's collar then held his arms out for their approval.

Anna narrowed her eyes then moved to the back of the minivan. She dug through her bag and came up with a plain gray scarf. "Tie this on."

"It's not *that* cold."

"No, but you want to look like you dressed with purpose, instead of grabbing whatever was closest to hand. Scarves are by default intentional, not accidental."

He obediently looped it around his neck, only for Anna to sigh, pull it off, and redo it herself.

"How about me?" Flint asked.

"You're fine. It's simple but not dirty. And since you won't be doing the talking, simple works great." She snapped her fingers at Hailey. "You're overdressed."

She sniffed and shook her hair back. "I thought we were trying to make a good first impression."

"We're trying to look like responsible, mature adults, not seduce the commander. Here." Anna zipped up Hailey's jacket to hide her cleavage then fished an elastic band out of her pocket. "Tie your hair into a ponytail, then you're fine. We ready to go?"

Chris retrieved the stack of printed photos from the back of the van then squared his shoulders as he turned toward the station. He hadn't had many chances to interact with the police before, just a couple of breath tests. Flint, on the other hand, had gotten into a not-insignificant number of altercations as a teenager and had spent a couple of nights in holding. The group had unanimously agreed that he should stay at the back and not say much.

Anna kept at Chris's side as they walked across the street. She was wearing her reading glasses, and he had to admit the librarian vibe made her look more mature.

"Remember, be calm." She spoke softly as she adjusted her jacket collar. "Be polite and respectful. You're part of Eileen's family, so you'll get more leeway than the rest of us, but only as long as you keep your temper in check and don't act like you know more than them."

"Even though I do," he grunted.

She pointed a finger at him as they climbed the two steps to the front door. "I'm serious, Chris. This might be our only chance to mobilize the police to find Eileen. Or at least, find out what happened to her. Keep your cool."

"Got it."

The door swung open. The reception area was already crowded, with a mother and her crying baby in the seats awkwardly placed in the room's corner and two officers at the reception desk.

Anna squeezed his arm and dropped her voice to a whisper. "Respectful. Polite."

As they approached the reception desk, the woman behind it tilted forward. She wore the same uniform as the other officers, but a sprig of lilacs had been tied into her bun. It was sharply at odds with the serious, formal atmosphere of the rest of the building. "Can I help you folks?"

"Yes." Chris clasped his hands ahead of himself and leaned closer to be heard over the baby's wails. "I'm Chris Hershberger. My sister—"

"Ooh, yes, Eileen Hershberger. Are you here to speak to the managing officer?" The receptionist had already dialed a number and lifted the phone to her ear, so Chris just nodded mutely.

The woman with flowers in her hair spoke into the phone briefly. Chris couldn't hear what was said in reply, but the tone sounded sharp. The receptionist listened for several moments, then she hung up and gave them a toothy smile. "All right, come with me."

Chris looked back at his companions. Flint shrugged, and Anna waved for him to hurry up. He followed the receptionist back into the depths of the station. Painted plaster walls gave way to old brick. The place seemed to have been designed by a madman; the hallway wove without any rhyme or reason, and Chris was sure they must be looping back on themselves before the woman pushed open a door for them.

"Officer Delago will be here soon. Can I get any of you something to drink? Tea, coffee, water?"

"We're fine." Chris waited until she'd dipped out of the doorway before looking about himself. They were in a kind of conference room. Pictures hung from the walls, showing how the town had looked a hundred years before. One large print of the mountain range took up the back wall. A large wooden table filled the middle of the room. Smaller benches and filing cabinets lined the walls. Chris approached the seats on one side of the table but had only halfway sunk into the wooden chair before the door burst open.

A female officer marched in, her dark hair tied into a bun and a stack of folders under one arm. All of her movements were sharp and energetic, and her wiry frame seemed swallowed by her rumpled jacket. She dropped the folders onto the table, extended a hand to shake Chris's, then slipped into the chair opposite him before he could blink.

"I'm Officer Carla Delago. I'm in charge of your sister's case." Like her movements, her voice was sharp and clipped. Chris had the impression that she was overworked and silently seething at the intrusion, but she still smiled as she folded her hands over the folders. "Sorry, Mr. Hershberger, but Viv didn't catch the purpose of your visit."

"We have a lead," he blurted. Anna, to his left, nodded and looked as professional as she could. To his right, Flint and Hailey were keeping silent and trying not to draw attention to themselves.

"Oh?" The fake smile transformed into an expression of genuine attention. "I'd be glad to see it."

Chris slid the stack of printouts toward her. "You gave my parents these photos yesterday. We found some, uh..."

"Abnormalities," Anna interjected on his behalf. "A shape that appears in some pictures and not others. We believe it might be the reason Eileen was taking pictures in the darkness. And possibly the reason she went missing in the first place. She was trying to frighten off…whatever this is."

Delago took the sheets. She spent a moment examining the top one then exhaled and lifted her head. "You're going to need to point it out to me."

"Here." Anna reached across the desk to tap the shape between the trees, then she shifted the top page back to reveal the two beneath it. "Here, and here."

"All right. And this is…"

"It looks like some kind of face. We believe Eileen was trying to frighten it off with the camera flashes. It's moving around, almost like it's stalking her at the edge of the light."

Anna sat back down. Flint gave her a thumbs-up, and Chris quickly pushed his hand back down.

Delago didn't notice, though. She was bent over the pictures, examining them closely. Then she pulled one of the folders out of the stack, flipped it open, and looked at something inside. Chris craned his neck, but the folder's angle was too steep for him to see what she was reading.

After what felt like an eternity, Delago put the folder down and pushed the sheets of paper back to Chris. "Have you heard of pareidolia, Mr. Hershberger?"

Before Chris could speak, Flint pressed forward so eagerly that he nearly came out of his chair. "Is that what you call it? The monster in the mountain?"

Chris urgently kicked his friend's shin. It didn't stop Flint, though.

"Because I was thinking it was some kind of Bigfoot, you know. But if you already know about this *paradola* animal then you can—"

"Flint, *sit down*!" Anna hissed at the same time that Chris kicked him so viciously that he couldn't ignore it.

He blinked at them, looking both shocked and hurt, then swallowed and slid back into his seat.

Delago had her hands laced in front of her in a perfect visage of calm and control, though the impression was ruined by her wide eyes and the alarmed tilt to her eyebrows. She maintained silence for a moment, seemingly waiting to see if there would be another outburst, then she said, "I'm sorry, I didn't catch your friends' names."

"Anna, Flint, Hailey." Chris was careful not to use surnames. He didn't know if the police departments were connected enough that Flint's history could be brought up on their database. The last thing he wanted was for his friend to be incarcerated in another state.

"Right. Well, like I was saying...pareidolia is the phenomenon of seeing familiar shapes where there are none. You might look at the swirls in a wooden floorboard and see a dog. Or look at a house with strange windows and see a face."

"We know what pareidolia is," Chris said, unable to keep the edge out of his voice. Anna shot him a pointed look, and he cleared his throat. "Ma'am."

Her eyes narrowed a fraction, but her voice actually softened. "I understand the loss of your sister is...a horrific thing to go through. You're trying to make sense of it. Find closure. I can understand that. But I'm sorry to say, in this case, you're finding clues that don't exist."

"But..."

Anna pressed a hand over Chris's arm. "Ms. Delago, we've been careful not to leap to conclusions. We examined the photos closely and discounted every natural explanation before coming to you. Once you eliminate the impossible, whatever remains, no matter how improbable, must be the truth."

"Sherlock Holmes fan, huh?" Delago smiled, but it was gone within a second. "I'm sorry to be the bearer of bad news. But in this case, you discounted a little too readily. Have a look at the original photos."

She reopened the folder and brought out a stack of pictures. All four of them leaned across the table to get a closer look.

"Here are photos twenty-seven, twenty-nine, and thirty-four. Their timestamps match the sheets you gave me. Can you confirm they're the same photos you found the...phenomena on?"

Chris didn't speak. Delago had found the right images; he'd spent so much time looking at them during the previous night that he had them almost memorized. There was only one key difference. The face was gone.

"I scanned these photos for your parents then imported them onto a USB. You then printed them out again. Somewhere in the process—during scanning or during printing—artifacts were introduced into the picture. Maybe your ink was running low. Maybe the scanner malfunctioned. But what you're looking at...I'm sorry, but it isn't real."

"Bull." Chris felt his anger boiling. No number of concerned glances from Anna could silence him. "You've...I...there's a mistake. It's here. It's got to be here."

He snatched the other photos out of Delago's hands. She didn't protest, but the pity left her face. He spread the pictures across the desk, hunting through them with an almost manic desperation.

"There was something in the forest. Something stalking her. I don't know why it's not in your copies..."

"Mr. Hershberger, until your sister's case is concluded, those are still evidence."

"You're making a mistake." He slammed his fist onto one of the pictures. "There's got to be—you've got to—"

"Come on." Anna yanked on his sleeve. "We're going. Sorry for taking up your time, Officer Delago."

"No!" His voice cracked, but he had no control over it. "My sister's still up in that forest somewhere! You can't just ignore that! You can't just pretend it didn't happen!"

"I can promise you I'm not." Delago stood. All softness had fled her face, and her glare felt hard enough to cut. "We are taking measures to recover your sister. But you *must* reconcile yourself to the fact that she probably will not be found. If she left the path—and she must have—and became lost, then our best chances of finding her are when her *bones* wash downriver."

Chris gaped. The officer's words were like a punch to the gut. They snatched away his ability to think, let alone speak. Angry tears pricked his eyes.

Flint looked from him to the officer then rose out of his chair so aggressively that it toppled over behind him. “This isn’t just about Eileen! Other people are going to go missing if you don’t kill this monster, Bigfoot, whatever it is. Who knows how many it’s already eaten!”

“Monster, huh?” Delago tilted her head. “I’m sorry to disappoint, but there is no monster. I’m in charge of missing person cases in this station. We have perhaps one or two incidents each year, which is in line with the average for other hiking areas of our size, business, and difficulty. If there was a monster picking off tourists, I think I would know about it.”

“Just because you don’t want to hear about it, doesn’t mean it’s not happening.” Chris’s vision was turning black at the edges. He felt dizzy and wild, and not even Anna’s desperate yanks registered. “Eileen wasn’t an incident. She was *murdered*. Police are supposed to protect people, get justice for people, but you’re doing *nothing*.”

“Have a good day, Mr. Hershberger.” Delago slammed the folder closed.

Chris turned away before she could see how close to breaking he was. Anna corralled him through the doorway, with Hailey scrambling after them. Flint was the last to leave, and as he did, he twirled and waved his two middle fingers at the officer. Delago’s irritated sigh followed them down the hallway.

CHAPTER 18

Friday, 9:15 a.m.

TODD WOKE TO A horrible headache and a shooting pain in his leg. He rolled his tongue around his mouth, but there was no saliva to moisten it.

He crawled forward, leaving the safety of the hollow where he'd hidden. He didn't care if the monster found him. Everything hurt so badly that a quick death might actually be merciful. He sprawled out in a gap between the trees and groaned in relief as his body had a chance to relax its tight curl.

A nerve in his leg had become pinched. It stung every time he tried to move it. Rocks dug into his back, but he barely cared about them. He'd been an idiot to come into the forest.

No, that wasn't true. He'd known what he was getting himself into. He'd brought water, food, and even a change of clothes. He'd been prepared, damn it. *But...that monster.*

He hadn't accounted for that. How could anyone? There was nothing that could have protected him from that except perhaps a couple of guns and a machete.

He'd thought he lived in a rational world. He'd thought he could deal with anything Ashlough Forest held. But the creature that had followed him was like something that belonged in a twisted fantasy dimension of monsters and gods.

Todd still didn't know what it was. His glimpses had been brief and distorted by fear. He remembered the fur, thick and long, the claws that stretched to the ground, and the poison-green eyes. It was unlike any other animal he'd seen before.

The sun was up, at least. He would no longer be at a disadvantage against the creature in the dark. He felt around himself until he found a dead stick among the debris then pulled it close to his chest. He might not have the energy to engage in a proper duel, but he could at least poke its eye out before it sliced into him.

There were deep gashes in the tree opposite him. Three lines, about shoulder height, dug into the bark with a sharp blade. Sap bubbled around the scores.

He tried to remember if they had been there the night before. It had been too dark to see much of anything, except for where scraps of moonlight fought through the canopy and touched parts of his environment. That tree hadn't been one of them.

Todd waited. Squirrels chattered in the branches above him.

Insects crawled over his skin as they accepted him as part of their environment. Birds sang, and the trees rustled. It would have been almost pleasant if he hadn't been waiting for his death.

Yet minutes passed, and death didn't come. The pins and needles gradually left Todd's legs. He groaned, sat up, and threw the branch aside. The sap on the cut tree looked dry. It was probably old. The monster had left. Maybe it really hadn't seen him the night before. Maybe it had become bored of waiting. Or maybe it didn't like being out during the day.

That meant if Todd wanted to get back home, he would need to move quickly. There was no way he could spend another night in the forest. He was thirsty, but that couldn't be helped. He would just have to wait until he got back onto the trail and could flag down someone with a water bottle.

His two top priorities had to be defenses and figuring out a path home. Todd rolled to his feet and grunted as the aching muscles tried to expire on him. He didn't let them. The gym rats might be bulkier, but he had something they didn't: determination.

He staggered through the forest, head bowed, as he tried to find a suitable way to defend himself. The monster's claws were long, which meant he needed a ranged weapon. With more time, he could have built a small forge out of clay and rock then smelted a proper blade. He'd watched some videos on how to do it; they looked easy enough. But time was short, so he had to improvise.

Todd found a dead branch that seemed sturdy. It was longer than his arm and heavier than he would have liked, but it would do the job. He kicked around the rocks gathered on the forest floor until he found a smooth, flat one then bent and scraped the branch's tip across the stone to sharpen it. The wood splintered and stopped him from getting the sharp tip he wanted. Todd muttered under his breath as he worked on it, finally getting it to something like a point.

As an experiment, he tried stabbing at a nearby tree. The impact sent shock waves up his arm, hurting already-sore muscles and throwing off his balance. Todd swore.

It was the forest. He could have fashioned a deadly spear if he'd had the right materials, but Ashlough was too wet and too unruly. All along, the forest had sabotaged every effort he made. Begrudgingly, he picked loose splinters off the spear's tip. He might not be able to create a proper weapon, but the stick's edge was still pointed enough to hurt. It would have to do until he found something better.

Todd rolled his shoulders. With his weapon taken care of, the only other issue was finding his way out of the forest.

He lifted his chin and tried to get a reading on the sun's angle. Layers of foliage created a confusing mess of sunlight and shadow. He thought the sun might be coming from behind him. That meant he knew how to find north…but he didn't know which direction the town was relative to the forest. He swore again.

What else? Think. Problem-solving has always been your strong suit. It's just a forest. It can't be that hard to find your way out.

He scanned the trees and the ground. He was sick of looking at them both. But the forest floor seemed to be trending downward to his right.

Of course. Follow the slope. The ground could only dip so far before it reached the town or—almost as good—a river. It was just common sense.

Todd squared his shoulders and hefted his spear and strode into the forest. He'd survived the worst night of his life, but he'd conquered his fear and the forest and was back in control. It was time to return home.

CHAPTER 19

Friday, 9:30 a.m.

"DO YOU NEED A moment?" Anna asked.

"No." Chris pressed his palms into his closed eyes. He was shaking, but he wasn't going to fall apart. *Now isn't the time for weakness.*

They had returned to the van in the grocery store parking lot. The walk back had been almost completely silent, except for Chris's ragged breathing and the squeak of Hailey's shoes. Now, locked away in their personal, mechanical cave, Chris could finally start to think.

"I'm sorry, man," Flint said, sounding embarrassed. "I lost it. I know we said I wasn't going to talk, that I'd ruin everything—"

"You didn't ruin anything." Chris dropped his hands. "You were trying to help. I'm sorry for kicking you. That was really mean."

Flint's grin reappeared. "It's all good, bro. What's a bruised shin between friends, eh?"

Chris chuckled then let his smile drop. "And sorry, Anna. I lost my temper. The exact thing I wasn't supposed to do. We should have let you do the talking. I kind of blew our chance, didn't I?"

Anna took a deep breath then let it out slowly. She looked upset but not with him. "No. That officer wouldn't have helped us, even if we'd been the mayor. It was a lost cause before we even stepped into that building."

"I knew it." Chris ground his teeth. "She didn't care about Eileen."

"It's not that. She cares. She just...has no hope." Anna shrugged. "I've met people like her before. I've got two professors like that, actually. Ten years ago, when she first joined the force, I bet she would have chased down our phantom in the photos. But those ten years have worn her thin and killed the spark that made her want to become an officer in the first place. It's dragged her into a particular mindset, and now that she's there, she can't get out. 'What's the point of trying? It never helps. Things end up rotten no matter what I do.' She's not consciously thinking that, but I can promise you, it's been ground into every fiber of her being."

"That's a lot to read from a ten-minute conversation."

Anna's smile was sheepish. "Psychology major. People watching has kind of become my pastime."

Hailey shuffled around in her seat. "She wouldn't have helped us, no matter what, right?"

"I don't think so, no." Anna pursed her lips. "What do we think about the pictures now? That smudge wasn't in the originals."

"Ghosts," Flint said and drummed his hands on the steering wheel. "I read this creepy story about how ghosts move from photo to photo to curse you."

"I'm not sure I buy the ghost angle," Chris said, "but I'm sure there was something there. Why else would Eileen be taking photos in the one spot, in the middle of the night? She was fighting something in the best way she could without weapons. I don't care if you can't see it in the originals. It's there."

"All right," Anna said. "So we're still going into the forest."

Chris spat his answer emphatically. "Yes."

"Hell yeah!" Hailey and Flint chorused.

Anna nodded. "Then we're going to need some extra supplies. Hailey, I'm sorry to ask such a crass question, but I'm broke. Are all of your cards maxed?"

"Yep." She winked. "But don't worry about that. Daddy will give me some more. I just have to ask nicely. How much do you need?"

Anna's mouth twitched as she counted in her head, then she gave Hailey a sheepish smile. "Any chance you could wrangle five hundred?"

"You got it." Hailey pulled her phone out of her pocket and slid out of the van.

Chris leaned against the window and watched Hailey pace the parking lot, speaking into her phone. Her face was animated, and she laughed frequently. He could only imagine what lies she was spinning for her father. “Anna, we already bought a ton of stuff yesterday. What else do we need?”

“I’m not sure we’ll definitely, absolutely need them. But I’m sure as hell not walking into that forest underprepared. If there really is something attacking hikers—and that’s a big if, but we’re playing it safe, remember—then we’ll need something to defend ourselves with.”

“Guns?” Flint asked.

“No, no way to get them quickly or easily. Not unless we go the illegal route, and I don’t know about you, but I haven’t spent enough time in this town to become acquainted with any crime lords. But I have some other ideas.”

The passenger door opened, and Hailey leapt back in. She had a mischievous grin. “Am I brilliant, or am I brilliant? I told him I wanted to hire a private tour guide to show me the lesser-known attractions. You’ve got your five hundred and five hundred more. It’ll be loaded onto the card in about ten minutes.”

“You’re brilliant, Hailey. And please apologize to your father on my behalf once this is all over.” Anna pulled her seat belt on. “Let’s go, Flint. We passed a camping-supplies store not far back. We’ll stop there first.”

Flint pulled out of the parking lot. He glanced at them through the rear-view mirror. “Hey, do you think Todd will be mad when he finds out we’re here without him?”

Hailey answered on all of their behalves. “Oh yeah, absolutely.”

“Yeah. I’m going to need to smooth things over with him when we get home.” Chris wasn’t looking forward to it. Todd had a way of rubbing things in, even if he hadn't done anything wrong. Still, Todd was his oldest friend. It felt a little callous to go on the trip without at least telling him.

But deep inside, Chris knew it had been the best choice. Todd liked being right. The democracy would have devolved into the rest of them fighting with a dictator if Todd had been part of the group. He'd started to develop an obsession with Eileen too. If she said anything to him, even if it was as innocuous as good morning, he would try to spend the rest of the day trailing around beside her. Talking to him didn't help. Getting angry with him didn't help. And calling him a creep definitely hadn't helped.

Chris pulled his phone out of his pocket and checked for messages. It was abnormal for Todd to go so long without texting him. Maybe the fight had upset him more than he'd shown.

Well, that's his problem, not mine. Apologies can wait until we get home.

CHAPTER 20

Friday, 10:30 a.m.

CARLA SWALLOWED TWO PAIN tablets. She'd already taken one dose before arriving to work, but her hangover migraine had developed into a stress migraine, and she was desperate enough to ignore the instructions.

She shouldn't have snapped at the kids. The look on Chris's face when she'd told him they were waiting for Eileen's bones to wash up was the stuff of nightmares. It was like telling a child that Santa Claus was dead and the town had shot his reindeer and cooked them for dinner.

The stress was getting to her. It had been getting to her for a long while, but she'd always thought she could just…cope. Like she always had. Push it down. Squish it into a little ball in the darkest, blackest part of her heart. Do her damn job like she was supposed to. But it had built up without her even noticing, and it was starting to spill out and hurt people around her.

She hadn't joined the police to yell at grieving kids.

Carla ground her palm into her forehead as she leaned over the conference desk. The migraine throbbed with every beat of her heart. She didn't know what to do with herself. She'd tried taking time off work, but that hadn't solved anything. Life at home wasn't exactly a joyride. Therapy hadn't helped.

Maybe she was broken, destined to grow more bitter and cold each year until she finally withered away. Maybe she would be the kind of person who had a funeral party of two—the priest and the undertaker. Maybe people would breathe a sigh of relief when she finally kicked the bucket.

"Carla?"

She jerked up and rubbed her hands over her eyes. There were no tears there—she hadn't been able to cry for nearly three years—but the motion was reflexive. "Hey, Viv. How are you doing?"

"I was going to ask the same thing." Viv leaned on the conference room door, concern twisting her face. "Do you need some pain tablets? I've got some spare—"

"Thanks, but I'm good. Just took some." She waved a hand at the table, as though the photos scattered across it gave an explanation for why she was falling apart. "Should kick in soon…"

"Did Hershberger and his friends give you trouble?"

Thinking of the double-bird the beefy one had given her on the way out, she cracked a smile. "No. They were energetic enough, but no trouble. I'm just…"

Viv slid into the seat beside her. Her expression was open and hopeful, silently promising to hear Carla's deepest fears without judgment. Not like that would ever happen. Carla had a strict no-personal-junk-at-work rule. She leaned back in her chair and stretched her shoulder muscles. "It's hard to disappoint people. They were so sure they'd found a clue for Eileen Hershberger's disappearance. But it just turned out to be a glitch."

"They must miss her," Viv murmured. "You should have seen their faces when they marched in. Like they were ready to beat down your door if you didn't listen to them."

"Yeah. I remember what it was like to be twenty. I felt like I could save the world." Carla began gathering the photographs and putting them back into order.

"And you don't feel that way anymore?"

Carla gave her a sharp look. They were treading dangerously close to the personal junk. "No. Once in a blue moon, I get to do some actual good. But most of my job is just...well, even busywork is too good of a name for it. You give people speeding tickets, but they don't stop speeding. You give help to battered wives, and they go back to their abusers the very next week. Do you know how many body bags I've watched be closed?"

Viv frowned. "How many?"

"Eleven. And do you know how many lives I've saved? And I mean really, genuinely saved, not just temporarily improved so that they could backslide the following month?"

Viv shook her head.

"Screw all." She spread her hands in a wide arc. "I'm not

anyone's hero. I'm not making the world a better place, like I vowed when I put on this uniform for the first time. I just clean up messes. I'm a glorified janitor with bonus paperwork."

"I don't believe that." Viv's voice had dropped to a whisper. "You do good. It's just hard to see because the effects aren't as obvious as a…a body bag."

Carla sighed. "You're a good person. And you're really trying. I hope working with me doesn't rub that shine off too soon."

She stacked the photos, returned them to their folder, and left the room without saying goodbye. Carla chewed on her bitterness the whole way back to her desk.

She needed something. Maybe a proper vacation. Maybe a hole through her head.

It was no wonder her co-workers didn't like her. And it was no wonder Decker incessantly stacked work on her desk as though it were a competition to see how high he could make the pile. Maybe he was trying to overwork her and get her to quit. She wasn't going to, though. She'd let the job absorb her identity. Without it, she would be no one at all.

Carla dropped into her seat. As was their unspoken accord, the man beside her, Lau, didn't acknowledge her, and she didn't try to initiate conversation. She just pulled the top file from her stack of work to do and opened it.

She tried to read the form, but her eyes glazed over. The photos didn't want to be forgotten. For a moment, when the girl had pointed out the shape buried in the image, Carla had felt a swell of the old excitement. If she hadn't seen the originals, she might have gotten swept up into the discovery, just like the kids had. The picture really had seemed to show a nightmarish face looming out of the darkness.

Carla put the form aside. She wanted to see the shape one more time, just to satisfy herself that it really was a glitch. There were two points where the artifact could have been introduced—during the scanning or during the printing. She had no control over the latter, but the scans should still be on her computer.

She navigated through her drive to find the right folder. Her mind insisted it was stupid to waste time, that she would drown under her workload if she didn't focus on it, but she couldn't help herself. She wanted to be *sure*.

Eileen's photographs were still in the scanner's folder. She counted through them to find the right number and opened it. The photo splashed across her computer screen.

There was no face.

That answered it, then. The printer had malfunctioned and introduced the inconsistency. Maybe a print head needed cleaning. Maybe data got corrupted on the USB. If she was being exceptionally cynical, she might think Chris Hershberger and his friends had Photoshopped the faces in to mess with her. No matter the cause, it wasn't her problem.

She pushed the folder of photos aside again and picked up the form. There were at least five pages to fill out. Some days, she felt like her job was nothing but a spiderweb of red tape.

Carla leaned back in her chair and stretched her neck, trying to work some of the knots out of her back and relieve the migraine. As she reclined, her eyes returned to the photo on her computer screen.

There was a faint, almost smoky shape between the trees. She snapped back up and leaned closer. As she did, the image disappeared. She froze, half fearing that she'd finally cracked and started hallucinating. Then, slowly and carefully, she rose out of her seat so that the computer screen was at an angle.

As she looked at it from a too-high viewpoint, the photo's colors distorted. A fuzzy shape materialized out of the blackness. Carla let her mouth drop open with a near-silent "Oh."

She sat back down and moved the picture into an image-editing program. The functionality wasn't advanced, but it let her adjust contrast, which was all she needed. She raised the contrast until the blacks were pitch-black and the colors seemed to glow, then flopped back into her chair, one hand pressed over her mouth.

The twisted, deformed face stared at her out of the picture. Part of its body was visible too. Not much—just the hint of wide shoulders below the monstrous head. It stood facing the camera square-on, chin lifted as it looked down at Eileen.

"They were right…"

Lau twisted toward her. "Say something?"

"No." She waited until he'd turned back to his own work to lean closer to the picture. The figure hadn't been visible in the original photos because the colors were all deep and natural. But when the pictures had been printed on a cheap machine, the colors had been distorted just enough to reveal its head. If she hadn't seen it with her own eyes, she wouldn't have believed it was real. Even with the contrast pumped up, the figure was too vague to get a good read on. But it was something…

No. She was getting carried away. She could see the shape, but its explanation hadn't changed. It was still pareidolia. She was so eager to see a monstrous figure that she was letting perfectly normal, coincidentally connected leaves trick her eyes. It was the same effect that made people see shapes in haunted building footage and assume they'd captured a ghost.

"Delago!" Decker's fist slammed into the door. "Where's the Crispin paperwork?"

"On its way, sir." Carla plastered a smile onto her face and pushed the photos away for a final time. Decker was in a bad mood, which meant everyone else—including her—would suffer. Her best option was to pretend there was no world outside of her work and hope he picked on a different underling that afternoon.

She closed the image-editing program. The visual effect had almost gotten a rise out of her. But it couldn't be real. No more real than the pictures of Bigfoot or the Loch Ness Monster—because what the photo showed was a monster, and monsters didn't exist.

CHAPTER 21

Friday, 12:00 p.m.

KNOTS TIGHTENED CHRIS'S STOMACH. It had been easy to say they were going to storm the mountain when they were safe at home, but now that it was actually happening, he felt fear.

Their van wove through narrow, bending roads in its climb up the foothills. Trees already clustered around them on all sides. Up ahead, the mountain ridge towered into the sky like a behemoth. Its summit looked an eternity away.

"Don't worry." Anna was fidgeting with her jacket's sleeve. The nerves seemed to be affecting her too. "We're not going up into the really steep part. Ashlough Forest has lots of bumpy sections, but it doesn't involve mountain climbing."

"Great," he managed.

They took a corner too quickly, and the van rocked. They

had only passed two cars coming in the opposite direction. The trails were an hour from Helmer, and most hikers wouldn't be returning home until later in the afternoon.

Chris didn't think he'd ever seen so much nature in one place. He lost count of how many plant varieties clustered on the roadsides. They had passed a gravel stopping point with three deer lurking at its back, waiting for visitors to bring food offerings. Birds circled overhead, and they were larger than the ones he saw out of his bedroom windows.

"My phone isn't getting a signal," Hailey said.

Chris gaped at her. "You're *driving*."

"I'm being safe," she insisted. "I just wanted to see if there were any messages."

"Put your phone down and focus on the road," Anna said. "It won't work up here. No reception. There were talks of putting in a phone tower a few years ago, but it was decided it would be too expensive."

Flint scoffed. "That's stupid. What about people like Eileen? A phone tower might save lives."

"I agree. But the woods are so dense and vast that a single tower would struggle to hold even a poor connection. Plus, you'd need to run electricity up the mountainside, and the locals were strongly against anything that would involve deforestation."

"You know a lot about this place," Chris said.

She shrugged. "I did a lot of reading after Eileen first went missing. It was my way of coping, I guess. I wanted to understand how it could happen."

The road took a hairpin turn, and Hailey had to slow to a crawl. They'd taken longer to get to the mountain than Chris would have liked. If he'd known the police were going to be so dismissive, he wouldn't have waited for the station to open and would have driven straight to the mountain.

The road opened up, and a massive archway passed overhead as they entered the Ashlough Forest parking lot. The space had markers to fit thirty cars and several tour buses, but Friday wasn't a prime hiking day, and only a half dozen cars sat in the gravel lot. Hailey pulled into an empty corner and parked. Chris, relieved to havc a chance to stretch his legs, leapt out of the van before its engine stopped.

The entrance to the forest waited on the other side of the parking lot. A painted map stood beside it, along with a brightly colored warning sign. Chris squinted to read it from a distance. It warned against leaving the paths, walking alone, and not bringing enough water. If it was anything to go by, the trails weren't as safe as the officer seemed to think they were.

"All right, let's check we're ready." Anna hauled hiking packs out of the back and passed one to Chris. It was bulky and heavy. She also handed them all sheathed, serrated knives to attach to their belts. "Hailey, you're wearing the wrong shoes."

She looked down at the sandals. "But these are more comfortable."

"You won't think that when sticks start poking through your skin and the soles fall off. Go change them." She scanned Chris and Flint. "Arms and legs covered, good. Hats, good. Put your pack on securely. It shouldn't be putting pressure on any single point in your back."

"This is excessive," Flint muttered.

"You know what's excessive? Dying because you were stupid." Anna glared at him. "You've never camped in a place like this. You have no idea how many risks it can hold, and not all of them are easy to see coming. Plus, we have the risk of some monster-like being roaming the forest, so yeah, I'd rather be excessive than underprepared."

"Still…" He shuffled, simultaneously looking resentful and apologetic. "Did we really need to get four maps? And four compasses?"

"Do you want to try getting home without a map if you get separated from the group?"

"No." He scowled and snatched up one of the hunting knives from the back of the van. "But we're not separating. Not after you drilled that into us for, like, twenty minutes."

"Accidents happen. We've just got to be prepared for all of them."

Hailey returned from the passenger's seat, now wearing hiking boots. Anna nodded. "All right. Let's go."

As they passed the sign beside the park's entrance, Chris gazed across the map for the final time. Eileen could have followed any of the twelve trails. No way to track her, and no way to know at which point she had stepped off the road.

Even though Anna was acting like they were trying to find Eileen, he knew she didn't expect it. For her, it was a charade to help them all get through their grief and guilt. And for the first time, he was starting to feel like she might be right. It would take years to search the forest thoroughly and decades, perhaps, to become familiar with it. They were essentially stepping into the woods and *hoping* they stumbled into Eileen. If they did, it would be almost pure chance.

He tried not to think about that as the shadows enveloped them. There had been greater coincidences. At least now, Eileen's chances were better than they had been before.

Ten minutes into the trail, their chosen path speared off to the right. A large sign had been positioned beside it, warning tourists of the risks.

CAUTION. Advanced trail. Not recommended for inexperienced hikers.

He hesitated. Eileen had gone on a few camping trips during her teenage years, but she was far from experienced. Maybe they had picked the wrong trail to follow. Maybe she really had stuck to one of the intermediate paths.

Anna seemed to be thinking along the same lines. She stared at the sign. "If Eileen read this, would she think it was a caution? Or a challenge?"

"A challenge," Chris said. His hesitation vanished. "You're right. She was looking for a challenge."

He led the way onto the dirt path. Anna followed. Flint and Hailey held hands and stepped in after them. Almost instantly, the atmosphere changed. The trail became rougher and narrower, with more rocks poking out of the compact dirt. It wove so aggressively that they couldn't see more than ten paces ahead at a time. The trees seemed to crowd in on both sides like walls. When Chris inhaled, he tasted air that had gone a long time without being disturbed by other humans.

Eileen had been gone for exactly five days. If she was still alive out there, he hoped she would hang on, just a little bit longer, for him.

"Advanced Trail" hadn't been an exaggeration. They walked for hours. Chris grew sweaty and panting. Every now and then, the path flattened out and tricked him into thinking they were through the worst of it, then it would turn back into an unending series of sharp, narrow stairs.

Though the scenery was beautiful, the initial thrill soon wore off. His hiking gear felt insanely heavy. He wished he had put more effort into maintaining his health.

Flint was powering on well. He barely even looked flushed. Behind him, Hailey's face had developed a permanent scowl, but she'd only complained once, when a spider tried to land on her. She and Flint went to the gym together, and both had built endurance. Anna was the least fit of them all, and it was showing. She bent forward, her breaths coming in labored puffs, her pink face glistening with sweat.

"Need a break?" Chris asked.

"Not yet. Better to…cover as much ground…as we can… while the sun's up."

He didn't argue, but he did slow the pace a little. She looked like she might throw up.

Before they had entered the forest, he'd harbored some vague, irrational dream of being able to tell where Eileen had left the path. Some sort of sibling sixth sense would lead him, or maybe they would find a muddy shoe print left in the ground. He'd found nothing of the kind. For most of the path, the ground to either side of the trail was so inhospitable that trying to leave the path meant either hiking up forty-five-degree angles or wading through prickly vines. It would have been pure insanity.

But realistically, the stretch of trail Eileen could have become lost on wasn't small. The shuttle bus had dropped her off at noon, and it would have picked up the last stragglers at six. That meant three hours into the forest and three hours to get back out.

Ahead, a sign poked out of the ground. They had already passed a couple like it, warning of slippery rocks and landslide risks. This one, however, pointed off the trail. Chris slowed as he got closer. "Kidney Pool."

"Yes, pool," Anna gasped.

Chris made the connection. One of Eileen's photos had shown her splashing in a body of water. The sign pointed down a trail that was even narrower than their current trail, if that was possible. Chris stepped into it and felt vines and branches scratch over his head and shoulders.

The path led them on for nearly ten minutes. It became so overgrown and erratic that Chris was starting to worry they had become lost. Then the cloistering plants opened up into a gorgeous natural pool.

Chris recognized the miniature waterfall and the small

crystalline lagoon. He took a few steps to the side and found the angle Eileen's photo had been taken from. He could even guess the branch the camera had been propped in.

"It's beautiful," Hailey said. She dropped onto a fallen log nearby and pulled her boots off to massage her feet. "Eileen would have loved it here."

"She would have," Chris agreed.

The waterfall made a soothing pattering noise as it hit the pool. The basin wasn't large but looked deep enough that a person could have a proper swim in it. Chris supposed its odd kidney-like shape had earned the pool its name. Water flowed over the right-hand lip to become a thin stream.

"At least we know we found the right trail." Anna collapsed onto the ground without bothering to find a seat. She leaned back and rested her hiking backpack against the tree behind her. "We had twelve choices, but we got it right. I think that's pretty darn impressive."

"Yeah," Chris agreed. He circled the pool, first looking inside the basin then toward where the overflow became a new stream. Eileen knew better than to jump into bodies of water without knowing how deep they were, but if she had, she could have broken her back and been trapped there. There was no trace of her, though, which he was grateful for. And he was fairly sure he didn't recognize any of the trees from her nighttime photos. She might have stopped at Kidney Pool, but she hadn't stayed.

"Hey," Flint called. "There's another path up here."

Chris rounded the pool to meet him. Near the waterfall, hidden among heavy growths, was the faintest trace of a trail. A metal chain had been hung from two posts on either side, cordoning it off, with a wooden sign suspended from its middle.

TRAIL CLOSED—UNSAFE

"Looks like it hasn't been walked down in years," Anna said. She'd gotten up to follow them, and Chris was glad to see her color was returning to normal.

"You don't think—" Chris started.

"She went down there," Hailey spoke over him.

"Oh, hell." Anna ran her hands over her face. "Yes. I bet she would have."

Flint squinted at the trail and snorted. "Nah. What sort of person would want to walk down there?"

"The sort of person who's on a mission to push herself," Anna said. "Damn it, it works out perfectly. She arrives at Kidney Pool and spends maybe an hour swimming and sketching in her art book. That leaves her with an hour to burn until she needs to turn back for the shuttle bus. She could go back to the main trail, or she could explore the long-disused path. What's she going to do?"

Flint swore.

"Yep, she would have gone down there." Chris's eyes followed the path, which twisted out of sight. "I don't especially like hiking, and even I'm curious about where it leads."

"And it's so old," Anna said. "I bet it would become really, really easy to lose the path."

"And never find your way back."

The four friends stood for a moment, staring at the chain and its gently swaying warning sign. Then Flint clapped his hands together. "I'm ready to get moving if everyone else is."

"Yeah," Chris said.

Anna shucked off her backpack and dug through its pockets. She came up with two balls of red twine. One she tucked into her pocket; she unthreaded a length from the other and tied its end onto the chain.

"Oh! Like that guy who got lost with the bull in the maze," Flint said.

"Theseus, Minotaur, labyrinth." Anna checked the knot was secure then began unraveling the twine. "But yes, basically, we're taking a note out of his book. If we get split up for any reason whatsoever, I want you all to use your own thread to mark your progress. It's incredibly easy to get turned around in this forest. But this should, at least, lead us back to our starting point."

One at a time, they stepped over the metal chain. The disused trail felt quieter and grimmer than the more-traveled paths. As the waterfall's gentle splashes faded from his hearing, Chris shivered. The trail felt wrong. He'd always expected untouched nature to feel pristine, but it didn't. Something about the path having once existed, but still not quite reclaimed, left it in a tight, uneasy limbo. He couldn't wait to leave it.

CHAPTER 22

Friday, 2:30 p.m.

TODD STAGGERED, FEELING DRUNK. The earth seemed to sway and ripple under him, and it was becoming harder and harder to stay upright.

He couldn't remember where he was going. It was becoming hard to keep track of what was happening, where he was, or how many days he had been in the forest. It felt like a lifetime, though he only remembered one night. The night with the silent, too-tall creature stalking him.

Maybe that had just been in his mind.

His makeshift spear hit a tree, throwing him off balance. He stumbled, staggered, and collapsed to his knees. His mouth was so dry. When was the last time he'd drunk anything? The thirst had gotten into his head and made it throb. He wished it would stop. He wished everything would stop.

He tried to whine, but it came out as a croak, so he let himself slide sideways to rest against the nearest tree. He was supposed to be doing something, he was sure. Finding a road. Or water. Water sounded good. He wanted water.

He hated the bloody forest and everything about it. He hated Eileen for leading him out there. Most of all, he wished he could go home.

Against his body's wishes, he hauled himself to his feet again. Somehow, he knew that if he let himself sit for too long, he would never get up again. At least he was going downhill. That had to mean he was near the park's entrance. Maybe another five or ten minutes would see him stepping out of the archway to greet the crowd of anxious searchers who had been looking for him. His friends would all be there—Chris and Hailey and maybe even Flint. Not his father, though. His father probably hadn't even noticed Todd was missing yet. But everyone else would be there, helping him into a car, giving him bottles of icy water, and wrapping blankets around his shoulders. They would be so impressed. It took a certain caliber of human to go through what Todd had gone through. And at least they would say he'd done his best to find Eileen.

He would probably be asked to speak at her funeral. It didn't seem quite right to sob over an empty coffin. But for Eileen's sake, he would. Her parents would appreciate it. Not even Chris would complain.

Todd hit another tree. He'd been holding the spear loosely, and it bounced out of his grip. He didn't bother picking it up again. The train of thought seemed irrational, even to himself, but he couldn't reel it back in. Something was seriously wrong. Maybe he'd gotten a fever after falling into the river the day before.

River...

He could hear water in the distance. He was so thirsty. Just a gulp or two would make everything better.

Todd's eyes drifted closed, but he kept moving forward. Each step stubbed his toe on some unseen obstacle, but his eyelids were too heavy to lift them. He relied on his senses to guide him forward, occasionally stepping through scratchy vines as he followed the enticing, gurgling noise.

It had better not be a mirage. He couldn't remember if mirages existed in the forest or only in the desert. He felt like he was in a desert. His lips were so dry. It was ridiculous. The forest was so moist that moss grew everywhere, but there wasn't a single drop for him to drink.

His foot landed in air, and Todd barely had the strength to gasp as he slid down a slope. Rocks and roots stabbed at him as he fell, tearing holes in his clothes and scraping off skin. He didn't care. When he finally came to a halt, his arms were in running water.

"Yes..." he croaked, crawling forward. The water wasn't deep. Unlike the earlier river, it wasn't crystalline or fast-moving, either. Bits of dirt and insects floated across its surface, and mud swirled up as he disturbed the riverbed. He didn't care. He plunged his face into it and drank and drank until he thought he was going to be sick.

Once his stomach was swollen with water, he dragged himself back up onto the bank. It was only waist high, but the effort was enormous. He collapsed into the ground and let his eyes fall closed. *When I find Eileen, she had better be grateful for everything I've gone through.*

Feverish dreams chased him for hours. When Todd woke, everything ached. He groaned and rolled onto his side. He wasn't sure how long he'd been asleep, only that the forest was growing dimmer. He was freezing cold. His jeans and sleeves were still damp from falling into the stream, but he'd lost his change of clothes when the monster had separated him from his backpack.

He squinted at the trees and tried to guess the light's angle. He didn't have many hours until sundown. Would the thing find him again? It had seemed to possess a sixth sense for his presence the previous night. But he'd been walking for so long, he had to assume he was out of its territory by that point.

He sat up and whimpered. He hadn't thought it was possible for a human body to hurt so severely. At least his mind was clearer. Most of the day had been spent in a fugue. Probably from dehydration, he realized. He looked toward the forest, the direction he'd come from. Water in Ashlough Forest wasn't as plentiful as he'd expected. He would need to leave the stream, though, if he wanted to retrace his steps.

He twisted to look downriver. Maybe he wouldn't have to leave the water. It was trending down, which meant it was leading toward the base of the mountains. It might take some extra time, but he would find his way to some kind of civilization as long as he followed the river.

That was a huge relief. He would still need food soon—his energy levels had plummeted—but at least he wouldn't have to suffer through another delirium.

His stomach was still full, but his mouth was dry. He knelt beside the stream, trying his hardest not to let his clothes dip into the water again, and scooped handfuls of the liquid into his mouth. Then he stood and groaned as he began the trek back into the forest.

The sun was getting lower. He didn't want to run through the woods at night again. His feet and shins still ached from the abuse. But he wanted to put at least a little more space between himself and the monster before sundown.

He found a dead branch that wasn't too decayed and used it as a walking stick. Eventually, he would need to figure out some kind of shelter, but he'd lost a large part of the day to the delirium and sleep. And the faster he moved, the sooner he would get home.

The sunlight faded. Birds sent up one final rally of screeches and chattering as they figured out their sleeping arrangements then fell silent over a half-hour span. Todd hoped they all dropped dead in their sleep. They were too loud, and his headache couldn't withstand much more of a battering.

He started tripping over obstacles again and reluctantly left the river's side to find a clear patch to sleep. That was more challenging than he'd expected. He'd entered a rocky part of the landscape, and any scrap of smooth ground was inevitably dotted with scrubby bushes and saplings.

Frustrated and tired, Todd used a stick to beat at some of the bushes. He cleared enough of a space that he could lie down in them. It wasn't exactly a five-star resort, and he knew they probably contained a multitude of bugs that would crawl over him as he tried to sleep, but at least they shielded him from sight in case the monster came looking for him.

Todd kicked off his shoes. He had blisters on both feet, and the shoes and socks were still wet. He couldn't see the skin, but he could feel the wrinkles. He knew they had to look horrible. Letting them air and dry out overnight would be smart.

He curled up with his arm under his head and his knees at his chin. He'd thought he would be exhausted enough to sleep, but as night animals chattered and insects whirred, he found himself too wired to close his eyes. The canopy blocked out everything except a hint of moonlight. He still had his flashlight in his pocket and turned it on. The bulb held a spark of life but soon fizzled into nothing. He grunted and thrust it back into his pocket.

A branch snapped. Todd's body stiffened. Not moving, he stared toward the source of the sound, willing his eyes to hunt out shapes among the darkness. The monster couldn't have found him again. He'd been walking for nearly a full day. It was impossible.

There was no scraping noise, but he could detect the scuffle of leaves being pushed aside. He imagined the monstrous form, tall and clothed all in black, and a spike of panic pulsed through him.

Taking his shoes off had been a bad idea. He sat up and felt for them in the darkness. The scuffling noise had stopped, but he sensed its source was still out there, possibly watching him, waiting to see what he did.

He fit the left shoe on first then struggled to pull on the right. His feet ached and protested against the wet clothing, but he made it work. If he needed to run, he would be in a lot more pain without any footwear.

The scuffling came again, a little closer this time. Todd hated the idea of waiting for it to come to him. If he made the first move, attacked it, maybe he could frighten it off—or at least give it second thoughts about fighting him.

Another twig snapped. There was nothing for it. Todd launched himself to his feet, snarling and yelling as much as his weary lungs could manage. A large rodent-like creature yelped and skittered away, darting between the trees in a panic.

Todd lowered his arms, laughing and shaking. He was safe. The monster hadn't found him. The relief even outweighed his irritation at being disturbed.

He took a few steps forward, just to make sure there was nothing else lurking around. A shape, unusually bright in the darkness, caught his eye.

A word had been painted on the massive, ancient tree trunk behind him. He didn't know how long it had been there or whether it had existed before he lay down and he just hadn't seen it, but it was large enough and bright enough that it arrested his attention and froze him in place.

Three letters had been painted across the tree. Whatever liquid had been used made the word glow an eerie seasick green. The effect made it look like it was floating in a sea of blackness. The message was simple, a single word. RUN.

He did.

Friday, 6:30 p.m.

"WE NEED TO MAKE camp," Anna said.

Chris obediently stopped walking, but he couldn't hide a frown. "The sun's still up. We can search for another half hour, maybe more, before it gets too dark."

"Yes. We can. If we're idiots." Anna collapsed against a tree. She was still red and sweaty, but he didn't think tiredness was the only cause for her irritability. "Twilight's hitting, which stops us from seeing clearly. Eileen could be lying two feet off the side of the path, and you would miss her. Besides, we've got to set up our tents, and I promise you, that's not going to be fun in the dark."

Chris unbuckled his gear and dropped it off his shoulders. He was grateful for a break but, at the same time, felt resentful. They had been hiking up and down the disused trail for most of the day without luck. But he felt like they were close. Eileen couldn't have followed the trail for more than half an hour or forty-five minutes before she tried to turn back.

They had found a marker proving Eileen had passed through the area. A magnificent pine tree, old and haggard, stood a few feet off the path. Hailey had noticed it first. When they pulled Eileen's photos out of Chris's backpack, they had been able to identify it as the behemoth captured in one of the daytime photos.

The discovery had been like molten energy running through Chris's veins. He'd led them on farther and faster after that, certain they would find another clue if they just looked hard enough. That had been three hours ago.

The routine was the same each time; they set out to follow the disused trail. It led on for about fifteen minutes before the path started breaking apart and becoming confused by phantom trails. When they reached a patch where the trail forked, they would choose one, but no matter which path they pursued, it soon vanished into the jumbled confusion of the woods.

Chris could see how easy it would be to become lost. The first time they'd encountered the fork, they'd assumed the straight-ahead route was correct. But the farther they walked, the more uneven the ground became. They had to bend over double to fit under low branches, climb over jutting boulders, and awkwardly shimmy through narrow gaps between trees. Eventually, when they stopped, they saw the path had vanished a long while before. If not for Anna's string, Chris might have shared Eileen's fate.

By the time the sun started to drop, they had followed each

path three times. Each time, Chris had pushed them deeper into the wilderness before Anna called him back due to the dangers the terrain presented. Each time, he stopped at the farthest point, took his whistle out of his backpack's side pouch, and blew it as loudly as he could. The piercing, shrill whistle would travel through the forest better than their voices could. If Eileen was still out there, and if she heard it, she might be able to find her way to them.

"We'll try again tomorrow, early, when the day's fresh." Anna must have seen the frustration in his face. It didn't stop her from unrolling her tent, though. "This is a good place to stop, anyway. We're near the fork, and the ground's about as smooth as I've seen anywhere."

"Fine. But I want us to start again early tomorrow. As soon as the sun's up."

Chris knew he was letting his irritability bleed out, but he couldn't help it. Despite guessing the path right, despite following the disused trail, and despite walking over the same ground as Eileen, he still felt lost. He didn't know where else to go or where else to search. Covering the same ground again and again wasn't helping, but there were no more clues. Regardless of which fork Eileen had taken, she'd had days to wander and be swallowed by the dizzying expanse of forest. Chris felt like he was chasing a ghost.

He unbuckled his tent from his hiking pack. Anna had bought it for him; it was a minimalistic dome tent designed to be lightweight. The night temperature was relatively mild at that time of year, but they still needed protection from rain. He and Anna would be sharing one tent, and Hailey and Flint had the second.

"Do you think we can have a fire?" Hailey asked.

"No." Chris's retort was automatic and more mean-spirited than he'd thought he was capable of. He didn't want her to have a fire. He didn't want her enjoying herself while they were supposed to be looking for his sister.

"Sorry, Hail, but not in this tangle," Anna said. "The trees are growing too close together. We can't risk a spark lighting some dry wood, or we could get burned alive in a forest fire."

She sighed. "I guess our food will be cold, then."

"I guess so." Chris flapped his tent's material out and began dragging it to a clear patch. Bringing Hailey had been a mistake. She wasn't taking the situation seriously enough. And he didn't think it would take long before she started asking to go home.

Hailey flopped down beside Flint and whispered, "Is this what camping's normally like? It's not very fun."

Flint laughed. "Nah, babe. Normally, there'd be a lot more beer."

The irritated itch became unbearable. Chris slammed his pack onto the ground. "Sorry for being such a massive disappointment, guys, but getting buzzed isn't exactly my priority right now."

Flint held his hands up. "Hey, we're cool, man. I was just joking."

"How about you *don't* until Eileen is found? Do you think you can manage that? Huh?"

The words tasted like venom, and Chris immediately regretted them. Hurt flashed through Flint's face, and Hailey pulled her knees up under her chin.

"Sorry, man." Flint shrugged his massive shoulders. "Force of habit, I guess."

"Whatever." Chris's tent was only half set up, but he gave up on it, kicked the one pole over, and stalked into the forest. "I need some air. Be back soon."

"Hey!" Anna ran after him. He waved for her to leave him alone, but she didn't. "You can't just run off, Chris! We discussed this. If there's something dangerous in this forest, we need to stick together."

"Will you shut up for *five minutes*, please?" He swiveled.

Anna stood an arm's length away. She'd brought the ball of twine, unraveling it as she ran.

The sight of it made him roll his eyes up. "You think we're going to get lost twenty paces from camp?"

"What's wrong with you? You've never yelled at us like this."

His eyes were burning. He turned away and leaned his forehead against a tree. The bark was rough and prickly. "Nothing. I just need some alone time."

He waited to hear leaves crunch as Anna retreated to the camp, but she didn't. After a moment, he turned to face her. She'd sat on the ground, legs crossed, ball of twine resting beside her. She didn't look as angry as he'd expected. He extended his arms in a show of irritation. "Well?"

"You're dealing with a lot. I understand. You must be under so much pressure." She folded her hands ahead of herself. "It's making you lash out. And I don't think that's what you want. I was hoping we could talk about it."

"Thanks for the lecture." He tried to sound angry, but a lot of the frustration had already slipped away into exhaustion. He slid his back down the tree until he was sitting opposite her. "I don't want to talk."

"Are you angry because of something I did?"

"No." He shrugged. "Yes. I don't know."

"Is it because I made us stop to set up camp?"

A pang of the earlier frustration reared its head. He glared at the canopy above them as the words spilled out of him. "Not just that. You've been calling the shots the whole way. What we buy, when we start, when we stop. And I know there's a good reason for it. You actually know what to do. But…"

"You don't feel in control anymore?"

"I guess." He shrugged. "And I know that's irrational. I don't have a monopoly on Eileen, and you guys are trying to help. And I'm grateful! I swear I am! But once we got onto this path, our progress came to a halt. I don't know where to go from here. I don't have any clues left to follow. I'm basically sitting on my ass and achieving nothing. It's what I did at home, just in a more exotic location."

"I get it. So much of what happens is outside of your control, and that's stressing you, so you're fighting back whenever you feel like your power is being taken away."

He rubbed his thumbs into the bridge of his nose. "Would you stop psychoanalyzing me, please?"

This time, the words were said half in jest, and Anna's smile told him she understood. "Sorry. Psych student. It's like a compulsion. I can't turn it off."

He glanced toward the area they had planned to camp in. He'd walked far enough to muffle sounds, but he was fairly sure Flint was working on their tents. "Maybe you could use that analyzing to tell me if I'm right. I'm thinking it was a bad idea to bring Hailey. Maybe we should take her back to the town while we're still fairly close."

Anna tilted her head to one side. "You're worried she won't pull her weight?"

"Well…" He shrugged, uncomfortable. "More like she didn't realize what she was getting into."

"I'm pretty sure she did. She's smarter than you think."

Chris scrunched his face up.

"Yes, she is." Anna laughed at his expression. "She's actually really clever. She just pretends she isn't. She's pretty, and she's blond, so people usually assume she's brainless, as well. She just plays into their expectations. People like her more that way."

He shook his head. "I don't believe you. No one was ever liked for being stupid."

"Are you sure about that?" Anna lifted her eyebrows. "You yelled at me and Flint, but not Hailey."

"Uh—" He blinked, shocked. He liked all of his friends, but he had to admit, Hailey had a disarming naivete that made it hard to be mean to her. It felt too much like kicking a puppy.

"Yeah," Anna said. "Guys like her because she's pretty and

needs to be taken care of. Girls like her because they think she's not a threat. And her father thinks she's a perfect innocent princess and would let her get away with murder. Everything is easier for her when she acts dumb."

Chris squinted toward the camp again. The light was failing, and Flint had set up a lamp to light the area. "So she's manipulating us?"

"No. Of course not. It's a subconscious behavior." Anna shrugged. "I doubt she's even aware she's doing it. But like a cat that gets rewarded when it meows, she gets rewarded when she acts naive. So she just does, without realizing why."

"You're too much." Chris ran a hand through his hair and felt a small collection of dead leaves and spiderwebs that had become trapped there. "I've known her for six years. I think I'd have noticed if she was secretly a genius."

"So you know she got straight A's in high school, right? And you know she's planning on going to med school next year?"

"I…that…" He blinked then laughed. "All right. Okay. I'm not conceding the point, but maybe you're not wrong. What about Flint, then?"

"What about him?"

"If we're analyzing our friends, I want to know what secrets Flint's hiding."

She grinned. "Nothing that you probably haven't already guessed. He's wearing a mask just like Hailey, except this time, it's all about pretending not to care. He's the tough guy, right? The frat bro, the gym monkey. But secretly, he cares deeply."

"Yeah?"

"I'm sure you would have guessed that, if you'd thought about it a bit. He wears this as-hard-as-nails shell as protection. He'll destroy anyone who messes with his friends. But he's intensely loyal. You could ask him to walk over blistering coals for you, and he would."

The guilt over yelling at Flint doubled up. Chris couldn't bring himself to meet Anna's eyes, so he stared at the ground instead. "I'm almost frightened to ask what you think of me."

"Oh, you're easy. Just a reverse Hailey. You're *actually* dumb but pretending to be smart."

He stared at her, shocked, and Anna laughed. "I'm joking, idiot. Don't look so heartbroken."

"You're terrible."

"I sure am."

A yelp floated through the cold night air. Chris and Anna both twisted to look toward the camp. The flickering golden light bounced off tree trunks, but they couldn't see either Hailey or Flint.

Anna picked up the ball of twine and began winding it back in. "We should—"

Her words were drowned out by Flint's screams.

CHAPTER 24

Friday, 7:00 p.m.

CARLA UNLOCKED HER HOME'S front door. Her feet ached, which seemed unfair when most of her day had been spent on her ass, filling out paperwork. She kicked her shoes off in the front hallway and hung her jacket on the hook next to the door. Matt's suede shoes were already resting on the polished-wood boards. Beside them was a single blue sequin. Carla stared at it for a heartbeat then lined up her own shoes on the floor, a meter away.

The house's lights were on, but no one called a greeting as she moved through the dining room and into the kitchen. Matt's dinner plate, knife, and fork were drying on the sideboard. The table held no food. Carla opened the cupboard, pulled out a carton of premade soup, then put it in the microwave to heat.

She still carried her satchel and car keys, but she wouldn't put them down until she was in her room.

It was a beautiful house. Five bedrooms, three bathrooms. Ducted air conditioning. A pool in the backyard. Way too big for just two people.

The microwave pinged to tell her the soup was ready, and she grabbed a paper towel to wrap around the plastic container and keep her fingers from burning. She held the carton carefully so that it wouldn't slosh then wove toward the twisting metal staircase in the back of the house.

The TV played some kind of sports game in the rumpus room. Carla had meant to pass it without comment, but she hadn't been silent enough. As she neared the door, Matt called out, "Good day at work today?"

"Yes." She always gave him that answer whether the day had been amazing or ghastly. It was their little routine, a habit that never seemed to break down no matter how badly everything else crumbled. "You?"

"Fine." He turned the volume down on the TV. That was different. Normally, they parted ways after their nightly check-in, but turning the volume down was a signal that he wanted to talk.

Carla could really do without it. She pressed her eyes closed then, taking a fortifying breath, squared her shoulders.

Matt appeared in the rumpus room doorway, looking as handsome as ever. The clear blue eyes she'd fallen in love with held no smiles for her, though. "How is the house search going?"

"Slowly but steadily." That was a lie. She'd visited a real estate site a week before, but it had made her feel sick and shaky. She hadn't gone back.

He rested one hand against the doorjamb and seemed to examine his fingernails. "It's been six months. That's an awfully long time to find an apartment. Your wage isn't *that* bad."

"I'll find one." She hated the way he spoke to her, like she was a stubborn child. She was struggling, not stupid.

The house had never been hers; Matt had inherited it from his parents, so it was only right that he got to keep it after the split. Still, it smarted. She had called it hers for four years. Decorated it. Painted the walls. Retiled the floors. Carefully handpicked every piece of furniture for the room at the end of the hallway…

"Do you think you could figure something out by the end of the month?" Matt scratched his stubbled jaw. She'd thought the stubble looked rugged and handsome once. Now it just looked lazy. "I don't like to push you, but c'mon, Carla. Enough's enough."

She couldn't hold it in any longer. "What's her name?"

"Who?"

"The girl who dropped her sequins in the hallway."

Matt ran his tongue over his lips. He didn't look ashamed, but he didn't meet her eyes, either. "I thought you agreed not to ask questions like that."

"And you promised to be discreet. And not to bring them into our home."

His voice maintained the same flat monotone, but his eyebrows went up. "It would be *my* home by now, if you weren't stalling."

That was fair. It didn't stop it from hurting, though. Carla stepped around him and continued toward her room. "I'll figure something out."

Matt watched her go. As she neared the staircase at the end of the house, he called after her, "Sorry, Carla. I'll clean up better next time. Okay?"

She knew if she said anything, it would be hurtful, so she acknowledged him with a wave instead.

The rumpus room door clicked as Matt locked himself away for the evening. Carla stopped at the stairs leading to the loft and looked to the right. A blue-painted door waited for her there. She glanced over her shoulder, toward the rumpus room, but Matt showed no sign of reemerging. Carla put down her soup and twisted the blue door's handle as gently as she could so that he wouldn't hear.

She'd decorated that room with more care than any other space in the house. A beautiful, empty crib waited below the window. Its mobile hung in suspense, fluffy ducks and pretty fish ready to be twirled. They would almost glow in the window's light in early morning. Timothy would have loved them.

The dresser was still full of little blue booties, bonnets, and onesies that had never been worn. Matt wanted to donate them. He probably would, when Carla moved out. He'd promised not to touch the room, to leave it as a monument, but she had no uncertainty about what would happen to it once she was gone. It would be torn down and thrown away in a day. Thrown away to make room for his *new* life, as though Timothy hadn't been the most important thing in the world to them at one time.

If she was being honest with herself, that was why she clung on to a house she was no longer welcome in—as long as she stayed there, so would Timothy's room. And building that room was one of the few happy memories she could associate with him.

Her eyes burned, but she didn't cry. She hadn't cried in almost three years. Not since that week bent over the crib, howling without any way to control herself. It was like some part of her had broken then. She no longer remembered how to cry. She barely remembered how to laugh. She was a walking husk, an automaton, an unfeeling machine.

She could remember the man's face, though. He'd been on drugs. Methamphetamines, the tests later proved. He looked more like a rabid dog than a human as he thrashed and screeched in the officer's arms. They'd brought him into the station to keep him in holding until the morning. But he wasn't going easily. He lunged forward, then pulled back, and then tried to bite their arms.

Carla, seven months pregnant, had been put on desk work until her maternity leave began. She'd heard the commotion and came out of her office to see if she could help. The man had broken free from the officer's arms. Hands cuffed behind his back, he had bent forward and charged into the hallway blindly. His path had taken him straight to Carla like a freight train.

She'd had just enough time to wrap her arms around her belly. It hadn't been enough. Nine hours of labor later, she'd given birth to Timothy. He had been perfect. Even covered in her blood, even premature, even dead, he had been perfect.

Carla closed the door silently. She picked up her carton of soup. It was time to do the only thing she still did competently: pour herself into work and, when the hour drew late enough, pour herself into alcohol until she felt as though she could sleep.

CHAPTER 25

Friday, 7:15 p.m.

TODD MOVED AT A crawl. He couldn't breathe properly, and dizziness threatened to topple him. He was furious with himself for running. He was furious with whatever demented creature ruled over the forest. The word painted on the tree had frightened him enough to send him scampering into the woods, and he'd lost the creek.

The question of whether it had been painted while Todd tried to sleep or whether it had been there before he lay down plagued him but was ultimately immaterial. He was still in the creature's territory. And he wasn't welcome there.

Todd couldn't wait for sunrise. Night had barely fallen, but already, he felt desperately unsafe. Any hope of maintaining his sense of direction was gone. The grandiose dream of instinctually picturing the way out had vanished too. Todd had tried, but the map he'd been able to conjure before wouldn't reappear. Maybe he was too frightened. Maybe the monster had done something to the airwaves to mess with his senses.

For a rational person like him, that kind of belief was borderline insane...but he could no longer discount it. The creature, whatever it was, couldn't be natural. When he escaped, he would probably be able to write a book about his experiences in the forest. He wished he'd brought a camera to capture the monster. Convincing people he wasn't lying would be the hard part, since the story would sound so unbelievable.

The word had been written a fair way up the tree. Todd hadn't gotten close enough to see it clearly, but he thought he would have had to stretch to touch it. He didn't know what the monster had used for paint. Todd had heard of fungus that glowed in the dark; maybe the creature had somehow distilled its essence.

He stubbed his foot on another rock, and Todd spat out a swear word. He was done. He sat, pulled off the shoe, and massaged his tender, aching feet. The socks had rolled up and put extra pressure on the blisters, and he thought one might have burst. His foot was sticky enough.

He shouldn't have run. Now, he'd lost his place to bed down for the night, not to mention his stream, which was his lifeline to the outside world. Moving any farther at night would be stupid; he would only risk getting even more lost and possibly falling down a cliff and breaking his neck.

But that didn't mean he had to spend the night on the ground...

Todd tilted his head back to look at the nearest tree. The canopy had enough gaps in it to paint the trunk with dappled moonlight. He could see a forked branch about fifteen feet off the ground. If the monster came hunting for him while he was asleep, it wouldn't find him in the tree, would it?

He could scarcely believe his own brilliance. He didn't have a hammock or any rope to tie himself down, but he could make do with his jacket, and the branches looked wide enough and sturdy enough to keep him contained.

At least then, he wouldn't have to spend the whole night with one eye open, terrified that he would hear the scraping noise or feel stabbing claws in his back.

Todd pulled his shoe back on then began climbing the tree. The bark scraped sensitive skin on his hands, but it had enough low branches and knotty whorls that he could pull himself up. He'd been rock-climbing a couple of times as a child, and his body seemed to have maintained some muscle memory. Though he had to admit he preferred the sport when there was a harness and a spotter.

He got himself onto the lowest branch then reached into a hollow to pull himself up higher. A spitting, hissing noise came from the hollow, and something prickly and sharp attacked his hand. Todd screamed as he pulled back. His balance teetered, and he threw himself at the trunk to stop the fall. Even at that low height, a drop could mean very bad news.

The small animal in the hollow gave a low, throaty growl. Todd gritted his teeth as he clung to the tree. The fright had left already-weak muscles shaky, and it took a lot of willpower to start the climb again. This time, he avoided putting his hand into the hollow, but he had no compunctions about using it as a foothold. If he accidentally squashed whatever was in there, well, tough luck.

The animal continued to hiss at him as he passed it by, but eventually, it fell silent. The final stretch of the climb had almost no holds. Todd closed his eyes and rallied his strength for the leap. He'd always believed in the concept of mind over matter. He credited it with his survival in the forest up to that point. His mind was too sharp and too determined to allow him to fail, and now he called on its strength again to get him onto the forking branch.

He leapt, scrambled, scraped one wrist raw on the bark, and ended up with his torso thrown over the branch and his legs dangling off. He sucked in two quick breaths to reoxygenate his limbs then crawled up until he was wholly on the ledge.

It wasn't as wide or as stable as he'd thought it would be. But at least he was ten feet off the ground and away from the monster's prying eyes. It would be looking for him in among the shrubs and leaf litter, not up in the boughs.

The height gave Todd a surge of adrenaline. Not even the pain in his muscles and the aches in his feet could dampen the thrill.

He shucked off his jacket and shivered. It would be a cool night, but that couldn't be helped. He needed a way to make sure he didn't fall during his sleep. He lay back on the branch, wiggled until he found the most comfortable position—which was still awkward—then tried to reach the jacket's sleeves around both his torso and the branch. He'd planned to tie the sleeves around like a makeshift rope, but it didn't reach. Not even close.

Todd swore. He'd gone to too much effort to get up there; he wasn't giving up. He pulled off his shoes and unthreaded the strings. They were still damp, but when he tied them together, they made a tiny two-foot-long rope. He knotted one end of the shoestrings around a jacket sleeve, tossed it around the tree branch until he could catch the other end, and finally completed the loop.

He tied the makeshift rope firmly but not so tightly that it would restrict his breathing or disturb his sleep. Then he rested his head back and smiled as he stared up at the sky. From his position, he could actually see a couple of stars through the gaps in the canopy. He focused on them and reminded himself that they were the same stars he would look at from home. It helped make the distance feel less extreme.

"Tomorrow," he said. Tomorrow would be the day he found his way out. By that time the next night, he would be in his own bed, with a full stomach and his TV playing in the room's corner. He closed his eyes. The branches were uncomfortable, but sleep began to fall over him as he let his limbs relax.

A familiar noise rang through the forest: claws scraping across old trunks. Todd jolted awake. The sound came from almost directly below him.

No. How did it find me?

He twisted in his perch, trying to see movement in the

shadows. The sound came from his left. Then from his right. Then he felt the tree under him shudder as the monster's claws dug into it.

"No! Go away!" Todd couldn't breathe. He swiveled, trying to see the ground. The makeshift strap pulled tight. He didn't realize he was slipping until it was too late.

Todd yelped as he rolled over the branch's edge. He felt a second of resistance as the jacket and shoelaces fought to hold him. The jacket's sleeve pulled through the lace's knot, and Todd plunged toward the forest floor ten feet below, and toward the monster's jaws.

CHAPTER 26

CHRIS TORE THROUGH THE forest, his heart thundering. "Flint!"

Screams came from the camp as Hailey joined Flint's panicked, pained cries. Chris reached for the knife strapped to his side as he broke into the clearing.

For a second, his eyes couldn't make sense of the scene. Flint had set up both tents and placed the lantern on the ground between them. Its golden glow washed over the tent's exteriors and the closest trees, creating a dome of light.

Flint and Hailey were near their tent. Flint jumped like a madman, screaming and beating at his own body. Chris moved forward, knife extended, but he couldn't see what Flint was fighting.

"Move!" Anna yelled, shoving past him. She'd torn off her jacket. When she reached Flint, she shoved his chest, hard, to move him closer to his tent. Then she balled the jacket up in one hand and began running it over his legs and arms, pressing firmly.

Red welts were appearing on Flint's neck and cheeks. He continued to slap himself, though his screams had fallen into grunts. Hailey was no longer shrieking, but she stood by the lamp, bent over and shaking as tears ran down her cheeks. Chris began moving toward Flint.

"Careful," Anna yelled. "Ant nest."

He looked down. In the lantern's glow, hundreds of fat, juicy ants teemed across the ground near the log Flint and Hailey had been sitting on. The puzzle clicked into place, and he resheathed the knife and pulled off his own jacket.

Together, he and Anna squished the ants crawling over Flint's clothes and skin. Flint stripped off his pants and shirt with pained whines. A handful of welts had grown over his torso and face, but the damage was worst on his legs. The flesh had turned into a mass of red. Chris tasted bile.

"Move away from the ants," Anna said, herding both him and Flint toward the lamp. "Hailey, did you get bitten too?"

"A bit." She wiped at her tears. "Not too bad."

Flint, dressed only in his underwear, was shaking. He kept staring down at his legs then looking away, only to look back a second later.

"This is my fault." Anna left them to rummage through her pack. "I thought I scanned the ground to make sure it was safe from hazards, but I obviously didn't do a good job. I'm so sorry, Flint."

"I can still feel them," he mumbled. "They're crawling. Crawling everywhere."

Anna returned, carrying the first aid kit, and gently pushed Flint toward one of their rolled sleeping bags. "Sit on that. I've got some painkillers here. Chris, can you get some water? And give some to Hailey too."

"Right, right." He swallowed his horror and jogged to his backpack. The water was, by far, the heaviest part of their burden. Anna had insisted on bringing masses, though, and he pulled out two bottles. He gave one to Hailey as he passed her then took the packet of painkillers from Anna, popped out two, and held them out to Flint. His friend didn't respond.

"He's in shock," Anna said. "Help him swallow them, then get one of the sleeping bags."

Chris felt awkward as he tipped Flint's head back and poured water into his mouth. Flint choked on it but swallowed the tablets.

Anna was working on Flint's legs, painting disinfectant and antihistamines over the skin. She'd purchased an expensive survival first aid kit—it had eaten nearly two hundred of Hailey's dollars—but Chris promised himself he would never complain about her cautiousness ever again. The ant bites were looking vicious enough even with treatment. Chris didn't want to think what they would look like without.

He shook out one of their sleeping bags and unzipped it all the way, so that it became a large, quilt-like blanket. Then he draped it around Flint's shoulders, trying the best he could not to rub any of the bites.

Hailey was still sniffling. She approached, sat at Flint's side, and took his hand. He tightened his fingers around hers.

"I'm okay," he mumbled.

"Yeah, you will be." Anna's face was fierce as she focused on her work. "Chris, if you're looking for something to do, how about you move Flint's tent away from the ants and put it closer to ours."

"We're…" He hesitated, glancing between them. "We're not packing up?"

"We can't, really. It's too dark to leave the forest safely tonight—and I don't think Flint could even walk the distance right now—so we'll stay here." She smiled up at the shaking, quilt-swaddled man. "Tomorrow, we'll get you back home and into the hands of a proper doctor."

"I'm okay," he repeated, and there was a little more certainty in the words.

"Sure you are, tough guy."

Chris's nausea refused to abate as he undid the tent and dragged it across the rocky ground to a new patch of earth. He was careful as he cleared the scrubby shrubs away and made sure there were no ant nests, holes, or other surprises lurking there. Only once he was certain did he start setting up the tent. It was slow, hard work with only the lamp to light the area. Anna joined him as he finished strapping it down.

"How's he doing?" Chris whispered.

Anna shrugged. "They were fire ants. Painful bite. Too many, and you can get an anaphylactic reaction, though Flint should be all right. But damn, he really didn't need this."

"No," Chris agreed.

"I feel horrible. I should have paid more attention to where we were setting up our camp. Are you all right to go home tomorrow?" She squinted up at him, trying to read his expression in the dark. "I know it's not what you wanted, but Hailey will want to go home with Flint. I'll be helping them back, and it would be a really, really bad idea for you to explore this place alone."

His heart dropped at the thought of what that meant: abandoning the search for Eileen before it had properly begun. He tried to push the selfish resentment aside. Flint deserved a better friend than he was being. "Yeah. Of course. Getting Flint back home is the priority."

"Thanks, Chris. I know what this means to you. Maybe in a week or two we can come back, if you think it would help you find closure."

It wouldn't. The only reason he was in the forest was because he was clinging to the slim, cold chance that Eileen might still be alive. Surviving for six days wasn't unheard of. Surviving for three weeks...he swallowed. If he left the following morning, he wouldn't be coming back.

They ate a cold dinner. As Flint's shock faded, he regained some of his energy. He cracked a few jokes, including "This bites," and "You're making a mountain out of an ant hill," though Chris suspected a lot of the bravado was a coping mechanism. The ant bites had to hurt. He didn't move much and stayed swaddled in the sleeping bag instead of trying to put on clothes.

They went to bed early. Chris and Anna shared a tent. The

construct was small and had no room for their supplies, but he actually didn't mind. More than anything, he didn't want to be alone. Even with company, he couldn't sleep, staring at the canvas and listening to wild animals moving around them.

Anna's phone had no reception, but its battery still had charge. She set her alarm for every hour, and when it woke her, she went to check on Flint. He must have been improving, because after the fifth hour, she didn't set another alarm.

The beeping phone didn't annoy Chris. He lay with his back to Anna and stared at the gently undulating tent wall. Sleep was elusive. Light rain began to fall around three in the morning, and the soft patter lulled him to sleep. It didn't stop his dreams from being distorted nightmares, though. His mind wouldn't be still.

He didn't want to leave the forest. Leaving the forest meant accepting Eileen was dead.

Friday, 10:10 p.m.

CARLA SAT AT THE desk in the loft. Out of all of the rooms in her house, the loft felt the most hers. To reach it, she had to take the stairs to thc sccond floor then climb a ladder into the highest room. Matt hated ladders. He had a weak ankle and refused to climb them.

Up there, in what she had dubbed her "workroom," Carla couldn't even hear him moving through the house below her. They hadn't shared a bedroom in more than a year, and sometimes, she didn't go downstairs at all. She would sleep at the desk, warm thanks to the central heating drifting through the floorboards, then go to work the next morning in a ruffled uniform. The room was her sanctuary, the only place she was safe from the world. No Matt, no Decker, no problems that didn't have any solutions. It was cozy there. Soft yellow lamps lit the peaked wood roof above, and narrow windows gave her glimpses of the trees outside.

That night, she worked through her report for the Hershberger case. They still had two officers searching the woods and a volunteer organization searching the lower river, but she suspected Decker would pull their efforts back on Sunday. That would mark a week since Eileen had vanished. They had spent a respectable amount of time to search for someone and about as much as they could justify considering their limited resources.

If she had her report ready to go on the conclusion of the search, the case could be closed and Eileen's photos and camera returned to her family by Monday. Returning Eileen's effects was a pitiful way to comfort them, but Carla hoped it would help at least a little.

She reached into the folder for her case notes, and the stack of photos fell out. She bent to pick them up. The top one showed Eileen wearing a floppy hat and beaming in front of a local attraction. She looked so bright, so vivacious. Sometimes Carla felt as though life punished its nicest specimens just out of spite.

Underneath that beaming picture were the photos taken in the dark. As Carla picked them up, she couldn't stop herself from scanning the tree trunks, scraps of ground, and leaves brought into sharp, unflattering view by the harsh flash.

She still couldn't shake how strange it was for Eileen to take twenty-three pictures after she became lost. She hadn't been trying to see her way and probably hadn't been trying to signal anyone, either. Maybe she'd become dehydrated and delusional.

Or she was trying to frighten something off.

Carla frowned, half-angry with herself for entertaining the monster theory any longer than she already had. She put the photos to one side and went back to work on the report.

Her attention span lasted all of thirty seconds. She scooped up the photos again and carried them to the scanner in the corner of her room.

She put the nighttime photos through one at a time and told the machine to import them into her computer. It took nearly half an hour to process them all at the highest quality, and Carla had become irritated with herself long before they finished.

She flopped back into her chair, fully prepared to scoff at her own paranoia, and opened up the first of the newly scanned photos. She fiddled with the settings to brighten it and increase its contrast.

The tall, dark figure popped into view. It wasn't clear—even with the contrast pumped as high as the photo could handle, it still looked like an indistinct blob—but that proved the artifact hadn't been introduced by Carla's work scanner. More likely, the camera had created it.

Carla opened up the next photo and gave it the same treatment. The shape reappeared. This time, it seemed to be slightly to the left compared to where it had been before.

It could have been a slowly swaying tree. Or the camera's flash was bouncing off a trunk and producing the phenomenon.

Another photo. The blob had disappeared in that one. Carla lightened it until the trees were blocks of solid white, but there was no sign of the shape. But when she went to the next picture, it had returned…

This time, it stood in the far right of the frame, as though it had been circling Eileen.

"Ridiculous." Carla spoke to convince herself. The face was too high to be human. It wasn't an animal. And no matter what the kids tried to say, there were no such things as monsters. At least not in Ashlough Forest.

In another photo, the shape remained at the far right, though it was half-hidden behind a trunk. Carla kept moving.

The friends had only found the phenomenon in three pictures. Those were the three where it was closest to the camera and picked up more of the flash. The friends hadn't been using image-editing software, so they hadn't been able to see its more discreet appearances.

The phenomenon wasn't in every photo, but it appeared in at least half of them. Sometimes it was in the center of the frame. Sometimes it was in the far right or the far left. Sometimes it hid behind trees, and Carla could only catch the edge of its form.

She printed out the lightened photos, numbered them as they spat out into the tray, then knelt on the loft's wooden floor. Starting with the first photo Eileen had taken, she laid them out in chronological order. They created a story, showing the phenomenon weaving between the trees and growing closer with every step.

"There's no such thing as monsters." That should have been an easy phrase to believe. But as Carla stared at the tableau of pictures arranged in front of her, she was beginning to doubt herself.

There had to be a good explanation. There had to be. She just couldn't see it.

She rose, fetched one of the bottles of wine she stashed in the room's corner, and popped its cap off. She'd taken the wine glasses downstairs that morning to wash and didn't want to leave her loft to retrieve them. She drank straight from the bottle as she returned to the photos.

Eileen hadn't been taking the photos erratically, and she hadn't been taking them because of some kind of delusion. She'd been using it to see the creature and, perhaps, to ward it off.

"What *are* you?" Carla ran her fingers through her hair. It was greasy and needed a wash. It wasn't going to get one, not that night.

The shape—the monster—was big. It was tall, too tall for a human, and with broad shoulders and a thick, rectangular body. What she could see of its face was inhuman and distorted. In some photos, she thought she could see fangs, though that might have been more imagination than fact. It didn't have a snout, but it wasn't flat like a human face, either. Where its eyes belonged were pits of black.

She choked down a laugh. Until that day, she'd happily ridiculed TV shows that promised to hunt monsters or search for ghosts. She'd always believed that if there was something supernatural in the world, humanity and its obsession with cameras would have gathered ample proof by that point. But here she was, actually considering it.

"Cool it, Carla." She took another deep, long drink of the wine then set the bottle aside. There could be another explanation—a freakishly tall basketball player with a mask and a fetish for frightening lost tourists, for example.

Somehow, that was even more implausible than a monster living on the mountain.

It could be a prank. But rigging up a monstrous-looking creature and taunting Eileen would have involved a lot of time and resources for minimal payoff. They couldn't have known Eileen would get lost in that part of the woods on that day, either. And if it had been just an innocent prank, why hadn't Eileen come out of the forest?

If the human behind the creature was a killer rather than a prankster, then why would they leave the camera? Eileen should have been easy pickings for someone with malevolent designs. She would have been tired after walking the entire day, and the photos were all taken from one place, which suggested she might have been worn down or injured. The killer would have realized she was photographing them, and destroying the camera would have been a simple, obvious precaution to avoid being caught. And that was ignoring how implausible a killer scenario was.

"Ugh." Clara took up the wine again, but this time she sipped it. She didn't want the buzz to hit too quickly or too hard. Her brain was scrambled enough already. She felt like there should be an answer within grasp, but every time she reached for it, the thought vanished like smoke.

No matter which angle she looked at it from, though, there was one awful revelation. Eileen's death most likely hadn't been an accident.

CHAPTER 28

Saturday, 9:10 a.m.

AFTER SPENDING HALF OF the night unable to fall asleep, Chris woke later than he'd meant to. The sleeping bag next to him was empty, and when he looked through the tent's open flaps, the sun already seemed to be high in the sky. Chris cursed himself as he scrambled out of his sleeping bag.

Anna had joined Flint and Hailey in their tent, and Chris tried to shake the fuzziness out of his head as he went to them. They were sitting on the beds inside and eating bowls of the camping food Anna had bought. She smiled and handed him a bowl of his own as he ducked into the tent.

"Morning. I didn't know whether to wake you or not."

"Hey," Chris said, but his attention was firmly on Flint. "How are you doing?"

"Great, bro. Feeling recharged and ready to power on today."

"That's what we're arguing about." Anna sighed, and her smile grew strained. "He doesn't want to go back to town."

Flint looked better, at least. He had his color back and had dressed that morning. He'd worn long pants that covered his legs, but the bites on his face had subsided into small red dots.

Chris stirred the rehydrated slop in his bowl. "Huh? Are you sure?"

Flint snorted like he'd been personally insulted. "Course I am, dude. We didn't come all the way out here to spend a night and go home."

Anna scowled as she swallowed a spoonful of breakfast. "For the record, I think it's blockheaded and unnecessarily risky to keep going."

Chris rubbed a hand over the back of his neck. "Don't the bites hurt?"

"We've got painkillers." Flint winked. "C'mon, don't listen to Debbie Downer. We can keep searching, at least for one more day."

"I think we should put it to a vote," Anna said, a hint of danger in her voice. "We live in a democracy, after all. I say we do the smart thing and leave now. Flint wants to stay. What about you, Chris?"

Her stare was pointed. She wanted him to join her side. Chris remembered what she'd said the previous night; Flint's loyalty meant he would walk over hot coals to make Chris happy. He should be a good friend in return and insist they take Flint to a hospital.

But if there's even a slight chance of finding Eileen alive… Chris stared at his bowl, feeling uncomfortable. "If Flint says he's okay…"

Anna glared daggers at him then turned to Hailey. "You're going to back your boyfriend, aren't you?"

"Sorry," she squeaked. "If Flint wants to go on, what's the harm? We don't have to spend the whole day if we don't want to. But we can spare at least a couple of hours, can't we? For Eileen's sake."

Anna's inhalation was audible. "Fine. I can accept when I'm outnumbered."

Flint looked as though he'd won a competition and was trying not to gloat. "You can go back if you want, Anna."

"And leave you clot heads to wander around in circles? Not a chance." She shuffled out of the tent then turned a final, blistering scowl on them. "Finish eating. We've got a lot to pack."

Flint had set up Chris's tent the night before, so Chris offered to repack them both to make up for it. Flint alternately laughed and scoffed, refusing to sit still. It was almost as though he was still trying to prove his capability, and he tore his own tent down so quickly that Chris was concerned he would break it.

Packing up took longer than unpacking had the previous night. Anna was adamant about not leaving trash behind. None of their equipment seemed to roll up quite as tightly as when they'd bought it and didn't fit into their backpacks as efficiently. Chris was already weary by the time the patch of ground they'd camped in was clear.

"All right, your call, Chris." Anna hiked her pack a little higher on her back and squinted up at the trees. "The fork in the road is up ahead. Left or straight?"

"Straight," he decided. It was the direction they had first chosen. If Eileen had been following the path without paying too much attention to it, he hoped she would have missed the left-hand turn.

The pressure that morning was palpable. The day before, there hadn't been any strict deadline. Now, he could feel Anna's tetchiness even when he wasn't looking at her. She wouldn't be completely happy until they were out of the forest, and he could only keep going for as long as Flint and Hailey wanted to continue. Flint kept a stiff smile on his face, which suggested the painkillers might not be working as well as they would have hoped.

Chris pushed them farther than they'd gone before. Once he reached the area where the path had fully vanished into the wilderness, he stopped and turned to his friends. "I want us to branch out."

"Absolutely not," Anna said. "I was very clear that we cannot split up under any circum—"

"I know that. And I'm not asking you to. I want us to fan out. We're not going to go far. We're just going to look for any sign that Eileen might have passed through. We'll never be out of hearing range of each other."

Anna looked skeptical.

"All right, how about this? Every ten seconds, yell out your name. If at any point you stop hearing another person's name, stay where you are and blow your whistle. We'll reconverge. It's going to be impossible to get lost that way, right?"

She finally relented. "Okay. But you'll probably find our tether doesn't extend far. The forest swallows noise."

"It's better than what we're doing now, weaving back and forward as a clump." He turned to Hailey and Flint. "When you walk, pay attention to the ground and the trees you pass by. Look for anything that could have come from Eileen. Hair caught in a branch, a footprint in the mud. *Anything.*"

They both nodded, though neither of them looked hopeful. Chris wondered if they could see the desperation in his face.

Anna moved to Chris's left. She shot a final tight-lipped smile back at them as she began to unspool her twine. "Be safe, everyone. Don't go anywhere that looks dangerous. And use your whistle straightaway if you get into any trouble, okay?"

"Course we will." Flint went to the far right, parallel to Anna's path. Hailey and Chris gave each other a final smile then speared off into their own trails, covering the ground between Anna and Chris.

Being in the woods alone was a very different experience from hiking with friends. Within moments, their footsteps faded into the rustle of wind moving the branches above.

Then Anna called from his left: "Anna!"

From his right, "Flint!" followed by "Hailey!"

Chris added his own name into the chorus. It felt stupid, but he understood the need for precautions—and not just to avoid becoming lost. If one of them was hurt, it was vital that they knew straightaway, not ten minutes after the fact.

As he walked, Chris kept his eyes moving across the ground and branches. He knew it was probably his desperation and his imagination pooling resources to play tricks on him, but every broken stick looked like a possible clue.

The voices to either side started becoming fainter. He raised his own volume in response. The game of Marco Polo was secondary to his urgent need to find some trace of his sister.

It took him a moment to realize Hailey's voice had dissipated from the chorus. He fell still and turned in the direction he'd last heard her. The trees completely blocked his view of any of his companions. He cupped his hands around his mouth. "Hailey?"

Seconds ticked by without an answer. Sweat began to build across his back. Maybe Anna had been right. Maybe he was being reckless by splitting them up. *Maybe—*

A whistle blared. Its shrill, angry pitch cut through the forest's stillness, and leaves dropped down around him as startled birds left their perches. The whistle faded as its owner ran out of breath, then it repeated, louder. Chris started running.

Saturday, 10:00 a.m.

IT WAS, TECHNICALLY SPEAKING, supposed to be Carla's day off. But technically speaking, she didn't care. She pulled up in the station's parking lot then jogged across the asphalt and up the stairs to the front door. Carla wasn't on duty that day, but Decker was.

Carla held her folder of the Hershberger case close to her chest. She approached the reception desk, where Rieger occupied Viv's normal seat. He barely looked at her as he tapped on his computer. "You're not on shift today."

"I know. Is Decker in his office?"

"Nah. Meeting with the mayor." Rieger's fingers never stopped moving.

Carla drummed on the folder. "For how long?"

"Left about thirty minutes ago, so I guess he'll be another half hour, hour maybe."

She really, really didn't want to have to make small talk with her co-workers on her day off. Especially not when the file in her hands felt like it was seconds away from setting her on fire. "Can you call him back? It's sort of urgent."

Rieger finally looked up from the computer. His expression told her he wasn't enthusiastic about the request. "He's in a scheduled meeting. With the mayor. Who decides our budgets. And you want me to…call him back?"

"No." She stopped herself from finishing with "Damn it."

"He'll be back when he's back." Rieger returned to his computer. "Whatever bee is in your bonnet, I'm sure it can wait."

It wasn't often that Carla was tempted to punch one of her co-workers as much as Rieger was inviting it. She squashed that impulse and stalked into the back offices. If she was going to have to wait on Decker, she might as well catch up on some of her other work and get a head start on Monday.

Lau was still at his desk in their shared office. He barely glanced at her as she entered. Carla pressed her computer's power button, left the case notes on the table, and went to make a cup of coffee while her outdated machine powered up. No one paid her any attention as she poured boiling water into the Styrofoam cup in the canteen.

It was a bizarre sensation. She felt as though she was holding on to a secret, something huge and special, not yet ready to be shared. If her co-workers knew what she believed about the Hershberger photos, they would laugh her out of the office. She wasn't exactly winning any popularity contests as it was. How much worse would it be if they thought she was crazy, as well? But no one knew about her secret, and so no one bothered her. It was both emboldening and a little frightening.

She knew what she was about to share with Decker might not be received as enthusiastically as she proposed it. Decker liked to run a tight ship. He'd spent several years in the military before becoming an officer and had developed a penchant for coloring within the lines and sticking to the rules, both real and imaginary. Asking him to look at something that might very well be a cryptid wasn't likely to go over well. She just needed to dig her heels in and not take no for an answer.

Carla meandered back to her office. Now that she had to wait, nerves were starting to build. She blew on her cup of coffee and began clicking through incomplete documents that needed work. None of them were holding her attention. She glanced back down at the Hershberger folder. Her palms were starting to itch from the tension.

"Hey, Lau?"

He turned toward her, looking equal parts startled and cautious. He was a large man with broad shoulders but a gentle face. It must have been weeks since they'd last spoken outside of scheduled meetings. "Hello?"

"I'm working on a missing person's case. Lost in the forest, presumed dead. Now someone's come to me with some crazy theory about there being a wild animal that's killing people. You haven't heard any rumors like that, have you?"

She'd phrased herself in a way that would make her sound skeptical, but Lau still frowned at her. "No."

"No...urban legends?" At his confused look, she rushed to elaborate. "Every town has some. Monsters, vampires living in the forest... I'm just trying to find the source of this particular rumor."

Lau actually chuckled. "I don't know what I did to make you think I was the epicenter of town gossip, but I promise you, I'm not. I've never spent enough time in the pubs or clubs to hear stories like that."

"Right." She should have guessed he was as much of a homebody as she was. They both liked the quiet, after all. Carla turned back to her computer, opened a document, and pretended to focus on it. Her eyes glazed over as they skimmed words, then they flicked down to the clock in the screen's lower right corner. She would give it another few minutes then risk Rieger's disdain to ask if he'd heard from Decker.

"Hey." To her surprise, Lau hadn't immediately returned to his work. He looked cautious but shuffled his chair a bit closer. "Is the case bothering you?"

She weighed her answer carefully. "A bit."

"I know how it feels. The missing hiker cases always get to me the most. Someone went out with the intention of having a nice day, only to end up feeding the bugs..." He grimaced. "I'll be glad if I never see another one."

"Oh..." Carla bit her lip. She was supposed to be the lead officer for missing persons. Was she really falling so far behind in her workload that Decker was passing some of her cases on to other officers? A sense of guilt rose in her stomach. She was letting her personal failings damage her work again.

Lau coughed, looking faintly uncomfortable. "I know we don't talk much. You shut down a bit after...well. You stopped talking, and I guess I didn't know what to say. I've never been good at helping people through grief."

She managed a chuckle. "No. I'm not, either."

"I guess I wanted to say I'm sorry. I asked Decker for a different office, but he didn't have room for me anywhere else. You must have felt isolated. And having to sit opposite me every day..."

The memory of that final night with Timothy resurfaced. She saw the man, his face twisted in an animal-like snarl as meth stole his humanity. And she saw Lau's face too. He'd been holding the man back. He'd cried out in pain as he was bitten. That was when the man broke free...

She shut the door on that part of her mind. It hurt too much. Instead, she latched onto a question that had surfaced, desperate for a distraction. "How many missing person cases have you handled?"

"More than I'd like." Lau frowned. "At least two or three in the last year. I don't know if it's a phobia or what, but I hate having to go into that forest."

Eileen Hershberger was Carla's third missing person case in the past twelve months. If Lau had handled another three, suddenly

Ashlough Forest's missing-hiker ratio was significantly above the national average.

She stood. A shot of adrenaline pulsed through her, leaving her feeling scattered. Lau stared at her, looking concerned, and she mustered a smile for his sake. "You're a good guy. I'm sorry we haven't talked more. Let's catch up sometime. Later. Right now, I've got something important to handle."

Saturday, 11:15 a.m.

CHRIS FOLLOWED THE SHARP, urgent blasts of Hailey's whistle as he ran. The pack bounced on his back, yanking his balance off center and making each step riskier than it should have been. He misjudged the terrain and slid down a hollow, hissing as dead branches scratched his arm and caught at his clothes. As soon as the slide stopped, he righted himself and kept running.

Hailey kept up the pressure on her whistle until he was right on top of her. She looked pale but was still standing, which was a good sign.

Chris staggered to a halt and held a hand out to her. "What's wrong?"

At the same moment, Flint burst out of the forest in the opposite direction. Unlike Chris, he didn't stop running until he had his arms wrapped around Hailey. He lifted her off the ground and hugged her to him. "You hurt? Hail?"

"I'm fine! Put me down." She laughed and squirmed out of his grip. "Did I frighten you? I didn't mean to. But I found something. I think it might be from Eileen."

Anna emerged from between the trees, panting and flushed. "What?"

Hailey beckoned them forward. She looked sheepish under all the attention. "Okay, I don't one hundred percent know it's her, but I don't know how else it could get here. Look."

She pointed to a blackened tree. A white shape had grown on the lowest branch, about head height. Among the greens, browns, and grays of the forest, it was hard to miss, but Chris didn't know what it actually was. The object was about as big as his hand, but flat and oddly melted…

Anna approached it then gasped and touched it. "It's paper!"

"Oh!" Chris blinked and suddenly recognized the shape. A scrap of paper had been speared onto the branch. It was malformed, though, drooping and coiling over itself. The rain must have damaged it.

"What do you think?" Anna asked Chris as he neared the white lump. "Does this look like something Eileen might have left?"

He touched the paper. It was thick, more like cardstock than printer paper. His throat ached. "Yes. It's art paper. She must have taken her art book with her. Probably to draw some of the scenery."

"And when she realized she was lost, she started putting scraps on trees to mark her progress, in case she needed to backtrack." Anna nudged the paper, and her lips tightened as she tried to repress some emotion. "We're lucky it survived this long. Six days."

"If there's one, there's got to be more." Chris stepped around the tree and scanned the environment. A flash of white caught his eye. "There!"

They formed a line as they scrambled down an incline to reach the second sheet of paper. It had been speared onto another branch twenty feet away. Chris touched the paper then immediately looked around for more. His earlier despondency had vanished in a rush of excitement. Eileen had left a trail of bread crumbs.

"Spread out," he said. "Like before. Stay within hearing distance, but yell when you find a piece of paper."

This time, they followed his instructions without question.

A minute later, Flint called, "Over here!"

He'd found a scrap of paper half-buried in the leaf litter. Chris guessed the rain must have weighted it down too much and pulled it off the branch. Ants had already started to decimate it for their own purposes, but it helped show the direction Eileen had been moving.

Again, they fanned out. Again, they found more paper. It seemed to be following the easiest passages through the trees, which made sense. Eileen had been looking for the path again. She wouldn't have wanted to waste energy so would have followed the course of least resistance.

The trail led them deeper into the forest. Chris pushed them to move faster. He was aware that their late start meant fewer hours to search, and Eileen had a not-insignificant head start. Several times, they lost the trail completely and had to spend upward of twenty minutes scouring the area in ever-widening circles until they found a new sliver of white.

Then Chris stopped dead in his tracks. Someone had sliced into a tree. The elm was huge, its trunk already cracked from age. Three deep gashes had been cut into it at a forty-five-degree angle. Sap had leaked from them like blood. He tried touching the bubbling amber. It was dry and dark; the injuries were old. He blew his whistle and waited for his friends to converge.

"Eileen couldn't have done this, could she?" He looked to Anna and Hailey for confirmation. Since Eileen had been at college, he'd seen less and less of her. But the Eileen he knew loved nature and wouldn't have willfully hurt such an old tree without a good cause.

For a second, he was afraid they would have seen a different side to Eileen, but his friends all looked as confused as he felt.

"No way," Hailey said.

Anna approached the scores and felt inside them gingerly. "What would she even have used? You'd need a machete or chainsaw to do this kind of damage. And she wouldn't have brought anything like that on a day hike."

"I know what did it." Flint's whole face quivered but not with fear. Murder flashed through his eyes. "That monster. The one from the photos. This is where it got her."

Chris turned back to the tree in a panic. He looked for signs that blood might have been spilled on the bark, but he couldn't see any discoloration. The dead leaves below the tree looked undisturbed.

"I'm not so sure." Anna continued to probe at the cuts. "These are old. The tree's already hardened its bark and healed itself. I'd guess these are—let's see…at least three or four months old."

"But it confirms a monster, doesn't it?" Hailey clung to Flint's hand.

Anna sighed. "I have no idea what to think anymore, Hail. Do you guys want to keep going?"

"Yes," Chris and Flint said as one. Hailey only hesitated a second before saying, "Okay."

Anna unlooped some of the twine and wrapped it around the tree as a marker. "Then let's move on."

To Chris, the discovery felt like being dunked in cold water. His elation had evaporated in the span of a second. He kept the pace quick, but instead of feverishly hunting for the paper like children on a scavenger hunt, they were scanning their environment for any sign of the unnatural presence that seemed to live in Ashlough Forest. Flint tore a dead branch off a tree and snapped off stray twigs to create a spear-like stick taller than he was. He held it ahead of himself while Hailey stuck close to his side. Instead of fanning out, they clumped together. It slowed their progress significantly, but Chris didn't complain. He was feeling unsafe too.

The terrain gradually became rockier and steeper, and they had to choose each step carefully. The trail of papers continued to lead them downhill. Chris pulled his phone out of his pocket to check the time. They'd been hiking for nearly four hours. Instinct pulled his eyes toward the service bars, but of course, there were none.

"Why's she still walking?" Anna asked abruptly. Her face was scrunched up in distress. For a moment, Chris didn't understand her, but then she looked up at him. "Eileen would have lost the trail at least two hours ago. At what point does she realize she's going in the wrong direction and backtrack? That's exactly why she left the papers. To find her way back."

He didn't have an answer. "Maybe she wanted to explore some more?"

"That doesn't make sense. By this point, even if she turned around and jogged in exactly the right direction, she would still miss the shuttle bus home. The sun would be getting close to setting." Anna rubbed sweaty hair off her forehead. "She must have been frightened. And I know people do irrational things when they're frightened, but Eileen had enough presence of mind to leave a guide to get back. So why isn't she using it?"

"What if the monster was already following her?" Flint had appeared on Chris's other side, and his blocky face looked even more sullen than normal. "Maybe she heard it behind her, stalking her. Not close enough to scare her into running, but enough of a presence that she really didn't want to turn around and walk toward it."

"Maybe." Anna scowled at the nearest tree. "She didn't start photographing the...the *creature* until well after dark. There wasn't even a trace of sunset in her pictures. Assuming she reached Kidney Pool at around two in the afternoon, spent half an hour there, then went down the disused path, I'm thinking it would have taken her until about five or six in the afternoon to reach this point. That's if she's walking at a steady pace, not running. If she was panicked and moving quickly, it would be even earlier. Which leaves at least another hour or two before it was dark enough for the photos."

"And that's if the photos were taken as soon as the last light faded," Chris agreed. "For all we know, they could have been taken at four in the morning."

"Exactly. So, if the creature was following her at this point, it must have been stalking her for hours before she got out the camera."

Chris tried to picture how that would feel, stumbling through the forest with tired legs and thirst starting to make its presence known, while the sun slowly set and an unyielding, unrelenting presence followed. He shivered.

"Lost," Hailey said.

Chris snapped out of his reverie. His friend had come to a complete halt. "Sorry, what?"

She pointed to a tree. A word had been painted across its bark: LOST.

CHAPTER 31

A RUSHING NOISE FILLED Carla's ears. She must have looked like a madwoman, because any time she passed someone in the hallways, they pressed against the wall and gave her the right of way. She was holding a count in her head, repeating a number over and over. "Thirty-six…thirty-six…thirty-six…"

She burst into Jenny Redcliffe's office, startling the plump woman. "Have you investigated any missing person cases in the Ashlough Forest?" Carla barked.

Redcliffe gaped at her. Carla could only imagine how she looked: pale skin, hair in disarray from where she'd knocked it out of its ponytail, and her eyes bulging. She had no time for pleasantries, though. "Well?"

"Uh, yes. Of course I have."

"How many in the last five years?"

Redcliffe scowled at her. "I transferred in three years ago."

"How many?"

"I don't know. Maybe four?"

The chant in Carla's ears changed. "Forty…forty…forty…" She swore under her breath and stalked out of the office. Belatedly, she remembered she was trying not to antagonize any more of her co-workers. She yelled over her shoulder, "Thank you!"

Redcliff's voice floated down the hallway. "You're…welcome?"

The Ashlough Forest situation was worse than Carla could have imagined. Until that day, she'd assumed she was the only person handling missing person cases. That wasn't true. The workload had been spread across most of the staff in the office. She'd spoken to everyone on shift that day—about half of the total force—and the estimated number of disappearances was up to forty.

Forty lost souls in five years, at the minimum. That was beyond state park averages. It was beyond acceptable numbers. Without exaggerating, it was turning into a small-scale disaster.

No one in the station talked to each other like they should. In a healthier environment, they might have chatted about cases they were dealing with and asked for advice. But in Helmer Police Station, they were all so absorbed in their own work and so resentful of their job and fellow officers that they'd shut down anything more than basic communication.

Carla had to take her portion of the blame for that, she knew. She hadn't invited friendly banter. Or banter of any kind. Hell, until that morning, she hadn't even known her desk mate still harbored three-year-old guilt over Timothy's death. She'd been too brittle, too quick to snap, too irritated by small talk. People had been frightened to approach her, and worst of all, she'd considered that a good thing.

If she'd been less of a disaster, maybe she would have heard about some of the other cases and put the pieces together years before. She could have prevented the deaths.

She swerved around the hallway's corner and slammed a fist onto the reception desk. Rieger glowered at her. "Back again?"

"Is Decker—"

"No, Decker *still* isn't in, and asking me for the third time in an hour isn't going to change that."

She snorted and turned away. Her midyear resolution to be kinder to her co-workers didn't apply to Rieger. He was too much of a tool to waste time on.

Carla climbed the stairs to the second floor, where the station's archives were kept. The station rightfully didn't like throwing out evidence, no matter how old, and its hundred-year history meant there was plenty to hoard. The archives took up four of the upper-floor rooms, stacked on shelves, on tables, and on the floor. Organization was in the pits. If an officer wanted to pull up an old file, they generally had to hope they remembered where they'd stored it.

She used her key to unlock the first room's door and stepped inside. Dust coated every surface and tickled her nose. Even though the room was supposed to contain files from the past twenty years, it was so cluttered and chaotic that it was hard to know where to start. It was a disgrace. If the public knew what their archives looked like, Carla doubted the station would ever be respected again.

They needed digital archiving desperately. There had been several attempts to bring in a database, but those had all petered out fairly quickly. Most officers simply let files build up on their desk until they were inconvenient then carried them upstairs and shoved them in any nook that was free. It was easy. Databases meant more work, more forms, more red tape, and more wasted time.

Any larger station would have died under that kind of system. But Helmer's crimes were almost unanimously of the petty variety. Repeat offenders were usually easy to recognize by sight. The larger, more significant investigations were easy to find: they had their own cardboard boxes with labels scribbled on the sides. But most cases were so minor that they never made it out of the off-yellow folders that took up ninety percent of the space. The Hershberger case currently lived in a folder. Soon, it would have its own box.

Carla flexed her neck and started work. She pulled out stacks of the folders, flipped through them to read the labels on the front, then put them aside if they were irrelevant. She felt a small thrill when she found the first missing-person folder. She peeked inside. It had been filled out by Gould, the man who normally sat beside her and was currently sick. Sure enough, the hiker, a man in his late fifties, had vanished in Ashlough Forest. The theory was that he'd suffered a heart attack. The search for his body was called off after a week. By that point, animals, birds, and insects would have eradicated most of him.

She put the folder aside and kept searching. Dust got everywhere, in her hair, in the folds of her uniform, and in her throat. She couldn't stop sneezing and wished she'd thought to bring some tissues.

It didn't take too long to find another missing-person file. Then another. The stack at Carla's side began to grow. Each file made her heart feel heavier.

She still didn't know what to think was responsible. Chris Hershberger had said it was a monster. She didn't believe there was any unnatural creature living in Ashlough Forest, but if she took that possibility off the table, it left her with a lot of question marks. What was responsible? An animal or a human? If it was human, then who...and why? Could it be some kind of deranged hermit living in the forest, or someone from town who hiked into the woods? How would someone from town know when a hiker entered the forest? How come no one had realized what was happening until now? And if the killer was human, what was that thing in the photos?

Carla sneezed again, gritted her teeth, and dragged out another stack of folders.

CHAPTER 32

Saturday, 3:00 p.m.

"LOST." CHRIS FROWNED AS he read the word. It had been painted high up the tree's bark, within reach but above his head. The gray-green letters had been applied in broad, messy strokes, across an ancient tree's cracked bark.

"Is this from Eileen?" Flint fidgeted with his makeshift spear. He looked confused and unnerved.

Chris rubbed his hands over his aching neck muscles. "I… have no idea. I don't see why she would have written this. I mean, maybe she's trying to draw the attention of anyone searching for her, but why just write 'lost' and not include any instructions for where to look? At the very least, you'd think she would add an arrow so we know which direction to go."

"For that matter, what did she paint it with?" Anna asked.

"She brought an art book, so I can believe she'd have paints, but this much? You'd almost need a bucketful, but Eileen would have wanted to pack light for a hike. You know, watercolors and the like."

"You're right." Chris stretched onto his toes to get a closer look at the substance. It was thick and flaked off the bark in some places. He rubbed a finger over it, but it was long dry. "When I saw her before she left for the hike, she was super into pencil drawings. I assumed that would be what she was bringing."

"And this is closer to fence paint than art paint," Anna said. "So, my feeling is that it was left by someone else. Another person who was lost?"

"The monster?" Flint suggested.

Chris shook his head. "Would a monster know how to write? And even if it did, would it *want* to? What would it achieve?"

"We don't know that, man," Flint said. "I've seen some freaky crap in movies. There was this one where a bog monster drew pictures on his victims' windows before it killed them. It wasn't, like, smart enough to enjoy their fear or anything. It just *did* it. Sometimes you have to accept that, every now and then, things happen for no reason."

"Eh..." Anna pulled a face, but she apparently decided that was one battle not worth the energy to fight. "Regardless, we know for a fact that the paper comes from Eileen. It's too fresh and too Eileen-specific to be a coincidence. We should keep following that."

Chris nodded to the right, where their next bread crumb lurked, suspended on a branch. The scraps were becoming smaller and spaced farther apart, which made Chris nervous. Eileen's art book would have a limited number of pages, and he didn't like to think about what had happened when she'd run out.

They pressed on. The trail began to weave in unusual ways, taking sudden turns to the left or the right, and seemed less inclined to follow the path of least resistance. In some cases, they had to actually climb down steep, rocky slopes to reach the next scrap. It meant more lost time as they had to fan out and search a wider arc. Chris was starting to think that maybe Flint was onto something. The trail almost had the feeling of evasion, as though Eileen had been trying to shake something that was following her.

Finally, the bread crumbs seemed to vanish. They found one last scrap of paper, this time stuffed into a crack in the tree's bark as though stabbing it onto a branch would be too much work. There was no other paper in view, so they fanned out to search for it. Forty minutes later, they reconverged.

"I can't find anything," Flint said. He looked worn down, and Chris remembered he was fighting through the pain of ant bites as well as carrying thirty kilos on his back.

"Either we're missing it," Anna said, "or it's not there to find."

"Search again." Chris tried to smile to encourage them. "I'm sure there's something we missed."

Anna said, "Chris…"

He frowned at her, challenging her, and she sighed.

"I want to find what happened to Eileen, as well. But it's getting late. We need a break, we need food, and we need to start thinking about setting up camp for the night too."

Chris's backpack was an expensive brand designed to distribute the weight evenly and safely, but after wearing it for two days, his back felt like it was being crushed. His feet were developing blisters in spite of the ergonomic hiking shoes. He'd been drinking water aggressively, but he still felt dehydrated. The others had to be just as weary as he was, if not more. Even steadfast Flint looked like he was ready to put his hand up for a break.

But they felt so horribly, tantalizingly close to finding Eileen. If they set up camp then and there, they might all vote to go home the following morning. It could signal the end of the search, when he felt like they were just within reach of answers.

"A bit more?" he begged. "Ten or fifteen minutes. That's it. Then I promise we can set up camp wherever you want and sleep in as late as you want."

"All right." Anna didn't sound happy, but she hitched her backpack up. The other two followed suit and speared off in different directions. Chris chose his own path and prayed they would find either Eileen or at least a clue that could justify spending a third day in the wilderness.

The group had developed a weird dynamic, Chris realized. If he had been shown the four of them in a lineup, he would have picked Flint as the leader. But Flint was much happier being a follower. If Chris asked him to spend another week in the forest, he would do it without complaint. And Hailey followed Flint. She might not be as eager, and if Chris pushed too hard, she would probably start complaining, but her default position was to let other people make the choices. Until that week, that had been Chris's default position too. As long as the group was having fun, he followed along.

The only one of them with natural leadership skills was Anna. She wanted to be able to call the shots, and now that Chris was challenging her, she didn't like it. She kept prodding and poking, trying to get him to fall back into line. She gave orders then got upset when he didn't follow them. In the eight years they'd known each other, he'd done nothing but show her that he *would* follow orders. Not having control was as foreign to Anna as being the leader was to Chris.

But he had to fight. Knowing he was borderline abusing his friends' loyalty made him sick to his stomach, and even though Anna's disapproving glares made his skin crawl and Flint's weatherproof smile was flaking by the minute, he had to keep pushing. For Eileen.

A shrill whistle broke through Chris's thoughts. His legs were tired, but he made them run anyway. As he scrambled over fallen trees and around spiky vines, Hailey appeared beside him. They ran alongside each other until they rounded a bank of closely grown trees and nearly collided with Flint.

"I didn't know if I should call you or not," the taller man said, twirling the whistle between his fingers. "I know we mostly agreed this wasn't from Eileen, but it seemed important, anyway."

"Yeah," Chris said. He took a step back and looked up at the massive word painted across the tree. "Thanks. It is."

DEAD.

Saturday, 3:20 p.m.

CARLA HELD A STACK of nearly thirty folders. They weren't all the missing person cases, but they were all she could lift without dropping them.

She carried them reverently, despite the dust and the tiny spider that crawled out from between the paperwork. As she passed officers in the hallways, they stopped to stare at the stack of files. She hadn't told anyone what she knew yet—she needed to speak to Decker first—but they must have guessed something significant was happening.

Rieger saw her coming. Both eyebrows crawled down to rest heavily over his eyes. "No, Decker's *not* back yet."

"I'm done waiting. Call him. Tell him I have something

important I want to share, so if he's taking the afternoon off at the pub or seeing the mistress, he'd better get his ass back here."

Rieger's sigh wouldn't have been out of place in a melodrama. Carla turned on her heel and returned to the nest of offices behind the reception area. This time, though, she didn't go to her own small room. She went to Decker's.

It was pretty much a given that the senior officer would have the largest space, but the station was so cramped that it didn't make much of a difference. Decker's office was perhaps a few square feet larger than hers, but then, he had so much extra material stacked over the three desks and filing cabinets and taped to the walls that it felt claustrophobic.

The main desk was in the middle of the room, with one leather chair behind it for Decker and two plastic chairs on the other side for whatever unlucky officer was getting chewed out that day. The desk was one of the few empty flat spaces in the room, so Carla dropped her pile of folders onto it. Puffs of dust spread out from the impact. Tough luck; Decker would have to clean it up later.

She'd gone to Decker's office for two reasons. First and most obviously, it meant she couldn't miss her boss when he returned. But second, Decker held a vast array of maps pinned to his wall… including one of the Ashlough Forest.

Carla approached the map on the wall behind Decker's desk. It showed the hiking trails and the river, as well as topographic markings for elevation. It had already been pockmarked with holes and tiny text marks from previous investigations. Brightly colored pins were wedged into the corkboard beside it. Carla plucked one out then returned to the folders and opened the top one.

The missing hiker was Maybell Broome, seventy-four years old. Her family described her as an avid outdoors person and a lover of dogs. She'd been last seen by another hiker on the trail as she turned down T-7 with her border collie, Poirot.

Carla returned to the map and scanned it for T-7. It was one of the advanced trails that snaked deep into the wilderness. She stuck the pin into the point where it broke off T-5, an intermediate trail.

Next was an aspiring Instagram model, Hayden "Blaze" Wulf. Nineteen. He'd been doing a series on natural fitness and was traveling to some of the best-known forests across the world. He believed that a person's body gained muscle faster if it was trained outdoors, surrounded by nature, instead of in an artificial gym. The folder was full of selfies and posed photos he had shot in various parks, forests, and mountains. He'd posted on Instagram the morning of his disappearance that he would be traveling up T-12, one of the hardest trails in Ashlough. That was the last anyone heard of him, and the officer in charge assumed he'd gone off trail to get the perfect photo and never found his way back.

Back at the map, Carla stuck a pin into T-12. It was a neighbor to T-7.

The next folder was a newly single woman, Maureen, who was traveling the country after divorcing her husband. The investigation had gone on for several weeks as some people suspected foul play. Apparently, the split hadn't been amicable, and Maureen's ex didn't enjoy single life as much as she had. The investigation wrapped up after nearly three weeks, when the officer found a shuttle bus ticket on her credit card statement. The bus's path led to, no surprise, Ashlough Forest. By that point, it was too late to try to recover her, and no witnesses had been found. There was no comment about the path Maureen had taken, so Carla had to put her folder aside.

She worked through the stack methodically, looking for any kind of clues. Helmer had never had a serial killer, but she'd been trained on what to expect if the situation ever arose. Serial killers generally had a "type." Blond hair. College student. Looks like their mother. For most serial killers, their victims shared features, such as ethnicity, age, or appearance.

If the Ashlough Forest had a killer, and if the killer had a type, it was narrowed specifically to people who liked walking. The missing persons were from all nationalities, genders, and ages. Some were health freaks. Some were middle-aged and overweight, and a copy of *Eat Pray Love* had encouraged them to try something daring. The youngest victim was sixteen, and the oldest was seventy-nine.

Only children were excluded, and Carla thought she could guess why. Children were allowed to visit the forest, of course, but they were always accompanied by an adult. And based on the folders, only visitors who were hiking alone went missing.

That didn't mean they had to *arrive* at the trail alone. Married couple Barb and Andy Gunner had argued on the bus to

Ashlough, and after walking along T-5 for a while, the bickering resumed. They agreed to split up to save each other from a horrible day, and Barb had stormed down the offshoot, T-7. She never made it back to the parking lot.

Like with the dissatisfied housewife, Maureen, police had strong suspicions about Andy's involvement in his wife's disappearance. The only doubt came from the fact that Andy called the police shortly after nightfall. In cases of familial murder, the killer often tried to lie low and not draw attention to their partner's disappearance. Or if they were compelled to call, it would often be the following day, or several days afterward, to throw police off the scent of when and where the death occurred.

Still, the police had aggressively pursued Andy as Barb's potential killer, and the case had even gone to court. He had been acquitted on a lack of evidence. Barb was never recovered.

Carla popped a marker into T-7 for the last place Barb had been sighted. Even though less than half of the files noted which path the victim had taken, a pattern had emerged. They had all vanished on three trails: T-7, T-11, and T-12. Two were advanced, one was intermediate, and they all looped into the same part of the forest: the upper section of the map.

Carla stepped away from the wall and rested against the back of Decker's chair as she surveyed the image she'd created. She could draw a circle around an area of no more than two or three kilometers that intersected all three trails. If there was something to be found, it would be there.

"Delago."

Carla turned. She'd been so distracted that she hadn't heard Decker approach, and he stood in his office doorway, a carton of Chinese takeout in one hand and a deep scowl marring his face. "What have you done to my map?"

THE MESSY, STREAKY SCRIPT was the same style as the earlier message. However, it was no longer possible to interpret it as something innocuous. It wasn't a message or a request. It was a threat.

DEAD.

Flint slapped his makeshift spear into the closest tree, and they all flinched. "If I find the bastard, I'll—"

"Yeah." Chris put his hand on Flint's shoulder. He was grateful he had company. The messages were leaving him feeling nauseous and panicked as it was. He didn't want to imagine how he would be feeling if he were alone.

"Let's keep going a little way," Anna said. "I don't want to camp near this thing."

They put their backs to the ominous message and speared into the forest. Within two minutes, they hit a river. Chris would have thought it would be a good place to camp—they would have easy access to water, and the ground was clearer—but Anna wanted them to keep moving. She said the water was too stagnant to be safe to drink, but that the river would attract wild animals.

They argued about whether to stay on that side or try to cross over. Chris felt committed to walking in a straight line, but Anna said Eileen wouldn't have wanted to wade through the water, especially if it was close to nightfall. Instead, they chose to turn right, following the river upstream, and see if they could pick up any more clues. Anna wove her thread around a tree several times to mark the turning point. They had been walking for so long that she'd unraveled four of the spools.

The forest's atmosphere changed palpably as day began to fade. Chris could feel everything winding up. The birds chattered, enjoying their final hour of freedom before settling down, and even the trees seemed to be straining to catch the last of the dying light.

"Here," Anna called.

She'd been trailing him by a few paces, and Chris swiveled to see what she'd found. She crouched to point at something in the forest floor.

"What is it?"

"Shoe print." Very gently, she shifted leaves out of the way so that they could more easily see the mark. It had imprinted into the mud, which had dried, leaving a solid block of rectangles and zigzags from a hiking shoe's grip.

"It's got to be Eileen." Chris positioned his own foot near it. "That would be about her shoe size. And it's going in this direction."

He glanced at his friends. They all looked haggard. Dark circles lined Flint's eyes, and Hailey looked sickly with limp, frizzy hair and no makeup. But there was hope in their expressions as they watched him, expectant.

He swallowed. "Can we go on a little more?"

"It will mean setting up camp in the dark," Anna said. "But yes. I can go a little farther. But only for as long as there's enough light to see our way."

"Deal."

The footprint led away from the river at an angle. Chris got behind it, lining it up and visualizing which path a person might take through the trees, then they struck out in that direction.

His overactive mind latched on to everything he saw, no matter how insignificant. Broken branches, crushed leaves, places where the debris hadn't collected as thickly as elsewhere—he wanted to take them all as signs that Eileen had passed through. After coming so far, it would crush him to lose the trail again.

Periodically, they took out their whistles and blew them in case Eileen was close enough to hear. Five minutes on, following a funnel-like gully with sharp sides, they found another shoe print. Only part of the sole was visible, but it made Chris's heart leap. He increased their pace, pushing them harder in spite of their aching muscles. The sun was dipping. Soon, it would be too dark to see their environment clearly, even with their lamp.

"Look," Hailey said, tapping Chris's shoulder and pointing.

Above them, at the top of the slope, another tree had been marred by deep, clawlike slashes. Chris kept one eye on it as they passed it, and Flint thumped his stick on the ground threateningly. Nothing emerged.

The terrain led them slowly downhill. No matter how much Chris searched, he couldn't find any other shoe prints. That wasn't surprising, though. In most areas, dead branches and brown leaves had built up so thickly that there was no ground left to imprint on.

Anna called a halt so that she could retrieve a fresh ball of thread from Flint's backpack and tie it to the old, depleted one. Chris had to admit, at the start of the hike, he'd thought the twine was a cute gimmick to give them some peace of mind. Now, he was deeply grateful for their lifeline. He felt like an astronaut floating out in space, attached to the shuttle by a tether. They had left the proper trails thirty-six hours before, and their path had been far from straight. Even if he'd been shown a map of Ashlough Forest, he would have no idea where they were in it.

The ground flattened out again. Chris didn't like it. While they'd been following the gully, he could be fairly confident that they were tracking in Eileen's steps. The ground to either side had been too steep to climb without a lot of effort. On the flat ground, she could have gone in any direction.

"Look for more shoe prints," he said. "Fan out."

The sun was setting. Vivid red colors seeped through the canopy to distort the natural greens and browns. Before Anna broke away from him to cover her own stretch of forest floor, she gave him a pointed look. As twilight grew, visibility dimmed. It was time to set up camp.

"Just a little bit more," he muttered. "Just a little bit..."

A faint droning noise came from up ahead, like a beehive or a computer that had overheated. Chris frowned as he followed the sound. It came from behind a bank of shrubs. The droning was louder than other insects he'd encountered in the forest. Persistent. Almost furious.

Tiny black shapes swirled around the shrubs. It took him a second to recognize them. Flies. A whole swarm of them buzzed around a source of food. Something large. Something dead.

"Hey!" Chris yelled. His heart was in his throat, choking him. He felt for his whistle, but even though he'd tied it around his neck, his shaking fingers couldn't fix around it. His friends heard his call, though. They reconverged, the urgency in his voice making them jog.

He still couldn't move forward. He knew what he would find behind the shrubs. But he didn't want to see it. Because seeing it would make it real.

Anna clutched his arm. Her hands were tight enough to leave bruises. Flint came to a halt a pace behind him, with Hailey half-hidden behind his shoulder. They all looked at him. He'd become their leader. They were waiting for him to take the first steps forward.

His leg felt weak as he made it move. Then he took another step. And another. Circling the bank of shrubs, heart thundering, mind screaming, he craned his neck to see the source of the flies' feast.

"Oh," he moaned as a human head came into sight. Its skin

was pallid and graying. Flies danced across the open eyes and freely crawled through the parted lips.

Chris's world crumbled. He pressed a hand over his mouth and dropped to his knees as he stared at Todd's corpse.

CHAPTER 35

"DECKER. SIR." CARLA DIDN'T know whether to smile or yell. "It's nearly six. Where *were* you?"

"Working. Which is more than you could say, from what I see." He threw the container of Chinese takeout onto his desk and stalked around the room to loom over Carla. "What the hell is this? What gives you the right to be in my office?"

"It's important, sir. It's related to the Hershberger disappearance, but now, it's so much bigger than just Eileen."

She snatched the folder with Eileen's photos off the desk and began leafing through them. "I got a tip-off from one of Hershberger's relatives. They found some anomalies in her photos. Uh, did you get my report? Did you read the bit about finding Hershberger's camera?"

Decker's scowl grew heavier and more thunderous with every second she talked. Carla swallowed and belatedly realized the

Hershberger report hadn't made it to Decker's desk yet. It sat half-finished on her computer drive while she tried to get on top of the more urgent parts of her workload.

"Well, sir, the gist is, her camera was found washed downriver. She took photos before her death. I've got the originals here somewhere—"

"Stop babbling. You're making no sense." Decker snatched the folder out of Carla's hands and threw it across the desk. "Sit down and explain yourself without sounding like a retarded squirrel. Can you do that?"

Carla rounded the desk to take the seat opposite. She was too pumped to even mind the insult. "Yes, sir. I'll back up a bit..."

Decker looked seriously unimpressed all through the explanation of the photos. Carla tried not to be fazed. Decker wore a poker face. Some days, she thought she could tell him that his favorite grandmother had died, and he would still look bored. She laid out the series of events as cleanly as she could then showed him both the photos' originals and the enhanced, lightened scans. She laid the photocopies out on his desk—as many as would fit, at least—and pointed through them.

"This is in chronological order. You can see the shape weaving between the trees, like it's being cautious, but always growing nearer."

"I'm going to stop you there." Decker slapped his hand on the photos and pushed a clump of them back toward Carla. "If you think there's something in the forest that got Hershberger, you're barking up the wrong tree."

"But..." Carla looked from the photos to Decker, wondering if he'd somehow not seen what was clearly visible. "It's in more than half of the photos—"

"Yes. And do you know what I think it is? I think it's a stirring reinterpretation of Bigfoot. Do you remember those photos? Big, blurry, furred monster wandering across a field? Eventually revealed to be a guy in an ape costume. This is going to turn out the same, I promise. It's a prank."

"I considered that at first, sir." She shoved the photos back toward him. "But that doesn't make sense. If someone was wandering through the forest in a costume as a prank, why did they leave Hershberger there to die? Any decent human would have helped, or at the very least left a tip with our station."

Decker took a deep, heavy sigh, as though the world and its stupidities were too heavy to bear that day. "Did you consider that Hershberger and her brother might be in on the prank?"

Carla opened her mouth then closed it again. She hadn't.

"Picture this." Decker shoved the papers back in her direction for a final time. "Two kids want to be internet famous and decide to trick a police station. They go out a little way into the forest. Not even too far; just far enough that the landscape won't be recognized. One of them puts on a costume. They take a series of photos, being careful to keep the 'monster'"—he made air quotes around the word—"too far from the camera for the stitches to be visible. Then this Eileen girl holes up in her home for a few days while her family rushes to the police, crying that their daughter is lost."

"Sir..."

"Meanwhile, they plant the camera somewhere it will be found. It's brought in to you. But oh no, their carefully framed monster glamour shots haven't been noticed. They were too discreet. The investigation is about to be closed. So they send in the brother with some digitally enhanced versions to reignite the search. And poor you, you're the dunce who falls for it."

"I really—"

"Why do you think they did it?" Decker flicked grime out from under a fingernail. "Launching a prank video series? No, it was too much work for that. Maybe they're hoping for media attention. Or no, I think I've figured it out. Once the story has enough attention, Miss Hershberger will 'reemerge'"—more air quotes—"from the forest. She'll have a tale of harrowing survival against a mythical creature. Our police investigation will lend legitimacy to her claims. We found the camera with the photos, after all. Her face will be on every morning news show in the country. There will be book deals. Maybe even a movie. She'll be filling her swimming pool with cash by the end of the week." He scoffed. "Bloody social vampires."

Carla clasped her hands in her lap so Decker wouldn't see them shake. "That's believable. More believable than there being a real monster, which is the one part of the situation I wasn't able to reconcile myself to. And maybe it's even the reality. But Hershberger is only one small piece in the puzzle. Even if she is fake, the others can't be."

Decker's sour poker face finally cracked. He sat forward as curiosity lifted his eyebrows. "Others?"

Carla pointed to the map behind his desk. Three clumps of red pins stood out against the neutral greens and grays. "I have thirty so far, sir. But there are a lot more. Solo hikers who vanished on three of our trails. On their own, they are unremarkable. Tourists get lost and hurt in forests. That's just life. But together, they become a pattern. Something has been harming hikers on those paths. They've been vanishing for years, and we didn't realize."

He stared at the map, his gray eyes flicking across the image, then he turned back to Carla. "All right, you've got my attention. Talk."

CHAPTER 36

"THIS ISN'T POSSIBLE." ANNA dug her fingers into her scalp. Tears streaked down her face. "I don't…I don't understand…how…"

Chris had no answers. He knelt on the forest floor, hand pressed over his mouth to hold a scream inside. He wanted to scramble away, far enough away that he couldn't hear the flies any longer, but his legs were too weak to lift him.

Todd lay on the ground. One hand was thrown out to the side, the fingers curling up. The other rested over his chest as though he'd been clutching it before death. Frothy vomit had dried around the corner of his mouth. His eyes didn't look right. They were sagging, like deflated balloons, and flies were creeping between them and the eyelids.

Chris turned aside and threw up.

"What happened to him?" Flint looked from Chris to Anna, dumbly waiting for one of them to explain. His arm was draped around Hailey but without strength or purpose. She'd buried her face into his jacket. "How'd he get here?"

Anna turned and hurled her ball of twine at the ground. It bounced then rolled to a halt against a log. She muttered under her breath as she paced then kicked a tree. She turned back to Chris. "When was the last time you spoke to him?"

The question seemed simple, but Chris couldn't respond. The smell, thick and sour, was overpowering. Todd's skin was sagging like his eyes. For a second, Chris thought he saw a pulse leap in his friend's throat. But then he gagged and scrambled back as he realized it was some kind of insect crawling under the man's skin.

He didn't stop moving until his back hit a tree. Then he pulled his knees up and buried his face in them. The shock was coming in waves. Every time he thought he'd felt the worst of it, it returned, bigger and deeper, and threatened to drown him.

A thud made him look up. Anna had dropped her backpack. She rustled through it and surfaced with a bottle of water. She unscrewed its cap and passed it to him. "To clean your mouth out."

"Thanks," he mumbled and washed the taste of sickness off his tongue. Then he took two deep gulps of the water and leaned his head back against the bark. "I last saw Todd…when you did. When he stormed out of my house. He was angry because we weren't following his ideas. I thought it was weird that he hadn't texted me afterward, but I figured he was still angry."

"We thought he was at home, stewing." Anna wrapped her

arms around her chest. "But instead, he came out here to look for Eileen."

Hailey peeked around Flint's chest. Her cheeks were wet, but her expression held more anger than grief. "He was obsessed with her. I know you're not supposed to say bad things about dead people, but I've got to. He was a creep."

"Maybe." Anna held out a hand toward Hailey, silently asking her not to say anything she might later regret. "But the fact is, he tried to rescue Eileen, and he paid the ultimate price for it."

"I can't believe this." Chris dug his fingers through his hair. "Why didn't he tell anyone?"

It was a rhetorical question. Todd had liked being a lone wolf. He'd never fit quite right into their friend group, and that had encouraged a stubborn, independent streak that had probably led him on a solo rescue mission.

The shock was fading. Grief was coming to fill its place. Todd had never been Chris's best friend, but Todd had more good qualities than a lot of people gave him credit for. And he'd sacrificed himself to find Eileen. Whatever the motive, that deserved some gratitude.

"We must have been following his footprints." Anna dropped her head and groaned. "Maybe he even left the paper trail. For all we know, we've been on Todd's tracks this whole time, and Eileen could be at the opposite end of the forest."

Chris swore.

"What are we going to do?" Flint asked. "We're not just going to...leave him, are we?"

As one, they turned to look at the corpse. Some sort of brownish liquid seeped out from under him. The stench of early decay permeated the area. Chris tried to imagine how they could possibly carry Todd on the two-day hike back to town, and he had to bite his tongue to keep his nausea suppressed. On the other hand, Flint was right. It was beyond callous to just leave him in the middle of nowhere.

"Right now, we're going to set up camp." Anna was shaking, but purpose filled her voice. "Not here. But not too far away, either. It's already too dark to do anything productive tonight. Once we've gotten our tents built and some food in our stomachs, we're going to discuss this. Figure out what to do. What the best choice is...for us and for Todd."

She pulled the lamp out of her backpack and turned it on. The glow was surprisingly bright. The sun had mostly set without Chris even realizing it; shock had made everything seem dim and blurry.

Anna tied her twine off to mark Todd's resting place. Then they clustered together and walked into the forest. She led them on for several minutes, until the odor was no longer detectable and they couldn't hear the buzzing flies. They found a patch of ground that would hold their tents. It wasn't as large as their first camping spot, but there was no trace of ants, at least. They assembled their tents by lamplight without speaking.

Even though Todd was out of sight, Chris felt his presence, as though his friend had become a dirty secret that they'd hidden out of sight and out of mind. No one wanted to deal with him.

No one wanted to think about him. As he poured water into the packs of dried food that would be their dinner, Chris wondered if their attitudes would be different if they'd found *his* partially decayed corpse in the forest.

They would have treated him differently, he thought. They would have stopped at nothing to bring him home. Because they were loyal to him. They'd spent too many hours together to leave him behind. The thought made him feel even more awful for Todd, knowing how much the other man had wanted friends but how badly he'd struggled to make them.

Flint had propped two inflatable beds in a V-shape with the lamp between them. When they sat on the beds, it almost felt like huddling around a heatless bonfire. Only the atmosphere felt strange. Hailey sniffled every few seconds. No one smiled. They were all wrapped up in their own thoughts, none of them happy.

Chris passed out the packets of reconstituted food then took his seat between Flint and Anna. He knew what he had to do. It meant giving up on Eileen, and the thought was like a knife twisting in his stomach. But it was the only right choice. Eileen was beyond their help. "We should find a way to bring Todd home."

No one spoke, and they didn't meet his eyes. He stared at them expectantly, and Anna cleared her throat. "From the looks of it, he's already been…deceased for at least a day. We have a two-day hike back home, and that's if we're unhindered. I don't want to leave him, either, but taking him back is going to be a really, really unpleasant experience."

Flint stabbed his fork into his packet of reconstituted rice and beef. "Can't we leave the string trail, go home, and get the police to come in and get him?"

"I can almost promise he'll be gone by the time they reach him." Anna scowled as she chewed. "Wild animals won't leave him sitting there for too long. Even if his body decays, they'll drag off the bones to get to the marrow."

Hailey shuddered.

"So we've got to bring him with us," Chris said. "We can start first thing tomorrow. We'll have to stop looking for Eileen. While we were following the papers and footprints, I really hoped we might find her. But I think you're right—" His voice caught, and he swallowed to get past it. "We were following Todd's trail for miles, if not for the whole journey. As much as I want to find Eileen, we're back to looking for a needle in a haystack. But Todd is right here. We found him. We can at least bring him back and stop this whole thing from being pointless."

Anna bit her lip. "Chris…"

"I know you guys didn't like him, but he was my friend. And he doesn't deserve to be abandoned."

"I think…" She shuffled her feet, staring at their lamp. "I think maybe you're underestimating what you're offering to do. This forest has the perfect conditions for decay. He's already started rotting. The flies will have laid their eggs in him, and the maggots will start hatching soon. By this time tomorrow, he'll have started to liquefy. He'll literally be dripping as we carry him. He didn't look too bad from the top, but you'll see a different story if you try to roll him over. Ants and grubs will have eaten holes all through his back. You can't imagine what the smell will be like."

Chris swallowed thickly. His stomach flipped, but he clung to his resolve.

Anna leaned a little closer. Her voice wasn't harsh; instead, it was pitying, and that somehow made it worse. "How can you even carry a dripping, maggot-infested, seventy-kilo body? Over your shoulder? At the same time as holding on to your backpack?"

He hadn't so much as considered throwing a tantrum since he was ten, but at that moment, Chris wanted to scream and scream without stopping. Anna painted a horrible picture. But no matter how bad it got, leaving Todd was still somehow worse. The smell and the squeamishness would fade a few days after being at home. The guilt would never go away.

Flint licked his lips as he stirred his dinner. "What would you have done if we'd found Eileen?"

Anna lifted her eyebrows.

"You've had a plan for everything that's happened in this forest. I'm sure you'd have a plan for what to do if we found Eileen and she was dead. Would you have left her?"

It was a good question. Chris watched Anna closely. She swallowed and dropped her head. "No. We would have built a litter from tree branches and jackets and carried her back on that."

Flint gave Chris a firm nod. "Then that's what we'll do for Todd. You'll take one end, won't you, bro? I'll get the other."

“Thank you,” Chris whispered and clapped his friend’s shoulder.

Anna took a deep, slow breath and closed her eyes. When she opened them, she looked resolved. “That’s the plan, then. We’ll get up early tomorrow, and I’ll help you build it.”

CHAPTER 37

Saturday, 8:10 p.m.

DECKER STEEPLED HIS FINGERS as he stared across the evidence stacked on his desk. He'd lost the smug indifference that Carla had come to associate with his face. He finally looked seriously, genuinely alarmed.

"I can't see any other answer," Carla said. "There are simply too many unrelated disappearances. Something, or someone, is attacking our hikers."

She almost wanted to laugh at herself. *Our hikers.* She'd flipped from wishing Helmer's tourist population would collectively throw itself off a cliff, to feeling urgently protective of it. If a tourist was staying in her town, that meant she was responsible for them. She'd failed in her duty, but it wasn't too late to get justice.

"Yes. I agree." Decker pressed his thumbs into the inner

corners of his eyes. "Hell. I really didn't need something like this under my watch."

She waited, trying to be patient while Decker thought. It was a lot of information to absorb in one lump. It had taken Carla most of a day to reconcile herself to it.

"Who else knows about this?" Decker asked.

"No one yet, sir. I've asked other officers some questions but didn't tell them why."

"Good. Keep it that way." He ran his hand over his chin. "We'll establish a task force to investigate and resolve this. I'll head it, but I want you involved, along with two or three other officers. That's about as many people as we can have working on this without tripping each other up. Don't let the public catch wind of this until after it's resolved."

"They already know about Hershberger's disappearance, sir. There was a viral Facebook campaign—"

"That's fine. It's not a problem if they know about Hershberger. We just want to keep everything else"—he waved toward the map behind them—"under wraps."

He saw the look on Carla's face and sighed heavily. "*Think*, Delago. If word gets out, the media will beat this into a frenzy. Our station will come under fire. Why did we let this go on for so long? Why didn't we put the puzzle pieces together sooner? Are we lazy or just incompetent?"

Carla genuinely thought they were good questions, but she understood Decker's gist. "If the media is riding on our backs, it will be impossible to do our jobs properly."

"They'll hound our every step. Interview possible suspects before we get a chance to speak to them. And I wouldn't put it past those mentally incompetent reporters to go into the forest with the *intention* of finding the so-called monster."

Carla grimaced. Yes, she could see that easily. Most would probably come back out fine. But if even one became lost inside the nature reserve…

"Media attention begets public outcry. Public outcry turns into inquests. Inquests mean people lose their jobs, whether they deserve to or not. That's just how politics works. Something goes wrong, people cry for blood. So I don't want to let anyone know what's happened. Not yet."

Carla had been trying to bite her tongue, but she couldn't any longer. "The families of the people who were lost deserve to know what happened. Sir."

He scowled at the map. "Of course they do. What are you? Brain-dead? We're not going to hide this *forever*. It's not a cover-up. We just need time to arrest the bastard behind this. *Then*, and only then, do we announce what happened. It changes the narrative. Instead of being seen as the incompetent police force scrambling to find a monster who's picking off tourists, we identified and eliminated a threat before he could hurt anyone else. We become the good guys again."

Carla chewed on her lip. She knew her resistance was irritating Decker, but she couldn't help herself. "That sounds manipulative."

"That's because it is." Decker thumped a fist onto the table. "*Obviously*, it is. But manipulation doesn't have to be a bad thing.

Announcing what we know now won't bring those dead hikers back to life. All it does is frighten people and give the media ammunition to use against us."

"I agree, but—"

"More importantly, our killer is probably watching the papers." Decker squinted at the wall behind her. "Serial killers love reading about their crimes. They want to see whether they're being suspected or not. If this bastard knows we're hunting him, he's not going to stick around. And good luck identifying him and bringing him in once he's in another country."

Carla hadn't thought of that. She rubbed at the back of her neck. "Of course. He'll be easier to catch if he thinks his crimes haven't been discovered."

"Exactly. First thing tomorrow, announce that the Hershberger case has been closed. The papers have been following it since that viral social media nonsense. They'll publish its conclusion. With luck, it will make our perp complacent." Decker pointed toward the map. "You say he only targets people on those three paths. Are you sure about that?"

"Mostly sure, sir." She hopped out of her chair, moved around the desk, then waved her hand over the area she suspected the prey were being picked out of. "They all intersect this location, which I think is his…well, for lack of a better word, hunting ground."

"You have good instincts," Decker said. "Sometimes you make me think you were dropped a lot as a baby, but at least your instincts survived. Tomorrow, at the crack of dawn, we're visiting those hiking trails and blocking them off. Those three…and another two besides. The official narrative will be that there was a landslide and they're now too hazardous to use. I'll get one of our officers to hang around the site to make sure no one tries to hop the fence."

Carla breathed a sigh of relief. At least, with the paths closed, no new victims could be lured into the killer's arena.

Decker tapped his pen on the desk. "Closing five trails still leaves…what? Eight? That'll keep the tourists happy enough. Or stop them coming after us with pitchforks, at least. And with luck, the killer will think it was coincidence that his favorite trails were shut down."

"Do you think there's a risk he'll start targeting people on other trails?"

"Possibly. How frequently do the missing person cases occur?"

Carla flipped through her stack of papers. "I don't have all of them yet, but so far, the closest incidents were five weeks apart. That's excluding the missing person cases that were unrelated—just hikers getting lost for a day before being found. If I had to guess, the suspect would be taking a victim on average every eight weeks."

"Six victims a year. Which means he's cautious." Decker threw the pen down. "He must be letting hundreds of possible targets bypass him before locking in on one. These people often say killing is a compulsion, that the urge builds up and builds up until they can't stand it any longer. So, yes, it's possible he'll try to catch prey from another path. But I don't think he will. His behavior suggests a system. A habit he won't want to break, a routine he'll be nervous to alter in any way. If I had to guess, I'd say he'd wait for the so-called repairs to be completed before he starts hunting again."

"And he took Hershberger last Sunday," Carla said. "Which means he may not feel the compulsion again for another few weeks."

"*Allegedly* took Hershberger," Decker grumbled. "I still think those photos look staged."

Carla couldn't wholeheartedly agree, but she didn't argue, either. She would be nothing but grateful if she found out Eileen was safe and comfortable at home.

Decker chewed the inside of his cheek as he continued to think. "The officer we leave at the forest...I'll instruct him to pay attention to anyone who asks about the closed trails, especially if they ask when they'll be reopened. We'll get him to record a physical description and write down their car number plate. There will be a good chance that the killer will want to know the timeline for the closures."

"You're right. He'll care a lot more than regular tourists."

"Once we've blocked off the trails, and once we announce the closing of the Hershberger case to the media, we can start the real work. You and I will use the conference room as a temporary base. We'll need a few men to join us. They'll need to be clever and good at keeping secrets. Do you have anyone you want to volunteer?"

Carla thought for a moment. "Lau. He fits the bill."

"He works with you, doesn't he?"

She shrugged. "Next to me. I don't think we've had a real conversation in months."

"He's not a gossip, then. That's good enough for me." Decker scribbled a note and threw the pen aside. "I'll pick a couple others. We start work tomorrow. Consider all of your weekends and holidays cancelled until this is resolved."

She stood. Adrenaline ran through her, making her feel taller and stronger. For the first time in a long while, she had a purpose. Something worth fighting for. "I'm looking forward to it, sir."

For a moment, a smile lightened Decker's face and softened his permanent frown. "Well, look at that. We'd lost you for a few years there, but that's the overeager spitfire I remember hiring. Welcome back, Delago."

CHAPTER 38

Sunday, 7:00 a.m.

"LIKE THIS." ANNA KNELT beside their homemade stretcher, tying off the spare jackets that made up the litter. The clothes were all brightly colored. Meshed together, they looked like a playful art project.

The sides had been created from two long, straight branches they had sawed off trees. Chris had tried to pick dry branches from the forest floor, but Anna wanted them to be living. They absorbed shocks better that way, she said, and if put under too much strain would splinter instead of snap.

Hailey pushed the last air out of their inflatable beds as she helped pack up their campsite. It had been an unspoken agreement that the girls would have no part in Todd's transportation home. Flint and Chris had put up their hands to make it happen, so they alone would be responsible for the job.

Anna tied off the final jacket and tried applying pressure to it. "Okay, that should be secure. Follow the twine to get back to Todd. And…" She flushed pink. "I didn't have the strength to do this, but I'm glad you have."

"Thanks," Chris murmured. He nodded to Flint, and they picked up the litter and rested it, bundled up, on their shoulders.

The sound of Anna and Hailey dismantling their tents faded from hearing as they stepped between the trees. The rising sun lit the forest well enough, but its angle was so sharp that shadows, thick enough to look like they'd been left over from nighttime, gathered in every available gap.

Chris hadn't slept well. He'd dreamed about Eileen. He'd imagined seeing her walking toward him from between the trees. She'd looked like Todd, decaying, gray skinned, and hollow. When she'd opened her mouth, flies poured out between her teeth. He'd woken in a cold sweat. Anna, resting beside him, had been kind enough to pretend she didn't hear him crying.

He still felt the sting of guilt over giving up on her search. During the hours he'd spent lying awake, he'd looked at the situation from every possible angle. The chances of Eileen still being alive were slim. Perhaps one in a hundred. The chances of finding her were even smaller. Before, when there had been nothing to lose, they could pursue that tiny, faint hope. But he couldn't, not anymore, not while Todd needed to be returned to his family. If

Eileen was watching him from an afterlife, he hoped she would agree he'd made the right choice.

They were thirty paces from camp before the flies' hum became audible. The air was still, so it took another few steps before the smell hit them. Then the flutter of feathers made Chris's breath catch. He dropped his end of the litter and ran toward the bushes surrounding Todd.

Carrion birds had gathered over the corpse. A large one dug into Todd's neck. Two others worked on the inside of his elbow.

"Hey!" Chris yelled. He waved his arms to chase them off. They left with a whir of wings and a series of angry cries. Chris came to a halt beside Todd's head.

The smell was horrific. Inhaling it was on par with trying to breathe underwater; Chris's body revolted, making him convulse as it begged to be removed from the situation. He stayed put, though, as a mingled sense of guilt and duty fixed him to the spot.

Todd's eyes were gone. Chris tried not to look too much at the black hollows.

"Oh, man," Flint groaned as he caught up.

"The birds got to him." Chris wanted to kick something. "We shouldn't have left him out here. We should have—should have covered him, at least."

Flint had pulled his shirt over his nose. He squinted as he stopped at Chris's side. "Don't be upset. They would have found him anyway."

"His eyes..."

"I dunno if you saw, bro, but they were half-melted yesterday. And if Anna's right, plenty more of him will melt before we get home."

It wasn't the kind of pep talk Chris would have expected to cheer him up, but it didn't make him feel worse. "Okay. Let's get him packed up."

They placed the stretcher beside the body, and Chris pulled gloves out of his pocket. They were thick, designed for climbing cliffs, and he had concerns over how well the porous material would actually protect his skin.

"How do you think he died?" Flint whispered. Lingering a step behind, he still held his shirt over the lower half of his face.

"Anna thinks dehydration." Just speaking was enough to make Chris gag, but he fought through. "Maybe, when we get him back home, the coroner will have a better idea."

Todd's body had started to deform overnight. His stomach, which had been flat the day before, was swelling as gasses collected, trapped under the skin. His sunken cheeks fluttered, giving the appearance that he was trying to speak. When Chris looked into Todd's open mouth, he saw a nest of flies fighting over the exposed flesh.

He turned away and lost the fight to keep his breakfast inside. Bent over a shrub, retching and with Flint patting his back, he began to think that there was no way he could bring Todd with them. No way.

Chris straightened and looked back at the corpse. If they had swapped positions, if he had died instead of Todd, he would have wanted to be brought home, interred in a graveyard where his family could visit him, rather than his remains scattered through the forest and his bones broken down by wild animals.

He pulled on the gloves and moved toward the corpse. He wouldn't be able to go through with it if he did it slowly. The only hope was to rush, to get it over with in a second, to do it before he even knew what was happening.

Todd's body made a wet, sticky, tearing noise as Chris rolled him off the ground. Leaves and bark stuck to where fluids had leaked out of him. Strips of something that might have been his shirt or might have been his skin stayed behind. Chris retched, but there was nothing left to bring up. The smell was horrific. The visuals were worse. *Things* were dropping off Todd's back. Beetles, grubs, and squirming shapes he didn't have a name for. Flies swarmed around him as their feast was disturbed. He squeezed his eyes shut and held his breath, then Todd's body flopped onto the stretcher, face up again.

"Oh man," Flint groaned. "Oh boy. No. No."

Chris staggered back. He didn't look too closely at the wet patch that lay where Todd had once rested. Instead, he stumbled into the forest, prepared for more retching. The nausea began to fade as he put some distance between himself and the stench.

Flint joined him after a moment. They stood side by side, breathing heavily. Sweat ran down Chris's face. He still wore the gloves. Most of his contact had been on Todd's shoulder and hip, where clothes covered intact skin. There was one dark stain on the palm of the left glove, but it hadn't seeped through.

"You good, bro?" Flint asked.

Not trusting himself to reply, Chris nodded.

"I don't think Todd died by accident, you know." Flint swallowed and rested his arm against a tree. "If he was coming to look for Eileen, he would have brought water and food and equipment and stuff. But he's not wearing a backpack, and I looked all around the clearing, but there's no kind of bag or rucksack or anything."

"You think something separated him from it?" Chris rubbed the back of his hand over his nose, which was dripping.

"The monster, man. The monster separated him from it." Flint looked certain.

Chris wasn't convinced. A delirious, dehydrated person might drop his equipment to make walking easier, even if it wasn't the smartest long-term solution. Still, he couldn't discount Flint's theory.

"I'm ready if you are," he said, and Flint nodded. They returned to the stretcher. He almost didn't need to follow the red twine anymore; the smell was like a homing beacon that they couldn't turn off. "Do you want head or feet?"

"Whichever, man."

The head end was worse. Not only would it be heavier, but he would be closer to the writhing maggots. But bringing the corpse home had been his special request. He positioned himself at Todd's head. Flint took the feet. They picked up the wooden bars carefully. The branches and the jackets held Todd's weight.

Chris blinked stinging eyes and turned toward the thread. A

few minutes of walking brought them back to camp. The girls had finished packing up and stood together, wearing their packs and waiting. When they saw Chris and Flint emerging from the forest, they turned and began leading the way back along the trail left by the twine. They kept far enough ahead that they wouldn't have to see or smell Todd's body but close enough that the men wouldn't lose them. Chris and Flint put the stretcher down just long enough to don their own packs, then they picked up the corpse and stepped into the forest. Anna rewound the twine as she walked, slowly removing the last traces of their journey into Ashlough Forest. She glanced over her shoulder to make sure Flint and Chris were following, and she gave them a tight smile. "Let's go home."

CHAPTER 39

Sunday, 7:15 a.m.

CARLA STOOD JUST INSIDE the archway that marked the beginning of the Ashlough Forest hiking trails. The rising sun hadn't quite breached the mountain above them, but it was a weekend, and the parking lot was already starting to fill. Based on her research on the Hershberger file, she knew the first shuttle bus would arrive at nine in the morning, ferrying in holidayers and explorers for a day of nature and exercise.

Any time a visitor approached the archway, she held out her hand to halt their progress and told them, in her most authoritative voice, not to venture onto any of the five closed trails. Decker had already installed a sign below the main map then disappeared into the forest to hammer more of them into the entrances of the closed trails. There hadn't been time for a professional printing job, so they had bought wooden picket signs and hand-painted the messages. Running layers of police tape across the path like a giant spiderweb added a layer of legitimacy.

People would be stupid, Carla knew. Telling them they weren't allowed to go somewhere would only make them more curious. They would want to see the fictional rockslide, want to climb around the police tape, and want to feel adventurous. All she could do was try to impress the importance of staying on the safe paths and pray they listened to her…or that the killer would be too cautious to try anything.

A van pulled up to the parking lot, gravel crunching under its tires. A woman jumped out, staring at the new sign below the map. She was middle-aged and stocky but clearly toned. She visited the forest for exercise, not for relaxation, Carla guessed.

The woman frowned as she approached the entrance to the forest, and Carla held out her hand to stop her. "Ma'am, just a caution, five of our trails have been closed due to significant hazards."

"So I saw." The woman's beady eyes scanned Carla's uniform. "But I hike T-7 every weekend. I'm sure I can get around whatever's there."

Carla barely suppressed a shudder. The woman must have hiked the trail alone dozens of times. She might never know what kind of danger she'd been walking past. "Respectfully, ma'am, I will need to ask you to use a different trail this week. For the safety of others, as well as yourself."

She'd found that line worked better than most other things

she said. People tended to follow rules more if they thought their stupidity might hurt an unrelated party.

"Fine." The woman rolled her eyes, slapped the fitness tracker on her wrist to start her time, and jogged into the forest.

Carla watched her go then released her breath, letting some of the stiffness leave her shoulders. She wasn't enjoying sentry duty that morning. The forest was at her back, and she felt as though it towered over her. She wondered how many bones might live there. She had visited the forest a few times a year since moving to Helmer, but she doubted she would be back. The deaths had tainted it. Even if she stuck to the safe paths, she wouldn't be able to escape the feeling that she was surrounded by suffering.

She wondered if other people would feel the same way. The forest was a major tourist draw. If knowledge of the deaths spread far enough—and with the sheer scope of the situation, it would be impossible for it not to—then public perception would change drastically. Instead of being known for its lush hiking trails in summer and snow-topped mountains in winter, it would become the murder forest.

People would still come, but they would be cautious. Or worse, they would be danger junkies. In the same way that Japan's infamous Suicide Forest attracted a hefty stream of death-obsessed tourists, Helmer would become a draw for gritty documentaries and serial-killer fanatics.

She didn't think she wanted to live in a town like that. Constantly being asked for more and more gruesome details about the cases. Watching the quaint gift stores start stocking

"I Visited the Death Forest and Survived" bumper stickers. Her favorite eatery had named a burger in honor of a politician who had lived there. Would they name a burger after the killer now?

Her thoughts were spiraling into a grim place, and Carla wound them back. She couldn't try to peer into the future. Instead, she needed to focus on the present and on their purpose. If they could ensure no other tourists vanished in Ashlough Forest and ensure justice was brought for those who had perished, that would have to be enough.

A police cruiser pulled up in the parking lot's far corner. Rieger stepped out, looking deeply unhappy. Carla gave him a bright smile and a wave as he slouched his way toward her.

It was selfish and petty, but she'd been secretly delighted when Decker had picked Rieger for trail-guarding duty. The officer would be miserable away from his comfy leather chair and the social media accounts he wasn't supposed to use at work.

"You know the drill, right?" Carla asked.

"It's a bloody figurehead position. How much of a drill can there be?"

Her fake smile became slightly faker. "Just keep people off the bad paths, okay? Apparently, the landslide is nasty. You don't want a fatality on your hands, do you?"

Decker had insisted on a code of silence around everyone—including other officers. Rieger wasn't on the task force, which meant he was fed the same story about the hazardous landslide as everyone else. Part of Carla thought the secrecy was a little excessive, but another part of her recognized the wisdom. It wouldn't take much for rumors to start leaking. If Rieger knew about the killer, he might tell his wife to make sure she didn't visit the forest. She would spread it to her friends to keep them safe. Those friends would spread it further...and suddenly, an avalanche of whispers would be running through the town. The papers would be at Carla's throat within a day.

Rieger took up her position at the head of the trail and sent a long-suffering stare into the sky as Carla entered the path.

Within five steps, the trees began to close in around her and block out the light. After another few steps, sounds from the parking lot began to fade.

Carla passed the turnoff for T-12. Decker had already affixed the sign in the center of the trail and slung what looked like fifty meters of police tape from the trees. Hopefully, no one would think it was strange that the police were closing hazardous paths. Normally, the council was in charge of trail maintenance, but trying to go through their channels would have taken days. Still, it didn't matter if people were confused. All that mattered was that they obeyed the damn instructions.

She found Decker at T-9, one of the dummy trails. He'd thrown his jacket over a nearby tree as he looped tape around the trunks.

"Rieger arrived," Carla said. "Twenty minutes late, but at least he's here."

"Good." Decker grunted as he broke the tape off and put the roll back into his bag. "That's the last of the blockades. We can get out of here."

He threw his jacket at Carla to carry then hefted the bag of supplies over his shoulder. She had to jog to match his pace.

"I was thinking, sir."

"Oh no." It was said with sarcasm, but a hint of a smile softened the tone. Carla thought the change of environment was improving his mood.

She shuffled the jacket over her arm. "Assuming this is really a serial killer and not some kind of wild animal…once we find our suspect, do you think there's any chance we can recover some of the bodies? I know most of them will be long gone. But if he can tell us where he buried them, we might be able to find some bones."

"He probably didn't bury anyone," Decker said. "Forest this big, away from the main trail, he'd just drag the body behind a shrub or drop it into a gully or something. It would be hidden plenty well enough. As we've found. No bodies have been discovered in the last five years, have they?"

"Only a hipbone that washed downriver. We were able to extract enough DNA to match it to a woman who'd gone missing a month before."

Decker grunted. "That's your answer, then. He didn't need to hide the bodies because no one ever found them. Souvenirs, on the other hand. We might get lucky with those."

"Like jewelry or clothes?"

"Yes. Or body parts. Fingers. Hair. Heads. Sometimes the killer likes to keep mementos from each murder. Sometimes they bury them in the backyard, but sometimes they freeze them or preserve them in alcohol. If we find anything like that, it will at least give the families something to bury."

Carla squeezed her lips together. If she'd lost someone on the trail, she wasn't sure how appreciative she would be to have the killer's trinket returned to her, no matter how well it had been preserved.

When they reached the parking lot, Rieger was no longer standing at the arch. Carla turned in a semicircle and found him sitting under one of the trees at the forest's border, arms folded and head tilted forward as he tried to nap.

"*Rieger.*" Decker's voice took on a hard, vicious edge that Carla had heard directed at her too many times.

The officer startled, his hat slipping down over his eyes, and stumbled to his feet. "Sir."

"I know it's a stretch for you to do *anything* competently," Decker snarled, "but you better figure out how to do *this*, or so help me, I'll have you shoveling snow in your underwear all winter."

Rieger righted his hat and snapped to attention. Carla hid a smile as she followed Decker back to their car.

CHAPTER 40

CHRIS'S ARMS WERE ALREADY tiring. Anna led them along the twine trail, unwrapping it from the trees as they walked at a leisurely pace. Even so, he was winded. Behind him, Flint's breathing was deep and rasping, as well.

Before, the hike had only worn out their legs. Carrying the litter with Todd's decaying body was straining Chris's arms and torso, as well.

It had taken two days to get into the forest. At their current pace, it would take at least as long to get out.

He hoped his parents weren't panicking. The last time he'd spoken to them—when he'd told them he was staying with Flint—he'd implied that he wouldn't be looking at his phone or emails. He'd made it sound like it was his way of dealing with the grief. It hadn't been a kind thing to do, but it had been necessary. They wouldn't have slept at all if they'd known where he really was.

Anna followed the thread as it led to the right, and Chris breathed a small sigh of relief as the ground flattened out into a gentle slope. The only thing worse than having to carry the body through the forest was trying to carry the body up and down sharp inclines. Todd hadn't been a large person, but he hadn't been a fairy, either.

"Bro, I'm gonna need a rest soon," Flint whispered. His breathing was gasping and labored.

Chris nodded; he didn't feel much better. "Hey, Anna, can we stop for a break?"

"Sure. Put him down there, then come and join us."

Both Chris and Flint groaned as they dropped the pallet. Chris was wary of leaving it unattended, but he knew no one would want to eat lunch with the corpse within eyesight.

Flint flexed his arms over his head, muscles bulging, and groaned. "Toughest workout I've ever had, bro."

"Hah. Me too." Chris unbuckled his backpack and turned toward where Anna was pulling bottles of water out. "Poor Todd."

"Poor, stupid Todd," Anna agreed. Her tone only held sadness. "If he'd just told someone he was coming out here..."

"Do you think he told his family?" Flint asked.

Chris shrugged. "He doesn't get on well with his father. I don't know if he would have told him what he was doing." Knowing Todd, Chris thought he'd probably kept it a secret on purpose. He would have wanted to surprise everyone when he returned.

In retrospect, Chris realized he and his friends had done almost the same thing. No one knew where they were or what they were doing. It had seemed like a safe choice at the time, but now, it left Chris feeling a little chilled.

He dropped his pack onto the ground as they reached Hailey. Anna had already started preparing packs of food. She looked unhappy about something. Chris wondered if he smelled. After being around Todd all morning, it was hard for him to tell.

"Gimme a hug, babe," Flint said, stretching his arms toward Hailey.

She shrieked and jumped out of reach. "Ew, no, no, definitely no. You've got *juice* on you."

"C'mon. Just a little hug." A wicked smile curled over his face. "Show me how much you love me."

"Nooo!"

"Guys," Anna said, a hint of warning in her voice. "Maybe don't joke about this."

Flint dropped his arms, and Hailey cleared her throat as she took a packet of food from Anna. "Sorry."

Another day, Chris thought he would be more bothered by Todd's death being turned into a joke. But he was too tired to care. As he rested his back against a tree and kicked his shoes off sore, blistered feet, he thought he would never take his bed for granted again. Or his shower, air conditioner, fridge, kettle, or any other of a hundred conveniences he'd never had to live without before.

That included his parents. It was hard to be grateful for family while living at home and enduring death by a thousand tiny irritants, but two days in the wilderness was enough to make him miss them intensely. When he got home, he would hug his mother more and make a point to laugh at even the corniest joke his father made. Because he never knew when they might be sucked away from him in an instant. Like Eileen had been.

Finding Todd felt like a poor consolation prize when he'd set out to recover his sister. But in a strange way, Todd's body gave him the finality he'd been missing. Until then, he'd pushed his friends fiercely, demanding they keep searching just a little longer, walk a little farther, because he'd always felt as though Eileen was just around the corner. Now that he'd seen death, he knew that was all that the forest held. He could stop searching.

"Chris? Something wrong?"

He blinked at Anna. She nodded toward the pack of food he held limply. He managed a tight laugh and picked up the fork. "Sorry. Distracted."

"Well, I have some not-great news." She sat on the ground with her knees pulled up under her chin and her arms wrapped around her legs. "We're low on resources. Both food and water. We'll need to find a river pretty soon to fill our bottles up. And we have enough food to last to dinner tomorrow, but that's it." Her face scrunched up with frustration. "Sorry. I really didn't expect us to spend so much time out here."

"My fault," Chris said. "I know I made you go farther than you were comfortable with."

Anna shrugged. "We all wanted to find Eileen. As long as we get water, we'll be okay. We can live without food for a couple of days, though it won't be especially pleasant. And I brought a book to identify edible plants. Hailey and I will be keeping a lookout for them while we walk back."

Chris scraped the last pasta out of his pack then balled the package up and pushed it into the bag of garbage they were collecting. As much as he hated carrying around extra weight, Anna had been insistent that they didn't damage the forest. He gave Flint a grim smile. "Well, we won't get home any faster by sitting. Ready for another workout?"

"It would sure be a little easier if my girl gave me a hug," Flint said, but Hailey only pulled a face and shuffled away from him.

The girls waited while Chris and Flint retrieved the stretcher, then they stepped back onto the path. Anna led the way, bundling up the twine, with Hailey occasionally shooting glances back at them. They had entered an area with more pine trees, and Chris tried to distract himself by examining the way the light dappled through the boughs. It made it easier to ignore the squirming maggots a foot from his hands.

"Hey," Anna called over her shoulder. "Stupid question, but do you guys remember walking through here?"

Chris tilted his head. "Huh? We must have. We're just following the string, right?"

"Yeah." She was quiet for a moment then laughed. "It's just weird. I thought we should have gone through that trench-like area by now. Remember that? But instead, we've just been walking through pine trees. It's a bit…"

Anna had stopped to unwind the thread from where it had been looped around a tree trunk. As she tugged it free, a snapping noise came from the branches above. She had just enough time to look up before a blade plunged from the sky and impaled itself into her throat.

CHAPTER 41

Sunday, 1:10 p.m.

THE TASK FORCE, CODE-NAMED Redwood, had gathered in the conference room. Folders, photos, and maps were stacked on the main table. The door was locked and had a shutter pulled over its window.

Decker and Carla had spent the morning gathering their team and debriefing them. Decker sat to Carla's right, and Lau to her left. Their party was completed by Greg Peterson, a tall, spindly man Carla didn't know very well, and Hannah Quincey, a bull of a woman who was somewhat famous for tackling and restraining three rugby players who had gotten into a drunken brawl.

Carla hoped they would be a good team. They were all taking it seriously, which was a positive start. Peterson furiously scribbled notes about the case while Quincey sifted through the files.

"There are more, correct?" she asked.

"Presumably." Carla shrugged. "You've seen the state of the archives. These are what I found in an afternoon of searching."

"Then that should be our first priority. We need to gather as much data as possible to look for trends. Does he attack his prey on one particular day of the week? One particular time?"

"I can already tell you it's no to both," Carla said. "People have vanished on every day of the week. Sometimes they started their hike in the morning. Sometimes they start in early afternoon. It's unfortunately impossible to know the exact time they're taken, since they're usually gone for hours before anyone realizes they're missing."

Decker held out a hand. "We also have to keep in mind, as we gather data, that we might have some statistical anomalies mixed in. This is a massive, wild forest. People are going to go missing in it without any foul play involved. Perhaps one or two a year, which means upward of ten percent of our data could be irrelevant."

"Still..." Quincey tapped her pen on the table. "Just knowing that they can be taken on any day gives us a clue. Our perp is either out of a job or works flexible hours."

"Good." Decker scribbled in his notepad. "We should also look for any gaps in the deaths. Anything more than three months long that could correlate with a chronic illness or incarceration."

Carla chewed her lip. "That will mean finding every disappearance. It could take weeks to work through the archives thoroughly."

"There's no way around it," Quincey said. "I'm telling you, data is going to be the king here."

The weedy man, Peterson, blinked his sunken eyes. "Is there any chance we could use a honey trap? Reopen the paths and send plainclothes officers down them a few times a day, hope the killer takes the bait?"

"Too risky," Decker said. "Not only for the officers, but for civilians too. If the paths are reopened, they'll go down them and be as good as sitting ducks."

Quincey pushed her thick-rimmed glasses farther up her nose. "Can we afford to bring in a criminal profiler?"

Decker snorted. "For this, we can afford to hire the entire Russian Ballet Troupe if it means catching our man."

"We could set up a surveillance system," Carla said. "A discreet one. Rig it up in the parking lot to record every vehicle that enters. If there's another death—and I really hope there won't be, but if there is—we can figure out exactly who was on the trail when it happened."

"Yes. I'll see about getting one set up this afternoon." Decker made another note.

Peterson cleared his throat. "Put out a call for information."

"We can't let the public—"

"Give them the wrong details."

Decker scowled at him. "What? Are you having a stroke?"

"That's what I ask my wife every November when she puts up Christmas decorations three weeks too early," Peterson muttered. "But I am mentally quite sound, thank you. What I mean is, invent a crime. Take the date of the last disappearance and say someone was attacked outside of the town border. Not in Ashlough Forest, but near it. Ask people if they saw anyone acting suspiciously on that day. Give them an email address to send us tips and follow up on any that have legs."

"That's actually a decent idea," Decker said. "We're inviting in a slew of work, but it could bring something in without alerting our killer that we're looking for him specifically."

"There's a lot to do." Quincey looked down at her own notepad. "We're going to need to prioritize the importance."

Carla nodded. "We've also got a reasonably tight window. Assuming Hershberger was the last victim, our killer could be itching for a new strike within a couple of weeks."

"And we can't afford to keep the trails closed for long," Decker added. "The mayor will be breathing down our necks if we keep his precious tourist trap shut indefinitely."

"How are we going to split the workload, then?" Quincey asked.

Decker pointed to her and to Carla. "You two will be hunting through the archives for more cases. When you find them, bring them down here for Lau to compile the data and see if he can find anything significant. I'll organize a hidden camera in the Ashlough Trails parking lot. Bloody hell, there's no electricity out there, is there? It'll have to be battery. What a pain. Well, I'll do that and find us a criminal profiler. Peterson, you create a fake crime and an email address for tips. Once you've run the details past me and gotten approval, start distributing it. Flyers, announcements in the newspaper, the normal." He snapped his pen cap back on. "Everyone happy with that?"

"Yes, sir," they chorused, except for Lau. He hadn't spoken all meeting.

Decker gave him a narrow-eyed glare. "What is it?"

Lau shot Carla a glance and folded his hands on the table ahead of himself. "Something's bothering me about this case."

"Spit it out."

"Well, there have been at minimum thirty victims across the last five years, and very likely more. That's a lot of people."

Decker released a frustrated breath and spread his hands. "Which is exactly why we're desperate to catch him before he strikes again. What part of that concept are you having trouble with?"

"What I mean, sir, is that's a lot of people for our perp to bring down without a hitch. I've done some research into serial killers in my spare time, and very often, there are survivors. People who escape. People who play dead until they're alone then crawl back to civilization. People who manage to wrestle with their attacker and get the upper hand." Lau nodded toward the stack of files. "Some of these victims are formidable. Young, fit men. A club bouncer. One is even an ex-navy officer. But not a single one of them managed to escape."

"Gun?" Peterson suggested. "It could be a ranged killing. A sniping between the trees."

Lau shook his head. "Guns aren't infallible. People have lost parts of their skulls and still managed to crawl miles to the nearest town. No matter the killing method, I just find it strange that none of them, not a single one out of thirty-plus victims, lived to talk about it."

CHAPTER 42

Sunday, 1:20 p.m.

CHRIS FELT HIMSELF SCREAM more than he heard it. He didn't realize he'd dropped the makeshift stretcher until Todd's corpse rolled across the ground near his feet. His world felt like it was fragmenting, almost as though a nightmare had managed to crawl out of his subconscious and enter reality.

The event had taken less than two seconds to play out, but to Chris, it had lasted an eternity. He saw every detail, heard every sound. Anna had unwound the thread from a pine tree. The twine had become stuck in a rivet in the bark, and as she yanked it free, he saw a flash of something gossamer-thin and nearly invisible snake away.

An instant later, the blade had plunged down from the tree above. It had a curved, serrated edge, like half of a bear trap. It had hit Anna, smacking into the space just below her jaw, in the side of her throat.

She'd staggered into the tree as the impact forced her back. Her eyes widened. Bright-red blood flowed over her hands as she reflexively grabbed the blade and pulled it out.

That had been the worst part—watching blood spurt between her fingers like liquid out of a partially blocked tap. Red specks materialized on the trees, on the ground, and on Chris as he ran toward her.

Anna toppled. Her hands were over the cut, but they weren't doing much good. He yanked his jacket off so frantically that the fabric, designed for durability, tore around the zipper.

"Hang on, hang on, hang on," he yelled as he forced Anna's hands away and pressed his jacket into the cut. Her mouth opened, but the only sound that escaped was a gurgle. Her eyes were huge, though. They were full of confusion and fear. She stared at him, unblinking, begging him for help.

"Don't move," he said as her hands scrabbled at his arm. "Keep still. Just—just hold on—we'll—I—"

His mind spun out of control as it tried to find a way to save her. Their phones didn't work. They were still two days from the parking lot. No one was looking for them. Chris had no medical training. He pushed the cloth into Anna's neck firmly, but it wasn't stopping the blood. His hands were soaked. It was starting to dribble over the forest floor…

Flint was yelling incoherently. Hailey was screaming. But unlike Flint, who had dropped to the ground, Hailey was moving.

She tore into Flint's backpack, throwing clothes and ropes aside with wild abandon as she wailed. Then she leaped toward him, the first aid kit clutched close to her chest.

"Move, move, let me try," she yelled.

He wasn't sure if he should trust her. She was cracking, half-hysterical. Tears drenched her cheeks. He couldn't believe she was sane enough to help.

She shoved him and screamed in his face. "Move!"

Chris staggered back. Hailey already had the first aid kit open. Equipment scattered over the ground as she snatched implements out. She was still hysterical; keening cries came out with every breath. But she moved with purpose.

He remembered talking with Anna two nights before. She'd laughingly told him that Hailey was smarter than she let on. He'd listened to her but hadn't believed her. He'd known Hailey for years. She was shallow. Self-absorbed. Girly and obsessed with cute things. He liked her, but their relationship had always been like he was looking out for a child.

He'd never seen her take control so aggressively.

Hailey's wails dropped into miserable sobs. Chris crawled toward her. She was pressing a sanitary cloth to the gash in Anna's neck. When she looked up at him, her expression was begging him for reassurance.

"I don't know if it's enough," she moaned. "I clamped the artery, but I don't know if it's enough."

"You..." He looked down at Anna. Her eyes were still open, but they had lost their focus. The pupils rolled up, and her mouth was slack. She'd lost her color. But her chest still rose with jerky, erratic breaths. Chris swallowed. "Can I do anything? Anything to help?"

"Um…can you get her backpack off?"

Anna's hiking pack was still strapped to her, twisting her body at an awkward angle. Chris took his knife out from his hip sheath and used it to saw through the straps. Then, with one hand supporting Anna's body while Hailey held the bandage to her neck, he eased the rucksack out from under her. Anna made a soft gasping noise as she settled on the ground, but she didn't respond in any other way. She was sheet white. The bandage was saturated, but it was no longer dripping.

"Right," Chris said as he kicked the pack out of the way. "What now?"

Hailey looked miserable. "We wait and see."

They stayed huddled around Anna. Her eyes were open, but she wasn't awake. She continued to breathe in short, labored gasps. Her color remained a sickly gray.

Flint sat a few paces away, jaw slack and arms wrapped around his knees. Every few minutes, he muttered, "What are we going to do *now*?"

It was a scary question. Until then, Chris had been the force driving them along, but Anna had been the brains directing their energy. She knew where to camp. She knew how to find food. She knew what was safe and what was stupid. Without her, Chris felt like a toddler let loose on a busy highway with no parent to guide his steps.

As he sat beside her, he stroked her forehead. He didn't know if she could feel it, but he hoped she would know that she wasn't alone.

"You knew how to clamp an artery?" he asked Hailey.

"Kinda." She wiped her hand over her nose, which was dripping mucus. "Never done it before."

"Oh..."

"But I've watched videos. To get ready."

"Ready for what?"

She glanced up so quickly that he almost missed it. "Med school next year."

That's what Anna said. I never would have guessed. But then, I never asked. "Are you sure there's nothing else we can do?"

She looked horrified by the question. She wasn't used to pressure, he realized. "I don't know. I mean...there's a needle and surgical thread in the box, and I know how to use them, but I don't know if it's safe to stitch her up. That knife thing cut through her artery. That really needs to be repaired before we pay attention to the skin. But...I can't repair the artery. You'd need actual surgeons. And..."

And surgeons were days away. Chris clenched and unclenched his hands. They'd gotten bloody when he tried to help Anna. The blood was drying, and it cracked under pressure. He wanted to scream. *It's my fault.*

He'd dragged his friends out to the forest for a cause they no longer had any hope of realizing. And in return, Anna was slowly bleeding out beside him.

His eyes shifted to one side. The metal trap lay in the roots of the pine tree. Blood glistened on its teeth. Chris approached it and found what he was looking for.

"Someone set this up as a trap." He lifted a transparent thread, like fine fishing line, which had been tied around the metal. It was meters long. Someone had set the trap on the tree, so that when the fishing line was disturbed, it would be released and drop the blade. Anna had accidentally knocked it free when she tried to unwind her own red thread.

"The monster?" Flint asked.

"*Some* kind of monster." Human or otherwise, it had put up the hazard deliberately. *Only*…he didn't know if the trap had been intended for them. The blade looked old. It was tarnished and had hints of rust around its handle. There was the possibility that the knife had been poised in the tree for weeks or months and was intended to catch animals, not humans. But the chances of them tying their own thread to the same tree by accident seemed incredibly, impossibly small.

Chris glanced around himself. He no longer felt certain that they were alone. If the monster had set the trap for them, it could be lurking in the trees, watching and waiting for them to be vulnerable. He began circling the scene, paying close attention to all of his surroundings. He was searching not just for movement between the trees, but for any more of the gossamer threads, as well.

"Bro?" Flint asked. "What's wrong?"

"I don't think it's safe to stay here." Chris rubbed his sleeve over his face to clear some of the sweat as he moved back toward Anna.

"You think it's coming back?" Flint's lips twisted into a snarl. He drew his blade, and the metal shimmered as his hand trembled. "Good. I'm looking forward to meeting it."

Chris glanced from Flint to Hailey and finally Anna. He swallowed. "I don't know if it will come back. But…there was definitely *something* here at *some* point. And I don't think it's wise to hang around for long. Hailey, do you think we can move her?"

Again, a deer-in-headlights panic flashed over her face. "Uh—uh—"

"Let me ask another way. Will waiting a few more hours improve her condition?"

Hailey shook her head. Her voice was a squeak. "No."

"Okay. Then we make a stretcher and get her out of here."

Chris used his knife to saw a fresh branch off a nearby tree. Every action was carefully premeditated. He didn't touch anything unless he was sure there was no more of the fishing line running through it, and he used a branch to essentially minesweep his path whenever he ventured away from the small clearing Anna lay in.

In a perfect world, they would have grabbed their gear and started running. But he couldn't do that. Even if he carried Anna in his arms—and he wasn't sure he had the upper-body strength for it—the movement would jostle her too much and reopen the gash on her neck. Which meant they needed a stretcher.

They already had one, but Todd was on it. Chris had spent

several futile minutes trying to figure out a way to bring both of them home, but it was impossible. He and Flint had been struggling enough with just one body; there was no way they could carry two for any distance. And Hailey wasn't strong enough to help.

No matter how he looked at it, they could only bring one of their friends. And the living had to take precedence over the dead.

He had suggested moving Todd off the first stretcher and using it to carry Anna, but Hailey had looked horrified. After a moment of thought, he had to concede. An open wound would be at risk of infection; they didn't want to make it worse by putting Anna in contact with fabric that had been soaking in rotting meat and maggots.

The branch finally broke free, and Chris glanced over his shoulder to check on Anna. Hailey sat at her side, keeping the pressure on her neck, but she still hadn't stirred. He was worried. They had stopped the bleeding, but she looked terrible. He knew she was a fighter, but he wasn't sure if she had enough fight to last for the rest of the walk home.

Chris hurried to strip the offshoots from the branch then picked up its companion and brought them back to the clearing. Flint patrolled the area. He dragged a branch over the ground behind himself, knife held at the ready, as he scanned the forest for signs of company. Chris knelt beside their backpacks and began sorting through. To keep their packing light, they hadn't brought any changes of clothes—just spare jackets in case of unseasonable cold weather. And they had already used those on Todd's litter.

Chris muttered to himself then unrolled one of the sleeping bags. He made sure it was zipped up then slit a hole in its base and ran the sticks through it. The fabric would be strong enough to hold Anna's weight…he hoped.

"Ready?" he asked Flint. They moved the sleeping bag close to Anna. He eased his hands under her back while Flint picked up her feet, and Hailey held her head as steady as she could. They moved slowly and carefully as they transferred her. Anna's eyebrows contracted as she was laid down, but she didn't make any noise.

Hailey peeled up the cloth on Anna's neck then tucked it back into place. "So far, so good."

"All right." Chris ran his hands through his hair as he tried to think. "Here's the plan. Hailey, you go first. Look out for any wires. We're not going to walk alongside the twine anymore, just in case. If that trap was intended for us—and that's not certain, but it's a risk we can't ignore—then there's the chance that more traps will be planted along the thread. We're going to be parallel to it, five or ten feet away. At least for a while. Flint and I will follow in your footsteps."

Hailey mutely nodded. They repacked the first aid kit—which was now significantly depleted—and distributed Anna's supplies between their own backpacks, discarding anything that wasn't absolutely necessary to keep their weight down. Chris spent one final moment standing over Todd, saying a silent goodbye, then he laid the stretcher on top of his friend. It wouldn't do much to protect him from the birds, but it was the best they could manage. He intended to leave the thread up so that someone could return for Todd once Anna was safe.

Then Chris and Flint gingerly picked up Anna's stretcher and followed Hailey as she stepped into the forest.

Anna was lighter than Todd had been, but it didn't make their job easier. Nothing they did could have hurt Todd, but now, every jostle and bump made Anna's body rock and threatened to reopen the cuts in her neck. They struggled to keep their movements smooth and gentle for her sake. Ten minutes into their journey, her eyelids fluttered, and she moaned. Then her awareness faded again.

Chris's panic stayed at a constant, grueling level. He couldn't shake the fear that, despite their best efforts, they were carrying what would amount to a corpse by the time they reached the trails. The guilt was like a heavy rock in the pit of his stomach. It wasn't eased by the knowledge that Anna had been a borderline unwilling participant in his hiking trip.

She had wanted to go home but refused to leave as long as her friends remained in the forest. Chris had taken advantage of Flint's desire to help and Hailey's habit of following her boyfriend's choice. He'd added his vote to theirs to keep them in the forest, and Anna had been forced into going along with them.

If he'd just listened to her and taken them home like he should have, Anna would be fine. Maybe he would be clinging on to some regret about not finding Eileen, but at least he wouldn't have to face the horror of killing his friend.

They had spent longer in the glade than Chris would have liked. Night would fall in a couple of hours. Anna had been adamant that they not keep walking after dark, but he wasn't sure he wanted to make camp and sit still for eight hours, either.

Hailey stopped walking. Fading daylight painted deep shadows in the creases around her eyes. "Chris, I have an idea. It's probably stupid, but I thought I should ask, anyway."

"Yeah?"

She swallowed. "I'm not complaining, please don't think I am, but we're kind of going really slowly. Which isn't your fault. But it's still slow."

"I know." The pace was barely more than a shuffle, but Chris couldn't see any way to improve it without hurting Anna.

"My stupid idea is that maybe I could go ahead. Leave my equipment except for a water bottle so that I'm lighter, and jog home. I'm no good at strength, but I've got lots of practice at cardio. I could probably get there in eight or ten hours if I pushed myself. Then I could bring back paramedics and stuff, and we can follow the red string to find you."

She looked so hopeful. The idea was tempting, and Chris found it hard to answer. "I think we need to stick together. Anna made a huge point of that. We can't split up. Especially if this… *thing* is looking for us. It's a good idea, but it would be too risky."

Hailey nodded, but her shoulders dropped as she turned back to the path. Chris understood. It seemed almost like madness to know they could get help to Anna in less than a day and instead stick with their tortoise-slow route.

But when he looked to his left, he saw another tree marred with the deep, vicious gashes. He would have done anything to save Anna. Except risk Hailey's life too.

CHAPTER 43

CARLA'S EYES BURNED. IT was nearly midnight, and she was still sifting through the endless stacks of folders in the archives.

Her search partner, Quincey, had left hours before. Carla was grateful. She appreciated the other woman's obsession with perfection, but after the first few repetitions of "Have you checked these? Are you sure? I'll check them again just to be safe," Carla had been ready to scream. She didn't like having her work micromanaged. And if there had been a micromanaging category in the Olympics, Quincey would have won it simply by existing.

Now that she was alone, Carla felt as though she was making real progress. Instead of just fishing at random, Carla had jumped back in time to see if she could pinpoint the beginning of the disappearances. Knowing when the killings started would narrow down the perpetrator's possible age. The older archive rooms had been arranged with less madness. There had been more than enough space back then, so folders had been stored chronologically and in an orderly fashion. She had started with files that had been created thirty years before and was moving forward from that date.

She still found missing person cases but cast a critical eye over them. They could be discounted if the person had gone missing anywhere except the forest or if the case was solved because the subject was found. What was left over was minimal. One case a year, if that, and those statistics were easily within the scope of natural accidents.

Then she reached 2004 and found four unexplainable disappearances in the one year, all occurring on T-12, one of the problem paths.

"Hah, there you are." She made a note of the date and kept digging. Sure enough, the following year had another five. The killer had been operating for slightly more than a decade. Or at least, that was how long they had been living in Helmer.

Carla checked her watch. She was the last person left in the building. Even Decker had gone home hours before. He'd given them all his personal number in case there were any urgent developments, but Carla didn't know how welcome a call in the middle of the night would be. She'd made an important discovery but not one that necessarily moved them closer to finding their suspect.

They could at least eliminate anyone under about thirty, assuming the killer hadn't started until he was in his late teens. She couldn't imagine them being any younger when they took down grown adults. Carla used her teeth to bite the cap off a highlighter and painted a bright-green stripe down the edges of the folders she'd checked then stacked them back into their places in the shelves. By the time they were done, every folder that wasn't a missing-persons file would have the stripe. It wasn't the most elegant solution, but it was the best she could do without a database.

Carla collected the nine new cases and held them close to her chest as she climbed down the stairs to the meeting room. One desk lamp remained on, spreading its soft glow across the furniture. Carla stacked her new folders in front of Lau's seat for him to sort through the following morning, wrote a note for Decker about the timeline discovery, then yawned. She was ready for sleep but not ready to go home. The twenty-minute drive was unappetizing and the home at the end of it even more so. She could sleep at the office that night. She would feel grubby without a shower, but that was far from a foreign experience. At least in this case, the lack of self-care came from excitement, not apathy.

Boxes of half-eaten pizza still sat at the end of the table, and Carla took out a slice. As she chewed her way through the solidified cheese and pepperoni, she peered at one of the open folders in Lau's work area. The case was from eight years before, which meant it was on the earlier end of the killer's run. The managing officer had written his notes longhand, and several lines had been highlighted on the last page. Carla didn't dare touch it with greasy hands, but she bent over to read the message.

Officer reported finding claw marks in trees. Theory that some large animal may be present in forest. Photographs taken for evidence. Recommend caution for future search parties.

Carla tilted her head to the side and scanned the rest of the notes. The case had been closed the following day. The victim had been missing for six days at that point, and although search parties had strayed deep into the forest, they hadn't found any hint of which direction the victim might have gone.

The comment about the claw marks hung with her. As far as Carla knew, Ashlough Forest wasn't home to anything larger than a fox or a wildcat. But the note was the first piece of police-sponsored information that might possibly correlate the Hershberger photographs.

She threw the pizza crust into the bin and cleaned her hands with napkins. Once she thought she was respectable enough not to stain the dusty pages, she flipped through the folder. Two Polaroid photos had been tucked in the back. In the first, a man stood beside a tree and rested his hand against the bark. Three lines had been scored into the trunk. Carla tilted her head. "Wild animal? Are you blind, man?"

The officer didn't look short, but the marks were level with his head. Carla had never seen a creature that could create such even, sharp scores at that height, certainly none that lived in Ashlough Forest. She couldn't believe the officer had tried to explain it away so blithely. She didn't recognize him. For all she knew, he'd been fired for incompetence.

The marks were at just the right height to come from the figure in the Hershberger photos, though.

The second picture was a close-up of the scratches. Carla had owned cats as a child. They had loved their scratching post, and when they used it, they always crouched at its base and dug their claws in vertically. And yet the scratches in the photos were diagonal.

Carla raised one arm over her head and swiped it down and across her body. That was the kind of motion that would create scratches at that scale and angle. Not a stretch and not a habit to sharpen nails. An attack.

She flipped the pictures over. Numbers were written on the back. It took Carla a moment to realize they represented latitude and longitude. She scooted into the chair at the end of the table and opened its laptop. Carla typed in the coordinates and waited for the map to resolve over Ashlough Forest. She zoomed the image out to get some perspective and grimaced.

She wasn't surprised to find the bizarre claw marks had been found in the area she'd identified as Ashlough's danger zone.

Decker was a man of science and logic. Quincey wholesale rejected anything that looked like tomfoolery. Lau's idea of a good time was solving a crossword puzzle, and Peterson looked like the only kind of creativity he relished was shuffling some numbers around on his tax return.

It was a terrible thing to realize that she was the open-minded member of the group. Carla was used to crushing dreams, not indulging in them. Still, as long as evidence pointed to some kind of unnatural presence in the forest, she was duty bound to investigate as far as she could.

She left the folder on the table for her team to examine the following morning. Most likely, they would conclude the scores were a natural deformity in the wood or something equally mundane. Then she left the conference room and navigated the station's hallways in the dark. When she reached reception, she clicked on a light and scribbled out a brief note for Viv to pick up in the morning.

I owe you lunch. Meet me at the corner café, 12:30.

Sunday, 11:40 p.m.

"CHRIS, WE NEED TO stop."

Every step was painful. His lungs were burning, and sticky phlegm was catching in his throat. But he didn't cease moving his legs. "I can keep going."

"I *can't*." Hailey sounded like she was crying. "And Flint can't. We need to find something to drink. And we need to rest."

Chris blinked through the haze that had fallen over him. It was deep night; the sunset had faded hours before. Hailey carried their electric lamp to light the way. Animals skittered out of their way as they approached, but Chris could still hear them all around, gnawing on wood and digging through leaves. He felt ready to drop.

But he'd wanted them to keep walking. Every extra step carried them closer to home. And those steps might tilt the balance for Anna. She didn't look well. She'd woken once, tried to speak, and fallen unconscious again. The gray shade hadn't left her skin. They had been trying to carry her slowly and carefully, but her neck wound had started to ooze again.

There wasn't anything they could do for her…except get her to a hospital as quickly as they could. They were just so *slow*.

The terrain was uneven and even harder to see with just the swinging lamplight. Every step had to be considered before it was taken. Chris had hoped they could push through and walk for most of the night, but he had to admit, he was at his breaking point. His legs shook. His arms shook. He shifted his grip on the stretcher's rungs every minute, but the muscles were too fatigued to take much more.

"Okay," he said. "Let's find an empty patch of ground to put her down."

They scouted out a patch of dirt circled by young spruces. Hailey kicked leaves and branches out of the way then flopped to the forest floor and unhooked her hiking pack with a groan. Flint helped lower Anna then collapsed to his side. He looked ghastly…worse than he should have, considering how much time he spent in the gym. Chris prayed it was just regular exhaustion. He didn't have the skills to deal with anything worse.

Anna stirred. One hand flopped out from under the jacket they had draped over her, and Hailey shuffled to her side.

"Hey there," she whispered. "How're you feeling, pumpkin?"

"Water," Anna rasped. "I…need…"

"Okay, I gotcha, babe." Hailey turned back to Chris, fear reflected in her sunken eyes. "You're certain you don't have any left?"

Chris dragged his pack around and unzipped it. He pulled the bottles out and shook them. They were all empty. "Sorry."

Hailey turned back to her friend with a shaky smile. "You hang on a moment, cutie. I'll get you some water, okay?"

Chris grabbed her arm as she tried to rise. "Hail..."

"None of us are going to make it far without something to drink," she hissed back. "You think we feel bad tonight? It's going to be twenty times worse tomorrow, when we try to start walking again."

He couldn't argue. His throat was parched, and his head was foggy. It felt like a bad hangover, and he knew he wouldn't feel better until he had water. "What are you thinking of doing?"

"I'm going to leave the string. I'm going to see if I can find a river."

Chris swore under his breath. "We've been walking all day without passing so much as a puddle."

"No. But we've been following the string and moving like molasses." She turned her backpack over, shook out its contents, then began stuffing the empty water bottles back in.

"Okay." Every muscle in Chris's body groaned as he stood. "I'll come with you."

She sniffed. "You can stay and rest if you want."

"Nah. We can cover twice as much ground if we both go. Flint, you stay here and keep an eye on Anna, okay?"

Flint didn't answer. Hailey shuffled to his side and rubbed his shoulder. "Babe?"

He grumbled and kicked one leg out. He was already asleep.

Chris emptied out his own backpack, refilled it with bottles, then collected two balls of thread and two whistles.

"Use the string. Make sure you don't lose your tether back to here. And whistle if you get into trouble or find water. Okay?"

"'Kay. Good luck." Giving him a tight smile, she clicked her flashlight on and stepped into the woods, a line of twine trailing behind her. The trees swallowed her and nearly eradicated her light within a dozen paces. Chris took a fortifying breath before he picked up his own light, tied off his string, then moved in the opposite direction. He cast one final glance back at their makeshift camp. Flint continued to sleep, though the muscles in his face twitched. Anna was mostly hidden by the jacket draped over her, except for one outstretched hand that looked like a ghost beckoning him. The lamp made a small circle of light but couldn't reach past the banks of trees and trailing vines.

As he stepped deeper into the trees, a sense of isolation washed around him. For the first time since leaving his home the previous Thursday, he was truly alone.

He didn't like it. The trees were too tall. When he turned his flashlight up, its light struggled through the lowest boughs but died before reaching the canopy. He hadn't minded being surrounded by the green giants before, when his friends were with him, but walking among them alone wasn't anywhere near as easy.

The only small consolation was finally being able to move quickly. Even with the tiredness and the soles of his feet burning as though they were on fire, he felt like he was soaring.

He unraveled the thread as he walked. Every ten or so paces, he looped it around a branch in the same way he'd seen Anna do it. Night animals chattered to either side. Chris didn't try to spot them with his flashlight but kept the light on the ground ahead of himself to watch for hazards.

He hopped over a rotting log and yelped as the forest floor vanished from under his feet. He scrambled, arms flailing for purchase, and dug his hands into soft ground. He was sliding, but the slope was shallow. His grasping hands found a rock, and he latched on to it, gasping and desperate to keep from dropping any farther into the abyss.

He'd dropped the flashlight. It bounced out of his reach, its beam flashing over vines, ferns, and weeds, until it finally came to a halt lodged against a rock. Chris let his mouth fall open. The light shone across water.

The liquid wasn't rushing, and it wasn't sparkling, but it was moving, which meant it wasn't just a bog. Chris let go of his perch and let himself slide down the riverbank until his boots squelched in the mud surrounding the river. He snatched up the flashlight and scanned the space. The closest part of the river was nearly stagnant, but farther out, it flowed smoothly. Chris grabbed his whistle out of his pocket and sent out four sharp, loud blasts. Then he pulled his bag off his shoulders, rolled up the cuffs of his pants, and waded into the water.

It was shockingly cold, but that just made him break out into gasping, hysterical laughter. He reached the area where the water flowed more reliably and dunked a bottle into it. He swirled it around then poured the water into his mouth. He'd never tasted anything so delicious. It washed down the frothy phlegm and filled his stomach. He emptied the bottle and submerged it for another drink.

Branches snapped behind him, and Chris lifted his head. "Hailey! I found water!"

She didn't reply. He turned the flashlight toward the trees and panned it over the bank of plants that grew at the top of the riverbank. Something moved out of sight a second before his flashlight landed on it.

Chris's enthusiasm turned chilly. He cleared his throat and called again. "Hello?"

The environment suddenly seemed thickly, oppressively quiet. Chris's own breathing echoed around himself. The water was silent, the night birds had stopped calling, and even the ever-persistent insect chatter seemed to have gone mute. The world was holding its breath.

Chris took a step toward the bank. He'd started shaking. He shouldn't have left Flint and Anna alone, especially not when they were both vulnerable. Anna had been pedantic about them staying in a tight group, and now, alone in the river with some unseen presence watching him from the trees, Chris wished he hadn't ignored her golden rule.

Leaves crunched. A branch broke as something shoved past

it. Whatever it was, it was coming toward him, and quickly. Chris squeezed the water bottle so tightly that the plastic crumpled.

A figure broke out of the trees and held up its hands to shield itself from the light. Chris lowered his arms and exhaled something between a gasp and a laugh. It was only Hailey.

"You gave me a heart attack!"

"You? What about me?" She dropped her bag and crawled to the edge of the riverbank to look down at him. "You said whistle for emergencies. I thought for sure you'd fallen and impaled yourself on a branch or something."

"Well, I did fall, but it turned out to be a lucky break." He redirected his flashlight to the stream.

"Water!" Hailey made to slide down the bank to join him, but Chris waved her back.

"No sense in us both getting wet shoes. Throw the bottles down to me. I'll fill them and lob them back at you."

"Thanks." She unzipped her bag and shook bottles out. "Give me one quickly. I'm parched."

Chris chuckled and threw his bottle up to her. But as he did, he couldn't stop his eyes from roving toward the bank of plants where he'd seen movement. He would have thought Hailey was too tired to play pranks like that.

CHAPTER 45

FLINT WOKE WITH A gasp. Something sharp pressed into his back. He reached his arm around and swatted at a dead branch that was jabbing just below his shoulder blades.

It was very quiet. His friends hadn't talked much for the last few hours of walking, and he hadn't wanted to, but at least their breathing and crunching footsteps had always been close by. Now, he felt lonely.

He sat up and blinked in the low lamplight. Anna was still there, lying on her sleeping bag. Except for the wad of bandages at her shoulder, she looked like she was just napping. Flint rubbed the back of his neck and blinked. Anna was there, but Hailey and Chris were gone. They'd left him.

No. They wouldn't do that. They're my friends...aren't they?

He swallowed and pushed up onto his knees. He'd been trying so hard. Harder than he'd ever tried before. He'd carried his fair weight, walked as far as Chris wanted him to walk. He hadn't complained when the bites on his legs rewoke and burned like fire. He hadn't caused a fuss. But maybe they'd guessed how badly he was doing. That was why they'd dropped him. They'd realized he was deadweight.

His throat burned. He tried to call out, see if maybe they were still close enough to hear him and take pity on him, but the cry sounded pathetic. He slumped back and ran his hands over his scalp, digging his fingers in until his skull ached.

He couldn't panic. They hadn't left him. They wouldn't have. Hailey loved him…or she said she loved him, at least. And Chris was his best friend. They'd been buddies since middle school.

But deep down, he knew he was being stupid. Friendships stopped being important after a few days lost in the forest. When things went bad…and they had…friendship turned into survival of the fittest. Anyone who couldn't keep walking got left behind.

They'd made a good effort. They'd tried to carry Anna for most of a day. But Chris wasn't dumb. He knew that every sick person in their party was a liability they couldn't afford. So he'd left Flint and Anna, the two weakest, to fend for themselves. The backpacks were gone. A bunch of equipment had been dumped out, probably as a final kindness, and his two friends had continued along the road alone.

It was the smart decision to make, he guessed. At least now Chris and Hailey had a good chance of escaping alive. He wished they had at least said goodbye, though. He didn't want to die alone.

Flint's throat burned worse than ever, but now his eyes stung alongside it. His fingers were shaking. Anna stirred at his side, and he patted her shoulder.

"It's okay, shh. It's okay. I won't leave you."

She didn't properly wake. Flint wrapped his arms around his chest and blinked furiously. He was thirsty. They'd been out of water for hours. His legs ached, but he thought they would carry him a little farther to find something to drink. But that would mean leaving Anna by herself. And she hadn't wanted to be alone in the forest. She'd been very, very clear about that.

Something moved between the trees ahead. Flint perked up and squinted into the shadows. The lamp's light was dimming as its batteries ran low, and the shadows were playing weird tricks on his eyes. One second, he thought he saw someone standing there. The next, the figure was gone.

"Hey!" His voice croaked. He glanced at Anna then swallowed as he picked up a branch.

Leaves crackled. There really was something out there, just beyond his range of vision, watching him. But it wasn't Chris or Hailey. They wouldn't have stayed silent if he'd called to them. Flint's heart missed a beat as he slowly rose to his aching feet. The ant bites, which had been calm, started burning again. He took a stumbling step forward.

"I know you're there, freak," he growled. If the creature heard, it wasn't frightened. He could see a block of shadow, tall and thick, standing among the trees. It looked just like a massive tombstone, except when Flint stared at it, the figure turned and began walking away.

He didn't want to follow. But he couldn't spend the night huddled next to Anna, knowing that if he fell asleep, the monster would come for them. There was no right answer.

Flint took a careful step forward. The creature continued to walk away. As it moved, it reached out an arm, and a slow scraping noise made Flint shiver.

He could see it now, but what happened when it moved beyond his line of sight? Would it circle around? Come at him from a different angle? Or just wait, biding its time? He couldn't stand it. As tired as he was, he wasn't going to be a sitting duck for it to pick off at its leisure. It was probably used to people being scared of it. Well, he wouldn't cower, and he wouldn't give it that satisfaction.

Flint charged. The creature disappeared behind a tree. It was fast. Flint hefted his branch as he reached the area he'd last seen it, but it was already gone.

"You want a fight?" he screamed. "I'll fight you! Come and get it!"

Something metallic scraped against a tree. Flint swiveled toward the sound. He caught a flash of glowing green eyes, then the monster was gone again. He leapt toward it, determined not to lose to the creature. It had taken Eileen. It had hurt Anna. It had probably killed Todd too. He would make it pay. As long as it could bleed, he could win, and he would make it regret ever laying a finger on his friends.

The monster stepped out from between two trees. It loomed over him, nearly a foot taller than he was. Its eyes flashed a sickly green. In the permeating darkness, that was all Flint could see. It was all he *needed* to see. He ran toward it, a bellow building in his chest, weapon raised to smash it across the creature's face—

His feet touched air. Flint screamed as he plunged down. The eyes disappeared from view. His branch hit something solid and was torn out of his hands. He was falling into an endless pit. There wasn't enough air left in him to scream. Then his head hit a rock, snapping it forward and sending fireworks across his vision.

Flint tumbled to a halt. He couldn't see anything except black. His limbs felt numb. He was lying on something hard and rough…tree roots, maybe. He had one thought.

The monster had lured him there. It hadn't needed to fight him, because it was smart enough to use a trap instead. And it had won.

His head dropped, and his eyes fell closed.

CHAPTER 46

CHRIS LOOKED UP, A half-filled water bottle in his hand. "Did you hear that?"

"Hear what?" Hailey, up on the riverbank, glanced behind herself.

"It sounded like someone yelling."

In the insipid light from the flashlight, Chris saw a flash of panic in her eyes. "You don't think…"

"We need to get back."

He staggered out of the water, his shoes sticking in the mud, and threw the bottle at her. She stuffed it into the backpack then reached toward him to help pull him up the incline. He scrambled onto the weedy, rocky bank then snatched up his pack. Feeling like a fool, he jogged toward the red twine. They shouldn't have left Flint and Anna alone for so long.

Chris pushed himself to jog along the path the twine made

back toward camp. Hailey's crashing footsteps echoed behind him. Moving quickly, they reached the impromptu campsite within two minutes.

The lantern still glowed, lighting Anna's sickly complexion as she drew in shallow breaths. Chris rotated on the spot, looking for Flint. The space his friend had been sleeping in was empty. "No, no, no!"

"Flint!" Hailey screamed. Her voice cracked. "Flint! Babe! Where are you?"

Chris ran his hands through his hair. Panic was starting to rise. He couldn't see any signs of a struggle, but that wasn't much of a consolation when his friend had essentially vanished into thin air. He should have told Flint where they were going before they left to look for water. He should have made sure he was awake and alert.

Hailey was shaking at his side. She clutched his forearm hard enough to bruise. "Fli-i-i-int!"

He didn't know what to do. If Flint had woken, panicked, and wandered into the forest, why wasn't he answering their calls? And if he had been taken unwillingly, would it be stupid to run into the forest after him?

Hailey's grip became even tighter. Her breathing was more labored than the run warranted. She was hyperventilating. "We have to find him…we…"

"Okay. Keep calm. I need you to focus." Chris tried to ignore the note of panic rising in his own voice. "We'll find him. We just need to…"

A noise like an animal's muffled wail came out of the forest ahead of them. Hailey stepped toward it, still keeping her painful grip on Chris's arm. "Is that him? He's in pain—someone's hurting him. Chris, do something!"

He pulled the knife out of the belt strapped to his waist. The noise repeated, sending chills running down Chris's back and limbs. He stumbled through the forest, his heart beating so fast that it felt like it was about to explode. He didn't like leaving Anna, but if the noises really were coming from Flint... "Stay close behind me. Watch my sides and back. Yell if you see anything moving."

They paced forward together. Hailey kept one hand on his shoulders to reassure him she was there. He panned his light across the tangle of plants and fluttering bugs that intersected his path, while Hailey kept her own flashlight on the area behind them. No more noises came from the forest, but Chris thought he could pinpoint the direction they'd come from. He kept creeping forward, his pulse hopping, his light jittering, his footsteps as quiet as he could make them.

Up ahead, a narrow ravine cut through the ground like a crease. No more than eight or nine feet wide, it was jagged and rocky. Chris slowed as he neared it and directed his light into the hole.

There was something lumpy and strange at the bottom of the ravine. As Chris stared at it, it moved. Flesh-colored limbs twitched in his light. Then he caught sight of Flint's electric-blue boots. He remembered how pleased Flint had been when he'd bought them, excited and eager, bantering as they paid the checkout lady. That had been just a few days before, when they'd been prepping to enter the forest.

That felt like an eternity ago. They'd lived a whole lifetime in the Ashlough Forest. All other memories were so old that they had started to feel like a dream. The boots were mud-caked and already wearing down, but Chris still recognized them. He yelled Flint's name as he dropped to his knees at the edge of the ravine.

It was about eight feet deep at that point. The cliff walls weren't perfectly vertical but still too sloped to climb easily. Flint had stopped moving.

"Get a rope." Chris grabbed Hailey's wrist. "Be careful going through the forest. Scream if anything tries to come at you. But bring a rope back as quickly as possible."

She dashed away in a flurry of snapping branches and stifled sobs. Chris tried to eyeball the best path down the ravine, then he put his flashlight between his teeth and slipped his legs over the cliff's edge. He scrambled for a purchase, then his feet found a solid rock. He let himself slide down, took a quick breath, then dropped the rest of the way.

The ground was soft where it had collected rainwater. He jogged to Flint's side and gently touched his shoulder. "Hey. Buddy? Can you hear me?"

"Euhh." Flint's eyes cracked open, and he managed a twitching smile. "You didn't leave me."

"Of course I didn't. We found water." Chris tried to keep his voice bright and happy, but he couldn't stop shaking. Blood dripped down Flint's temple. He tried to keep the light out of his friend's eyes as he carefully felt around his skull. Flint hissed.

"Sorry. Sorry. Just trying to…uh…" Chris swallowed. "Do you think you can stand?"

Flint's legs slid through the mud, but the movements had no real strength in them. Chris bit his lip as he frantically tried to think.

"Chris?" Hailey's light reappeared at the top of the ravine. "I've got all the rope we have. Is he okay?"

Chris didn't answer the question. Instead, he stood and turned the light across the environment. "We need to get him out of here and back to camp. I don't think he's able to pull himself up right now. We could walk along the ravine and see if the walls get lower farther along…"

"But it might go on for kilometers."

He looked back at Flint. The man's eyes were open, but they looked dazed and glassy. A steady, seeping panic crept over Chris. For a moment, he considered bringing Anna down into the ravine with Flint and moving the camp there. But he couldn't see any way to get her down the cliff walls without hurting her more.

They couldn't stay split up. That was an open invite for disaster. Somehow, they had to get Flint up. He motioned to Hailey. "Tie the rope onto a really sturdy tree then send the rest down here. Okay?"

Her pale face nodded then disappeared from sight. Chris nudged Flint's shoulder. "Hey, buddy. I'm going to help you stand, okay?"

"Hhh..."

Flint's head lolled as Chris helped pull him up. He stood shakily, leaning most of his weight on Chris. They staggered closer to the ravine's walls. It was only eight feet. They could make it. Somehow.

Hailey returned and threw loops of rope down to them. Chris caught it and wound the cord around Flint's chest, under his arms. He tied the loop securely then looked up at Hailey. "When I say go, pull as hard as you can."

She looked skeptical but nodded.

Chris patted Flint's back. Sticky liquid had seeped into the jacket. He tried not to let it fan the flames of panic any further. "I'm going to need you to climb, okay, buddy? Try as hard as you can, just for a few seconds, then you can rest. Okay?"

Flint's eyes had dropped closed. He groaned. Chris wasn't sure if his words had gotten through, but the longer Flint stood, the worse he looked. They had to move. "Okay, Hailey, go!"

The rope went taut. Chris knelt and wrapped his arms around Flint's legs. He lifted as hard as he could, raising the other man off the ground. His muscles screamed. His vision flashed white. One leg threatened to slip, so he dug it in even more aggressively. He was bent double but gaining inches. Rocks and bits of dirt rained over him as Flint scrabbled at the ravine's walls. Then Flint's weight suddenly felt less impossible. Chris peeked his eyes open. Flint had gotten his torso over the ravine's lip, and Hailey had dropped the rope to grab under his shoulders and haul him up.

Chris changed position, letting go of Flint's legs and putting his back under his feet. Flint's boots dug into his shoulder blades, and he pushed against the pressure until it disappeared entirely.

"He's up!" Hailey yelled. "He's safe!"

There were no words from Flint. Chris picked up his flashlight and tried to see over the ravine's lip. As far as he could tell, Flint had collapsed as soon as he'd gotten onto solid ground.

"Here." Hailey threw the rope back over the edge. Chris gripped it and called on the last of his energy reserves to scramble up the slope. As he reached the top, Hailey helped pull him up. Tears were shining on her face, but she was laughing too. "You did it. You saved him."

As Chris looked at his friend, pale and with a smear of blood painted over his forehead, he prayed that was true.

"Let's get him back to camp." He patted Flint's back. "One last push, okay? We'll get you back where it's safe and warm, then you can sleep for as long as you want."

He didn't stir.

"You can do this, babe." Hailey stroked his cheek then bent to kiss his forehead. "You've been amazing. We're really close, okay? We can get you something to drink."

Finally, Flint shifted, trying to push himself up. Chris hooked him under one arm and helped lift him, and Hailey put herself on his other side. Together, the three of them stumbled into the trees.

For a moment, Chris felt a hitch of panic. They hadn't brought any twine with them when they were searching for Flint. For the first time since leaving Kidney Pool, they didn't have the red thread to guide them home. But the camp hadn't been far away, and within moments, the lamp's glow broke through the trees.

Chris adjusted their course toward it and let out a cheer of relief as they stepped into the clearing. Anna was where he'd left her. So were their backpacks holding the precious water. He lowered Flint onto the ground beside Anna then unraveled a sleeping bag to wrap around his friend while Hailey got him a bottle of water.

Flint drank deeply then collapsed back. Hailey curled up near him and stroked his hair back from his forehead. She looked like she was trying not to cry.

"Hey, Anna?" Chris brought another bottle of water and knelt beside her. When she didn't respond, he nudged her uninjured shoulder. She moaned, and her eyes opened. "I got you some water. Here."

Pouring the liquid into her mouth was a delicate balance. Chris lifted her head a little but didn't dare raise her too high for fear of damaging her neck further. When he poured too fast, she began choking, and he wiped water off her chin with hushed apologies. It took nearly ten minutes until she had enough water, then he lowered her down and let her slip back into her fugue.

The exhilaration of getting Flint back to camp had faded into a cold pit of fear. His friend was sick. Had been sick since that morning, probably…either with an infection or something worse. The fall down the ravine had put him out of action completely.

With Hailey's help, Chris could probably carry Flint back

to town in the same way they'd coaxed him through the forest: stumbling and slow. But that would mean leaving Anna behind. And he wouldn't do that, not while she clung to life.

But even if Flint managed to walk under his own power, Hailey wouldn't be strong enough to help carry Anna's stretcher for more than ten or twenty minutes. To keep moving, they would be forced to leave at least one friend behind.

And he wasn't leaving anyone.

Which meant, for the time being, they were trapped. There was water nearby, at least. When morning came, Chris could probably read through Anna's survival book to see if there were any edible plants nearby. They might make it a couple of days… as long as nothing hostile came their way. But that was it—a couple of days before hunger and sickness wore them down. He'd started shaking and kicked off his wet boots to keep the chill from spreading.

"I'm going to do it," Hailey said.

He squinted at her through the lamplight. She'd lain down with her head close to Flint's and continued to stroke his forehead. The tips of her fingers had gathered blood from where it seeped out of his hairline.

"What do you mean?"

"What we talked about yesterday. If I run, I can get home in half a day. I can bring help back for you."

Chris felt as though his heart were being squeezed.

Hailey guessed his thoughts and gave him a small smile. "I know we're not supposed to split up. But this is the best chance we have…for Flint, for Anna, maybe even for us. If I stick to the string, help will be here in maybe a day. Do you think you can look after them for that long?"

"Running in this forest is going to be dangerous. I should go instead."

"I'll be faster. And it won't be any more dangerous than sitting here." She patted the knife strapped to her waist. "Besides, I've got a weapon. I'll be okay."

Chris nodded. He'd fought to avoid separating their party. But now, Hailey was right. Someone needed to go. Otherwise, they would all die together. "Be careful."

"I will." She kissed Flint's forehead and gave his cheek a final stroke. "If he wakes up, tell him that I love him. And…and that he means the world to me…and I'm sorry for saying his shorts looked gay the other week. They were very flattering. Tell him, okay?"

Laughing hurt. "I will."

"Be safe."

Chris watched as Hailey picked up a backpack full of water bottles, a flashlight, and a handful of extra batteries. She smiled as she stepped away. Within a minute, both the sound of her footsteps and the light from her flashlight were swallowed by the forest as she followed the thread's lifeline to home.

He sent up a silent prayer that she would make it back safely, then he pulled his knees up under his chin and prepared for a long, lonely night.

CHAPTER 47

Monday, 3:00 a.m.

HAILEY LIKED CARDIO. FLINT had always preferred weight training, but Hailey gravitated to anything that got her heart thundering and her legs moving. She flew through the forest now, leaping over logs and ducking under low branches. The thread danced in and out of the flashlight's beam.

She'd run marathons before. She knew she needed to pace herself, or she would burn out too early. But even though she'd been running for close to an hour, it was hard to slow down. Her beautiful Flint, the rock she'd thought would never crumble, lay unmoving and unspeaking in the middle of nowhere. He had a concussion at the very least and possibly a hemorrhage. If it was a hemorrhage, it needed to stop quickly…or she had to run like the wind.

A rock threatened to trip her, but she glided over it. Her mouth was dry already. She would need to stop soon for water, but she pushed it off a little longer. It was easier to run without a full belly.

The earlier drink had fought off dehydration, and now her sweat glands had reopened and were saturating her clothes. Her hair had clumped into something that was starting to resemble a massive dreadlock. None of her clothes retained their original colors. The grit and grime burrowed into her pores and under her fingernails. She'd been grubby for so long that she'd started to forget what it was like to be clean. She'd known the search for Eileen wouldn't be easy, but she hadn't expected it to be quite so brutal, either.

Hailey corrected her course to nip around a large bowed tree. The red twine dipped toward the ground then rose up above Hailey's head. She slowed then stopped, her breathing ragged and her head foggy. She couldn't see which direction the twine was leading. She followed it with her flashlight, and her heart plummeted.

The thread had been tied around an enormous oak. The knot was higher than her head, at least seven feet off the ground. And painted above the cord was a word written in a fluorescent green liquid: LOST.

Hailey clutched at her throat. A ringing noise started in her ears. She stumbled to the side and let the momentum carry her around the oak. There was no mistake. There was no hidden loop of red leading farther into the woods. The thread ended there.

Just before Anna had been hit by the spiky trap, she'd been asking if they recognized the area they were walking through. By that point, Hailey had spent so long in the woods that the environment had begun to blend together. She simultaneously recognized every tree and was familiar with none of them.

Then the metal had fallen, and Anna's question had been forced out of their minds. They'd been so preoccupied with trying to save their friend that when they started walking again, they'd continued to follow the thread blindly.

"No, no, no," Hailey moaned. The sweat coating her was turning cold.

At some point—probably on the night they'd found Todd and were arguing over whether they could bring him back—something had cut the thread, rolled it up, and then rethreaded it into a new path. A path leading them away from safety. Deeper into the forest.

Hailey couldn't breathe properly. Hope had been carrying her and giving her legs the energy to run, but now it had been stripped away from her in an instant. They weren't hours from safety. They were hell-knew-where, probably days from any kind of human life, with no idea of which direction to walk and no way to get out.

She pressed her hands over her mouth to silence the miserable, frightened wails that kept escaping. They had hoped they were moving away from the monster's territory. But it must have been following them the whole time. For all she knew, it had lured Flint to the ravine and made him fall.

And she'd been following its lure, walking right into its arms.

A branch snapped. Hailey shrieked and swiveled so fast, she felt dizzy. Her flashlight's beam jittered over trees, rocks, weeds. No sign of movement. That didn't stop her feeling as though she was being watched.

She needed to get back to the group. She needed to warn them…and protect them, if she could. The monster might not have had its eyes on her; it might have been waiting for the people left at the camp to lower their guard. Anna was unconscious. Flint was in bad shape. And Chris was so tired that he looked like a walking corpse. He wouldn't be able to keep his eyes open for long. And then they would be all too easy to pick off.

A skittering noise above her made her flinch. *It's just a night animal. Something foraging through the canopy.* Still, her skin crawled, and her mind buzzed with fear. She turned back to the thread, back to the way she'd come, and started running again.

Before, hope had carried her. Now fear moved her legs instead. She didn't pause for a drink break but ran as fast as her limbs could carry her. She was small and light, at least. She could fly around obstacles.

Her flashlight kept picking out flashes of the red thread. It sickened her to think that Anna's careful creation had been replaced by some psychopathic monster's. The creature had mimicked Anna's methods of laying it; the twine looped around a tree branch every twenty or so feet.

Then, abruptly, the thread dipped toward the forest floor.

Hailey kept running, her light trained on the sliver of red coiling among the dead leaves. Then it vanished.

She stumbled to a halt. Her lungs ached but not as badly as her overtaxed heart. Tears spilled over her lower lids and streaked through the grime on her face as she backtracked and found the thread again.

It had been cut. The jagged end lay limply on the ground. She turned and scanned the trees surrounding her. There was no sign of the other end.

The monster had been following her after all. It had wanted to divide her from her friends.

More tears came, and she couldn't stop them as she turned in a slow circle. The forest seemed more alive than normal; tree branches moved, vines swayed, and leaves twitched in the slow wind. Two trees nearby had been hacked into with the same deep, angry gashes. Hailey sucked in a hiccupping, gasping breath as a pair of green eyes flashed out of the darkness.

CHAPTER 48

Monday, 11:20 a.m.

LOUANN KENT, CRIMINAL PROFILER, looked as though she'd stepped out of a big-budget Hollywood movie. A hint of lace added a feminine touch to her navy-blue suit and crisp white blouse. With golden-red hair swept back from an impeccably made-up face, she was glamorous without looking gaudy and had the confidence to pull it off.

Carla sat opposite her, back pin straight and neck lifted high as though good posture might disguise just how disheveled her uniform was and how her hair had reached that awful crux where grease made it clump and frizz made it look wild.

She hated comparing herself to other women. Partly because she believed it didn't need to be a competition in the first place, and partly because she always came off second best. She wasn't ugly, she knew; she'd been enough to hook Matt. But she was all hard angles and harsh words. People preferred women like Louann: softly spoken, well put together, and gently persuasive.

Louann's red nails—the same shade of red as her lips—tapped on the notes in front of herself. The men all listened attentively as she spoke, and she made eye contact with each of them with an almost practiced regularity.

"Sadly, our evidence is quite limited right now," she said. "Without bodies or crime scenes, we won't be able to build a complete profile. Normally, I would be able to look at what had been done to the victim to build up an accurate picture. Was she raped? Was she mutilated? If so, did it occur before or after death? Details like that can inform us whether the perpetrator is sadistic or insecure, or whether he is acting out of suppressed emotions or a negative relationship in his life. Without those, I'm largely in the dark."

Decker nodded to the case files. "You have everything we know. The forest will have swallowed up every possible crime scene by now, and the only bones we recovered—bones washed downriver—showed signs of being gnawed at by small animals but no marks that could indicate knife wounds."

"I'll share my best estimates, but most of them will be quite general. Our suspect is most likely in the thirty-to-sixty age range and male."

Carla spoke under her breath, so that no one else would hear. "I could have told you that."

"He might be a functioning member of society, but the

location of the attacks suggests he is most comfortable when he's alone. He may feel cut off from social groups or stressed in a busy urban environment. The forest would be somewhere he feels safe and at home."

Peterson lifted a finger. "Are you sure the forest is significant? Wouldn't it just be a convenient place to kill people without being seen?"

"There are a *multitude* of convenient sites," Louann said. "He could pick up hitchhikers and take them somewhere secluded. He could travel into the farming regions that surround here, where there are very few people per square mile. Even in the town, there are plenty of quiet alleys and empty buildings he could choose to work in. However, it takes *effort* to visit the forest. Even the closest residents would need to drive to reach it. Killing in the forest is a conscious choice, and that gives us insight into his personality."

Not much *of an insight,* Carla thought. Then she reined herself back in. She was becoming irritable and snappish, just because she was drowning under her workload. It wasn't Louann's fault that she was wasting everyone's time.

"If you *do* recover a body, the coroner's report could help me build a mental profile," Louann continued. "If a woman is killed slowly, it means the perpetrator craves power and relishes a feeling of control. If she is killed quickly, it can come from a frantic, almost mindless compulsion. If the body is mutilated after the fact, we can glean that the killer may struggle with feelings of inadequacy around women or that he is bitter and resentful toward them. In a relatively high number of cases, the killer is acting out of resentment toward his mother. He may intentionally pick women who look like her, or modify them to make them resemble her. Cutting hair, making them wear specific kinds of clothes, the like."

Carla had been itching to speak, and when Louann paused for breath, she cleared her throat. "The victims include men, not just women."

Louann's smile didn't change, but her eyes narrowed a fraction. "Yes, but if you look at the cases, you'll see there's a preponderance of female victims. Enough that, statistically—"

"No," Carla said. She looked to Lau for support, and he gave a quick nod. "As far as we can work out, sixty percent of the victims are women. Forty percent are men."

"Exactly—"

"But that doesn't mean there's a…a *preponderance*, as you want to call it. About sixty percent of the people who visit the park are women. The victim ratio is pretty much in line with the ratio of visitors. It's almost like the killer picked his prey by chance."

"Prey?" This time, Louann's smile twisted a little higher. "That's what you're calling them?"

"Potential victims." Carla swallowed, feeling all eyes on the room focusing on her. "We only referred to them as prey because it feels so much like an animal stalking its food."

"That is actually an interesting thought." Louann turned to a new page in her notes. "It lines up with one of my own theories. Since the perpetrator has taken victims of all ages and genders, we can assume he's probably not sexually motivated. He may still achieve some sexual satisfaction from the act, but not in a direct, physical way. More psychological. Based on my assessment of this limited data and what I have observed in previous cases, it's possible the perpetrator has grandiose fantasies of himself."

Quincey tapped her pen on the table. "Can you elaborate?"

"In this scenario—and again, I must stress, we don't currently have enough clues to conclusively say this is accurate—the killer's home life would be unpleasant." Louann steepled her fingers and glanced at her companions, seemingly checking that she had their attention. "He would feel stifled and crushed, possibly by a nagging wife, an unreasonable boss, or both. He longs to break free. To be wild and driven by impulses, the way he imagines life should be lived. When he enters the forest, he slips into a fantasy world where *he* is in control. *He* is the most important person. *He* gets to decide whether Ashlough Forest's visitors live or die. He goes from emasculated to all powerful, and although he knows it's wrong, those killings provide a rush that he cannot get anywhere else."

"So it's like a way to cope with his miserable life?" Decker asked.

"Exactly. After committing the murder, he can return home and endure his wife or his boss for another few weeks, because he feels like he's back in control. 'I killed a person,' he says to himself. 'I could kill them, too, if I wanted.'"

"Will he?" Peterson asked. When Louann raised her eyebrows, he coughed. "Kill his partner or his boss?"

"If something pushed him too far, potentially. But as long as life maintains its regular unpleasant routine, no. He will have a clear divide between his personality at home and his personality in the forest. He is not a killer at home. He is weak, subservient. It's only when he can enter his fantasy in the forest that he can become something greater, so to speak." She clasped her hands together. "That is one possible theory, at least. There may be others. He could be suffering from a mental disorder such as schizophrenia. We might even be dealing with a group working under a cult mentality."

Peterson spread his hands. "So, at the end of the day, you're saying it could be anyone."

Louann smiled, but her words held a slight clip to them. "Until you can present me with evidence I can glean more data from, I'm afraid that's where we're stuck. Possibilities, likelihoods, and generalities. If it is a single perpetrator, they are likely to follow the behavioral patterns of other killers with antisocial personality disorders. Abusive or absent mother. Bedwetting as a child. A history of hurting animals. Those are all of the usual warning signs. But that is about the limit of what I can give you based on our current data."

"Well, you've given us some stuff to work with." Decker rose and extended his hand, signaling the end to the meeting. "Thanks for your time, Ms. Kent."

She said goodbye to Decker then smiled at the rest of them as she waltzed her way to the door and let herself out. Peterson waited until Louann's footsteps had faded before speaking.

"What an absolute charlatan."

CHAPTER 49

Monday, 11:35 a.m.

HAILEY STIRRED OUT OF a dazed, uncomfortable sleep. She was worn down both mentally and physically. An image stuck in her head. It had followed her into her dreams. She thought, even if she lived to be a hundred, she would never forget it.

A monster had stepped out from between the trees. Green eyes like fireflies emerged from the shadows across its face. It was focused on her, unblinking.

She'd only felt that level of intensity once before. Her father had taken her on safari for her sixteenth birthday. A lioness had fixated on her as she strayed too far from the group. For a moment, it had risen, ears down and eyes round, as it stalked toward her.

Except then, the guide had pulled Hailey back into the safari buggy. The vehicle had been reinforced. The lioness gave up.

That night, though, there had been no protection between her and her hunter. No safe barrier. No guides with guns in case of emergencies. It was just Hailey and the predator, a creature that was bigger and stronger than even the lioness. Any fight would have been over in seconds.

Then Hailey had remembered the photographs. Eileen, devoid of any other weapon, had used the camera's flash against her assailant. Hailey turned her flashlight toward the monster.

It had flinched back from the light. In that second, she had gotten her first good look at it. The monster stood several heads above her. Its broad shoulders were covered in long dark fur that blended into the shadows perfectly. The fur draped to the forest floor, making it look like a tall block of darkness. Only its face and eyes held color.

The face was gray and deformed. Part human, part animal. Bulging eyes. That was all Hailey had been able to glimpse before it had twisted away from her flashlight. A massive, jagged claw-like appendage had swiped toward a tree. It sent flecks of bark trailing to the ground as it gouged out a chunk of wood.

Then the monster had retreated deeper into the forest, into the shadows. Hailey had been too terrified to move. She was shaking, her legs like jelly, her hands squeezed around the flashlight that had become her lifeline. The monster might be hiding, but she knew it wasn't gone. She could still feel its eyes. It was watching, waiting. Her flashlight's batteries wouldn't last forever.

She had started running. She hadn't given any thought to the direction, just that she wanted to be *away* from it. As she ran, she heard its pursuit. A sharp blade dragged against trees to create a low, ominous scraping noise. It didn't seem to be hurrying. In fact, the faster Hailey moved, the fainter the noises became. She'd eventually dropped to her knees, breathless, and turned off her flashlight. The forest was silent except for the ever-present insects and night animals. She thought she would be safe, hidden in the dark.

It had found her, though, somehow. The wicked blades scraped over a tree barely ten meters behind her. Hailey had turned on her flashlight and pointed it toward the noise. The beam had only picked up the greens and browns of plant life. She had been forced to flee again. She'd kept moving—not quite running but at least stumbling along—as the sun rose and brightened the environment.

The exertion had half killed her. She'd collapsed into a state somewhere between sleep and a coma. Hailey didn't know how long she'd been out of it, but she thought it must have been at least a few hours. She squinted against a headache and struggled to orient herself. Her flashlight lay at her side, still turned on but with dead batteries.

Her limbs ached from where she had bumped into trees and pushed through branches. Her feet hurt worse. She was frightened to pull her shoes off and see the damage. But at least the creature hadn't caught her. Either she'd outrun it, or it had given up the chase. One of her last memories was of sunrise lighting the environment. Maybe it only wanted to hunt during the night.

She fumbled for her backpack. A dehydration headache beat

at her brain like a war drum. She emptied one bottle into her open mouth, threw it back into the pack, and pulled out another.

The awful truth about her situation was starting to sink in. She had been at least an hour away from her friends when she'd lost the twine trail the night before. That gap could only have widened. There was no hope of locating them with her whistle. Or of warning them. If Flint woke—if Anna recovered enough to walk—they would follow the same path she had, into a dead end and the waiting claws of the monstrous freak trailing them.

She had no energy left to cry. She searched for some escape—any glimmer of hope, no matter how thin—but she couldn't see it. How long would Flint, Chris, and Anna survive? A few days? A week? They had water, at least, but no food. If the monster didn't return for them, they would sit there patiently, waiting for the rescue she had promised, a rescue that would never come. Hailey screamed, kicking at the ground, hands pressed to her forehead as the grief and guilt overwhelmed her. For all of their preparations, for all of Anna's meticulous planning, they seemed no more equipped to survive than Todd had been.

Hailey fell quiet. A memory had surfaced. Anna's planning… so meticulous, so obnoxious at the time…might give them the slim chance they needed.

She dragged the backpack closer. Before leaving her friends, she'd emptied out all of the equipment except for a few spare batteries and five bottles of water. She hadn't thought to touch any of the pockets, though. When they'd been at the store the morning of the trip into the forest, Anna had stuffed a collection of odd sorts into each pack. Hailey hadn't paid much attention to it; she'd been too focused on the store clerk who was flirting with Flint. But she thought she remembered two items that might mean the difference between life and a slow, horrible death.

Hailey unzipped the pockets and sifted through the equipment. A small notepad and pen. A packet of painkiller tablets; Hailey popped out two and washed them down with more water. A Swiss Army knife. That would be useful. And finally, at the back of the pocket, a folded-up square of paper and a small glass shape.

She pulled the paper out and carefully, reverently, unfolded a map of Ashlough Forest. Then she placed the compass on top of it and wiped dirt off her cheeks. If Anna survived, Hailey would never make fun of her pedantry ever again.

CHAPTER 50

Monday, 12:40 p.m.

"CHARLATAN, HUH?" DECKER ASKED.

Peterson looked wholly unrepentant as he spread his hands. "She basically presented us with a fiction of what a killer *could* be like. And even if her fiction bears a resemblance to reality, it doesn't exactly narrow it down, does it?"

Carla was silently glad she wasn't the only person who had been rubbed the wrong way by the slick criminal profiler. She knew there wasn't much the woman could do with such limited data, but still, she was charging the taxpayers a hefty price for her services.

Peterson folded his stick-like arms over his chest. "What are we going to do? Interview every person in the town with a cranky wife or domineering boss? Because that describes literally everyone in this room."

"I agree that her profile was… How shall I put this? Completely underwhelming? But she did give us some ideas." Decker flipped through his notes. "None of you suggested that we could be dealing with multiple killers. Considering your cumulative years of experience and training, that's honestly embarrassing."

"Do you really think multiple people could keep a project of this scale silent?" Quincey asked. "Kent suggested it might be a cultlike operation. But I've lived in Helmer for most of my life and never heard so much as a hint about anything like that."

"No," Peterson said. "I've yet to stumble onto any ritualistic sacrifices or notice black robes in my friends' closets."

Decker released an irritated sigh. "I agree it seems a little far-fetched to believe we have a cult in this town, especially one that has been operating for twenty years. But we might be looking for a family. Have you heard of folie à deux?"

Carla had, but Lau and Peterson both shook their heads.

"The idea is that when two or three people spend all of their time together, they can become wrapped up in their own crazy fantasy. It was named after two sister maids in 1930s France who, over several years, developed co-dependent delusions. They ended up murdering their employers and mutilating their bodies and never recognized that what they'd done was wrong."

"So we might not be looking for a traditional cult," Carla said, "but a tightly knit, cultlike family."

"Still…" Peterson looked unconvinced. "In crazy families, the children eventually grow up, move out, and become at least a little less crazy. Over twenty years, no one's ever come forward.

Not even an anonymous tip saying, 'Hey, there's some weird stuff happening in the forest. Maybe you want to check that out.'"

"It *is* easier to keep secrets with only one person involved," Carla agreed. "But I guess the takeaway is that we're not looking exclusively for miserable loners."

"No. How helpful of Ms. Kent," Peterson muttered. "To sum it up, we need to keep our eye on Helmer's entire population."

Carla snuck a glance at her phone under the table. It was nearly one in the afternoon. She smothered a curse. "Hey, I'm going to head out for lunch before I starve."

Decker glared at her. "What? You think you still get proper lunch breaks? That's a luxury reserved for people who catch their perps."

He was joking. At least, Carla hoped he was. She stood and hooked her jacket off the back of her chair. "Somehow, I doubt going on a hunger strike will guilt him into giving himself up."

"Fine. But don't lounge about. And bring me back a coffee. Our machine is garbage."

Carla threw a wave over her shoulder as she left the room, then she jogged down the hallway. She hadn't seen Viv that morning, but Matthews had already relieved Viv for her lunch break.

As she stepped outside the building, Carla relished a lungful of clean, fresh air. Peterson was a smoker, and although he didn't smoke in the conference room, he still reeked.

Carla jogged down the cracked walkway to the little café at the street's end. She usually brought lunch and ate at her desk, but on days when she really, really hated her fellow humans, she visited the café as a treat. The cakes in the display cabinet were always verging on stale, and the deep-fryer oil wasn't changed as often as she would have liked, but the owners never failed to greet her with a smile and sometimes gave her free biscuits.

As she entered the little brick building with blue-painted walls, she spotted Viv sitting at a table by the window. She'd put daisies in her hair that day, and they matched the paintings behind her. Carla was late, and she'd worried Viv might have given up and left, but she looked quite happy as she chewed on a sandwich.

"Hey," Carla said, sliding into the seat opposite her. "I'm so, so sorry I'm late."

"It *was* you!" Viv beamed. "You've really got to sign your notes. I figured there was a fifty percent chance the letter was from you, and you were running late, and fifty percent I'd been asked on a date and then stood up."

"Sorry."

"Don't worry about it. I've been enjoying an excuse to get out of the building." Viv wiped her mouth with a napkin and settled back in her chair. "But I'm guessing you didn't invite me out here to talk about girly stuff like which guy in the office is the hottest."

"None of them are hot. And you're right. I wanted to ask your advice on something."

One of the waitresses approached just as Carla was pulling the sheet of paper out of her pocket. She subtly pushed it back in and faced the woman. "Burger and fries. Thanks."

"Anything to drink?" A smile created dimples on the waitress's cheeks and chin.

"Uh…"

"Get a chamomile tea," Viv hissed. "It'll do you good."

Carla pulled a face. "No. I'll get a latte. And a black coffee. Make it all to go."

The waitress bustled off, and Carla turned back to Viv. "You're socially active, aren't you?"

"I go on dates, if that's what you're asking. But I won't go on a blind date. I agreed to one of those once, and the guy was a total creep."

"I mean…" Carla pulled the paper out of her pocket again. "If there were any strange rumors floating around, you'd be pretty likely to hear about them, right?"

"Probably. I'm not a hermit. What kind of dirt are you trying to dig up?"

"Well, this is going to sound crazy, but have you heard any stories about a large animal in Ashlough Forest? Something that could create this?"

She unfolded the paper and pushed it toward Viv. It contained a photocopy of the two photos she'd found in the file the previous night: one showing the officer standing next to the gashes in the tree, and the close-up.

Viv whistled as she scanned the images. "I'm sorry, but I've never heard of anything like *this*. Like, one guy swears he saw a herd of deer in the woods, but they're not supposed to live in this part of the country, and most people figure he's full of it. But this? No. Never heard of anything in the area that could cause this type of damage."

Carla had guessed that would be the answer, but it had been worth a try. "All right. Can you do me a favor? I'm time-poor at the moment, and I need to know who this officer is. The photo would have been taken about twenty years ago. Do you think you can have a bit of an ask-around in your spare time? See if anyone recognizes him?"

"Sure, I can do that."

Carla tore the paper in half, carefully removing the claw marks, so that only the officer was left. Then she handed it to Viv. "Thanks. I'd like to get in touch with him, if he's still about."

Viv's eyebrows were raised, and curiosity sparkled in her eyes as she folded the paper and tucked it into her purse. "What's this about, anyway?"

"Eh, I'm not really supposed to say right now. Decker wants to keep it under wraps. You'll know soon enough, though."

"Is it…" Viv glanced around to make sure they were alone then leaned closer. "Is it about the Hershberger case? The weird pictures you were worried about?"

Carla swore. She should have guessed Viv would make the connection. "Keep it quiet, okay? Decker will have both our necks if this starts circulating."

"Sure. I can keep a secret."

"I'm serious, Viv. Don't even tell your mother."

"Hey, I'm not some snitch." Viv winked. "You can count on me. I'll keep my button zipped and see if I can figure out who our mystery officer is, as well."

"Thanks. Lifesaver."

"One question, though. Have you called Hershberger's brother? The one who visited you?"

Carla had mostly put him and his friends out of her mind. She shook her head. "I can't tell them, either. Not until this, uh, situation is wrapped up."

"It's just..." Viv fidgeted with her napkin. "They looked so upset when they visited, and it wouldn't have been a cheap trip, either. Maybe you could let them know you're not just ignoring them. I bet they'd appreciate it."

"Maybe," Carla said. The waitress behind the counter waved to let Carla know her order was ready, and she pulled her credit card out of her pocket. "I'll cover your meal. Thank you again."

"You can't stay for a bit?"

"Sorry. I need to be fast, or I'll get eviscerated for wasting taxpayer money." She chuckled. "Not like we haven't done enough of that lately."

CHAPTER 51

HAILEY BENT LOW OVER her map as she tried to figure out a way home. She'd read maps before. She'd just never tried to read one without knowing where she was on it.

The map showed the twelve trails, the parking lot, the border of the closest towns, and the rivers. It didn't cover all of the mountains. For all Hailey knew, she might have already gone past the edge of the map. That was a terrifying thought.

Depending on where she was, she would need to walk either south or southeast to reach civilization. If she'd moved too far to the west, walking south would add an extra day at minimum to her trip.

Another issue would be the rivers and lakes. She needed to make sure she passed some to refill her water bottles. But if she bumped into the *wrong* ones, she might get stuck if there was no way to cross over. Some of the river lines were hair-thin, but others looked threateningly thick.

It all boiled down to the one problem: she was basically blind until she found a landmark to give her context. And the map was sadly thin on those. If she found a river, she could follow its bank, try to keep track of its bends, then see if she could match it to any of the dozen squiggly lines on the map. There were some lookouts marked on the map, but they all branched off the trails. The only other signifier was a little arrow at the top of the sheet, pointing up and slightly to the right. It read Cobb Mountain.

Hailey took a sharp breath. If she could see the mountain, she could at least know which direction it was in and maybe even guesstimate how far away it was. That wouldn't give her a precise location, but it would at least narrow it down.

The canopy was miserably thick. She'd barely had a glimpse of sky since they'd entered the forest. But there was no shortage of trees, many which had plenty of branches to climb.

Hailey refolded the map and pushed it and the compass into her jacket pocket. She slung the backpack over one shoulder then began walking. Instead of searching for a path, she was looking for the largest, tallest tree she could find.

After a few minutes, she settled on an ancient pine. Its trunk was so thick that it had developed deep cracks, and it had branches at regular intervals. She looked up but couldn't see its top. It seemed to grow higher than anything around it, though. Hailey dropped her backpack on the forest floor, rolled her shoulders, hooked her arm over the lowest branch, and pulled herself up.

She wished she hadn't left all of her equipment at the campsite. At the time, it had been important to drop as much weight as she could to increase her speed. Water had been a necessity, but she'd been expecting to get back to town before the next evening, so she hadn't even brought anything to sleep with. Now, she wished she'd at least brought gloves. The spiky bark scraped skin off her hands.

Hailey clambered from branch to branch, raising herself a foot at a time. The lower part of the tree was covered with thick ledges, but as she moved higher, each perch began to feel more precarious. The branches became thinner, and the trunk narrowed.

She kept moving, arm over arm, leg over leg. Glimpses of sky were growing more frequent. She pushed on, even when the trunk began swaying under her weight.

Scraps of bark and pine needles spiraled toward the ground as her hiking shoes knocked them loose. Hailey spared a glance toward the forest floor, and her heart constricted. It looked incredibly far away. She'd never been frightened of heights before, but the view made her wrap her arms around the trunk in a death grip. Rough bark jabbed at her cheek, and she closed her eyes as the tree's gentle swaying made her queasy.

She had to keep climbing. There was no backing down, not when she was so close to seeing above the canopy. The upper leaves from the nearest trees surrounded her, scraping over her arms and back as the wind moved them. *Another five meters might be high enough...*

Hailey took a sharp breath and forced herself to loosen her

grip. She reached for a new branch and pulled herself up another rung. And then another. And another…

The branch under her foot snapped. Hailey screamed and grabbed the tree again. She'd been lucky. She'd only just started to shift her weight from one foot to the other, and she managed to regain her balance on the lower branch. The tree rocked her farther than she'd thought was possible as the broken limb tumbled away. It bounced off a dozen of its counterparts before hitting the ground with a thud that Hayley felt but didn't hear.

She took quick, shallow breaths. She couldn't stop shaking and couldn't let go of the trunk. A small bird flitted past her, chasing insects, and Hailey watched it without moving her head.

When she glanced up, she saw the sky. Blue, stretching forever, with a scattering of clouds building toward her left. She was very close. Her mind screamed, trying to lock her limbs into place, but she forced the screeching voice of panic into the back of her skull and lifted her leg again.

The new branch held her. She chanced a quick glance over her shoulder. She could see the tops of some trees. Another step. The limb groaned, and the tree swung horribly. But she could see the mountain.

It was just a tiny glimpse of the highest peak. That was all she needed, though. She fixated on it and slowly, carefully, released one hand from her hold on the trunk and pulled out her compass.

The mountain was northeast of her current position. Hailey managed to keep her hand still long enough to get the exact angle then stuffed the compass back into her pocket.

Now, she only needed to get back down.

She began shuffling her body lower, still clinging to the trunk. Not daring to look down, she extended her leg and felt around until her boot touched something solid. She held her higher leg on its branch while she tested the lower perch. It took her weight. Slowly, gingerly, she lowered her right leg then her torso and repeated the process.

Moving her second leg to the branch, she felt it cracking. She tried to pick her leg back up, to get it onto a more stable perch, but she was too late. The bough broke, splintering away from the tree, and Hailey gasped as her grip on the trunk failed.

Her stomach flipped at the sudden drop. Then her breath rushed out in a gust as a branch slammed into her torso. Even through the pain, Hailey tried to grab it. She could feel herself sliding off, the branch bowing under her weight, and scrabbled for purchase. It slipped out of her grip. She was falling again, more branches smashing into her thighs and her back, each one slowing her descent a fraction, only for the speed to pick up again in a heartbeat.

One arm looped around a branch, and momentum smacked her into the trunk. She felt herself slipping again. Her legs scrambled and miraculously found purchase. Hailey hung there, balancing with her toes on one branch and her arm looped around another. The tree continued to sway, threatening to rock her free. Her back ached. Her head ached. She couldn't breathe. She could barely believe she was still alive.

Hailey held that pose for several moments. She was terrified of letting go, but as the spike of adrenaline faded, her calves began to cramp. Slowly, gingerly, she loosened her hold on the higher branch and let herself rest fully on the lower limb. She then returned to holding the trunk as she lowered herself back down.

The branches were becoming wider and stronger again. The trunk swayed less, then finally, it didn't at all. Hailey dropped off the tree's lowest branch and let herself crumple into a ball among its roots.

She couldn't stop shaking. She wanted to see Flint. Whenever she was upset, he always pulled her into the biggest, roughest hugs. The gesture was so comically exaggerated and heartfelt that she could only hold out for a minute at most before she started laughing. He would have been able to make her feel better. To feel safe. Like she might actually survive.

The tremors faded, but the aches refused to abate from where she'd hit branches while falling. She unrolled from the ball and flinched as a dozen brand-new bruises twinged. Mucus dripped over her lips, and she wiped it away furiously. She pulled the map and compass out of her back pocket then crawled to the backpack. She took the pen from the zippered pocket and flattened her map.

The mountain was past the edge of the map, but she used the arrow to guess its direction. Then, using the angle she'd taken on the compass, she drew a line across the map. She hadn't been able to guess how far away the mountain was from the brief glimpse she'd gotten, but she knew she had to be somewhere on that line. Based on that, her best odds of reaching a town quickly came from walking southeast.

She wanted to sit longer to let her aches settle and her pulse slow. But only a few hours of daylight remained, and she needed to get the best head start she could. She stuffed the map back into her pocket and the water bottles back into her backpack then stood, swallowed around the lump in her throat, and let the compass guide her course.

CHAPTER 52

Monday, 3:15 p.m.

CARLA SAT AT THE bus stop down the street from the police station. Every few seconds, she snuck a glance over her shoulder to make sure none of her co-workers emerged from the old building. What she was doing would earn her a few choice words at the very least, and possibly suspension, depending on how bitter Decker was feeling.

She'd excused herself from archive duty to deliver three new folders to the conference room, then, instead of returning, she'd picked up the Hershberger case file and slunk outside.

Viv's words had been hanging with her since lunch. Chris Hershberger deserved to know that his photos hadn't been forgotten. She wouldn't tell him about the other disappearances, but a brief mention that she was still working on finding Eileen might go a long way.

The Hershberger family had been notified that the case had been closed the previous day. Like the rest of the world, they were supposed to think that was the end of the story. Eileen had been given up on. The photos were being ignored. They needed to turn their attention to organizing a funeral and trying to pick up the pieces of their lives.

But Carla worried about the youths who had visited her. Chris hadn't been alone. Three of his friends had come along, too, and that made Carla uneasy.

She remembered what it was like to be twenty, full of fire and the need to solve every problem that came into her life. Chris wouldn't have yet learned the painful truth that a single person fighting for what was right rarely improved the world. Now that the case was closed, Carla hoped they weren't thinking of doing anything drastic.

The Hershberger case files contained cell phone contacts for the parents but not for Chris. Carla chose Mr. Hershberger's number, and with a final cautious look back at the station, she dialed it.

Mr. Hershberger answered after three rings. "Hello?"

"Good afternoon, Mr. Hershberger. This is Officer Delago. I'm sorry for disturbing you during this painful time." Carla cringed at her own words. They were the perfect mix of awkward and inappropriate.

Mr. Hershberger didn't seem put off, though. "It's fine."

"I was hoping to speak to your son, Chris, if he's available."

Mr. Hershberger sighed. He sounded worn down. "He's staying with a friend right now. And not answering his cell phone."

"Oh." Carla frowned. "Did he seem all right the last time you spoke to him?"

Mr. Hershberger made a grumbling noise in the back of his throat. "Well. He's upset, you know? His sister's dead. He misses her."

"Of course." Carla hunted for something soothing she could say, but everything sounded too much like a cute phrase plucked out of a sympathy card. In the end, she simply said, "I'm sorry."

"To be perfectly honest, I'm disappointed. He's never ignored me or his mother like this before. They say that everyone has different ways of coping with grief, and I know he's an adult now with his own life...but our family always used to stick together. It's not like him to ignore us for so long."

Carla licked dry lips. "How many days...?"

"He was going to stay with his friend. That was on Thursday. They had better not be spending all of their time drinking." Mr. Hershberger's voice quavered. "I raised him better than that."

Carla had spoken to the friends on Friday. Her palms were growing sweaty, and she shifted her grip on the phone. "And you haven't spoken to him since?"

"No." The energy drained from Mr. Hershberger's voice. "We've booked a flight home for tomorrow. When we see him, I'll tell him you called. Will that be all right?"

"Yes, thank you." As Mr. Hershberger hung up his phone,

Carla dropped hers into her lap and tried to swallow around the tightness in her throat.

Chris Hershberger had traveled to Helmer without his parents' knowledge. He'd brought three friends with him. They had come, convinced that their photos depicted a monster attacking Eileen.

And now, he was uncontactable. She didn't need to be Sherlock to guess why.

Carla forced her phone back into her pocket and walked back to the station. Viv beamed and waved as she passed the reception desk, but Carla could barely manage a thin smile in return. She felt ghastly. Chris Hershberger had come to her for help...possibly as a desperate last-ditch effort before taking matters into his own hands. She had blown him off. She had berated him. And she hadn't recognized any of the warning signs until it was far too late.

She burst into the conference room and slammed the folder onto the table. Her four teammates were gathered around the laptop at the other end of the conference room, and they all looked up at her explosive entrance.

"We need to organize a search and rescue mission," she said. "Immediately."

Decker's expression clearly conveyed how little patience he had for her at that moment. "No."

"Sir..." Carla took a deep breath and collected herself. "I strongly believe Chris Hershberger and three of his friends went into the forest to search for Eileen. According to his parents, he's been unreachable for four days. He—"

"All right, calm the hell down, Delago. You're giving me a headache." Decker sank back into his chair.

Peterson blinked at her. "Four days. Chances of survival drop significantly after just one, don't they?"

"For an unprepared day hiker!" Carla slammed her fist onto the table. "These kids weren't day hikers. They would have planned to spend time in there and come prepared. Tents, water, food. If they were very smart, they would have marked their path, as well. It might not be too late for them!"

"All right, enough yelling!" Decker massaged his temple. "You will have your bloody rescue mission, Delago."

"Thank you—"

"Shortly. Right now, we have a more pressing issue."

Carla glared at him. "What? Sir, we *cannot* delay—"

He lifted his hand, and his stare was so hostile that Carla bit her tongue.

"If they're as prepared as you say they are, I'm sure a couple of minutes won't kill them. In the meantime, I want you to read this. We may have just found our killer."

CHAPTER 53

CHRIS FELT HELPLESS. HE sat with his back to a tree and a knife in one hand, watching the environment. It was all he could do.

Anna had stirred twice through the day. She wasn't getting better. Each movement seemed feebler, and even though she asked for water, she barely drank any before lapsing back into unconsciousness.

Flint wasn't in good shape, either. Chris had tried to make him as comfortable as possible. He'd rolled up a backpack under his head to cushion his damaged skull and wrapped him in a sleeping bag. He'd stopped bleeding, but it still frightened Chris.

He hated being alone. He'd tried to stay awake through the night, but sleep had claimed him during the early morning. When he'd finally clawed his way back to wakefulness, the sun had already risen. Nothing had tried to attack them, at least.

At first, it had been a relief to sit and let worn-out muscles recover. But as hours passed, Chris began to feel edgy. Soon he rose and started pacing the area in a kind of patrol. He couldn't leave the camp, but after days of walking, it felt wrong to sit and do nothing.

"Hailey…"

Chris jolted as his friend spoke. He scrambled over to Flint's side and patted his shoulder. "Hey. Can you hear me? How're you feeling?"

"Ugh." Flint squinted even though the light in the forest was muted. "Bad. Where are we?"

"Still in the forest. Hailey's gone for help. We're just waiting for people to come and collect us, now."

"Oh." Flint blinked, sluggish, then his eyes popped open. "No. No! Get her back!"

"Wha—"

"It's not safe." Flint tried to sit up but toppled back down almost immediately. "Call her back. You've got to—she can't—"

"Careful. Don't move too much. You cracked your head." Chris licked his lips, knowing that the news wouldn't make Flint happy. "I can't call her back. She left hours ago."

Flint released a string of swear words. He swung a fist at Chris, but the motion was slow and easy to duck.

"Hey! Calm down! It was our only choice. You were hurt, and Anna's getting worse by the hour. Hailey thought she could follow the thread and jog to town. She's probably already at the parking lot by now."

"She can't be out there alone. I saw it. The monster. It caught me… It tricked me…" Flint's eyes rolled back in his head. Then he coughed and grabbed Chris's shoulder. "It wanted us divided. It's gonna get Hailey. We've got to save her."

Chris looked over his shoulder. The forest seemed deceptively peaceful. A bird flitted through a tree. Tiny insects looked like dust particles dancing in the sun. And yet he could feel it—the sensation that something evil lived in the woods.

It was psychological, he knew. In the same way that he imagined he had a scratchy throat any time he came in contact with someone with a cold. Anna probably could have explained the phenomenon, if she'd been awake.

Still, Flint's panic wasn't helping him feel at ease. Chris shivered. "I'm sorry, man. We didn't know what else to do. She's not defenseless, though. She's got a knife. And she's fast. You've seen her run, right?"

The consolation was feeble at best. Flint didn't reply, but he rolled over, putting his back to Chris. His shoulders were shaking. Chris reached out to touch him but thought better of it and pulled back.

He'd been trying not to think of all the ways Hailey's rescue mission could go wrong. The path shouldn't have held any unexpected surprises like cliffs. She was following the string they'd laid out on the way in, after all. But if the monster had found her and chased her away from their lifeline, she wouldn't need to stray too far from it to lose the trail.

Chris shuddered. He looked in the other direction, toward

the river. Sitting still was doing him no good. "Hey, I'm going to refill our water bottles. Will you be okay here for a moment?"

Flint didn't answer. His shoulders continued to shake. Whether from anger or fear, Chris couldn't be sure. He gathered the empty bottles into his bag then slung it over his shoulder.

His twine from the night before still trailed through the forest, leading the way to the riverbank. As Chris followed it, he glanced up. His watch said it was still midafternoon, but the light was failing. *Clouds,* he thought. *We might be due for more rain.*

He stepped out from the trees and looked over the river. His unplanned slide down the bank the previous night had left a scar in the soft dirt. The river wasn't wide, but it would swell with the rain.

Chris bent forward to try to see where the water led. It traveled on a little way before a bend put it out of sight. The river most likely traveled to the gully, where it would pass through tourist locations and farmland. For one crazy moment, he imagined building a raft and sailing them out of their predicament. But just looking at the water, he could clearly see why that wouldn't work. The river wasn't wide enough for them to float far without getting stuck on the weeds or fallen branches. And if the craft overturned, it could easily drown them—especially Anna. Both rapids and waterfalls were likely.

But the rocky journey wouldn't hurt a bottle.

Chris felt through his backpack's compartments. Anna had given them all pens and paper. They had seemed pointless at the time, but now he was only grateful. He sat on the riverbank and crafted his message.

On one side of the paper, he wrote SOS in big thick letters. On the other, he briefly explained what had happened and described the area they were in to the best of his ability. He mentioned that they were alive so far, but members of his party were injured. He finished with a plea for help. Then, shaking, he rolled up the note and poked it into one of the empty bottles.

The note uncurled inside the barrel, with the SOS on the outside. Chris gave it a few nudges to make sure the letters would be visible even if the plastic fogged up, then he screwed the cap on as tightly as he could. He staggered down the riverbank and continued on until his boots were soaked in the icy water.

Chris dunked the bottle underwater and shook it. The cap was watertight. That was the best he could do. Chris sent up a quick prayer, kissed the bottle for good luck, and threw it into the river.

It landed with a splash then bobbed on top of the slow-moving stream. Chris watched as it wove between weeds and rocks. He didn't stop watching until it had drifted around the river's bend and out of sight.

CHAPTER 54

Monday, 3:35 p.m.

CARLA CAUGHT HER BREATH. "You what?"

Decker beckoned her toward the laptop. "We think we might have found the killer. The email address asking for tips has been running hot all morning, since Peterson put a public call in the newspaper and posted some flyers around town. Most of the tips are garbage, of course. They're responding about a fake crime, so thankfully, it's easy to weed out the chaff. We've had amateur spirit mediums, one guy who seems to have a crazy grudge against his neighbor, and a couple of emails from just plain psychos. But then, two tips came in about the same individual. Sam Gabon."

Carla bent to read the computer screen. The email window was full of messages, but two had been highlighted.

"The first email names him. He claims he saw Gabon walking

down Glenview Lane, dragging some kind of large sack. He says he's friends with Gabon and offered to give him a lift home. Gabon declined and, according to our lead, seemed *shifty* about it."

Decker scrolled down to the next highlighted email. "Then, about an hour ago, we got this message. It claims to have seen a man, forty to fifty years old, walking down a road with a heavy bag behind him. He doesn't name the man, but with the description of the bag and the time frame, they have to be the same. He says he noticed the man's pant legs seemed to have blood on them, and he stopped to see if he was hurt. The man laughed and said he'd only been doing some hunting in the forest."

Decker lifted his eyebrows at Carla as he waited for her to catch the implications. She bit her lip. "There's nothing to hunt in Ashlough, is there? No deer. No rabbits. Unless he's hunting humans…"

"Exactly." Decker slapped the desk. "It's a bold-faced admission."

She'd heard of killers who did that. They made jokes or offhanded comments about their crimes and relied on the fact that most people would assume they were making a strange joke. It was a thrill for them. They loved boasting about what they had done and getting away with it. For some of them, it was also a way to absolve guilt. They'd confessed. When no one punished them, that meant they were free to do it again.

"This is a strong lead," Decker continued. "The street, Glenview, runs alongside Ashlough Forest and connects with the entry to the trails. If you follow it, it also leads to Sam Gabon's house. He lives on a rural property a fair way from town. It's less than an hour's walk to the trails."

"What do we know about him?" Carla asked.

Peterson sighed. "Not much so far. He was in the military when he was younger but dishonorably discharged. Since then, he's apparently hopped from job to job, usually working in low-skill labor industries. From what we can work out, he doesn't trust the government and has made a point of keeping all of his personal information offline. He lives alone. No kids, never married."

"It's enough to get a search warrant," Decker said. "Is everyone on board with nailing this louse? I want to strike quickly, tonight, before he has a chance to scuttle away and hide."

"Yes," Carla said. "But we also have to try to get those kids out of the forest. It's been four days. They'll probably be safe against the weather, but if one of them gets hurt or a cut becomes infected—"

"Enough, Delago, you've made your point. Do you know which trail they went down?"

"No, sir."

Decker chewed on his lip. "That's a problem. It's going to take me at least an hour to get that search warrant, and until we bring Gabon in, I want to be careful. We don't know how closely Gabon is watching his trails. And if we start an aerial search, he'll probably see it. His home's that close."

Carla stared at him, trying to convey her sense of urgency without irritating him further, and Decker sighed. "I'll send some men out to scope the trails. They'll be under instructions not to leave the path but to look for any sign that someone else might have. Tape on the trees or rope or anything of that kind. Will that satisfy you, Delago?"

"What if they can't find anything?"

"Then you had better hope Gabon is our man. If we can make an arrest, we'll move to organize proper search parties and a rescue helicopter." He grumbled to himself as he shut the laptop. "You had better hope this isn't part of their monster-in-the-forest prank."

Carla was sure it wasn't. The strain in Mr. Hershberger's voice had been palpable. He didn't know where his son was, and despite trying to act like it wasn't a big deal, he was growing worried.

Decker stood. "Get ready to leave. We're going out as soon as I have that warrant. If our criminal profiler was on the right path, Gabon probably won't try to put up a fight. But be prepared anyway. Bulletproof vests, guns, the works."

Lau's eyebrows had risen. "*We're* going to make the arrest?"

"Of course you are," Decker snarled. "Why? Is that making you nervous? Would you like to call your momma and have her hold your hand?"

"I—" He looked from Carla to Decker then swallowed. "No, sir. I'll be ready, sir."

Decker snatched his jacket off the back of his chair and swept out of the room.

Carla waited until he was gone then patted Lau's shoulder. "You okay?"

He laughed, looking shaken. "Sure. I've just never done a raid before. I'm really more of a desk person. I suppose I just imagined Decker would send someone…more qualified."

"It's probably a precaution in case our tips are duds," Carla said. "If anyone outside this group participates in the arrest and the target turns out to be innocent, then the Ashlough Killer would no longer be under wraps."

Lau's smile was strained. "As long as I can get through tonight without being shot, I'll be happy."

Carla understood. She'd spent more time on the streets than Lau had—responding to domestic disputes, making arrests, and breaking up fights—but she'd never expected to arrest a serial killer in her career. Helmer just wasn't the kind of town where those things happened. She'd become aware that a murderer was in their midst and was going to take him down, all within a few days. It was as though she'd become trapped in an unpleasant dream.

She joined her co-workers in donning their rarely used bulletproof vests and strapping on holsters. Other officers stared as they walked through the halls, but no one asked what was happening, as though they could feel the change in the atmosphere and knew better than to get in the way.

Carla took her seat at the conference room's table. With nothing left to do except wait, nerves began to rise. She hadn't felt nervous in years—cranky, resigned, and occasionally alarmed, certainly. But the butterflies were back, beating through her stomach, just like they had during her first day on the job.

Everyone started when Decker shoved the office door open. He very rarely smiled, but now, a vicious grin spread across his face. "We've got our warrant. Let's go nail this bastard."

CHAPTER 55

Monday, 6:30 p.m.

READING THE COMPASS BECAME harder as the sun set. Hailey had thought she would only need to glance at it every ten or twenty minutes, but as she fought her way through the undergrowth, she kept it in her hand and obsessively checked her angle every few seconds.

The forest wanted to throw her off course. Walking in a straight line was impossible, and even when she thought she was, she inevitably became bent to the east or to the west.

She was running low on water. Depending on where she was on the map, she might bump into a stream within the next few hours, or she might need to hike on without a drink for another half day.

Hunger was practically burning a hole in her stomach, and

her limbs were growing shaky. She'd thought she could jog to the forest's exit, but now, after moving for a whole day, she'd crumbled. If she'd been alone in the forest, she would have stopped there and found a place to camp for the night. She hadn't brought a tent, sleeping bag, or food, but she was tired enough to curl up against a tree and sleep for twenty hours. But her friends were relying on her to bring help as quickly as possible. She couldn't let them down, not when failure meant death.

And they weren't the only company she had in Ashlough Forest.

As the daylight faded, messages started appearing on the trees. The text held a luminosity that made it seem to float in the shadows. She'd passed one tree that ominously told her "RUN." Up ahead and to her right was another that said "DEAD." She tried not to read them and kept her head down, following the compass.

Cliffs and slopes that were unscalable kept obstructing her path. Sometimes, she had to walk for half an hour or more before she could find a way around. Her stress grew with every delay.

A patch of dark vines blocked her passage. She hated them; they had hooks that always caught in her clothing and scratched her bare skin. This was a thick clump too. She looked for a way around it. To the right, the vines ended in a sharp slope. Hailey eyed the incline, trying to see if there was a safe way to slide down, but it would carry her a fair way off the path.

She turned and walked in the opposite direction, trying to find an end to the thorny plants. They seemed to go on forever, and the trees grew thicker, creating a natural wall. Eventually, she returned to her starting position, an area that was mostly free from trees but swallowed by a clot of the vines. She could glimpse clear ground on the other side of the tangle, no more than one or two minutes away.

"Damn it." She gripped the straps of her backpack and waded into the tangle. She instantly regretted not getting a branch to beat down the plants. The highest claws scraped over her neck and cheeks, and others plucked at her pant legs and sleeves. She squeezed her eyes closed, holding one hand over her face to protect them, and launched herself forward.

The claws were small but hard, like rose thorns. Their vines looped over each other in an impossible puzzle, and when Hailey tried to snap them, she only succeeded in bruising the green shoots and covering her aching hands in sap and pricks of blood.

Hailey stopped, breathing heavily, and opened her eyes. The patch of weeds stretched farther ahead. She looked over her shoulder but couldn't see her starting point. She tried to take another step. The multitude of hooks held her in place. It had caught her, like a human-sized fly in a gigantic spiderweb.

Panicking, she thrashed, desperate to get out of the snarl, but the harder she fought, the more the thorns dug in. Each inch was a battle. The vines refused to let her go.

She tried to back up, but that only made it worse. The vines cut into her when she pulled against them. She felt surrounded, swallowed by green. Insects crawled off the vines and wormed their way under her sleeves and the collar of her jacket.

Hailey tried to scream. It came out as a terrified yelp. There was no one to hear her. She was sweating and panting, and fear made her irrational. She could see herself in a week's time, whittled down to a skeleton, with her bones still permanently entombed in the mass of grasping vines.

"No, no, no!" She began struggling again. Adrenaline pumped through her, lending her additional strength. The hooks sliced into her hands and her face, but she barely felt them. Something snapped, and she lurched forward an inch. The vines stretched too far ahead of her. She would never have the strength to battle through to the other side. But to her right, they only lasted another couple of feet before the cliff halted their growth. She could make it that far.

Hailey scrambled for freedom. Two vines looped around her throat, and she had to dig her hands under them to keep herself from being strangled. She alternately tried to duck between the vines and climb on top of them, in a crazy, helter-skelter dash.

Then the ground sloped away sharply. She hadn't thought it would be so soon—the vines had blocked the ground from view—and she cried out as she fell. The vines tangled over her went taut. The two around her throat cinched tightly enough to choke her. Hailey struggled, kicking her legs and battering against the plants, then with a snapping, tearing noise, she broke free and plunged down.

Stones dug into her side as she fell, but the drop wasn't as far as she'd thought. She tumbled to a halt in the hollow where a massive tree had once existed. Its roots had rotted out of the ground, leaving an indent in the forest floor. Hailey looked up and saw the vines on top of the hill above her. Their tendrils waved cheerily, almost as though they were beckoning her back in.

Hailey dropped her head back. She was breathless and shaking. Now that the fear was passing, pain made itself felt. A thousand tiny scratches had been scored into every available inch of flesh. Her hands were the worst. She hadn't brought gloves, and now they were a map of red lines.

"Stop it." She didn't want to cry, but she couldn't stop tears from leaking down her cheeks and stinging raw skin. She flexed her hands, and fresh drops of blood beaded in the scores.

Twilight was almost gone. In a moment, Hailey would be stranded with her flashlight in an ocean of black. She wanted to curl up there, in the hollow, and close her eyes. *Things might be better in the morning. People might come, wake me up, and airlift me out.*

"No. No one is coming." Hailey gingerly pushed herself up. She couldn't afford to rest.

The pulse of adrenaline had drained the last of her strength, and Hailey stumbled as she tried to walk through the forest. A drop of blood tickled her skin as it ran down her neck, but she didn't have enough strength to wipe it away.

Up ahead was a tree with a message scrawled across its massive trunk. It was barely visible in the twilight, but she knew, as light faded, it would float out of the darkness like a ghost.

DIE.

CHAPTER 56

Monday, 8:00 p.m.

CARLA RODE SHOTGUN BESIDE Decker in the first police cruiser. Nerves made her jittery. She knew too much fidgeting would irritate the commander, so she tried to expend energy by wiggling her toes in her boots and kept her hands clasped tightly on her knees.

Decker's expression had lost its typical apathy. He reminded her of a wolf on a hunt. Light glittered in his steely eyes, and every angle of his face was sharp. He drove a fraction over the speed limit and took the curves a bit too quickly.

Peterson sat in the seat behind them, gaunt and as silent as a ghost. Quincey and Lau shared the second vehicle, a wagon. Carla watched them through the rear-view mirror.

Gabon, their target, lived outside of town. His rural property backed onto Ashlough Forest. Carla couldn't help but wonder if he had a private path leading into the woods. The forest was a protected area, and damage by civilians could result in prosecution, but that was hard to police when hundreds of properties connected with the forest's edge. It was possible Gabon had been picking off visitors without ever going through the official entrance or following the proper trails.

The sun had set some time before. Now that they'd left the city proper, stars splattered across the sky as though an artist had flicked his paintbrush across the heavens. Carla hadn't appreciated the stars in years, but she couldn't stop herself from watching them now. It was amazing how much more she could appreciate life when faced with possible death. Not that she was in serious danger…but Decker thought there was a good chance Gabon was illegally armed, and the bulletproof vests didn't cover their heads.

"Is this it?" Decker slowed the vehicle to a crawl. A thin trail led off the main road, marked only by a wooden post and a mailbox without a number. Dense plants grew on either side of the road. Carla couldn't see a house.

Peterson leaned forward, and his bony hand squeezed the back of Carla's seat. "I think so. We passed 165 a while back, so this has to be 167."

Decker turned the cruiser down the road, nearly clipping the mailbox. The rural road they'd been following was narrow but smooth. This new road tested the car's shock absorbers and rattled Carla's bones.

"If he's *really* paranoid, he'll have some kind of detection system on the driveway," Decker said. "Cameras or motion sensors. Be prepared that he may know we're coming."

Carla tightened her grip on her knees. The butterflies in her stomach had turned into a riot.

The wagon followed behind them, matching their slow speed. The driveway stretched farther than Carla had anticipated. It bent and twisted multiple times, each turn masking the terrain ahead. Finally, the heavy growths let up and opened into a weedy clearing. Three cars dotted the space, all of them old and eaten by rust and two partially deconstructed. Clumps of wood—old fences and floorboards—were stacked to one side, apparently being dried for a fire. At the back of the clearing, nestled near the forest, was a shack.

The building didn't look large—three or four rooms, maybe—and its roof was made of tin. Newspapers had been plastered over two of the windows and wooden boards over a third, but one was left open. A light shone out of it.

Decker let the car inch forward as he examined the building. Carla watched the lit window, but there was no motion inside. Decker pulled up at the opposite side of the clearing and parked, then he opened his door and stepped into the night.

"Guns at the ready," he whispered as the team assembled around him. "Quincey, Lau, you two loop around the back and check for a rear exit. There's probably going to be one, but knowing this guy, it might be concealed. When you find it, radio through. Delago, Peterson, you two are with me. Once any rear escape is covered, we'll go through the front door and sweep the building."

Carla nodded. She wasn't certain that she could answer without her voice cracking, so she didn't try. She wasn't alone in the nerves, at least. Lau's skin was glossy with sweat. Even Quincey, who looked like more of a bulldog than a human, had lost her perpetual flush. Only Peterson and Decker didn't seem frightened. Peterson never showed any emotion, but Decker looked alive in a way Carla had never seen before.

"Go," he whispered, and Quincey and Lau disappeared toward the building. They moved around opposite sides, both holding their guns at the ready, though Lau's steps were a lot slower and more measured.

Carla watched the lit window. Still no movement. She wondered if Gabon was already aware of their presence. He could have bolted as soon as he saw them coming down the driveway; if he was truly paranoid, he would have had a camping kit prepacked, ready for an extended hideout in the forest. That would be a horrible end to their case. They had enough trouble recovering lost hikers who *wanted* to be found. If Gabon vanished into Ashlough Forest, they might never see him again.

Decker held his walkie-talkie expectantly. Seconds passed. Carla's stress increased exponentially with each heartbeat. She breathed through her mouth, trying to minimize noise as she listened to the environment. Insects whirred in the tall, weed-riddled grass. Two birds chattered angrily as they fought over a nesting spot. No noises came from the building.

Then the walkie-talkie crackled, and Quincey's whisper floated through. "Back exit secured."

"Be ready if he tries to run," Decker whispered back. Then he tucked the black box into his belt and nodded to Carla and Peterson.

They approached the front entrance in an arrow formation, Decker leading the way with Carla to his left. The yard was absolutely saturated with junk hidden among the tall grass, and Carla had to muffle a curse as she tripped over the remains of an old bike. Decker ascended the single step leading to the front door and pressed his ear to the scraps of paint that still clung to the gray wood. After a second, he nodded to them and waited for a nod in return. He tried the handle. It didn't turn. He backed up a step and took a deep breath.

"Police!" Decker's cry boomed through the night air, loud enough to make Carla flinch. It was followed by a crash as his boot connected with the door. The wood, cheap and old, splintered away from the handle. A second kick sent it banging into the shelter's internal wall. Decker flicked his flashlight on and stepped into the room. Carla brought out her own flashlight and held it in her left hand, resting it on top of the hand holding her gun as they swept the space.

A TV in one corner of the main room was turned on but played only static. The gray light flickered across the space, confusing Carla's eyes and highlighting a sagging couch and a small folding table with one seat. A bowl of soup, partially eaten, sat on the table.

Decker motioned for Carla to go left and Peterson to go right while he crossed to the door at the back of the room. Carla tried to swallow, but it caught in her throat. A plain-white door occupied the left wall between two large maps pinned to the plyboards. One map showed the town. One showed Ashlough Forest.

Both of her hands were occupied with the gun and flashlight. Carla lifted her boot and slammed it into the door, forcing it open with a bang. The room inside was dark, its windows covered in boards and newspaper, but her flashlight picked up a metal bed frame and bookcase stacked with odd boxes and handmade trinkets.

"Clear over here!" Peterson yelled from behind her.

Carla opened her mouth, but her voice caught in her throat. A thin man stood in the corner beside the bed. His hands were at his gray, unkempt beard, which trailed down to his collarbones. He was bony, his ribs visible even under the greasy tank top, and his hair was matted. Wild, angry eyes glared at Carla. His lips parted in a grimace, and his hands moved an inch higher.

The bony fingers weren't empty. A pistol was embedded in the snarled beard. The barrel pointed upward, into his chin.

Carla took half a step forward. "No!"

The gunshot deafened her.

Monday, 9:50 p.m.

CHRIS STIRRED OUT OF his doze. Sleep came in fragments, teasing him then darting away. Aching muscles made it difficult to rest properly, no matter how weary he felt. He'd turned on the lamp to light their little clearing, and although it let him see his companions well enough, it also added to the sense of isolation. His ten-foot circle of light was a pitiful refuge in an eternity of darkness.

Flint sat upright with his back against a tree. He'd crossed his arms over his chest, and his expression was cold. He hadn't talked all day except for grunts.

Chris rubbed his eyes as he stretched. "You okay?" he mumbled.

"Anna's not breathing."

Sleepiness fled like a blanket being ripped off him. Chris jolted up and crawled toward the bed where Anna rested. She was gray. He touched her cheek, but she still felt warm.

"Anna?" He gave her a gentle shake. Normally, she stirred when he disturbed her. But now he couldn't get any response.

"Hasn't been breathing for a while," Flint said. He didn't move, not even to turn his head, but his eyes followed Chris. They glittered in the flashlight's beam.

"No." Chris let his hand drop to the side of her neck that wasn't swaddled in bandages. He felt for a pulse then felt again and again, certain that he must be doing it wrong. Anna's muscles felt oddly slack. Chris swallowed, and emotions rose in him like a tidal wave. Before he could stop it, he was crying.

He bent low over Anna. The grief caught him by surprise and overwhelmed him. Until that moment, he'd believed that she was going to be okay. They would get her out of the forest and into a hospital. Blood transfusions would fix her color. Surgery would repair the tear in her neck. That had been their goal, their reason to fight. Get out of the forest alive. Save Anna.

She'd put up with more than she should have, following him miles farther than she'd wanted to because she'd cared about him enough that she'd wanted to keep him safe. She'd never even expected to find Eileen alive. At least there, she'd been more practical than Chris. She'd only come to help him. To support him. And his blockheaded stubbornness had killed her.

Chris beat his fist against his forehead. He'd never hated himself before. But it was hard to be at peace with his own existence when he'd snuffed out Anna's. She would never get her degree or open a clinic like she'd wanted. Her parents would have to bury their baby.

He couldn't bear it.

Chris cried until his throat was raw and his eyes burned. Every time he thought he was done, the misery returned, deeper and harsher, drowning him. It took a long time for the noise to fade. Then he curled up in a ball by Anna's side as he tried to stop shaking.

Flint remained deathly silent. When Chris finally dared to meet his eyes, they weren't friendly. Chris turned away again.

A fly buzzed down to land on Anna's cheek, and Chris, revolted, brushed it away. It was a warning of things to come, though. He hadn't forgotten Todd, riddled with maggots within a day, slowly liquefying as they watched.

He didn't want that to happen to Anna. The crazy part of his mind said it wouldn't, as long as they kept her close by and looked after her. She would be fine then, bundled up and perfectly protected until rescue came. She would look like she was just having a nap. They could have a proper, open-casket funeral.

But he knew that wouldn't work. Not unless rescue came very, very quickly. Either they would need to move Anna, or they themselves would need to find a new camp.

"How's your head?" Chris asked, his voice croaky and raw.

Flint's reply held no hint of emotion. "Fine."

"Do you…do you think you could walk? We could start following the red string. Meet Hailey halfway."

No response. Chris glanced at his friend. Flint's expression was hard and cold, like it had been carved out of stone. There was something wild in his eyes, though. An emotion that Chris couldn't pinpoint.

"Flint?"

"Of course I can walk."

"Oh…oh, okay. Good. It'd probably be a good idea to make a plan. D'you want to rest a bit longer, or…?"

Flint was already rising. He moved in twitches, and color drained from his face as he stood. His muscles must have been aching, Chris guessed. His own still weren't happy, even after a full day of rest. He started to throw their water bottles back into the backpack but stopped as Flint collapsed.

"Hey," he said, crossing to Flint's side. "Are you—"

"Get *off* me." Flint swung a fist at him and narrowly missed Chris's chin.

Chris backed off, hands held up, as Flint struggled to get his feet back under himself.

This was something more than a cracked skull or concussion. Flint seemed okay until he tried to put weight on his feet, then his whole face tightened. A vein popped out in his neck, and perspiration built on his forehead. He was in pain, Chris realized too late. He moved closer again, more slowly, wary of his friend's new aggressive streak. "Hey, sit down a minute. I want to have a look at your feet."

"I can stand," Flint spat between gritted teeth.

"I know! Of course you can! I just—we need to check your shoes." He felt like he was talking to a child, mixing lies into a sugar-sweet voice to talk them off a ledge. "It'll just take a second."

Flint's eyes didn't soften, but he slowly lowered himself back to the forest floor. Chris, painfully aware that he was within striking distance, bent at Flint's feet and began untying one of the hiking shoes. As he moved, the end of Flint's pants flicked up, and he caught a glimpse of red skin.

A horrible sense of foreboding rose through Chris. He gently, carefully rolled up the pants and pressed his fist to his mouth. "Hell. Flint. I…" He looked up, but Flint's expression showed no softness. "How long have they been like this?"

"I'm fine. I can walk."

Chris's hand trembled as it hovered over the red skin, oozing and slowly rotting. There was no way Flint could walk out of the forest. Chris doubted his friend could walk more than a pace. The injuries must have been festering for days, probably since the ant bites. Infection had gotten into them, and without treatment, the skin was literally decaying off the bones.

"I…I'm sure there's something in the first aid kit…" Chris scrambled toward the pile of equipment near the lamp and riffled through it to find the white box. "I'm not good at this stuff like Anna, but we can use the disinfectant and painkillers, at least. And there's a booklet here that might help…"

He turned back to Flint but froze. Metal glinted at Flint's side. He'd drawn his knife and clutched it in a white-knuckled fist by his thigh.

Flint had always been a little intense. Anger, loyalty, love—he seemed to feel every emotion deeply. The intensity had swung too far, carrying him toward madness.

Chris swallowed and put the box aside. "It's okay. We can worry about that later. Right now...right now, I think the best thing would be to sit a while. It wouldn't be smart to move when Hailey's sending people to look for us. So we'll stay here. Okay?"

He hadn't been expecting an answer, and he didn't get one. Chris's attention kept skipping from the patch of oozing skin visible under Flint's pant leg to the knife to Flint's stony face. Something about the expression told him Flint wouldn't let him close to the wounds again, so he sat back against his own tree.

It was nearing midnight. He was tired, the grief over Anna having wrung him empty, but he didn't know if he would be safe if he tried to sleep. Flint hadn't raised the knife, but his fist was still tight on its handle.

They were stuck in a stalemate, separated by the lamp and the corpse.

CHAPTER 58

HAILEY LET HERSELF WHIMPER. It didn't matter if she sounded pathetic; there was no one around to hear, so she let herself whine and cry as much as she wanted, just as long as she kept moving.

She felt sick from tiredness. The scratches continued to burn, even though she'd left the thicket behind hours before. Her neck was stiff in the kind of way that told her a migraine wasn't far off. When she moved her limbs, the dried blood crackled and itched. She'd wanted to wash the cuts, but she couldn't spare the water. She was down to her last half bottle.

That wasn't the only resource she was low on. She'd changed the flashlight's batteries when the bulb dimmed too far, and she was on her last set. Once they ran out, she would be blind. She just had to find the forest's end before that happened.

The longer she walked, the more her doubt grew. She was following southeast on the compass religiously, but everything around her looked identical to the path behind. For a few hours, she'd tried to keep her energy up by imagining that the trees would end soon. *Just over the next hill...or the hill after that...or the one after that...*

It had worked at first, helping her move faster as eagerness drove her, but soon, it had become an exercise in disappointment.

Over the last hour, a bleak idea had started to form. She knew it was irrational, but the longer she walked, the more she began to feel as though she might never escape the forest. The nature reserve had grown while she was inside it, she thought. The edge kept spreading outward, swallowing up the town and then the entire country. She could walk a lifetime and never escape it.

An angry laugh escaped her. It was a nice change from the whimpers, but even despite the exhaustion, she recognized it as sounding hysterical. She needed to stop soon. Even though her friends were relying on her, she needed a rest, or she would go insane.

Soon, she told herself. *Just a few more minutes. A few more steps. Maybe once you get over the next hill you'll be able to see the forest's edge.*

The ominous messages floated about her, painted in thick, glowing strokes. She'd stopped trying to read them. Sometimes, she only saw a few letters at a time as other trees covered part of the word. Sometimes, she thought the floating messages might exist entirely in her mind.

Occasionally, she thought she heard leaves crackling behind her or the sharp snap of a breaking branch. She kept her eyes ahead. If she was being followed, knowing how close her stalker was wouldn't help her. She was worn down and had nothing but a knife strapped to her side. The monster had claws made of metal. There would be no contest. The best she could do was keep moving southeast and hope she found the forest's edge before her pursuer caught up to her.

If the forest's edge still exists.

Another gasping, miserable laugh hurt her raw throat. She wanted Flint with her. She wanted to hug her father. She was starving for human contact. A kind word…no, even an angry word would be a relief. The forest, simultaneously so quiet and so loud, was driving her insane.

She stumbled down an incline her flashlight had failed to pick out of the gloom. The soles of her feet ached from the sudden extra pressure, and she clenched her teeth. When she lifted her light, her breath caught.

The land ahead seemed different from the ground she'd passed through. For the first time in what felt like days, she was being shown a variation in the endless, repeating pattern of trunks, leaves, and vines.

Hailey's pace picked up. Finally, she'd found the forest's edge. She could see where the trees ended. She could see bare ground. There was wood in the distance, but it wasn't in vertical lines. It was horizontal. Planks. A house.

"Hello!" The word was a rasp. She moved faster, shoving her way through the final vines blocking her access. "Help! Hello!"

The trees disappeared, and she was standing on clear ground.

She looked up and saw the stars above her. They were unspeakably beautiful.

When she looked back down, her thumping, leaping heart fell. She wasn't at the edge of the forest. She was in a clearing.

A single house stood among the trees. Its walls were made of rough-hewn logs. Its windows were covered with shutters, not glass. An ax was embedded in a log near the front door.

Hailey clutched her hands to her neck. Dried blood flaked off under her fingers. Something was very wrong with the scene. As her flashlight's beam jittered over the clearing, she searched for a car but couldn't see one. She looked for power cables. She looked for a fence, a letterbox, or a road. None were present. It was a house, yes, but a house without any signs of civilization.

She'd walked through kilometers of the ominous floating words. Claw marks marred the trees ringing the clearing, sometimes two or three on each tree. She turned off her flashlight. Her legs had lost their strength, and she sank to the ground, coiling into the smallest shape she could make.

Somehow, she'd stumbled into the monster's lair. There was no other explanation for the building. Her eyes were drawn to the sheen of metal. Moonlight, no longer suffocated by the canopy, reflected off the wickedly sharp ax near the front door.

If the monster was inside and had seen her light, she wouldn't be able to run fast enough to escape. Even if her muscles hadn't been worn down and her feet weren't screaming, she doubted she could outpace it. She could only pray her presence hadn't been detected.

She didn't think it was asleep. It was a nocturnal creature. So then, it was either awake inside the house…or out stalking prey.

Minutes passed. Goose bumps grew over Hailey's skin as she began to feel the cold. She kept her eyes moving between the shuttered windows and the door but saw no sign of motion. At last, she couldn't stand the wait any longer and turned on her flashlight again.

The house was small, probably a single room, and looked as though it had been built by hand. Even the shingles on the roof had a rustic feel, as though they'd been baked in a homemade furnace. There was no sign of a garden, which didn't surprise Hailey. She was fairly certain the monster was carnivorous.

Hailey rose from the forest floor, moving slowly and watching the shack's door. She circled the building, searching for any signs of life. No smoke came from the chimney at the back of the cottage. Behind the building, a small trail led into the forest, but it was too narrow for a car and looked rough, like it wasn't used often. The house had only three windows, all of them closed.

She completed the circle of the building and found herself facing the front door again. Her heart wanted her to take the path and hope it led back to town. But she couldn't. Not yet.

Hailey crept up to the nearest window. It had been built high, and she had to rise onto her toes to see through the cracks in the shutter. There was no light source inside the building, and she couldn't see anything. She pressed her ear against the wood and held the pose as long as her feet could stand. There were no noises…that she could detect, at least.

She stepped back and approached the door. Like the walls, it was made of slabs of hand-sawed wood held together with loops of what might have been vines or old rope. The door wasn't locked, just shut with a simple latch. She lifted it and held her breath as the door drifted inward.

CHAPTER 59

CARLA'S MOUTH OPENED, BUT she didn't think she was making any noise. Her heart hammered loudly enough to echo in the shack's stuffy bedroom. There was no threat, not anymore, but she still held up both hands, the gun and the flashlight shaking uncontrollably.

Gabon slumped against the bedroom wall. His gun had dropped from his hand and slid across the dirty wood. His open eyes stared at Carla, even though the insides of his head were painted across the plyboards.

"Move," Decker barked, shoving Carla aside. She hit the wall and finally lowered her gun. Decker stepped past her but didn't go far. There was no rush anymore, even though everyone seemed to be moving with a frantic energy. Footsteps thundered through the building, and soon Peterson and Quincey were cramming themselves into the cramped room too. With the bed taking up most of the space and Gabon's body filling one of the remaining corners, there was barely enough room for the four of them to breathe.

Carla backed away slowly and bumped into Lau just outside the doorway. Even in the poor light, she could see he was sheet white.

He squeezed Carla's arm. "Better put that away now," he whispered.

It took a second for Carla to realize what he was talking about. Then she swallowed, nodded, and tucked the gun into her holster. "Wasn't me. He shot himself."

"Decker thought he might be armed."

Loud voices came from the bedroom, but they were so jumbled that Carla couldn't make out the words. Quincey retreated first, wiping her sleeve over her forehead, then Peterson stalked out, resembling a ghoul even more than he normally did. When Decker followed, he was already barking directions into his walkie-talkie.

Carla felt numb. It wasn't her first time seeing the results of violent death, but it was her first time being in the room when it happened. Gabon had been looking right at her when he pulled the trigger. It had been over so fast, she hadn't even seen the shock waves move through his face. One second, he was a human. The next, his expression had fallen slack, and there were gray and red *lumps* splattered across the wall behind him. She'd watched him drop, though, crumpling down like an accordion. His legs had gone first and left him propped in an unnatural sitting position, like a doll that had been carelessly discarded.

She could feel shock creeping over her. She slipped away from Lau's hand and stumbled outside. There were plenty of things to sit on in the yard, but they were all rusted, so she lowered herself onto the shack's step. The voices continued behind her as Decker sent instructions to the station, and Peterson and Quincey became locked in a debate. Then someone turned on the main room's light. It flowed through the open door and around Carla, spreading across the long weeds and twisted metals ahead of her.

The voices gradually softened into murmurs. Carla didn't know why, but people always seemed to talk quietly when there was death about. She tried to tell herself that Gabon didn't deserve that kind of reverence, but meeting him, however briefly, had pulled the conviction out from behind her righteous anger.

He'd been smaller than she'd expected—weedy, almost sickly. And there had been fear in his eyes. He wasn't the evil bogeyman she'd been building up in her mind. He wasn't some lecherous monster who would laugh in her face and gloat over his victims.

In that second before he'd pulled the trigger, she'd felt like she was looking at a child. Lost, confused, and scared. Based on his appearance and the condition of his house, she suspected some kind of mental illness had been at play. It didn't excuse his crimes. They were still heinous, no matter who the perpetrator was. But it did make it hard not to feel a small kernel of pity for a man whose life had probably been twisted by demons outside of his control.

The step creaked as weight was applied to it, then Decker sighed as he sat down at Carla's side. "You okay, Delago?"

Her mouth was dry. "Sure."

"Not going to be sick on me, are you? Because this whole area is a crime scene. If you're going to throw up, try to do it in the woods."

She managed a shaky smile. "I think I'm good."

He took a deep breath then let it out slowly. "I think we've confirmed that he's the killer. We found a note in the kitchen. It's a list of names. About sixty of them, lots that are familiar. Eileen Hershberger is the most recent."

Carla closed her eyes. She was grateful. After seeing Gabon face-to-face, after seeing how frightened he looked, she'd been afraid that they might have zeroed in on the wrong man. But at least now, they could have closure. The deaths would be over.

"Not ideal that he killed himself," Decker mumbled. "But maybe it's for the best. No long court proceedings. No slimy lawyers trying to get him off on technicalities. The families can have the closure they deserve."

"Maybe you're right," Carla murmured. "But…I wish we knew his *why*."

Decker lifted his eyebrows, and Carla shrugged.

"Why he did it. What compelled him. Schizophrenia? Paranoia? Hatred of humanity? It's hard to understand how someone could kill so often…so consistently…across so many years."

"Sometimes there's no answer." Decker laced his hands over one knee and stared at his fingers. "Before I transferred here, back when I worked in the city, I had to bring down a couple of serial killers. They confessed to their crimes. Weren't ashamed of them. But when we asked them why, they didn't have an answer. Not because they were trying to be difficult, but because they genuinely didn't know."

Carla chuckled. "That's a tough pill to swallow, isn't it? Some people are killers, and that's just the way it is."

"It certainly didn't help me sleep at night."

Carla glanced up at her commander. Decker had never been so candid with her before. While he'd been on the hunt, his whole focus was absorbed in bringing down the killer. But now, with Gabon dead, all of that energy had bled out of him. He looked older. Tireder. And for the first time since she'd known him, his sharp tongue wasn't biting. His walls weren't up.

"Can we send out the helicopter now?" Carla asked.

Decker actually smiled. "I knew you'd be on me about that. I already radioed it through to the station. It's too dark to do any good tonight, but it'll be prepped to start the search at the first light of dawn. We're also launching additional search parties. If those kids are still out there, we'll find them."

"Thank you, sir."

"You did a good job with this, Delago. I honestly thought you'd gone loopy when you first came to me. But you'd caught on to clues that everyone else in my station missed, and your intuition was solid. I'll be chasing a promotion for you."

"Oh." Carla didn't know what to say. She'd only dug deeper because of Chris Hershberger's belief. And even then, she'd been horribly close to ignoring the photos. If anything, she deserved to be demoted for negligence.

"Or I could arrange for a transfer to a different station," Decker said. He was watching her out of the corners of his eyes. "Sometimes, when our lives go off the rails, the best thing we can do is to shake free of the past and find a fresh start."

She thought of Matt, growing increasingly impatient that she hadn't found an apartment. She thought of the beautifully decorated room at the end of the hallway, with the crib that would never hold a baby. She'd been loath to let them go. The more they slipped away from her, the harder she'd tried to cling to them. They'd been the last scraps of meaning in her life.

That had been before. Something had changed over the last few days. The butterflies. The fire in her stomach. The sense of purpose and conviction she hadn't felt in years.

"Yes," she said, so quietly that she wasn't sure Decker could hear her. "I think I'd like that."

Someone yelled from behind the shack. Both she and Decker twisted, but from their angle, they couldn't see anything. Then the walkie-talkie came to life, and Quincey's snapping voice crackled through.

"Sir. Get over here. We found something."

Decker's familiar scowl slid back into place. He groaned as he pushed off the step. "She found something, did she? Couldn't wait for the bloody backup. Damn idiot's gotta play Nancy Drew, probably screwed up the crime scene..."

Carla smiled then stood to follow Decker. Quincey and Peterson were no longer in the house, so they circled the building until they found the two officers in the strip of ground at the back. It was a narrow passage, no more than ten meters wide, between the house and the forest's edge. Quincey dragged a bundle of cloth out into the open.

"When we were securing the back door, I thought I saw something strange in the forest," she said. "Lookit this."

The bundle flopped open, and Carla squinted as she tried to understand what she was staring at. "It's a..."

"Costume," Decker whispered.

Carla blinked, and the medley of shapes and colors became clear. It was some kind of long cloak, so long that it would trail on the ground if she tried to wear it. Strips of fabric had been sewn over it. From a distance, they might have looked like fur. The cloak had a hood decorated in the same way, and secured inside the hood was a homemade wooden mask.

She ran her hand over her face. "The monster from the photographs. He must have been dressing up whenever he went into the forest, just in case anyone saw him or photographed him."

Decker growled. "Smart bastard."

"These were beside the costume." Peterson stepped forward and dropped two boots on the ground beside the cloak. Leather and sturdy, they had immensely thick soles. Carla thought they would have added at least five inches to his height. "He wanted to look more intimidating..."

Quincey picked up the cloak and shook it out. Carla tried to visualize how it might look, if she found herself lost late at night in the forest. The jacket was oversized, and the fabric strips would add to its bulk. The mask, barely visible under the hood, would look monstrous. And the boots would have made him appear unnaturally tall. If she'd been alone with Gabon in his costume, she would probably have panicked too. The mask was likely the last thing most of his victims saw. She reached for the jacket's sleeve and felt the rough fabric sewn over it.

Then Decker's barking voice made them all flinch. "Stop rubbing your filthy paws all over the evidence. At least have the brains to put on some gloves, damn you."

CHAPTER 60

Monday, 11:00 p.m.

HAILEY PANNED HER FLASHLIGHT across the cabin's insides. Like she'd suspected, it was an open-plan room. Most of the furniture looked handmade or constructed with bits and pieces of broken fittings. Nothing looked new, and nothing looked factory made.

There were no light fixtures, but a kerosene lamp rested on the square wood table in the middle of the floor. Hailey waited a moment to make sure she was alone, then she crossed to the table, set her flashlight upright so that its light diffused over the ceiling, and shook a match out of the box beside the lamp.

The glass-and-metal tube was still full of fuel and lit easily. Its light spread better than her flashlight's, and she had her first clear look at the space.

A bed stood against the back wall. It didn't have blankets,

but a sleeping bag had been draped over the foam mattress. A counter ran along the wall to Hailey's left and included a sink but, strangely, no taps. Four large plastic jugs of water stood beside it. Hailey went to the counter and opened the cupboard below the sink. The basin's pipe ended above a metal bucket. Whoever lived there had to throw the water outside by hand after washing up. The space held buckets and a bottle of bleach. Cloths, most of them closer to rags, hung on hooks beneath the sink. There were a lot of them, and they were all lined up in perfectly straight lines.

Hailey stepped back and looked around the room. Everything was like the cloths: old but arranged carefully, well worn but not grimy. The dust was minimal. The floor was swept. She frowned. It was hard to reconcile the impeccable shack with the barbaric creature she'd seen following her.

A dark shape stood by the door. Hailey squinted at it. Fur ruffled as a breeze came through the open door, and Hailey screamed, lunging backward. Nestled in the shadows, hidden in the corner behind the door, stood the monster.

Its pale face stared at her, its teeth bared in a snarl. Its arms hung at its sides. It stood perfectly still, black eyes unblinking.

Hailey tasted blood as she bit her tongue. She scrambled for a weapon, her hands grasping for anything heavy or sharp that might, at the very least, make the monster wary of her. The counter held nothing of substance, but she knocked over a jar and a small pot in her frenzy. She belatedly remembered the knife strapped to her waist and yanked it out so fiercely that the strap bit into her hip, then she turned back to the monster.

It continued to stare at her, unmoving. Its eyes looked cold and dead. Its jaws, parted in that horrible snarl, didn't even quiver.

Hailey slowly lowered the knife. The monster looked different from the one she'd seen in the forest. It was just as tall but thinner, almost as though it had been deflated. The longer she stared at it, the more convinced she became that it wasn't alive.

Her legs shook as she crept around the table. The monster was motionless, but she still couldn't escape the fear that it was waiting for her to get close enough to lunge. She got within four feet of it, knife still held out protectively, then with a burst of courage, Hailey darted forward. The blade pushed through the fur. There was nothing for it to sink into, until it hit the wall behind the monster with a dull thud.

Hailey stepped back. She pressed her hand to her chest as she choked out a laugh. Even though she knew it was harmless, the monster still looked too real—too terrifying—for her to turn her back to it.

She tucked the knife back into her sheath and steeled herself to touch the fur. It was thick and shaggy, and the hair felt slightly greasy. She gave it a yank, and the figure rippled under her touch.

It was a costume. When she moved it, she saw it was hanging from a hook on the wall. The arms ended in open sleeves. The base, which trailed on the ground, was hollow.

Hailey craned her neck to see the head more clearly. She was looking at a mask. It was well made, though, realistic enough to look convincing when blended with the costume. She tapped a fingernail against the flat black eyeholes. It felt like glass.

It took her a moment to realize she was looking at night-vision goggles. Hailey pressed her hand to her forehead and moaned. It was no wonder the creature had been able to follow her without a light of its own. Its glowing green eyes had given it a deadly advantage. And that explained why it had hidden when she'd turned her flashlight on it too. The beam must have blinded it.

Hailey swore under her breath then began laughing. She didn't know why. She wasn't feeling happy, and the situation was a long way from being funny. All she felt was shock, shame, and a lot of anger. The emotions hit her at the same time, and they were too much to hold inside, so they burst out as miserable, howling laughter.

She punched the costume then punched it again for good measure. She was too tired. It was hard to think. She was aware that every minute she spent in the cabin multiplied her risk of encountering the monster in its lair, but she also couldn't waste the opportunity. She'd discovered the magician's backstage room. She had access to all of his tricks. She couldn't just leave, not when it might mean the difference between life and death for her friends.

The discovery gave her one good, strong piece of knowledge. She was no longer fighting a monster. She was fighting a man. If he was human, he could bleed. And if he could bleed, he could die.

But she needed to level the playing field. The monster she'd seen in the forest had steel-like claws. The costume's sleeves were empty. The cottage was small, though, and it didn't take much searching to find the weapons. A large wardrobe stood next to where the costume was hung, and when Hailey opened the doors, she found massive blades—two feet long, at least—suspended from hooks inside. They had straps at their hilts so that the wearer could fasten them to his arms. She pulled them down and grimaced as she staggered under the weight.

She carried the blades through the open door and dragged them into the forest. If the monster didn't have his weapons, he wouldn't be half as much of a threat. They were heavy and kept catching on roots and in bushes, but she carried them as far as she could manage. Then she dropped them into a hollow and covered them with dead grass and leaves. The stranger might eventually find them, but it would take him a lot of searching.

Hailey returned to the cabin and approached the costume. The stranger's second advantage was his ability to see in the dark. She tried to wrestle the goggles out of the hood, but they had been attached firmly. Muttering swear words under her breath, Hailey punched at the glass. It achieved nothing except to bruise her knuckles. She pulled her knife out of its holder and prepared to cut into the costume but then froze.

A noise disturbed the still night air. It blended into the drone of the insects but had a mechanical, man-made undercurrent. Hailey's heart missed a beat. The noise was growing nearer. As its volume increased, she recognized it. Flint owned a motorbike that sounded almost exactly like it.

Hailey took one step toward the door then swore and turned back. The lamp was still on. Even with shutters over the windows, the glow would stand out like a beacon in the dark night. She scrambled for the light and blew out the flame. The engine was growing closer. She snatched up the flashlight and mashed the power button. Finally, darkness enveloped her.

She clenched her teeth and prayed she'd been fast enough and that the trees had been thick enough to hide the light. If the stranger had seen it, he would search for her. Her best chance—really, her only chance—was to slip away unnoticed.

She stumbled as she felt her way toward the open door. Moonlight helped guide her. She made it as far as the threshold then pressed herself back against the doorframe.

Headlights flashed between the trees. They were moving toward her. In a second, they would turn around the final bank of trees and light the clearing.

Time seemed to freeze. Her mind raced through a dozen different scenarios. She could run for the forest's edge. It was twenty meters away, and in another couple of seconds, the headlights would be cutting across that ground. She might be able to make it…but it would be close.

Or she could try to scurry around the cottage's corner. It was nearer and would hide her from the driver's sight but still left her out in the open. The stranger would only need to drive around the building to park, and he would be looking right at her.

If the cottage had a back exit, she could slip out that way. It would give her an uninterrupted run to the forest's edge and buy her the precious seconds she needed to hide herself. She twisted to look over her shoulder, desperately hoping to see a door in the back wall.

There wasn't one. That second-long glance cost her dearly. The lights flashed out from behind the trees and arced toward the cottage's door. Out of options, she lunged back and slammed the door behind herself. A heartbeat later, light glinted between the door's hinges as the headlights flooded over it.

She was trapped.

CHAPTER 61

Tuesday, 6:25 a.m.

FLINT HATED THE MAN opposite him. He'd thought he hated plenty of people before. The guys who had tried to hit on Hailey. The police who took his friends in for drunk driving. The middle school teacher who had failed him when he talked back.

But they had all been nothing. Strong dislike, at best. This… this was true hatred.

Chris matched his stare. He sat with his back pressed to a tree on the other side of the lamp. His eyes were sunken and ringed in black shadows like bruises. He looked tired. He would have to fall asleep eventually. And Flint would be ready when that happened. He rubbed his thumb over the wood on his knife's handle.

Flint had thought he knew his friend. If someone had asked

him about Chris before the trip, Flint would have said he and Chris were like brothers.

But he'd been manipulated. Chris was pure evil. He saw that now. Saw it so clearly, he couldn't believe he hadn't seen it before.

Anna lay to his right. She'd been dead for less than six hours, and flies were already gathering around her. Chris had pretended to care. He'd tried to make a show of shooing away the flies, but that had only lasted for a few minutes. Now, he let the flies consume her. Just like he'd let her die.

No…he hadn't let her die. That made it sound like it wasn't his fault. He'd killed her. He was killing them all, one by one. Smiling to their faces and digging knives into their backs when they weren't looking. He'd killed Todd first. Probably sent him into the forest alone then led the rest of them in so that they could find his body. Chris had been so eager to carry Todd's corpse around with them, like some kind of trophy.

Then he'd killed Anna. He'd tried to say a knife had fallen out of a tree, but he'd been the only one to see that happen. Probably, he'd waited until Flint was distracted then stabbed Anna himself. He'd convinced them it was an accident. Flint only had himself to blame for believing that.

Then he'd tried to kill Flint by luring him into the forest and tricking him into falling over the cliff. Flint had spent the whole trip believing in a monster, but there wasn't a monster. Not a real monster. Just a human. A sick, twisted human who had made a game out of murdering his friends.

Flint hated himself for not realizing it sooner. If he had, he might have been able to save Hailey. Chris claimed she'd gone off to find help, but Flint knew better. Chris had done her in. His beautiful, sweet little Hailey. Murdered by a man he trusted. Whenever he thought about it, he became so angry that all he could see was red. He couldn't give in to his rage, though. Not yet. His legs were bad. He had to wait until Chris couldn't run away. Flint had to wait until he fell asleep.

Now that he thought about it, the sick bastard had probably even killed his own sister. Their whole reason for being in the forest must have been a setup.

Had he, though? Flint blinked. He thought Chris had been in a wholly different state when Eileen went missing. Had they traveled to Helmer before or after she stopped calling home?

It was getting harder to remember what had happened. Events were starting to run together in an unending loop. Holding on to reality was like trying to grasp water. But it didn't matter if he went insane, just as long as he held on to that one kernel of truth: Chris had killed his friends.

Flint didn't think he was getting out of the forest. He couldn't walk, and even if some miracle saved his legs, he didn't know the way to the exit. That was fine. He was resigned to dying. But he didn't want to go before he got revenge. He wanted to dig his knife into Chris's throat and listen to his gurgle as he drowned in his own blood. For Hailey. For Anna. For Eileen. And even for Todd, the little weirdo.

Chris refused to close his eyes. He'd probably had the same

idea. He was waiting for Flint to sleep, so that he could finish him off. *Well, let him try.*

Flint had endurance. And he had anger fueling him. If it came to a battle of who could stay awake longer, Flint would win. He would make sure of it.

The flies hummed. One flew past Flint's cheek, but he didn't try to swat it. His energy was low. He had to conserve it as much as he could. He was thirsty and had been for a long time, but he couldn't reach the water without exposing his back to Chris.

But Chris was flagging. His eyes were starting to droop. Flint silently urged them to drop lower, to give in completely, but every time they nearly shut, they fluttered open again. Chris rolled his shoulders and shuffled a little farther up the tree, apparently realizing that he'd been slipping down.

That's fine. I'll be patient. He won't last much longer.

The buzzing noise seemed to be growing louder. And it wasn't all coming from Anna anymore. Flint blinked. The sound seemed to be above them. He wanted to look up, to see if he could spot any bees in the branches above them, but he didn't want to look away from Chris. Any sign of weakness would be a mistake, he was certain.

Chris broke eye contact first and tilted his head back. He frowned, then his eyes widened. He yelled something Flint didn't understand and lurched to his feet.

Flint snarled and lifted his knife, but Chris wasn't moving toward him. Instead, the man was waving his arms above his head, chin tilted back to face the canopy. Flint couldn't understand.

Chris had gone mad. He pulled his aching legs a little closer to himself, wary.

"Here, down here!" Chris screamed. He looked at Flint, and a wide smile restored some life to his sallow face. "It's a plane! Hailey sent a plane!"

"Hailey..." Flint swallowed and clamped his lips together. Chris was trying to distract him, to make him drop his guard. The bastard was actually using his dead girlfriend to manipulate his emotions. *Well, it isn't going to work.*

Chris was facing the sky again, waving his arms and staggering in a semicircle. His grin began to fade. The buzzing noise was growing fainter. "Here...We're here..."

He was moving closer. Facing away from Flint but taking slow steps back, he'd circled around the lamp and stood in Flint's section of the clearing. That was a mistake. His legs were nearly within striking distance.

"They can't see us," Chris babbled. He ran his hands through his hair as he shook his head. "The trees are too thick... How are they going to see us?"

He was committed to the part. But in his efforts to be distracting, Chris had compromised himself. He took another half step backward, putting his left leg beside Flint's tree. Flint let a small, vicious smile grow. He lifted the knife.

"How are they going to see us?" Chris asked.

Flint lunged.

CHAPTER 62

HAILEY PANTED, AND SHE couldn't stop. She was suffocating in the small room. She'd been too frightened to run for the forest's edge, and that fear had damned her. In a moment, the cottage door would open, and she would have to engage in a fight for her life.

The element of surprise was in her favor. As long as the stranger hadn't spotted her when she darted back inside, he wouldn't know she was there. She pulled out her knife and clutched it tightly. She should be able to get in one good jab, maybe even two, before he realized what was happening. She had to make them count. She was going to have to kill.

The quickest way to kill was to get the blade into his brain, but that wouldn't be an easy task. She would need to stab through the eye—a small target—or up under his chin. That would need just the right angle to work. And she couldn't get that angle unless she was right up against him, virtually standing on his toes.

The heart would be the next most effective target, but she knew enough about anatomy to understand how tough that mark was. If she could slot the knife between the ribs and push hard enough to get through the cartilage, she could pierce the heart. He would bleed out in seconds. But that was a gamble, at best. If the knife hit a rib, it would hurt, but the wound wouldn't be fatal. At least, not quickly.

That meant the neck was her best target. She would have to aim for the side, between his ear and his chin, where his jugular vein ran up to supply his brain. It wouldn't be an instant death. But as long as she did better than nick it, and as long as he didn't get medical treatment, he would bleed out in two or three minutes, tops.

That was two minutes when he could still be active and aggressive. Two minutes was plenty of time to hurt her, maybe even kill her. She just had to hope the element of surprise—and the element of pain—would keep him distracted long enough for her to elude him. Best-case scenario, she could deliver the crippling blow, dive around him, and race for the forest. Then all she needed to do was keep running for two minutes. She could do that.

The motor's roar slowed to a purr as it coasted around the cabin's corner. Hailey lowered the knife and glanced to the side. There was another option. She could hide. The sink had a row of cabinets under it. She crossed the room in two long steps and wrenched open the doors. Inside was a large bottle of bleach and a bucket filled with plastic gloves, scrubbing brushes, and washcloths.

The engine cut out and was replaced by the softer, more patient chant of insects. Hailey looked back at the front door. She only had seconds to choose between fighting and hiding. They were both gambles. If she fought, she was betting on being able to cut his throat—and cut it correctly—before he disarmed or injured her. Then she had to avoid him until he collapsed from blood loss.

If she hid, she was gambling on the idea that he wouldn't look in the cupboard. If he opened the wardrobe where the claws had been stored, he would know someone had been in his home. But he wouldn't know when. With luck, he would think the invasion had occurred hours before. He might even leave to look for the intruder in the forest.

And if he didn't leave…the bed in the corner proved that he slept in the cabin. She just had to wait a few hours until he was unconscious, then she could slit his throat. No gamble necessary.

She dropped to the floor and crawled into the cupboard. It was cramped, but if she kicked the bucket under the plumbing, she fit. Hailey pulled the cupboard door closed then bit her tongue as she heard the cabin's front latch rattle.

The cupboard was homemade, like a lot of the furniture in the cabin. Its door wasn't a perfect fit. A half-inch gap existed around its edge, and when Hailey leaned forward, she could see the cabin's front door opening.

A tall, bulky shape stepped through. She tried to glimpse the stranger's face, but it was above her line of vision. He dropped a large backpack on the floor just inside the cottage. Then he crossed the room, walking straight toward Hailey.

Panic choked her. She shrank back, pressing her shoulder into the cupboard's back wall, and held the knife ahead of herself.

She was a sitting duck inside the cramped space. If he opened the doors, she had one chance to do some damage. Crouching put his throat well out of reach. But his hamstrings were close by. Cutting one wouldn't kill him, but it would sure slow him down, maybe enough that she could get around him before he grabbed her and smashed her skull.

His feet stopped right outside her hidey-hole. She could see denim muted in the moonlight. That would be tough to cut through. But she had to try. Her heart threatened to choke her as she held her knife at the ready.

He didn't open the cupboard door. Instead, something heavy and wooden clattered above her. *The shutters,* she realized.

He was drawing back the wooden boards over the windows to let in more light. His legs shifted as he moved something over the counter, making a scraping noise. Then a sloshing noise. The whine of a bottle cap being screwed back on.

Then he stepped away, and Hailey finally managed to take a thin breath. He'd been getting a drink. That was all. The drive into the forest must have taken a couple of hours, and he'd been thirsty.

She bent forward again to see through the door's gap. The stranger stood by the table with his back to her. He wore a simple gray T-shirt, but the fabric didn't do much to hide the muscles underneath. The stranger was tall, broad-shouldered, and weighed easily three times as much as Hailey. Probably even more than Flint. Her chances in a fair hand-to-hand fight would be as good as nonexistent.

He smacked something onto the table. Hailey squinted. It looked like a water bottle, but not one that contained liquid. It held something white. A piece of paper, she thought. Someone had scribbled a word onto the paper. From her angle, she could see an *S* but nothing more.

The stranger reached for the box of matches next to the lamp. He struck one then opened the glass door to light the wick inside. As the flame caught, something about the stranger's demeanor changed. It was subtle, but his back tensed, and he seemed to rise an inch higher.

Hailey pressed one hand over her mouth. She wanted to scream. She'd been so preoccupied with hiding that she hadn't thought about the lamp. It would still be warm from when she'd used it less than three minutes before.

"Hah. This is a pleasant surprise, little mouse." The man's voice was deep and gravelly, and it held a note of laughter. He stepped toward the backpack he'd dropped and pulled something out of a pouch in its side.

Hailey had to lean forward to see what he'd fetched. A meat cleaver.

She swallowed a moan. The man turned to scan the room, and she finally caught a glimpse of his face. He had to be in his late forties, maybe fifties. His face was blocky, and the creases around his eyes and mouth might have looked friendly in another situation. Now, they just looked cruel. "Here I was, thinking I'd need to spend the night hunting you down. But you came to me instead. Why don't you step out of your hole so we can talk?"

A tear ran down Hailey's cheek. She kept her hand over her mouth and nose in a desperate effort to silence her breathing. Her heart felt like it was going to break her ribs.

"I know you're here." The man's voice was light, even friendly, but he kept the meat cleaver swinging at his side. "You can't have blown out that lamp any more than four or five minutes ago. And you can't have run away. Because if you had, you would have triggered one of my motion sensors." He tapped the top of the blade against a black box strapped to his belt.

Bile rose in the back of Hailey's throat. She ran through a dozen different scenarios, but none of them had a good ending. She could leap out of the cupboard and run toward the door. He would catch her easily with a slash across her back. She could try to jump onto the counter and escape through the open window. His paw-like hands would fasten around her ankle before she even got her torso through the hole.

"No? Committed to the game, huh? All right, I'll make the first move." He wrenched open the wardrobe doors and stepped back. The wood rattled as it banged against the walls. His head tilted as he saw the knives were missing, and his voice lost the playful tone. "Those were expensive. You'd better not have damaged them."

Hailey bit her tongue hard enough to draw blood. She could rush him and try to slice her blade into his throat. She'd sacrificed the element of surprise, though. Even if she managed to get close enough to touch him, she would lose her arm to the cleaver. But even that slim chance was better than doing nothing—because doing nothing meant certain death.

He circled the room like a shark, and she watched as his eyes moved from the bed to the kitchen cupboards, the only two hiding places left. He stopped at the bed first and crouched to look underneath. He was being careful. There was a gap of at least two feet between himself and the frame. If Hailey had been hiding underneath, he would have been outside of her striking distance.

She squeezed her knife's hilt so tightly that the muscles in her arms ached. If she was going to die, she wanted to at least die fighting. But her body felt horribly feeble.

"Game over, little mouse." Floorboards creaked as the man circled the table to approach the kitchen cupboards. He was out of view again, but she could hear his approach. Hailey's eyes focused on the bucket she'd kicked back to make room for herself. He'd been prepared for corpse disposal. The gloves, the scrubbing brush, and the bleach were all ready to mop up her blood.

Hailey's hand dropped away from her mouth. She stared at the bleach. Then she lunged for it and unscrewed the lid.

The door flew open with a bang. Hailey flinched against the rush of air and light. The man stood just out of reach, grinning down at her as he tapped the meat cleaver against his thigh. "Hello, little mouse."

She put all of her strength behind the bottle as she heaved the bleach at his face. Liquid arced out, splattering across his shirt, his throat, and the side of his face.

He screamed and staggered into the table. Bleach had gotten into his mouth and, more importantly, his left eye. He clawed at it. Hailey dropped the bottle and ran toward him. He was taller than her, and she had to get close to reach his neck. Her knife sliced into the skin.

Blood splashed out, mixing into the bleach running down his throat, but it wasn't enough. She'd grazed him, but there wasn't the high-pressure gush that assured a killing wound. She tried to stab again. Her knife never touched him.

His fist slammed into her torso, winding her and throwing her to the ground. Hailey gagged and retched as she rolled onto her side.

"You *bitch*," he roared. The meat cleaver came down. Hailey screamed as pain exploded through her leg. Her vision went black then came back in flashes of angry white.

She curled over. Breathing was no longer possible. She flinched away from the stranger, knowing any second would bring another flash of blinding pain. His shadow loomed over her, then suddenly, it was gone.

Hailey tilted her head back. Tears half blinded her, but she saw the man at the sink, pouring water from one of the large jugs over his face. The bleach had to be hurting him. Maybe even blinding his left eye. She looked in the other direction. The door wasn't far away. Her leg wouldn't move. He'd done exactly what she'd hoped to do to him—cut through tendons. But escape was too close to give up on. She began to crawl.

The man dropped the water jug. It banged as it hit the sink, then she heard a scrape as he picked up the cleaver. His voice deepened into an animalistic growl. "Where do you think *you're* going?"

CHAPTER 63

Tuesday, 8:30 a.m.

FOR THE FIRST TIME in a long while, Carla turned up to work early and without any hangover. She wished it were from some renewed sense of purpose or the restoration of her faith in the system. In that ideal world she sometimes dreamed about, she would be grinning as she jogged up the steps to the station, full of joy at the knowledge that she'd made the world a better place.

Fantasy wasn't reality. In her reality, she was frowning. There was no gratification, just a throbbing, low-level headache from a night of broken sleep. Every time she'd tried to drift under, nightmares dogged her. They'd grown worse with each iteration. She would wake, thrashing, gasping, and covered in cold sweat, with only a vague sense of what her dream had been about.

She'd spent the night in the loft, alternately trying to sleep and pacing the barren space. The longer she stayed awake, the more the sense of wrongness grew. It itched at her like a bad infection. And dawn hadn't dispelled it like she'd hoped it would. So she was at the station, early and sober, to try to work through the trauma.

Trauma wasn't the right word, she corrected herself. She wasn't suffering from PTSD over Gabon's death. She knew what PTSD looked like, and it wasn't this. It felt more like guilt…vague, intractable guilt.

She didn't understand what was causing it. Search parties had been deployed into Ashlough Forest early that morning. A helicopter circled the area, searching for signs of life. She was doing everything she could to retrieve Chris Hershberger and his friends. If she was lucky, they would be found even before she called his parents.

What she felt was something more than that. Something that worried her subconscious. She just couldn't figure out what it was.

Viv was at the reception desk and waved to Carla as she came in. Carla, distracted, gave a wave in return. Viv called her name twice, but Carla was so absorbed with her worries that she didn't realize she was being hailed until Viv started chasing her down the hallway.

"Sorry," she said as Viv snagged her sleeve.

"Jeez, you're really out of it today." Viv brushed strands of loose hair back into place. She was wearing pansies that morning. "Are you okay?"

"I had trouble sleeping." Carla wanted to say why, but she

bit her tongue on the Gabon case. Decker wanted to retrieve the missing friends and compile details about the victims before going public with the announcement.

"Well, you asked me to tell you as soon as I found something out." Viv offered her a slip of paper with a name and a phone number, and Carla frowned as she took it.

"Sorry, just remind me. This is about—"

Viv's eyebrows lifted. "The scratch marks? On the trees? You wanted me to find out who the police officer in the photos was."

"Oh. Oh! Right!" Carla laughed and pressed a hand to her forehead. She felt like she'd lived half a lifetime since the lunch with Viv. "Of course. Thanks."

"You can thank Peter at the pub. The officer moved out of state a while ago, but Peter remembered him. That guy must have a photographic memory. His name's James Aberdeen. He's retired now but still alive. Took a while to find his phone number, but there it is."

"Thanks, Viv. I'll get you lunch later this week. Sometime when I'm a bit more awake."

"Looking forward to it, chief." Viv waved as she returned to her reception desk. "Don't work yourself to death, now."

Carla took a deep breath as she entered the office she shared with Lau and Gould. They hadn't arrived yet. Despite her resolution to get along better with her co-workers, she was grateful for the quiet as she slid into the chair at her desk.

The guilty, uncertain feeling continued to niggle. She tapped Viv's message on the tabletop. Now that they'd found Gabon, speaking to the officer from the photo was no longer a high priority. But it was better than contemplating the stack of forms waiting for her attention. She dialed the number, lodged the phone between her shoulder and her ear, and hoped James Aberdeen liked to wake up early.

He did. He sounded surprised to be contacted by his old station but was happy to talk. Carla spent nearly fifteen minutes speaking with him, and by the time she said goodbye, the vague sense of wrongness had solidified into a heavy, sickening lump in her stomach. Carla set the phone back into its cradle and stared at the wall. Her mind was churning. Her mouth was dry. She felt like she might finally be on the edge of a mental breakdown.

The door behind Carla creaked as it opened, and Lau entered. He gave Carla a small smile as he settled into his desk. "Good morning."

"Morning," Carla echoed. The word sounded hollow to her. She was starting to feel dizzy. "Is Decker here yet?"

"No. He's off today. Don't you remember? Last night, he said we could all take a break if we thought we needed one. I wanted to catch up on some work, and I guess you did too."

Carla swore under her breath and stood. The dizziness increased.

"Is something wrong?" Lau asked.

"Yes." Carla paced to the door then returned to her desk, her hand pressed over her mouth. "Cripes, yes."

"Uh...we have an emergency contact number for Decker if we need—"

"It'll take too long to get him here." Carla jogged back to the door. "It's okay. I think I know what to do."

Lau stared at her as she ran down the hallway. She was behaving irrationally, she knew. But the world seemed a lot less rational than it had the day before.

She shoved into Decker's office and approached the map of Ashlough Forest at the back wall. Her pins still marked the paths the victims had vanished from. She scanned the rivers and blocks of green, running her fingers over the worn paper, and muttered a series of furious words under her breath. Decker had a notepad on his desk, and she tore off two sheets and began scribbling coordinates. Then she turned and ran back to the hallway.

"Oh, hey!" Viv beamed as Carla skidded into the reception. "Did the phone number help?"

"Hah. It sure did." Carla slapped the paper onto the table and pointed at her messy scrawl. "I need you to do something for me. It's really important. Contact the helicopter and send it to these coordinates. They'll have a two-way radio. Make sure they search the area thoroughly. The missing people are here, but they might be hurt."

Viv's smile grew tighter. "Uh, for something like this, I'm supposed to get authorization—"

"That will take too long. There are four people lost out there, and it might already be too late. Just...just fake Decker's authorization. You can do that, right? If you get in trouble for it, say that I forced you."

Viv took the paper. Her smile had vanished. "Carla, you're

frightening me. What happened? How do you know where they are?"

Carla waved her hands, frustration and panic making her incoherent. "There's a pattern! He made a pattern! They're going to be there. I'm sure of it. Just…just make sure the helicopter gets them. If they're not at that spot exactly, they'll be close by."

Without waiting for Viv's confirmation, she jogged to the door. She held a second slip of paper with its own set of coordinates in her pocket. She had limited time to confirm that her suspicion was correct.

CHAPTER 64

CHRIS STAGGERED. HE WAS so absorbed in the sky—or, rather, the tiny scraps of sky interspersed like stars among the stifling canopy—that it took his over-tired brain a moment to figure out why he wasn't moving forward. Something had snagged his jeans, near his calves. Cold metal pressed into his skin. He looked over his shoulder and saw Flint glaring up at him. "Wha..."

He tried to pull his leg free, but it was held in place. Not by Flint's hand, but by the knife he held. It had stabbed through his jeans and nicked his skin—not enough to hobble him but enough that the sting was starting to make itself known. Flint held the knife at an angle to pin Chris. His eyes narrowed, and his lips peeled back from his teeth.

Cold sickness washed through Chris. He'd been stepping away from Flint when the knife struck. It must have been aimed at his flesh.

He met Flint's gaze. He'd never seen his friend stare at him like that before. Something wild and insane flashed through his eyes. The kind of madness that couldn't be talked down. Couldn't be reasoned with.

Fear spread through Chris's insides and squeezed. They both kept still, unbreathing, unblinking, waiting for the other to make the first move. Chris was acutely aware that the next few seconds might decide whether he died that day. The knife continued to dig into his calf. A drop of blood rolled down, tickling his skin, and soaked into his sock.

Chris wrenched his foot away. He made the movement as sharp and forceful as he could, hoping the jeans would tear and free him…or, if he was lucky, pull the knife out of Flint's hands.

It did neither. With the sharp edge of the knife facing Chris's skin, the jeans strained but didn't break. Flint used the blade like a hook as he yanked back. It pulled Chris's balance out, and he fell forward, landing on his hands and knees. Flint finally pulled the knife free from the fabric, and Chris gasped as the blade sliced across his thigh.

He tried to crawl forward, but Flint had grabbed him around his knees and pulled him back. Chris squirmed onto his back in time to see the knife rise. He yelled and kicked at Flint's arm. The other man grunted as he took the impacts, but he didn't drop the knife.

"Stop! Get off me! What the hell is wrong with you?" Chris's voice rose into a scream as Flint crawled higher, pinning him to the ground, the knife seeking out his torso.

Flint's lips were peeled back, and his teeth clenched. A fleck of saliva flew free as he slashed the knife down. Chris yelped and jammed his hand into his friend's elbow, forcing the blade's arc to one side. The knife embedded in the ground beside his left ribs.

"There's a helicopter!" He already knew Flint was too far gone to be reached with reason, but he had to try. "They've come for us! We're safe. We can go home. Stop, you idiot!"

The knife scattered dirt as it came free from the earth. Flint had lost the use of his legs, but his upper body had more than enough strength to compensate. He pressed into Chris's chest, pushing air out of his lungs and pinning him. His mad, unblinking eyes fixed on Chris's throat as he aimed the knife again.

Chris was desperate. He reached up and hooked his fingers into the back of Flint's head. It wasn't hard to find where his skull had cracked; the area was swollen into an egg-sized lump. Chris pressed his fingers into the bulging flesh and cringed as Flint screamed.

The knife came down. The blade hit him just below his collarbone. The strike had lost its force, but it was still heavy enough to break skin.

Chris dug his fingers in harder, and Flint's manic eyes finally closed. His face contorted in agony. The knife slashed erratically. Hot blood sprayed over Chris's cheek, but he couldn't tell where it came from. Streaks of pain flashed over him, burning everywhere—his arms, his neck, and his chest.

Flint screamed again, lurching back as he tried to escape Chris's fingers. Chris finally let him go and rolled. He used arms and legs to propel him as far as he could and didn't stop moving until he hit a tree.

He'd come to a stop beside Anna. Flies droned all around him. He didn't need to look at her to know they were creeping around her eyes and mouth. Flint lay a half dozen paces away. He'd curled onto his side and was shaking. Chris watched him, cautious in case he attacked again, but Flint didn't try to move. As the pained grimace slackened, he started to cry.

"I'm sorry, man. I didn't want to hurt you." Chris looked down at his fingers. Blood stained them, but he couldn't tell if it was from the swelling on Flint's skull or from the cuts in his own skin. None of the gashes were too deep, but they hurt like hell. There were at least eight of them across his arms and upper body. He couldn't slow his shallow, frantic breathing.

He crept a few inches closer to Flint to grab the first aid kit. Without bothering to disinfect the cuts, he wrapped bandages around the ones on his arms and taped cotton pads over the ones on his chest and neck. He did the job quickly, mostly focused on trying to stop the bleeding.

He glanced to his left, half expecting Anna to sigh and roll her eyes at him for dressing the cuts wrong. Her expression stayed slack. A fly crawled out of her mouth and over her lip. Chris swallowed and faced forward again.

"I guess you hate me. And that's fine. I don't need us to be friends. But there's a helicopter out there, which means they're looking for us, which means safety is really damn close. But they won't be able to see us if we just sit here. So I'm going to need you to sit tight for a while. I'm going to try to save both of our bloody lives."

He got to his feet. The cut on his thigh hurt, but he could at least put weight on it. Flint lay on his side, eyes closed as tears leaked down crevices in his face. He looked sheet white. Chris silently prayed he hadn't done any serious damage by putting pressure on the fracture. But it had been the only way. He needed to save both of their lives.

He picked up one of their sleeping bags and stepped into the forest as he let the red twine lead him downhill. Trying his hardest to ignore the burning cuts, he tried to look for the good. Having a rescue party look for them meant Hailey had gotten out of the forest. It had taken her a little longer than she'd promised, but that didn't matter. She was safe. And they would be soon too. He hoped.

Chris tilted his head back to squint through the treetops. The helicopter had passed over only once. He considered the possibility that they didn't know where he was and were canvassing the forest in blocks. That was a frightening thought. *With only one helicopter, how long will it take them to pass over the campsite again? Hours? Days?*

He stumbled over an exposed root and returned his focus to the ground ahead. Hailey wouldn't have been able to mark their position on a map; she'd only been following the twine, and that wove through the forest in an erratic, nonlinear path. Without an exact or even approximate location, the most reliable way to find them would have been by following the thread.

He'd told his parents he would be uncontactable for a few

days. Even though they did a good job of giving him space when he asked for it, they would still worry eventually. He tried to remember how many days it had been since he'd entered the forest. Time had started to blur eerily. It was becoming harder and harder to remember what sunlight or clean skin felt like. Picturing his parents' faces was even becoming difficult. He could still see Eileen's, though. Sometimes, he felt as though her eyes were watching him from every shadowed hollow.

He reached the riverbank, dropped the sleeping bag, then slid down the slope to the water's edge. He couldn't control what had happened to Hailey. Or Flint's head. So he shut his mind down in the face of those impossible problems and focused on what he *could* help. The helicopter had no chance of seeing them if they stayed under the canopy. And there was only one place within walking distance that forced a break in the smothering trees.

Chris unrolled the sleeping bag and unzipped it. Its outside was a dark, muted green, but it was lined with bright red. He shook it out so that the color faced the sky, then he dragged it behind himself as he waded into the river.

Even with water cutting a band through the trees, the branches still tried to bridge the gap. Chris roved up the river, face pointed toward the sky, as he looked for an opening wide enough to give the eyes in the sky more than a split second to see his bag. When he found the best that he could, he laid the bag out flat and weighted its top end down with rocks. The river was slow but persistent and dragged the fabric out like a flag.

Chris crawled onto a large boulder that rose above the water and drew his knees up under his chin. His shoes and part of his jeans were soaked and made squelching noises every time he moved. When he glanced down at his chest, he saw a map of red blooms coming through the makeshift bandages. He felt dizzy, but he hadn't lost enough blood to explain it. Hunger was a likelier cause. He hadn't consumed anything except water in a while, and a ravenous pain burned in his stomach.

But that didn't matter. None of it would matter. Just as long as the helicopter came back.

He dropped his chin onto his knees. While he was moving, it was easy to ignore everything wrong. Now, it was impossible. Doubt and fear were screaming in his mind. Everything ached. He hated himself for hurting Flint. He hated himself for what had happened to Anna.

Time passed strangely. He knew the sun must be rising higher, but the sky was so overcast that it didn't make any difference. His eyes fluttered closed. He caught himself just before he slipped into the river, and shook his head in a useless attempt to clear it.

The insects were growing louder. Chris lifted his head and stared toward the patches of overcast sky. A tiny black speck drifted across the tableau of gray. His lips parted as the speck flew closer and the whirring grew louder. Then he leapt up and began waving his arms, screaming so loudly that his voice cracked and his lungs burned. "Here! We're here!"

The helicopter flashed its lights to acknowledge him. Chris started to laugh and cry, and he couldn't stop until he was nearly drowning in the emotions.

CHAPTER 65

Tuesday, 10:00 a.m.

CARLA HUNCHED OVER HER steering wheel as she followed the narrow roads to Ashlough Forest. She couldn't stop herself from running through the same series of painful questions and doubts, even though answers felt impossibly far out of her reach. She kept visualizing Gabon in the brief seconds they'd shared while he was alive. Those bugged-out eyes, lips pulled away from receding gums, panic and anger informing his every movement.

She hoped she was right. No, she *believed* she was right…and hoped she wasn't. But the more she played through the spiraling events of the past week, the feebler that seemed.

It wasn't enough to convince herself of the truth. She needed to convince other people. That meant she needed evidence. And based on the costume they'd found behind Gabon's cottage, evidence was likely to be thin on the ground. He hid behind the mask, never revealing his face, so even if Chris Hershberger and his friends were still alive, their testimony likely wouldn't be enough.

Carla swallowed around a lump in her throat. If any of those kids were dead, it would be her doing. She took a corner too quickly and nearly scraped the rails. Carla sucked in a deep breath and held it as she counted down from ten then eased her foot off the accelerator. It wouldn't help anyone if she killed herself in her recklessness. But it was hard to drive slowly when every minute made the weight of her revelation feel heavier.

When she'd realized what she was looking at, the pattern on the map was obvious. She knew where to find the missing search party. She knew where to find every single resting spot of all unaccounted-for hikers—including Eileen Hershberger.

Eileen had been smart enough to take photos of her attacker. She'd lost her camera, possibly by accident or possibly because it was forced from her, but Carla didn't think it was accidental that the camera had washed downriver.

Nearly ten days had passed since Eileen went missing. There might not be much of her left by that point. But if there was evidence, even something as small as a tear in her jacket where a knife had pierced her, it could be instrumental in resolving the case. Carla just had to find it before she shared her theory with anyone.

The road straightened as it entered the parking lot. Carla turned to the right and rolled to a stop underneath a large tree. There weren't as many cars there as normal.

The mayor would be leaning on Decker, Carla knew. The town survived on its tourists, and any kind of tourist attraction closure hurt all of their wallets. He would want Gabon's posthumous conviction rushed through, the paths reopened, and public trust restored.

Carla stuffed her equipment into her backpack and mentally double-checked that she'd brought everything she needed. Her map, with a path highlighted. A camera for capturing the scene. Evidence bags and plastic gloves. A GPS tracker and bright-red tape to mark the location. Her battery-powered two-way radio to hail for help if she got lost. Her compass, in case the radio failed. A first aid kit. Water to last for two days.

She wasn't taking risks. Even though she was familiar with the forest and knew enough to protect herself, she had backups for every safety measure. A last-ditch measure in case of a true disaster was an email set to be delivered on a timer. If she didn't return home by sundown and disable it, the message would automatically be sent to the entire police department as well as emergency services with explicit instructions for how to find and retrieve her.

As she crossed the parking lot, she saw a van near the opposite side of the clearing. Even with other vehicles in the parking lot, it stood out. Leaves blanketed its roof. A branch had fallen beside it and rested against the passenger door. It must have been there for at least three or four days. She could guess who owned it.

An officer continued to stand sentry at the park's entrance. He was a new hire, and Carla didn't know him well, but she still waved and smiled as she passed him. He gave an unenthusiastic wave back.

Carla zipped her jacket up as she entered the shadows. She followed the trail until she found the path she wanted—T12. Police tape was strung over its entrance like streamers, and Decker's homemade warning sign created an extra layer of protection. Carla ducked under the tape and set a fierce pace. Moving quickly helped burn off some of her anxiety.

Twenty minutes into the hike, Carla took out her map and checked her position. The fastest way to reach Eileen's resting place was to spear off the main road and onto a little side trail to a pool. The path was so overgrown and the sign so worn down that, moving at a jog, Carla nearly missed them. She caught sight of the post as she passed it, backtracked, and followed the offshoot.

She recognized the pool. Carla had never visited it before, but Eileen had, and it had been immortalized in her photos. Carla circled the pond to where an old, disused trail continued into the forest. She checked her map and confirmed that it led straight into the red zone where their lost hikers had disappeared. She would have bet a month's wage that Eileen had gone down the trail. Carla didn't intend to, though. Even though the trail would make for an easier hike, it created a circuitous loop to Eileen.

Carla centered herself with her compass and stepped off the trail into the heavily overgrown forest. That section led uphill, and even though Carla was fit, she had to hold on to her anger to maintain the blistering pace.

Now that she knew where to find Eileen, she felt an additional measure of pain in the discovery. Eileen had only been an hour from the pool and the trail that would have led her home. Knowing someone had died deep in the forest with no hope of rescue was unpleasant, but knowing someone had died within a short walk of safety was infinitely worse.

As the slope tended uphill, Carla had to unzip her jacket and tie it around her waist. She was breathing heavily and drenched in sweat, but the exertion helped silence her mind. She continuously checked her compass to ensure her route was correct and used her watch to track her progress. Right on cue, she caught the gurgles and muted roar of rushing water.

Carla stepped out from behind a curtain of vines and found herself on the edge of the Upper Andrea River. She looked in both directions. To her right, the river cascaded down a rocky slope. A hundred meters to her left was a cliff. Mist floated over the lip, caused by the churning waters below.

She consulted her map again. Based on the curve of the river, she worked out that she'd arrived not too far from her destination. Carla turned left, toward the waterfall, and struggled through the plants growing close to the river's edge.

The cliff was steep and high, and it led down to a bowl-shaped pool at the base of the waterfall. Carla looked for an easier way to get down, but the cliffs continued as far as she could see. She pursed her lips and pulled a rope out of her bag. Climbing back up would be a bitch, but it was her only option unless she wanted to spend the rest of the day in the forest, which was a strong negative.

Carla tied the rope around the sturdiest tree she could find and turned the other end into a makeshift harness. She double- and triple-checked her knots, taking no risks, then stepped up to the cliff's edge and leaned back.

The ground was soft and the rocks prone to collapsing. Carla took the climb slowly, only feeding herself enough slack on the rope for one step at a time. She didn't loosen her harness until she was at the ground.

Something bright blue had been tied onto a shrub to Carla's right. She approached it and felt the fabric. It was stretchy, and she guessed it had come from a swimsuit.

"Oh," Carla moaned. She looked around. Strips of the fabric had been tied to dozens of trees in the area. One larger piece of cloth had been spread out like a flag between two saplings. Eileen had lived at least long enough to hope for rescue and to take measures to make her location visible.

It was an exercise in horror to wonder how many days the girl might have lived, but Carla couldn't stop her mind from going there. If she'd wandered through the forest, her odds ended at one or two days. Dehydration was usually the culprit, closely followed by hazards and exhaustion. But camped in one place and with water close at hand, Eileen might have lived longer—four days, five, maybe even as long as a week.

Carla fetched the gloves out of her backpack and pulled them on. She began taking photos of the strips of fabric, gradually working her way toward the river's edge. Under an overhang of rock at the cliff's base were a tattered backpack and two empty water bottles. Carla photographed them then turned around to look toward the trees. She took a step to her left, and they lined up perfectly, just like in the pictures she'd spent hours examining.

She turned back to the overhang and reached for the backpack. A shadow moved in the back of the nook. Bony fingers flopped down to land on Carla's own. They squeezed weakly. Carla followed the emaciated arm up toward a sunken face and two familiar blue eyes.

Carla swore.

CHAPTER 66

HAILEY FOUGHT HER IMPULSE to scream. Her arm was wrenched painfully behind her back as the stranger dragged her into the forest. Each bump jarred the gash on her leg. A trail of blood marked their progress. The stranger dragged her with one hand, his cleaver swinging menacingly in his other. She didn't try to shriek but instead poured her energy into staying conscious.

He dropped her, and the impact forced Hailey's breath from her. Lights flashed across her eyes. She flopped onto her back. The shapes around her were fuzzy and swirling. She could see the man, though. He loomed, his left eye tinged red from the bleach and his teeth bared in a snarl. The cleaver continued to move in slow, smooth sweeps as he flexed his muscles. The blood from the cut on his throat was staining his shirt.

She didn't want to watch her death coming. She'd lost. But that knowledge wasn't as bitter as it might have been. At least she would go down knowing she'd fought back. She'd hurt him. It hadn't been enough, but it had been something. Flint would be proud. Her father would be proud.

The tip of the cleaver pressed into her cheek. Its metal was cold, and Hailey shuddered.

"I'm not going to kill you," he said.

Hailey peeked her eyes open and caught sight of his grin.

"You've got some resourcefulness in you, and I respect that. I respect it enough to let you go." The blade pressed harder, pushing her head back. "Enjoy your freedom. While you have it. That leg isn't looking too good. I'll come back in a few days to check how you're doing. I'm not much of a fan of disposing of corpses, so I'm hoping nature will do my job for me. Until then, have fun, little mouse."

The blade disappeared, and leaves crunched under his boots as he strode back toward the shack. Hailey tried to watch him go. She was becoming nauseous. She pulled her legs up and felt around her ankle. Even touching near it sent blinding pain coursing through the limb.

He was letting her go, but he'd correctly surmised she wouldn't last long. The blood loss was too severe. Even if she managed to stem it, she had exactly zero percent chance of walking out of there.

That wouldn't stop her from trying, though.

Vines grew near her head. Hailey wrapped numb fingers around one and pulled it down. She managed to tear it out of the tangle then wrapped it around her leg below the knee. She looped it around several times, making it as tight as she possibly could. The pain was excruciating, but she clenched her teeth and pulled harder. She needed to cut off the blood flow to that leg—and that meant not just the surface veins, but the deep artery, as well. It exposed her to a big risk of killing the limb, but it was better than doing nothing.

She tied the vine off. It was an imperfect tourniquet, and the skin around it began to throb. Hailey forced herself up to sitting and pulled her top over her head. She whimpered as she pressed it to the gash on her ankle. The sleeves were long enough for her to wrap them around and tie off. That bandage was also imperfect.

Hailey took thin, panting breaths. The man was gone. She was free to try to escape, if she could. She'd seen a path behind his cottage. That had to lead back to civilization. The only question was how long the walk would take. It was probably a long way if he used a motorbike to reach the cottage.

The motorbike...

It was a slim chance, but that was better than nothing. Hailey used a tree to pull herself to her one good foot. She stumbled as she hopped toward the clearing, using trunks and vines to keep herself upright despite the vertigo. The man was injured. He would want to return home quickly. The only question was who would get to the bike first.

He hadn't dragged her far into the forest, probably because the exertion had been making his own blood loss worse. Hailey reached the edge of the clearing and leaned against a thick trunk as she squinted toward the cottage. A glint came from light reflected off the motorbike. It rested against the side of the cottage, around the corner from the door. She couldn't see the man. He'd probably retreated inside to bind his own cut and try to wash any lingering bleach off his skin. He wouldn't stay for long, though.

Hailey tried to run forward. It was impossible. She couldn't put any weight on her bad leg and didn't have enough sense of balance left to hop unassisted. She fell forward onto her hands and knees then crawled toward the bike.

The tourniquet had slowed the flow of blood but hadn't stopped it. She couldn't afford to waste precious seconds stopping to retie it, but the nausea was growing worse, and it was being accompanied by a rushing noise in her ears. All bad signs. But the bike was close. Very close. The man had left the keys in its ignition. He'd thought he was alone in the forest. He'd thought Hailey would die quietly in the woods. That had been a mistake.

She could hear him moving around inside the cottage, slamming things on the counters and grunting. The sound of splattering water confirmed that he was trying to clean himself. Hailey reached the bike's side and used it to pull herself up.

She'd ridden Flint's bike plenty of times, but his had been smaller than the stranger's. Hailey tried to throw her injured leg over the seat but doubled over from the pain. She pressed her lips tightly together, breathing through her nose, trying to stay silent as the waves of agony washed over her and faded. Her shoe was soaked, and drops of blood had started to drip onto the ground. Time was running out. She took a sharp, quick breath then tried again, throwing her leg over the seat and letting it flop down the other side. This time, a whimper escaped her.

The noises inside the cottage fell silent. Hailey blinked through the lights invading her vision as she hunted for the key and turned it in the ignition. The motor roared as it came to life. The cabin's door slammed open.

There was no time to get her balance or to familiarize herself with the bike. Hailey kicked the prop up, tucked both legs in as well as she could, and fed power into the throttle.

The bike lurched forward faster than she'd anticipated. It careened, wobbling wildly, and Hailey tried to use her uninjured foot to keep herself from tipping over. It scraped on the ground, twisting it, and she shrieked. She felt something tug on the bike, slowing it, and turned the throttle farther. The bike broke away from the resistance, and she heard the man yell. Then she was racing down the pathway, rocking dangerously and bouncing over roots. Strength was bleeding out of her limbs, but she clung to consciousness, fighting to keep the bike stable. When she glanced in the rear-view mirror, she saw the man. He stood at the end of the trail, arms hung limply at his side, shock and pure, raw fury twisting his expression.

Hailey managed a smile as she hung low over the handlebars. She didn't know if she had enough strength to get back to a main road. Her life was dripping out of her by the second. But she'd won. Even if just for a few moments, she'd won. She managed a chuckle as the bike jolted over the narrow, twisting trail.

CHAPTER 67

Tuesday, 6:40 p.m.

CARLA SAT IN A dimly lit living room. The recliner was leather—real leather, not the fake stuff that fell apart after a couple of years—and made of dark colors to match the rest of the room's décor. Its seat was thick and plush, which was convenient. She'd tucked a small object down the gap beside her thigh, where only she could see it.

The clock in the hall marked each passing second with a tick. A streetlamp sent light through the curtained windows to highlight the living area's furniture. Dark woods. Plush carpet, either recently refurbished or rarely trodden on. The house wasn't large, but it was expensive. There were no photos on the walls.

The front door's lock scraped as it was unbolted. She listened to the creak, the scuff of shoes on the mat, then finally, the gentle snap as the door was closed. The hallway lights turned on. A man came into view, pulling off his jacket. He tossed it onto the hallway's empty side table then moved toward the kitchen. The living room's shadows were so heavy that it took him a moment to see Carla. When he did, he took a sharp breath. "Delago?"

"Hey," she said and smiled. "How're you doing?"

Decker stepped into the living room and hit the switch to turn the lights on. "What the hell? What are you doing here?" He glanced toward the front door. "How did you get into my house?"

"You forgot to lock your kitchen window. I hope you don't mind. I made myself at home."

He stared at her, incredulity and confusion written over his expression. For once in her life, she'd caught him flat-footed. "*Why?*"

"There have been a couple of big updates in the Hershberger-Gabon case. You probably haven't heard them yet, so I wanted to tell you personally."

Irritation was rapidly replacing his shock. "This is out of line, Delago. You should have radioed me."

"It's too important to tell you over the phone." She motioned toward the leather seat opposite her. "Got a minute?"

He eyed her, sizing her up, then slowly sank into the chair. For a moment, the only noise in the house was the persistent ticking of the hallway clock. Then Carla took a deep breath and let it out slowly. "We found the missing search party. The ones that lived, at least. Chris and Flint are in the hospital. Anna is in the morgue. And apparently, there was another one we didn't know about, Todd. We're working on finding his remains now."

"Hell, at least *some* came back alive." Decker scowled. "Media's going to have a field day regardless, but it would be worse if they were all dead."

"That's not all. Eileen Hershberger is alive."

"What?"

Carla swallowed. The memory still hurt. It would probably hurt for a long while. "I found her. Dehydrated. Muscles wasted away from starvation. Delirious and incoherent. But she's alive and getting treatment now."

Decker's frown tightened. "You said she would be dead."

"I thought she would be. Finding her alive was a miracle. She only survived because she landed near shelter and water—and was injured too badly to move from there. Hailey made it back too. A construction worker found her on the side of the road, next to an unregistered motorbike. She looks awful. They think she'll probably lose her leg, and she's in an induced coma."

Carla let her gaze slip to Decker's swollen, bloodshot eye and the bandage taped to his neck. "Looks like she gave you hell, though."

Decker held perfectly still. His cold gray eyes, unblinking, fixed on Carla's and refused to waver.

"I only figured it out this morning," Carla said. "You hide your tracks well. It took a lucky phone call to a retired officer to help me put the pieces together. Do you remember Aberdeen? He responded to one of the very first disappearances. They found scratch marks on a tree. He thought it warranted further investigation, but the station's chief wanted him to wrap up the case quickly. I asked who the chief was. He said it was you. You'd held the position for just over a month when that all happened."

Decker still refused to speak, but the corners of his mouth twitched into a thin smile.

"So I started thinking," Carla continued. "This whole time we were investigating the mass disappearances, I kept asking myself how we'd failed to realize our town had a serial killer. Why hadn't we noticed so many people were going missing? Why had no one, in the ten years it was happening, put the pieces together? The answer was you. Any time a case came into the station, you chose who to assign it to. And you'd been spreading the cases out so that no one officer ever received enough to raise suspicion. And my own missing person cases always landed on my desk when I was absolutely swamped with work. I'm sure that wasn't on accident. You were careful to only assign us the cases if we were too busy to give them the attention they deserved."

Decker's smile was gradually growing wider.

Carla picked a stray hair off her pants. "On top of that, you tried to shut down communication. You belittled us, picked at us, pitted us against each other. Working in your station is hell, and that's deliberate. You wanted us to resent each other. To avoid talking to each other. You sabotaged our efforts to update to a digital records database and kept all of your dirty secrets lost in those storage rooms on the second floor."

"You seem to have spent a while thinking about this."

"You took a while getting home," Carla countered. "Must have been a painful walk after Hailey took your bike."

His eyes darkened.

"After talking to Aberdeen, pieces of the puzzle started falling into place. The only person capable of killing for a decade without being discovered was someone with insider knowledge of how police investigations worked. Someone who could ensure the files never got linked together. Someone who could nip speculation in the bud before it got out of hand. *You.* So I went to your office, where you keep a map of Ashlough Forest in a place of honor behind your desk. The first time I looked at it, I remembered noticing how well worn the map was. The paper had been broken by dozens, maybe hundreds of pins, and had markings scattered over it. At the time, I hadn't thought they might be connected to the disappearances. But they were."

She clenched her hands in her lap, a small motion to disperse some of her anger. "You'd marked numbers over the map. Tiny numbers written in red pen. I realized they were marking the resting places of your victims. And so I found the latest numbers. I sent the helicopter to one and went myself to another. But I really want to know…how did you keep track of people once they were in the forest? How did you follow them and find where they fell?"

"Motion sensors," he said simply. "I have a network spaced through the forest. Not too close together, but near enough that I can pinpoint someone's location down to a square kilometer."

"And you didn't think anyone would notice them?"

"They're hidden well."

Carla sighed. "You must have known your activities would be discovered eventually. That's why you had a backup plan. When I came to your office with proof that people had been going missing, you at first tried to put me off course by suggesting it was a prank. When you saw I had too much evidence for that to work, you switched tactics and set up that sham investigation. You must have thought you wouldn't be suspected if you were the most enthusiastic one about it. And you were right. I blindly trusted you. We all did." She scowled. "I should've guessed something was wrong when we got those anonymous tip-offs about Gabon. They were a little too good to be true. I wonder, if we trace those emails, will we find your IP address behind them?"

"Am I a fool, Delago?"

"No, of course not. You'd know how to hide your trail. Burner email on a public library computer, maybe? VPN? Whatever your method, I'm sure it will be hell to trace."

He folded his hands across his knee. "You didn't believe Gabon did it, huh?"

"I did at the time. It was all so convincing. A list of missing persons on his kitchen counter. Costume hidden behind his house. Of course you planted them…the costume ahead of time, the paper during the confusion around Gabon's death. He was a good choice to take the fall. Unstable, neurotic, a loner on the fringe of society. You probably had him picked out years in advance, ready to take the blame for when someone asked too many questions. Only one part of the setup wasn't convincing."

"Oh?"

"The costume. I guess it must have been a spare or maybe an old edition you no longer used. You're what? Six-four? Wearing the boots, you'd be nearly seven feet tall. Gabon is only just over five feet. Even with the boots, he wouldn't have filled out the costume."

"Hah. I was worried you might notice."

"And that's why you wanted to promote me. To a different area. You wanted to move me out of the station, get me distracted with another city's work, and hopefully make me forget the whole ordeal. I guess you would have done the same to Quincey, Peterson, and Lau, right? Maybe not immediately, but over the next few months, they would all be retired or transferred. And once everyone directly involved in the investigations was gone, you'd start killing again."

He tilted his head to the side. The smile almost looked friendly.

"I guess you thought it was a lucky break that Gabon was paranoid enough to shoot himself. He couldn't protest his innocence that way, right? You'd told us to keep a tight lid on the situation. You kept saying that you wanted to compile a complete report of the lost hikers before releasing the news. I'm sure that was a play for time. Once we were transferred away, no one in the station would know it had even happened. I'm sure you had a plan for what to do if the news leaked, but it would have been easier for you if it hadn't."

"The mayor is a nightmare to work with," Decker growled.

For the first time since Carla had started talking, he showed real emotion. "Incessant nagging. So much red tape that I sometimes feel like I'm drowning in it. I would rather transfer myself than deal with him."

"Okay. So you would have moved to a new station. Waited a few months until you had a measure of the place, had worn the officers down to miserable shells of themselves, then started killing again."

"That's one thing you're wrong about, Delago." The smile had grown wide enough to show teeth. "I *never* killed anyone. I never so much as touched them."

She scoffed. "Are you sure about that? Hailey's been sliced up pretty badly."

"What I did to Hailey was self-defense. She attacked first. Bleach in my face. In my own home. I had every right to defend myself by whatever means necessary. And once she was subdued, I let her go."

"Let her go to bleed out in the woods. Lovely."

He spread his hands. "Like I said. I have never killed a person."

"You just put them into a situation where they killed themselves." She blinked, her mind scrambling to reassess what she knew. "You frighten them off the trail. That costume…it's not just to hide your identity. It's supposed to be intimidating. People don't know what you are—human or monster—but you look threatening, so they run. And you herd them into the forest. Deep enough that they can't find their way back out. You created a bank of sinister markings on the trees to deter them from walking in the right direction. Then you leave them out there. Lost. It's just a matter of time until they die from natural causes."

"No blood on my hands." Decker scraped grime out from under his fingernail and flicked it away. "It's not my fault if they don't find their way out."

A flush of anger burned through Carla. "It is, though. What you do is intentional. It may not be murder, but it's still manslaughter."

"Can you prove that?" The wolflike teeth glinted. "There are no laws against being scary. It's perfectly legal to wear costumes while you visit the forest. Motion sensors are fine, even in the numbers I was employing. Perhaps, at a stretch, you could get me for vandalism, for cutting and painting over the trees. But even then, you may find that the knives and paint were bought with cash in shops without surveillance, several towns away. Have fun trying to link them to me."

She shook her head. "You planned this so well."

"I've had a long time to think through possible outcomes."

"Your loopholes and excuses won't be enough, though. If this goes before a jury, they'll convict you, no question."

"Perhaps." He adjusted his position. "*If* it goes before a jury."

"Explain that."

"I have some good friends in this town. The DA and I have drinks every Friday. He wouldn't want to see me go through court on some flimsy, vexatious claim."

"He'll have no choice in the face of the evidence."

"Delago, exactly what evidence do you have?" He leaned a little closer, eyes laughing, eyebrows raised. "That little mouse who stole my bike is hardly a reliable witness… I can argue that the trauma has damaged her memories. The photos the Hershberger girl took show something that might be a mask or might be a blur. Yes, I visit the forest. But so do hundreds of people in this town, yourself included. You can't tie the deaths to me. You can't tie the paint, the knives, or the vandalism to me. I'm an officer, Delago. I know all of the methods I would use to nail a perp. And I've protected myself from them all."

"I'm sure you have," Carla growled. "You probably have alibis set up too. Layer upon layer of protection."

"Correct." He shifted a little closer. Even though their legs were more than a meter apart, she felt as though he was pushing into her personal space. "And right now, the only person who knows the truth is *you*."

She met his eyes—one gray and laughing, the other bloodshot.

"You're bright, so I hope I don't have to explain the situation for you, Delago," he murmured. "Right now, it's your word against mine. People in this town respect and like me. You haven't made too many friends lately with your attitude. So, already, the scales are tilted against you."

"You think so?"

"I *know* so." His eyes flashed, and his smile tightened. "If you even whisper a hint of what you know, I will *ruin* you. There are so many ways I could do it. I could fire you for having sexual relations with prisoners. I could raid your home and discover a shipment of drugs. Or…" He licked his lips. "You're married, aren't you? How would you like it if we found some kiddie porn on your husband's computer?"

She and Matt were as good as divorced, but Carla's stomach still tightened. Matt wasn't an angel, but he didn't deserve to have his life destroyed like that.

"Yes," Decker purred. "You understand now. Break your silence, and your name becomes mud. I'll make sure you never work again. Your friends will turn on you. The media will eat you alive. You could try to counter it with what you know, but your evidence is so scarce that people will think you're lying in a sad attempt to divert attention from yourself. I hold all of the power in this situation."

"Hah." Her palms were sweating. "I was afraid our conversation might end up like this."

"Then why come?"

"Because I wanted to know."

He tilted his head, a silent question.

"I wanted to be sure that I was right. There's always that tiny itch of doubt, you know? We've worked together for so many years… I respected you… I guess I wanted to be wrong. So thank you for putting that to rest." She ran her hand over her face then dropped it again. "I have one more question. It's the same one I had for Gabon. I want to know your why. What makes you do this?"

His eyes narrowed. He seemed to be judging whether the question deserved an answer. Finally, he took a deep, slow breath. "I have two nephews. They're twelve and fourteen. I visit my sister twice a year during my annual breaks, and while the other adults get drunk, I watch the kids play on the computer. They love simulation games. Theme park simulations. Zoo simulations. Life simulations. The games seem innocent; the purpose is to build the best park or zoo or home you can manage. Then you watch simulated people interact with what you've created. But inevitably, those kids always turn to the same question…can we kill someone?"

Carla frowned, and Decker chuckled at her expression.

"They build a roller coaster with no end and watch as the patrons sail across the screen before crashing in a ball of fire. They build a lion enclosure in their zoo then delete the fence and watch the visitors be mauled. You send your avatar to go swimming in a pool then build a wall around it and watch them drown. When the game creators added those features, they were intended as a punishment. You did something wrong, and now people are dead, how horrible. But the kids playing the game don't see it as a punishment. It's a challenge. How many creative ways can you kill those simulated humans?"

She couldn't believe what she was hearing. "This is a game to you?"

"No. It's basic human nature. Remove our inhibitions—remove consequences—and we want to watch someone die. If you can get over the squeamishness, it's surprisingly satisfying. Like cracking your neck. Releasing tension. Feeling a little rush of exhilaration. And once you're past the initial thrill, it just becomes a question of *how many*."

She felt queasy. "You want to see how many you can kill before you lose the game."

"Exactly."

"You're at sixty. Isn't that enough?"

He raised a finger. "Sixty *here*. I've been doing this for a while longer than I've been chief of your station, Delago."

"Bastard," she spat.

"Watch your temper. Don't forget what's at stake for you." He rested back and regarded her through heavy-lidded eyes. "I'm not a monster. I don't expect you to continue working for me, knowing what you know. So I'll let you choose. Early retirement or transfer?"

"What?"

"It's not a challenging question. This is in exchange for your silence. Do you want to retire early and take a substantial bonus or transfer and get a raise?"

She choked on her laughter. "You think I want either?"

"I *think* you don't have a choice." His voice deepened. "I *think* you will be grateful for this concession. I'm not trying to ruin your life. But I won't hesitate to do so if you fail to comply."

"So that's it, huh? You pull some strings, get me a raise or a bonus to buy my silence, and I just have to…forget?"

"That's right." His smile was back. "Once you walk out of here, you'll never have to speak to me again. I know you can put this whole business out of mind. You're not an idealist. You're practical. Cynical, even."

"I guess I've made that pretty clear over the last year or two."

"And I respected you for that." He gestured toward her. "If anyone else had confronted me, I would have gone ahead and ruined them preemptively. I have no time for bleeding hearts and martyrs. But you're practical. Even if it's unpleasant, you're capable of making hard choices. Which is why I know you'll be able to accept *this* choice. Compartmentalize it, just like you've compartmentalized all of the other unpleasantness in your life."

"I..."

"Remember, for me, the outcome will be the same whether you speak out or stay quiet. The only person you can hurt here is yourself."

He was a monstrous human, but he knew how to be persuasive. She looked toward the window. The curtains blurred the street, but she could see kids playing in the yard opposite Decker's house. As much as she hated it, he was right about her. She *could* compartmentalize. She *could* shut her eyes to the atrocities in the world. She had plenty of bottles of wine to get her through the unpleasant nights.

"Can't decide?" Decker said. "I'll make this easier. Go home, sleep on it, and send me an email when you know what you want. I'll put you on paid leave until then."

"All right."

"I'll just need one thing before you leave. Your recorder."

She startled. "What?"

"I'm not stupid, Delago. All of your evidence is flimsy at best... but a confession from my own mouth would be irrefutable. You didn't come here to put your mind at ease or to understand why

I did this. You came here to wrestle an admission out of me. Catch me off guard, confront me with the evidence, then let me confirm my guilt. You'll have a recorder on you somewhere." He held out his hand. "So I'll have that now, please."

She glanced down at the small black shape nestled at her side, hidden behind the cushion. Then she managed a weak laugh as she shook her head. "You have a pretty good measure of me."

"Of course I do. I've had years to get inside your head."

"But you slipped up in two places."

"Oh?"

"First, you've overestimated my intelligence. I didn't come here to play mind games and try to outsmart you. I knew that would be impossible before I even stepped in here." She sighed. "And second, perhaps I'm more of a bleeding-heart martyr than you gave me credit for."

Carla lifted the shape from behind the cushion and held it toward Decker. She waited just long enough for his eyes to widen and his lips to part. Then she pulled the trigger and watched the back of his head scatter across the beautifully decorated room.

CHAPTER 68

CARLA HAD BEEN SICKENED when Gabon killed himself. Decker's death was no easier to handle.

She placed the still-warm gun on the carpet beside her chair. Squeezing her hands together, she closed her eyes and waited for the shaking and nausea to pass. The hallway clock's steady ticking helped ground her. She didn't cry, even though she wanted to. She would save that for later that evening, once she was out of Decker's house.

A long time passed before Carla felt ready to move. Finally, she lifted her head and examined her ex-boss with the most analytical eyes she could manage. His jaw hung loose, and his eyes were open. The entry wound, just above his nose and a little to the right, was small. But gore painted his chair's back and sprayed across the carpet behind him like an impressionistic painting by an exceptionally troubled artist. She tried not to stare at the flecks of bone.

Carla reached behind her own chair and pulled out her backpack of supplies. A packet of disposable gloves sat atop the pile, and she pulled on a pair. Then she took out a microfiber cloth and began polishing the gun, being careful to cover every inch, not just the handle.

Decker had been right about her: she could make hard decisions. Unpleasant decisions. The kind of stuff that had to be done. Stuff no one wanted to be responsible for. She could get her hands dirty if it was really, truly necessary.

And it was necessary in this case. Decker wasn't young, but he was fit and healthy for his age. Left unchecked, the killings could have continued on for as long as a decade. And he'd left her with no doubt of his intentions.

She carried the gun up to him and lifted his right hand. His skin was still warm, and she tried not to squirm. She manipulated his fist to wrap the hand around the gun and coat it with his DNA then picked up individual fingers to create prints over the trigger and the barrel. Then she held both the gun and Decker's limp hand up to the front of his face and dropped them. The hand fell into his lap. The gun skittered over the floor. She left them where they fell.

The gun was Decker's. She'd found it hidden under his mattress while searching his home. If a ballistics expert took the time to examine the bullet wound, they would realize the shot had been fired from a distance. But Carla hoped no one would bother digging that deeply. Decker was, statistically, at a high risk of suicide. Police officers with long histories almost inevitably suffered from PTSD and depression. On top of that, Decker was single with no children. He lived alone and had just concluded a stressful, horrific case with Gabon's death. People would be upset to hear he'd killed himself, but no one would be surprised.

Carla stepped back and examined the scene. Even though she'd worn gloves when entering the house and had kept her hair tied back, it was impossible to prevent traces of her DNA from dotting the building. If anyone realized Decker's death wasn't self-inflicted, she fully expected she'd be caught eventually.

She could live with that. She was, after all, a murderer. No point in sugarcoating it. She wasn't going to give herself up—she wasn't that much of a martyr. But she would accept her punishment if the system caught her.

It was walking a very, very fine line between justice and vigilantism. She didn't like how close to the edge she was standing. But then she didn't *need* to like it. She just needed to be sure that it was the right thing to do.

Decker had been right—there wasn't enough evidence to put him behind bars. He'd been too clever to leave bread crumbs. And even if she managed to cobble together more evidence, get past a defensive DA, get past a biased jury, and manage to get a conviction, the town would never be the same again. A serial killer was horrific enough. Knowing that their police chief had been a killer would shake anyone.

This way, a minimal number of lives would be hurt. Gabon would take the blame for the murders. Decker would go down as a tragic hero. People would feel safe again. It wasn't justice, but it was the best she could manage in a messed-up world.

Carla closed her eyes and bowed her head. Throwing up would pretty thoroughly ruin the scene, so she swallowed her nausea. Her heart ached, but she couldn't tell if it was from the horror of what she'd done or relief that it was over.

The only element that put her at risk was Hailey. The girl had been attacked six hours after Gabon's death. And even though Decker had doubts her memories would survive the horrific trauma, it was far from a certain thing.

Carla was still in charge of the Hershberger investigation. She planned to pay the girl a visit once she was out of the induced coma. She wouldn't ask Hailey to conceal the truth, but she would explain the situation and let the girl make up her own mind on what was justice.

She hoisted her backpack over her shoulder and moved through the house to the open kitchen window. Just like when she'd entered it, the building was unpleasantly quiet. Carla climbed onto the counter and eased herself through the window, being careful to touch the sill as little as possible. She lowered herself onto the grass gingerly to protect it from damage, then she took a cloth out of her bag and reached through the window. She brushed down the counter to remove any fibers from her clothes then checked that no hairs had been caught in the window frame. She pulled the pane down into the position she'd discovered it in. A pinch of dust brushed off the walls and blown across the sill made it look like it hadn't been touched in weeks.

Carla retreated from the house, keeping her footfalls soft and checking that she left no prints behind. Decker's house backed onto a nature reserve. It wasn't officially part of Ashlough Forest, though it had once connected to the mountains before civilization had built roads through it. A hiking trail through the nature reserve led to the main road, which ran along the forest's edge. Not far from that was where Hailey and the bike had been found. Carla suspected that Decker had used his private passageway rather than the main entry to access the forest.

She pulled a cap out of her bag and tucked it onto her head to hide her face. Then she entered the pathway and left Decker and his property behind.

Friday, 11:30 a.m., Willow Grove Cemetery

THE SUN WAS WARM, but it was still fighting to dry the traces of moisture that had gathered in shady hollows and on the dark side of the tombstones. The previous night's rain had changed the atmosphere and left the air feeling fresh and crisp.

Chris stood behind Eileen. Simple white-painted wooden seats had been provided for members of the party who wanted to sit. Eileen's leg was encased in a thick cast, and their parents had ushered her into a chair as soon as they arrived at the graveside. They'd wanted her to stay at home, in bed, but she'd insisted on coming.

She looked like a skeleton. Her muscles had atrophied, and movement seemed to exhaust her. Sometimes, Chris barely recognized her. Then she would smile, and that sensation would fade. Her grin was just the same as ever, big and carefree, and let him know that his sister was still hiding inside.

Hailey sat beside Eileen, but she had a different kind of seat. The wheelchair dug into the soft ground. She'd become more subdued since losing her leg, and it was too soon to fit her with a prosthetic. The stump, amputated below the knee and swaddled in bandages, was discreetly hidden under the blanket covering her lap.

Her bubbly, girly attitude had evaporated following her experience in Ashlough Forest, but she had gained confidence in its place. She seemed to have aged ten years. Chris remembered one of his last discussions with Anna, where she'd said that Hailey's ditzy personality was a mask. He hoped this new personality—assured and calm—was closer to the real Hailey. She said she was still planning to attend med school the following year.

He glanced to his left, where Flint stood with his hands on the wheelchair handles. Flint looked strange in a suit. Chris had never seen him in anything more formal than a T-shirt. His tie was a little crooked and looked too tight, but he'd obviously put a lot of effort into tying it. He saw Chris looking and gave him a quick smile in return.

They hadn't really talked after the rescue. Flint had spent two days in the hospital being treated for a concussion, a fractured skull, and dehydration. When Chris had finally gotten up the courage to visit him, they'd sat in silence for several minutes.

Flint had simply said, "It got weird out there, didn't it?"

"Yeah," Chris had said.

"Sorry, man."

"Same."

And then they had started talking about the football game playing on the hospital's TV. It had seemed almost laughably blasé compared to the girls' reunion—which had involved a waterfall of tears and affection—but Chris didn't mind. Things weren't quite back to normal yet, but he thought, with a bit of time, they would be.

The damage to Flint's legs had been caused by an infection. They were recovering quickly with antibiotics. People had offered him a chair, but he'd refused, preferring to stand behind Hailey. The two of them seemed closer than they'd been before going into the forest, and Flint made a point of pushing Hailey everywhere, even though she laughingly said she could wheel herself.

The priest finished speaking, and Chris took a slow breath as he watched the casket sink into the ground. Anna's parents had chosen a good plot for her. She'd never been a big fan of flowers, but there were plenty of spreading trees and ornamental shrubs around her. A river was visible from the grave. He hoped she would like it there.

They would need to have another funeral soon for Todd. The police were still working on trying to retrieve his remains. Parts had been found—Chris didn't have the stomach to ask which parts—and he didn't think it would take long for a funeral day to be scheduled.

The priest kept his head bowed until the winches stilled, then he led the group in a final prayer. When he finished, he invited friends and family to take a handful of dirt from the mound beside the grave and throw it in. Anna's parents, an older couple with gray faces and bowed shoulders, went first. Then Eileen rose out of her chair. Their father took one of her arms, and Chris hurried to support her other side as they helped her to the grave. Her breathing was laborious as she bent to pick up a fistful of dirt. Chris heard her whisper, "Goodbye. I'm sorry," as she threw it, then she let them carry her back to her seat.

Flint pushed Hailey forward next, and they threw their dirt in together. Some of Anna's friends from college followed then neighbors and acquaintances from around town. It hadn't been a small funeral gathering. Their experiences in the forest had made national news, turning them semifamous overnight. Hundreds of people had arrived for the funeral, and a camera crew lurked near the cemetery gates, waiting to pick up interviews from the departing attendees.

They were the rescue party that shouldn't have survived, the victims who had escaped a serial killer. Eileen's photographs had captured imaginations, and even though they were still supposed to be police property, they had spread far and wide.

Chris had been approached for interviews, and one agent had eagerly tried to sell him on a book deal. He'd rejected them all so far, as had the others. Chris thought he might feel ready to talk about the experience one day. But not quite yet. Not until his lost friends were buried and his surviving friends had healed. And there was a lot of healing still to happen.

Officer Delago approached the grave, one of the last. She took a handful of dirt, and he saw her lips twitch as she whispered something, then she scattered her offering. As she turned away, Chris thought she glanced in their direction. Hailey lifted her head to return the look. He didn't think it was his imagination that they shared something private. Hailey had barely talked about her ordeal, but she'd had several private meetings with the police officer. Delago's glance only lasted a second, then she retreated to the back of the gathering.

Chris's bad opinion of Delago had been reversed. Apparently, she'd been instrumental in the killer, Gabon's, discovery. Even though she'd dismissed his photographs during their meeting, she had followed up on them afterward and was perhaps the only reason he and Flint had been rescued. Her station was in chaos following the superintendent's suicide, but she'd been almost aggressively determined to be helpful. She'd given him her direct phone number in case he needed anything in the next few weeks. She'd mentioned she was planning to move away from Helmer the following month. He hoped she was going somewhere nice.

The priest said a final goodbye, and the funeral party began to disband. Chris waited until the bulk of the group had drifted away, then he bent over Eileen's shoulder. "Ready to head home?"

"Actually…" Flint cleared his throat. "It's the first time we've all been together outside of the hospital. Do you remember that pub Anna used to like? The one where she tried to explain how nuclear propulsion works on a napkin?"

"And almost started screaming because we didn't understand."

Chris laughed. "Yeah, I remember."

"It was one of her favorite places. I thought we could have a drink in her honor."

"That sounds nice," Eileen said.

Her mother, sitting on Eileen's other side, tugged at her arm and began speaking in a hushed voice. Eileen laughed and patted her hand.

"I'm not made of glass, Mum. And I'm feeling a lot better today. I'll be fine."

Her mother sighed. "Stick with your brother. And don't drink anything alcoholic."

"Sure." Eileen stood, and Chris offered his arm for her to lean on. Her cheeks crinkled as she smiled. "Let's go."

"All right," Flint said, his grin broad. Hailey unlocked the brakes on her wheelchair, and he turned her around. They wove through the remains of the funeral gathering and followed the path leading to the gates.

The grief still burned and probably would for a long time. Chris was acutely aware that his life would never return to what it had been a month before. But he also knew that change was not inherently bad. Anna had once told him that. She'd said that life had sections, like walking through doors. People had to choose when to walk through them, but no one could see what the next room held until they were in it. Some new rooms were painful. Some were happy. Some seemingly had no purpose. But the fullest, happiest lives were lived by those who walked through many different doors, unafraid of what they would find.

He didn't know what his next room would hold, but he wasn't alone. The four friends, clustered together tightly, walked under the cemetery's arch and into the next stage of their lives.

Read on for a sneak peek at *Dead Lake*, coming August 2020

CHAPTER 1

SAM'S BREATH CAUGHT AS she stepped back from the car, jacket in one hand and a luggage bag in the other, and turned to face the densely wooded hills behind her. The strangest sensation had crawled over her, as if she were being watched.

That was impossible, of course. The lakeside cabin was the furthest from civilization Sam had ever been. Nestled deep in Harob Forest and situated at the edge of a large lake, her uncle's property was a two-hour drive from the nearest town. Her uncle Peter had said hiking paths snaked through the forest, but only a couple of them came near his part of the lake, and they weren't used often.

Despite that, Sam couldn't stop herself from running her eyes over the dense pine trees and shrubs that grew along the rocky incline. Only a colony of birds fluttering around a nearby conifer and the steady drone of insects broke the silence.

Sam turned back to the two-story cabin. The sun caught on the rough-hewn wood, making it almost seem to glow. It sat as close to the water as it could without compromising its foundations, and a balcony overlooked the lake. The rocky embankment rising behind it merged directly into the mountains, which grew more than a kilometer into the sky.

Peter had built the cabin nearly a decade before as a hobby to keep himself occupied on the weekends. He was proud of it, and rightfully so; Sam knew Peter made his living as a woodworker, but she hadn't expected him to be so proficient at it. The cabin looked as natural as the rocks, as though it could have sprouted out of the ground fully formed.

Sam shifted the luggage bag to her left hand and approached the front door. Her key fit into the lock and turned easily, and a grin grew across her face as the door creaked open.

The cabin's lower level was a single large room. A fireplace sat to her right; a stack of kindling waited for her near the soot-blackened hole, with a bracket holding aged firewood and an ax beside it. Two stuffed armchairs stood on thick animal furs, facing the fireplace. A polished wood table and chairs sat to Sam's left, near the kitchenette that took up the back part of the room. A stairway above the kitchen led to the upper level.

Sam dropped her bag beside the open door and marveled at how clean the room was. Peter said he visited it at least once a month, and he must have been scrupulous with its maintenance. Sam felt in her jacket pocket for the letter he'd given her then unfolded it to re-read the characteristically abrupt chicken-scratch scrawl.

Sammy,

Have fun at the cabin. Don't get eaten by bears.

The lake's good for swimming. There's a canoe in the shed. And dry wood. Light a fire when the sun goes down—it gets cold at night.

There's no electricity or phone reception, so don't get into trouble, but if you do, there's a two-way radio in the kitchen cupboard. I wrote the most important codes beside it.

Don't go on the dock. (This line was underscored twice.) *The wood's rotten. I'll fix it next time I'm up there.*

There's food in the cupboards. Eat it. You're too skinny.

Love,
Petey

Smiling fondly, Sam tucked the note back into her pocket. The drive from the city had taken most of the day, and the sun was already edging toward the top of the mountains surrounding the lake. Sam hurried back to her car and began bringing in the rest of her luggage.

An easel, watercolors, oils and acrylics, a large wooden box full of mediums, charcoal and pencils, copious brushes, sketchbooks, and a dozen canvasses had filled the boot and both back seats of the car. Sam brought them inside with significantly more care than she'd shown her travel bag, which held only clothes and towels. She placed most of her equipment on the table then opened the easel in the empty space in the room's corner.

Sam adjusted the angle of the easel so that it caught the natural light from the window, and set a canvas on it. It looked good there, she thought. *Like an artist's dream retreat. If this doesn't get you back into your groove, nothing will.*

The sky was darkening quickly, and Sam knelt in front of the fireplace. She found matches and clumsily lit the kindling in the grate. She hadn't started a fire since her parents had taken her camping when she was a child. She used up most of the kindling before the blaze was strong enough to catch onto the larger pieces of wood.

Satisfied that her fire wasn't about to die, Sam went to explore the second floor. The steep, narrow staircase turned at the corner of the room and led straight into a bedroom, which, like the ground floor, was open-plan. There was something resembling a bathroom at the back wall, with a sink, cupboard, mirror, toilet, and a bathtub—but no shower. The sink and bathtub had plugs, but no taps. On examination, Sam found a pipe coming out of the wall, with a drain and a bucket underneath it, set next to a hand pump. She guessed it was connected to a rainwater tank behind the cabin.

Of course. No electricity and no running water.

That meant she would have to heat the water over the fire if she wanted a warm bath. It wouldn't have bothered Peter. He was a mountain man through and through; he loved hunting, fishing, and woodworking, and he probably relished ice-cold showers, too.

A large double bed took up most of the room. It held several layers of thick quilts, topped with animal furs. Sam hesitated, felt the furs gingerly, then folded them up and placed them in the cupboard opposite the bed. Sleeping under the skins of dead animals seemed strangely macabre.

The door leading to the balcony stood to her left. Sam opened it and leaned on the sill to absorb the view. The sun had set behind the mountains, but most of the sky was still a pale blue, with tinges of red showing just above the tops of the trees on the west mountain. The glassy lake, which seemed to stretch on forever, reflected the patchy white clouds. Peter's cabin was set at one of the lake's widest points, but to her right, it narrowed and curved around the sides of the hills that cradled it.

The dock protruded from the shore below the cabin, running twenty meters into the lake. Something large and misshapen sat at its end; Sam squinted in the poor light, trying to make out what it was, then her heart faltered as the shape moved.

It was a man, on his knees, bent over the edge of the dock. His broad shoulders trembled as he stared, fixated on the water below.

ABOUT THE AUTHOR

Darcy Coates is the *USA Today* bestselling author of *Hunted*, *The Haunting of Ashburn House*, *Craven Manor*, and more than a dozen other horror and suspense titles. She lives on the Central Coast of Australia with her family, cats, and a garden full of herbs and vegetables. Darcy loves forests, especially old-growth forests where the trees dwarf anyone who steps between them. Wherever she lives, she tries to have a mountain range close by.

VOICES IN THE SNOW

NO ONE ESCAPES THE STILLNESS.

Clare remembers the cold. She remembers dark shapes in the snow and a terror she can't explain. And then…nothing. When she wakes in a stranger's home, he tells her she was in an accident. Clare wants to leave, but a vicious snowstorm has blanketed the world in white, and there's nothing she can do but wait.

They should be alone, but Clare's convinced something else is creeping about the surrounding woods, watching. Waiting. Between the claustrophobic storm and the inescapable sense of being hunted, Clare is on edge…and increasingly certain of one thing: her car crash wasn't an accident. Something is waiting for her to step outside the fragile safety of the house…something monstrous, something unfeeling. Something desperately hungry.

For more info about Sourcebooks's books and authors, visit:
sourcebooks.com